Heart-Glow

Heart-Glow

A NOVEL

SHEILAH R CRAFT

STARLIGHT BOOKS

STARLIGHT BOOKS

Cover photograph taken by Sheilah R Craft. The dolls in the photograph represent the two main characters, Eric and Angilia. The dolls were manufactured by the Tonner Doll Company. Based on the author's descriptions of the two characters, Laurie Lenz customized the two dolls to resemble the characters. The author does not have any business affiliations with either Tonner Doll Company or ANGELS Doll Studio.

ISBN-13: 978-0615720869

ISBN-10: 0615720862

ACKNOWLEDGMENTS

Writing itself may be a solitary task, but no author writes any novel alone. I have many people to thank who all in some way helped me to write this novel. Foremost, I owe the genesis of this project to God, who revealed the entire story to me one night in early 2012. A waking dream began playing in my mind, much like a film, as I looked up at the ceiling. Throughout the night, I watched the story unfold, from beginning to end, and knew that this was the novel I was born to write. From that moment, I knew that God had gifted me this story and these characters, and although I had to do some research—mostly medical and some angelic—this project has been a true blessing, as my character Angilia would say. I did the medical and angelic research, I created the country of Valdavia and the DeBruce Martineau family tree, and I wrote detailed character sketches for each character. I then wrote a detailed outline of the twelve chapters. I began writing chapter one on 20 August 2012, and I completed chapter twelve on 20 October 2012. Two months. Never has any writing project come as easily or as quickly as Heart-Glow. The credit goes to God.

My family planted the seeds which enabled me to take God's gift from dream to novel. I was born surrounded by readers, writers, educators, and books. Reading and writing are in my DNA. My mother read to me from the time I was born, and I began writing stories as soon as I could hold a crayon or a pencil. Throughout the months of this project, family members have listened to my progress reports, ideas, and joys as it all came together. I spent the duration of this project going to my job as an English professor and coming home to sit at my computer and type, type, type. I thank my family for enduring these months so that this novel could come to life.

My friend and co-worker, Nicole Conrad, shares an office with me, and she has kindly listened to my progress, updates, plans for the sequels—yes, there are three sequels that also appeared in my waking dreams—and even the customized doll project for the characters. Nicole's support and encouragement remain valuable and much appreciated. Thank you, Nicole, for your God-sent friendship. As Angilia says, you and I know that nothing happens by chance or luck. Everything happens for a reason, including our being brought together.

Yes, while writing the detailed outline, the idea to have dolls created of the characters entered my already full brain. I do collect dolls, beautiful dolls. The characters were clearly defined and real to me from that first night of the waking dream. I know what they look like, how they dress, what they sound like, and everything about them. My favorite collector dolls are manufactured and designed by the Tonner Doll Company, which was founded and is helmed by the inimitable Robert Tonner. I selected some of his dolls to become the characters of Angilia, Eric, Marisol, Alejandro, Juanita, Eduardo, Patrick, Matthew, Mitchell, Katherine, Susan, and Miss Yost. You may see Robert Tonner's creations at www.tonnerdoll.com.

To transform those dolls and to bring them to life as the characters, I turned to the talented Laurie Lenz, who operates ANGELS Doll Studio. Her first task was to bring Angilia to life based on my descriptions. Eric followed, and the others are in progress or soon to follow as I write. I look at Eric, Angilia, Marisol, and Eduardo, and I see my characters lifted from the pages of this novel and looking as they did in that initial waking dream. The creative freedom to work with Laurie in making dolls of the characters has energized me and brought dimensions to this project that I had not anticipated. Laurie's one-of-a-kind transformations can be seen at the ANGELS web site, laurielenzdollstudio.com.

Finally, I thank my ancestors. Genealogy remains extremely important to me. When I confirm and discover information about those people who preceded me, that is always emotional, personal, and truly insightful. Their individual stories touch my heart and soul and bring an indescribable richness to my life. My ancestors contribute to the story of my life, a story that is still in progress. Each of them contributes to making me the person I am. Without them, I would not exist. As you read Heart-Glow, you will recognize their influence.

DEDICATED TO MY GRANDPARENTS

HENRY MORGAN AND MAGGIE ALICE HOLBROOK

AND

IVORY BOLEN AND MAXINE CRAFT

GREATER LOVE HATH NO MAN THAN THIS,

THAT A MAN LAY DOWN HIS LIFE FOR HIS FRIEND.

--JOHN 15:13

THE HISTORY OF VALDAVIA

Before becoming an independent sovereign state, what we now know as Valdavia belonged to France. King Philippe VI de France created the kingdom of Valdavia on September 16, 1331 and declared, by virtue of a Royal Grant, his most trusted, loyal, and ardent supporter, soldier, and friend, Christophe Alexandre Martineau, Duc d' Evreux, the first King de Valdavia. The Royal Grant stipulated that King Christophe's first-born or eldest surviving son be the sole heir to the throne.

King Philippe VI de France strictly enforced what much later became known as the Salic law, and stipulated that in the Royal Grant. Under the Salic law, no female relative—not even if she were the King's eldest or only child—could become monarch. That never became an issue for any King de Valdavia until recently, and the Salic law remained in place for many generations, even though the King de Valdavia is an absolute monarch and has full authority to change and to create laws.

The first king of Valdavia, King Christophe, remained loyal to and supportive of Philippe VI and his successor Jean II. Christophe's loyalty and support before and during Philippe's reign prompted the French King to grant Christophe two honors. In fact, the kingdom was the second and grandest honor bestowed upon Christophe by his friend. In recognition of Christophe's friendship and public support after the unexpected death of the predecessor, Charles IV on February 1, 1328, Philippe granted his friend a dukedom, making him the Duc d' Evreux. Several generations of the Martineau family, including Christophe's father, hailed from Evreux.

When Charles IV died suddenly, the French throne was claimed by England's King Edward III, whose new wife Philippa of Hainault was the daughter of an ally of the recently-deceased French king. In Edward's mind that tenuous family connection entitled him to Charles IV's throne. The French aristocracy felt much differently, however, preferring Philippe. Christophe stood strongly behind his friend and publicly voiced his support of Philippe as King de France. An essay proclaiming Christophe's support and explaining why Philippe deserved the crown was written by Christophe and published in the Paris newspapers. Christophe was never afraid to stand with his friend, and when Philippe was coronated on May 29, 1328, Christophe sat with the new King's family at their invitation.

Christophe's bravery, encouragement, diplomacy, intellect, and leadership during the Battle of Cassel in 1328 spurred Philippe to grant his friend the kingdom of Valdavia in 1331. Christophe served as a knight in Philippe's household, and was valuable during the King's first major battle. The Battle of Cassel was but one plague (literally) that troubled Philippe's reign. Flemish rebels opposed French taxes and laws, which they refused to pay and to obey, respectively. This resulted in an uprising in early August 1328, and Philippe garnered the military support of several rulers. In preparation for the impending battle, Philippe gathered an army consisting of 2500 armed knights and 12,000 infantrymen and archers. Among the knights, leading them to victory with his model courage and military skill, was Christophe. The battle began on August 23, and the Flemish rebels were soundly defeated.

After working to establish the new kingdom, Philippe granted Christophe the kingdom and the title HM King Christophe de Valdavia on September 16, 1331. When Christophe was coronated on November 17 that year, Philippe and many members of the French aristocracy attended to show their personal and public support of the new King and his kingdom. Christophe and his family had their sorrows—their first two sons died young—yet they lived happily and peacefully in the Palais Royale de Valdavia (formerly a palace belonging to the French monarch) and enjoyed the beginning of the new country as citizens moved to Valdavia from neighboring France, Italy, Monaco, and Spain. Christophe reigned for 48 years, dying on October 22, 1379, when his only surviving son—and sixth child—inherited the throne and became King Philippe I de Valdavia. Yes, Valdavia's first heir to the throne was named for his father's friend and ally, King Philippe VI de France.

The current King de Valdavia is the 19th and arguably most beloved of the country's monarchs. Eric Richard Constatin DeBruce Martineau was born in the capital, Valmondois, on November 17, 1954—on the 623rd anniversary of Christophe's coronation. The birth of his only child and heir, Angilia Erica Charity DeBruce Martineau, on January 3, 1996, prompted Eric to eradicate the Salic law days after her birth. Angilia will, in due course, become the first hereditary Queen de Valdavia, a coronation which will make history. In 2012 Valdavia celebrates 681 years as a sovereign state, and although a relatively young country, the history is impressive.

The direct lineage traces the Martineau family to Robert the Bruce, King of Scotland, a lineage established when Robert's descendant Muriel Darrell married the man who became HM King Leon II de Valdavia on November 20, 1578. Robert the Bruce, the brave King who battled King Edward III's grandfather King Edward I, inspired Leon to change the family surname officially when he assumed the throne. The Martineau dynasty henceforth became the DeBruce Martineau dynasty.

In its 681 years, Valdavia has grown in every conceivable manner, not just in population, but in industry, banking, education, the arts, and in global recognition and respect. While the future is largely unknown, Valdavia remains in the most capable hearts, minds, and hands of its King and Princess. Eric and Angilia may be monarch and heir of an absolute dynasty, but they are no tyrants; both believe in and practice what is technically called benevolent tyranny—putting the needs of Valdavia's citizens first, making decisions and creating laws which are in the best interest of the majority of the people. Eric and Angilia are less concerned about increasing their personal wealth or holdings than they care about making sure every Valdavian's life remains as secure, safe, free, and unfettered as humanly possible. That compassionate approach, as inherited by Eric, is ingrained in his heir, Angilia, who in time will instill the same altruistic mindset in her children, the next heirs of the kingdom of Valdavia.

A testimony to the 19 Kings de Valdavia is the fact that in 681 years, the country has not been troubled with wars, uprisings, challenges for the throne, depressions, or crises. Though Valdavia does not have the equivalent to a parliament or cabinet, King Eric's first major task upon his ascension was to assemble a team of experts in various fields—military, finance, education, the arts—as well as a Chief Advisor. This team meets monthly to apprise and advise the King and to—in Eric's words—guide him in formulating the most effective and benevolent polices and laws. Eric is the first King de Valdavia to create an Advisory Board, a tradition Angilia states she will continue.

Due in large part to the compassionate approach of each succeeding King—and future Queen—Valdavia and its people exist largely in peace, harmony, liberty, and happiness, causing some in the media to dub Valdavia the 21st century's Utopia. Despite the running joke that the water must contain fairy dust—how could any country not have serious issues or crises?—the truth is that each King made his primary goal the well-being of his people. Valdavians do not pay taxes, and entrepreneurs pay nominal taxes annually primarily as a business license renewal fee, for example; the telephone, postal, and communications commerce remain monopolies, the profits all going into the public funds which are used to pay for programs, maintenance, and projects. Poverty is all but nonexistent in Valdavia as a result. Valdavians in return remain fiercely loyal to and supportive of their King and Princess; the citizens understand how blessed they are to not have many of the burdens and problems endured by those in other countries.

Eric is known globally as the King of the People for his unending dedication to assisting and providing opportunities for his fellow Valdavians. Understanding how blessed his family has been for several generations, Eric's driving desire and philosophy remain consistent: pay forward the kindnesses and blessings shown to him and his family. With such inherent compassion and concern at its core, Valdavia might just be as close to a modern Utopia as one country can become.

5

CHAPTER 1

Early-morning light filtered through the rose-patterned curtains as Angilia opened her eyes and reached for the radio switch. Standing and stretching, she heard the end of an old Ricky Nelson song, and then the voice of the morning disc jockey, Dave Rodan. "Happy Tuesday, everyone! It's January 3, 2012—and our darling Princess Angilia's Sweet Sixteenth Birthday! This one is for you, Princess. Happy birthday!" She smiled as The Crest's "16 Candles" filled her bedroom. How sweet. She picked up her cell phone from the bedside table and called Dave at the radio station to thank him for remembering her birthday.

She stood looking out the window at the beautiful sunrise when she heard a gentle tap on her open door. "Come in, Daddy," she beamed. She turned to see her father bathed in the golden glow and smiling at her. He went to her and held her in a tight, close hug, as tears filled his eyes and choked his voice. "Happy birthday, my beautiful daughter Angilia. I love you so much."

"I love you, Daddy. More than ever. I am so happy God made you my father."

"So am I, Angel. So am I. I want to give you this now," he softly said as he pulled a package from his suit pocket and handed it to her. She took it and carefully opened the burgundy velvet box to reveal a stunning green agate cameo. She gasped at the beautiful image carved into the stone. Tears slid down her cheeks as she grabbed her father in a hug, affecting him by choking out, "Mommy's so beautiful! I love her. And you. Thank you, Daddy. Thank you."

"That is from a picture of Mommy when she was 16. She is beautiful. And she is with us today, too, Angel. On your 16th birthday."

"Mommy is always with us, Daddy. Always. I feel her all the time, in here," she whispered through her tears as she placed her hand over her heart.

He kissed her forehead and cleared his throat as he reminded her that breakfast would be ready soon. "Abuela and Abuelo will be up soon, too, you know. It's a very special day." He winked as he left her to shower and dress.

Twenty minutes later, Angilia walked down the marble staircase to the faint sound of her own voice drifting to her. As she entered the dining room on the first floor, she realized the radio was on in the background—and that Dave Rodan played her songs that morning, one after another. Her father and grandparents were already there, and her grandmother welcomed her with a hug and a kiss. "Feliz cumpleaños, mi amada nieta. Le amo muchísimo."

Angilia kissed her grandmother's soft cheek and held her close. "Le amo muchísimo, Abuela. Abuelo, le amo muchísimo también," she said as she greeted her grandfather with a hug and a kiss. "I love you both so very much. Thank you for everything."

Suddenly, her grandmother was crying, and Angilia looked at her father in alarm. "Marisol. Mi hija. Tan hermosa. Tan hermosa. Alejandro, nuestra hija Marisol." Her grandmother was tenderly fingering the cameo Angilia's father had given her earlier. Angilia held her grandmother as they smiled at one another. Alejandro put his arms around his wife and his granddaughter as they admired Marisol's beautiful, smiling profile carved so perfectly into the stone. "Si, Juanita, nuestra hija es tan hermosa."

"Daddy had this made for me. He gave it to me a few minutes ago in my room. Mommy is so beautiful and perfect."

"I have never seen anything more beautiful, Eric, mi hijo," Juanita said with a tearful smile. "I have always been so proud of you, mi hijo."

Eric embraced his mother-in-law and gently wiped away her tears with his handkerchief. "I love you both, I hope you know that. Marisol is the love of my life. Angilia told me this morning that she feels her Mommy with her always. Marisol never left us really. Her soul is here and her love remains in our hearts."

The four of them embraced, and as they did, Angilia spoke a loving prayer. "Dear God, thank you for making us a family. Thank you for the gift of eternal life which keeps those who have left this world with us in spirit and which will reunite us. Mommy, Uncle Patrick, Grandfather, Grandmother, and all of our ancestors. We love them all, and we know they are with us always. We are so grateful for your many blessings to us. Amen." Eric kissed the top of his daughter's bent head, and echoed her "Amen," as did Alejandro and Juanita.

§§§§

"Eric, the car is ready. We need to leave in ten minutes."

"Thanks, Roger. Angilia and I will go in my car. The rest of you can follow in the other car."

"All right. I'll have everything ready by the time the four of you come down."

"Thanks buddy," Eric said to his close friend and personal assistant, a job Roger had held under Eric's father, King Gerard IV.

Eric knocked on the door to his in-laws' suite and greeted them with a smile as he reminded them they would all leave for the museum in a few minutes. They were so excited and happy, and he adored watching them together. He wished his own marriage could have been as long, but he was truly grateful that Marisol had graced his life as she did. Their love was true, eternal, and living through the daughter they celebrated on her 16th birthday.

Angilia stepped into the hallway from her suite as if on cue, and walked to her father's open arms. She smiled at her family, her small but love-filled family, and felt her chest ache with the pain of unshed tears. She could not cry now, not when they had a public engagement in a few moments. As they walked down the stairs and headed toward the garage, Angilia stopped to give her father and grandparents a group hug and said, "I love you all so very much."

"Mi amada nieta, we love you, but if you start this now, you will turn us all into slobbering messes before we enter the museum."

"Abuelo, you are just as emotional as I am. I cry over everything, it seems."

A few minutes later, she kissed her grandparents, and then Roger and Eric assisted them into the Rolls Royce. She followed Eric to his car, a 2012 Aston Martin convertible—a gift from Angilia on Christmas Day 2011. She smiled at him while he opened the passenger door for her. He settled behind the steering wheel, and her smile broadened. "What are you smiling about?" he asked her.

"You look like James Bond, Daddy, only more handsome."

"Is that why you got me this car? So I can play James Bond?"

"Maybe. You are handsome, and dashing, and powerful. You need a car like this one."

"Here we go, baby. Let's make our grand arrival at the museum in this cool car. It's our first drive outside the gates."

He pulled out of the garage, turned into the main courtyard, and when the guards opened the huge iron gates, he drove onto the street to thunderous cheers from the hundreds of people who were crowding the mall in front of the palace. Everyone screamed her name as the car turned the corner, and with the convertible top down, they could see her. Eric and Angilia waved to the well-wishers as they made their way to the Musée National de Valdavia, trailed by the Rolls Royce carrying her grandparents, Roger, Daniel, and Susan to the museum. A third car contained security officers, who were present at every public appearance.

Eric pulled up in front of the main entrance and parked, and as he reached to open his door, Angilia touched his arm and gently reminded him to wait for security to exit their car first. He smiled; she was always so protective of him. A moment later, officers stood on either side of the Aston Martin and opened the doors. Eric and Angilia exited the car to hundreds more people behind police barricades across the street from the museum, all of them cheering, screaming for them, and waving flowers and signs. Angilia quickly crossed the street to tell them she would come over when they were finished inside, which elicited even more applause and screams.

By the time she rejoined her father, he and her grandparents were standing there beaming with pride and love. She slipped her left arm through her father's right, and they walked up the wide staircase to the open doors. Inside, the royal family and their guests were greeted by the Musée director, Muriel Laperen, who curtsied to both Eric and Angilia and bowed to Alejandro and Juanita. She greeted Roger, Daniel, and Susan with handshakes, then escorted the party to the Royal Portrait Gallery.

The room was filled to capacity with reporters, photographers, and guests who had purchased tickets to attend the unveiling. In honor of Angilia's birthday, one hundred percent of the ticket proceeds were donated to her education foundation. Ms. Laperen stepped to the podium to welcome everyone and to explain the importance of the day's unveiling. "As you know, we are here to unveil the first official portrait of Her Royal Highness The Princess Angilia de Valdavia. Her Royal Highness' portrait, to commemorate her 16th birthday, hangs alongside the most recent official portrait of her father, His Majesty King Eric de Valdavia, which was unveiled on his 50th birthday. The artist who received the great honor of painting Her Royal Highness' first portrait is here today, Mr. Michel Remais."

Mr. Remais waved briefly to the applause, and Angilia went to him and encouraged him to stand with them in the front of the room. Ms. Laperen followed Angilia's lead and offered the podium to the artist so he could make a brief public comment about the portrait. He smiled and nodded in appreciation. "Merci, merci. Thank you all. I cannot express how honored I am to have been chosen to paint Her Royal Highness's first official portrait. Her Royal Highness is the most beautiful, kind, and gracious young woman whom I have had the privilege to meet, and while she was an easy subject with which to work, my challenge was to capture her true beauty. When I first met her, I realized that no photograph has ever captured her truthfully. There is something truly rare and mystical about Her Royal Highness that is ethereal. I sincerely hope that Her Royal Highness and His Majesty are pleased with the portrait and that all of you will enjoy viewing it when you visit the Musée. Thank you." The audience politely applauded Remais, and he smiled at them. He stood aside as Ms. Laperen introduced Eric, who came to the podium to make a formal statement prior to the unveiling.

The guests stood as Eric approached the podium, and Angilia beamed with joy as her father received a standing ovation. She always enjoyed seeing peoples' love for her father. Eric smiled, too, and thanked everyone for coming. "I am thrilled and honored to be here today, on my beautiful daughter's 16th birthday, as her portrait is unveiled and she takes her rightful place in this gallery amidst her ancestors. Angilia is the light and love of my life, and words fail to express the joy, love, and blessing she gives to me every moment. I am so blessed to have her, and so are you. My little girl is your next Queen, actually the first hereditary Queen of Valdavia. What an amazing Queen she will make one day. Her love, her empathy, her compassion, and her joy in helping others inspire me. I think she teaches me far more than I teach her." Some people clapped in agreement while others wiped tears from their eyes.

"Before I unveil her portrait, there is one gift I want to give to Angilia publicly, if you do not mind indulging a proud father." The guests applauded their approval as Eric thanked them and turned to Roger, who handed him a parchment sheet. Angilia appeared surprised by her father's comment, not expecting a public birthday gift. She wondered what he had planned. "Ladies and gentlemen, it is my distinct honor to issue this Proclamation:

Royal Proclamation

by

King Eric de Valdavia

Whereas HRH The Princess Angilia's dedication to and love for Valdavia and its people have led her to devote much of her energies and time to improving the educational systems and to helping all people through her foundations and patronages, and whereas HRH is a wise and valuable unofficial Consort to the King, I have thought fit to issue this Royal Proclamation.

On this 3rd day of January 2012, I, King Eric de Valdavia, do confer upon HRH The Princess Angilia the title of Duchesse de Valmondois. Henceforth, her full official title shall be HRH The Princess Angilia Erica Charity, Duchesse de Valmondois.

Signed: King Eric R

Dated: 3 January 2012

The crowd again rose to their feet in a more boisterous standing ovation, and Angilia stared at her father in stunned silence. As he motioned for her to join him at the podium, he saw her touch the cameo pinned to her dress, above her heart. Her heart pounding with love and gratitude, Angilia walked to her father and embraced him. The crowd chanted, "Speech, speech," so Eric lowered the microphone for her and stepped aside. She clasped his hand, though, pulling him back to her side as she fought back tears. "My father is far too kind. I don't deserve this honor, but I hope I live up to it and to your expectations." She smiled at her father and a man in the crowd shouted, "You already do!" which prompted shouts of agreement. Eric smiled, while Angilia motioned them quiet and thanked them. "I love you all, and I am honored to serve you. I could never have a better, wiser, stronger teacher than my father. Thank you, Daddy. I love you." She kissed his cheek and brushed tears away as she rejoined Michel and Ms. Laperen.

Eric cleared his throat of impending tears. "Without further ado, I am so proud to officially unveil Angilia's first portrait." Eric stepped over to the huge portrait, pulled the golden cord, and opened the red velvet curtain to reveal a gasp-inducing portrait of

Angilia. Cameras flashed and clicked as hundreds of pictures were taken, and the guests stood in a thunderous standing ovation. Michel beamed with happiness that the people appreciated his portrait of their princess, and Angilia's grandparents stood with tears of happiness trickling down their cheeks.

Eric hugged Angilia and kissed her cheek, while the applause continued. Photographers shouted for them to pose with the portrait, and as they did so, Angilia called for her grandparents to join them. "Marisol's gown. You wore Marisol's gown for your portrait," her grandmother softly said through tears as Angilia again touched the cameo and kissed her grandmother. While the four family members smiled and hugged, Angilia looked at the faces in the room and felt her heart skip beats when she saw her doctor standing amongst the people. Why was he there? He had paid to come? Why? The smile vanished from her pretty face, and the doctor shot her that evil sneer that always sent chills and terror down her spine. He saluted her as he stepped from the crowd and walked out of the gallery.

Eric noticed the change in her demeanor, the look that flashed in her eyes, and he held her close. She stood in front of her father instinctively, as if to shield him, and forced a smile. As the ceremony ended and guests approached to greet them and to wish her a happy birthday, Angilia scanned the crowded room constantly. She stole a moment to pull aside a security officer and ask him to look for Dr. Jamieson; she had spotted him, but now could not locate him in the crowd. Reluctantly, the officer agreed and left for several minutes. When he finally returned, she looked at him expectantly, trying to hide her fear. "I asked the guards outside, and they said the doctor got in a car and drove away. Sorry."

Angilia took a deep breath of relief and thanked the officer. She rejoined her family with a sincere smile, and Eric was puzzled by her mood shifts. They left the gallery and walked outside, and he whispered to her, "What happened in there?"

She smiled up at him and held his hand, knowing she could never tell him the truth; that was far too dangerous. "Nothing, Daddy. I just got very emotional. I was trying so hard to fight it all back. You really got to me. You're very sneaky, you know."

"A surprise has to be sneaky," he replied with a giggle as they stepped down the stairs to more screams and applause.

"Daddy, I promised them I'd go over when we were done. Is that okay?"

Eric smiled his approval. "Of course it is. Alejandro, Juanita, our Angilia wants to greet everyone who's been standing here for hours waiting to see her on her birthday. Let's go with her." He knew his in-laws would enjoy the attention and talking with people. Security officers followed closely, and Angilia turned and told them to stay close to her father. Eric was used to her protectiveness by now, and he did find it touching, though he wondered why she felt the need to be that protective of him. He forgot that, though, and he beamed with love and paternal pride at the reception his daughter received from the hundreds of people who came just to see her. Her kindnesses toward all of them warmed his soul.

Angilia talked to as many people as she could, accepting cards, flowers, gifts, stuffed animals, and well-wishes from them all. Susan busily took armfuls of gifts from Angilia and placed them in the trunk of the Rolls Royce. Eric, too, talked with people, who showered him with love and praise, much to Angilia's delight. Angilia had seen the love and respect people had for her father since she was born, and it never failed to touch her emotional core.

An elderly man in a wheelchair caught Eric's attention, and when Eric bent to speak with him, the gentleman grasped Eric's hand and smiled at him. "I am 96 years old, son, and I remember your great-grandfather King Gerard III. I was 10 years old when he died, and my family stood outside the church to pay our respects the day of his funeral. Your grandfather King Stefan was a man then, and he was coronated later that year. We stood outside the church to watch the procession that day, too. I was 47 when he died in 1963 and your father was coronated King Gerard IV. I watched you as a young boy at your grandfather's funeral and your father's coronation, solemn and composed even in your grief, and I thought then that you were going to make a fine king when your time came. And you have, Sir, you have. I have watched you grow up into a fine man." Eric thanked him while Angilia moved closer to hear more of the conversation.

"Your great-grandfather was a great king, your grandfather was a great king, as was your father, but you are the best king Valdavia has ever known." Eric blushed as the gentleman squeezed his hand and Angilia put her arm around her father.

"Daddy is far too humble, so I will take the praise on his behalf. Thank you. I agree with you wholeheartedly, sir. He is the absolute best king, and I really could never have a more perfect father and teacher."

The elderly gentleman reached for Angilia, hugging her as he wished her a happy birthday. He touched her cheek and told them through tear-filled eyes, "I only regret that I shall not live to see you crowned as Queen of Valdavia, my dear. You are a very special girl, and I can tell how splendid a queen you will make."

"Thank you," she replied and kissed his cheek. "No offense, sir, but I pray that day is many, many decades in the future."

He patted her cheek with a smile and a wink, and they thanked him and walked on to greet other people. "He knew grandfather, great-grandfather, and great-great-grandfather. He has lived through four kings. How amazing and history-filled his life is, Daddy. I wish I could have known grandfather and great-great-grandfather, too." She panicked, realizing she had not mentioned her great-grandfather. What would her father think and say? Thankfully, Eric seemed not to have noticed.

"Your grandfather was very wise and kind, Angilia. He must be looking down from Heaven with pride and love today. Your great-grandfather and great-great-grandfather, too, darling. I was old enough to know your great-grandfather, and I loved him dearly. We all did. And they love you. I know that, as they look down on you and watch you. You are not just my future, you are their future. Our family's legacy grows even stronger through you, Angel."

Roger finally mentioned to Eric that it was time to leave, as it was already afternoon. Eric and Angilia thanked everyone for coming and told them how much their support meant to them. As they waved, they could feel the palpable love flowing from the people who stood there for them. Angilia blew them a kiss and slid into her father's car.

"This is all too much for me, Daddy. I don't deserve all of this." She looked at everyone still standing there waving, cheering, and yelling "Happy Birthday." She waved until the car turned the corner.

"Yes, you do, Angel. You are so mind-blowing, you do so much. It's hard for me to wrap my head around everything you've done in just 16 years."

"I haven't done anything really, Daddy. Nothing earth-shatteringly important. Not like you. You take my breath away."

He smiled. "Let's just call it even, huh? I love you, you love me, and we're a happy family," he sang as they neared the palace.

She smiled and giggled. "We are happy, Daddy. You make me so happy."

§§§§§

During lunch, they could hear—even through the thick palace walls—the continuous shouts, screams, and chants of the hundreds of people who filled the mall. "They have been there since dawn, haven't they? You are much loved, mi nieta querida. Much loved."

Eric squeezed his father-in-law's shoulder and smiled at him. "She is. Everyone loves our Angilia." He nodded in the direction of the mall. "They are certainly persistent and devoted. Are you up for another walkabout, everyone?"

Juanita smiled and smoothed Angilia's long ash-blonde hair. "I am very happy and very proud today. My heart and soul could not hold anymore love if they had to right now, they are so full. I would enjoy meeting everyone with you again, mi hijo."

Eric called Roger and Susan to accompany them, and Angilia walked arm-in-arm with her adored Abuela to the front entrance. Eric, Alejandro, Roger, and Susan followed, and when the door opened, the screams increased in volume. Hundreds of cameras whirred and buzzed as the royal family approached the gates. Angilia asked the guard to unlock the gates, and then told the guards to stay close to her father, just as she had done earlier.

Angilia was instantly surrounded by screaming teenagers and young adults waving CDs, magazines, pictures, and newspapers at her, as well as birthday cards, flowers, and gifts. She looked over at her father, her eyes showing her amazement at the reaction. She accepted their cards, flowers, and gifts with tear-filled eyes and gratitude, then signed their CDs, newspapers, magazines, and pictures. Several fans wanted pictures taken with her, and she was thrilled to have her grandparents included in the attention. Press photographers asked if the family members would pose for some pictures, and they did so.

After four hours, Angilia had greeted every person who had come to wish her a happy birthday, had signed hundreds of autographs, posed for hundreds more pictures, and thanked each person for thinking of her. Susan and Roger were overwhelmed by the sheer number of cards, bouquets, and gifts, and made several quick runs to the foyer to empty their arms.

The last person to greet Angilia gently tapped her arm. She looked down and her smile seemed a mile wide. "Billy! Oh, it's so nice to see you, dear!"

"It's so nice to see you, too. Happy Birthday, Princess darling." He held up a single white rose and a wrapped gift. "When I grow up, I want to be one of them," he said as he pointed to the guards. "I want to protect you."

"I'm very flattered, Billy. You will make a strong, trustworthy guard."

"Thank you, Princess darling." He took her right hand in his and bowed as he kissed her hand in a gallant gesture. Everyone oohed and ahhed at the sight, some even shedding a tear or two. Cameras captured the moment, which was splashed across the next morning's newspapers.

Eric stepped forward to shake little Billy's hand and to thank everyone for coming on his daughter's birthday. "We love you all, and we are so grateful for your love and support. We have a very important birthday party to begin soon. Thank you all so very much." He put his arm around Angilia's shoulders and they walked through the gate into the courtyard, followed by the others. The guard locked the gate, and when the family reached the main entrance of the palace, they turned and waved to everyone again. Finally, they were inside, surrounded by piles of cards, flowers, and gifts.

"Someone has a lot of gifts to open," Eric smiled at her.

She looked at the piles and shook her head in awe. "I can't believe all of this is for me."

"You deserve it more than anyone does, Angel. Everyone truly loves you, baby, especially I." He hugged her close and kissed her cheek. "Let's all refresh ourselves after that long walkabout, and then we can begin the birthday party. What do you say we change out of these formal clothes for the rest of the day?"

The four of them climbed the stairs to the third floor, where they went to their respective suites. Daniel was waiting for Eric, and the friends smiled as they entered Eric's suite. Daniel was one of her father's closest and most trusted friends, someone he had met at university. After they received their degrees, and Eric returned home, he brought Daniel with him as his newly-appointed valet de chambre. Angilia was happy that her father had his closest friends around him; he needed their company, companionship, and fun. His job required much of his time, attention, and energy; he was always working to make life better and less demanding for the people of Valdavia. Regaining her thoughts, Angilia asked Susan to assist Abuela, since she must be exhausted after such a long time of standing and walking.

Angilia walked through her private sitting room and bedroom to her large wardrobe/dressing room. She sat on her vanity stool and unpinned the cameo her father had given her that morning, looking at her mother's beautiful image and crying. She had never gotten to meet her mother, but she felt as though they knew one another. She loved her mother so, and knew that they would be reunited one day, when Angilia died and her soul entered Heaven. Until that day, she vowed to live a life that would earn God's and her family's approval. With her beloved father guiding and teaching her, that would not be too difficult. Who and what she was at that moment was due to God and her father, not to her. She knew that.

Sighing, she stood up and removed her clothes, then selected jeans and a blouse. She quickly dressed and slipped her feet into comfortable ballerina flats. As she rushed into the hallway, she ran straight into her father, who smiled at her and then furrowed his brow and asked why she had been crying. "Does it show? I'm sorry. I was thinking about Mommy and how much I love her. Not sad tears, really, Daddy. I thought about how we will be together in Heaven one day in the future. It will be so beautiful, it really will, Daddy. Imagine all of us together in the most exquisite, loving, peaceful place, for all eternity. Forever."

Eric sighed deeply. "You are so wise, Angel. Yes, it will be beautiful and wonderful. Plus, we will finally meet all of those ancestors you research so diligently."

She smiled, and they were joined by her grandparents, Susan, and Daniel to walk downstairs to the second floor sitting room.

§§§§§

The door was closed and Eric gestured for Angilia to open it and enter first. "You're the birthday girl, after all."

She did, to see the room decked in banners, flowers, streamers, balloons, the gifts, stuffed animals, and cards from the foyer and car trunk, and several familiar faces. Everyone burst into a loud rendition of the happy birthday song, while she stood looking at her friends and fighting tears. When they finished she thanked them, then thanked her father for planning such a wonderful party for her. Closest to her stood her boss, the President of Wolfson College at the University of Oxford, Dr. Christopher Dalton. They embraced as he wished her a very happy birthday and said how amazing it was for him to watch her grow up, literally, as first his youngest student ever and then as his most esteemed faculty member. "I'm so proud of you, Angilia," he said, tears choking him. She hugged him again. "Oh, Chris, I'm so happy you're here. Really."

Next she hugged Sam Burton, her record producer and manager, then the band members she had inherited from Tom Greenfield: John Herbert, Joe Arnold, Tim Hanley, and Greg Smithson. "I love you all, and I am so happy you're all here today."

Tim put his arm around her and kissed her temple as everyone settled onto the sofas and chairs, and he said they had a very special gift to present to her. Greg handed her a rose-printed gift bag as John cleared his throat. "This is from Tom. He bought it about a week before the accident, and said it was the perfect 16th birthday present for his Angel girl." John struggled to fight his tears, as Joe patted his back and spoke on their behalf. "Tom wanted to share this day with you, Angilia, but since he can't be here physically, we are giving his gift to you today."

Angilia's eyes filled with tears, and Eric handed her his handkerchief. She wiped her eyes and managed to thank them and to say, "I know he's here, though. I can feel his spirit. Tom's always with us, guys. Always. Thank you." They sat quietly for a moment, their heads bowed, before Tim cleared his throat and echoed Angilia's comments that Tom's soul lived on and stayed with them. "Open it," he finally said.

Angilia pulled a beautifully-wrapped box from the bag and carefully removed the ribbon and paper. She opened the box, her eyes filling with tears again. She gently lifted a snow globe from the box. "Christopher Robin and Pooh," she whispered. "He told me that I made him feel like Christopher Robin, so I must be his Pooh Bear. He said I made him feel like a boy again. It was the movie we watched together after shows, the book I read to him on the bus or plane. It was something we shared. It's also something Daddy and I have always shared. This is beautiful. I will treasure this for the rest of my life." Everyone was tearful by then, and Tim held her for a few moments, until Joe broke the mood. "How about our gifts next, huh?"

Joe handed her a wrapped box, which contained a rare book of Italian poetry. Greg gave her a gold charm bracelet with the first charm—a gold guitar. John's gift contained five charms for her new bracelet: a gold piano, a gold pen, a garnet—her birthstone, a gold horse, and a gold 2012 to commemorate the year of her 16th birthday. Tim placed a black velvet jewel case in her lap, which held a pearl and amethyst choker. Tom's birthstone was amethyst, and this was another gift that honored their dear friend who had died so suddenly and tragically almost one year earlier. Angilia kissed them each, touched by their kindness and thoughtfulness.

Sam stepped over and handed her a gift, which she opened to reveal a carving of her handsome Palomino, Starlight. "Sam, he's gorgeous! Thank you!"

He explained that he had met an artist in Mexico whose talent was hand-carved wooden animals. Sam had given the man a picture of Angilia and Starlight and commissioned the carving for her birthday gift.

Christopher handed her a gift, which, when opened, revealed an extremely rare first edition of Percy Bysshe Shelley's poem Adonais from 1821. She looked at him in shock, stunned he had tracked down a nearly-pristine copy of her favorite poem. "Christopher, thank you! I don't know what you did to get this, but I can never thank you enough." He smiled, happy she was pleased.

Daniel gifted her with a pink briefbag for her official meetings, which would increase in number as she assumed even more royal duties. He joked that a pink briefcase was meant for Angilia, which caused a round of laughter. Pink was her favorite color. Roger gave her a first edition of Winnie-the-Pooh from 1926, which brought tears to her eyes again, especially in light of Tom's posthumous gift. "I had no idea, Angilia. I know the books are very special to you and your dad, and when I saw this one for sale I had to get it for you." She hugged him, thanked him, and told him it was a wonderful present, one she would treasure and share with her children someday. Eric found himself tearing up at the mention of his future grandchildren, and she gently wiped the tears from his eyes.

Susan gave her a heart-shaped silver evening bag, perfect for Angilia's gala events. Alejandro moved next to his granddaughter and gave her an engulfing hug and a kiss as he placed a small package in her hand. "Oh, Abuelo, you are going to make me cry again." She was right—when she opened the small box and saw the pearl necklace with the emerald clasp, she hugged him tightly and cried. Eric had known; the strand of pearls had been Alejandro's gift to his own daughter, Marisol, on her 16th birthday many years earlier. "Muchas gracias, Abuelo. I love you more than you know." She wiped her tears away with her father's handkerchief, again, and kissed her grandfather on both cheeks as her grandmother squeezed between Angilia and Eric.

Juanita was crying, too, and as she struggled to stop her tears, she kissed her granddaughter and handed her a tiny gift wrapped in a delicate linen and lace handkerchief with a tiny green M embroidered in one corner. "Abuela, not you, too. I'm going to cry all afternoon and evening. Mommy's handkerchief is more than enough."

"Just open it, mi amada nieta. I want you to have this."

Angilia untied the green ribbon that held the corners of the handkerchief together, to reveal an emerald and diamond bracelet. Angilia was indeed crying again at the sight of her beloved mother's birthstone bracelet. "You wear this and enjoy this, just as your mother did, yes?"

Angilia nodded, unable to speak for the tears choking her, and hugged her Abuela close. "I will, I promise," she hoarsely whispered.

As Angilia dried her tears once more and kissed her grandparents again, Eric got up and walked across the room. He returned with a huge wrapped box, and placed it on the floor in front of his daughter. Juanita moved over so that Eric could sit beside Angilia. "Happy Birthday, my beautiful daughter Angilia. The past sixteen years have been filled with such love, happiness, fun, and amazement. I am so in awe of you, baby. To say that I love you seems so inadequate compared to what I truly feel for you.

I don't know what I did to be blessed by God with the gift of you, but I am eternally grateful."

Now Angilia was sobbing, her tears seemingly uncontrollable, and Eric held her close. Her tears stained her father's shirt, as his own slid down his cheeks. Juanita and Alejandro could no longer fight their own tears, and within seconds everyone was tearful, too. After several moments, Eric took his handkerchief from her lap and dried her face, then gently kissed her tear-filled eyes. "Daddy, that is the best gift of all, really. All I really want and need is you and your love and all of my family and friends here. Besides, you already gave me a wonderful, gorgeous gift this morning. I don't need anything else."

"Maybe not, but I want you to have this, Angel. Open it."

She untied the large pink ribbon and unfolded the pink paper, then removed the lid from the white box. Eric stood and lifted the contents out of the box and placed it on the table between the two sofas. Angilia looked at the large white wooden jewelry chest, with her insignia inlaid on the top in garnets. She lifted the top and gently placed the pearl necklace in one compartment and the emerald bracelet in another. Next she placed the charm bracelet and charms in a third compartment. "I knew Abuelo was giving you the pearls and Abuela was giving you the emerald bracelet, but not about the charm bracelet. But as you take on more duties, you will likely receive many gifts of jewelry. My mother was given many and your mother was, too, after we married. Open the other drawers, darling."

Angilia was stunned to see the box filled with a dozen lovely pieces, which Eric told her were her mother's and grandmother's jewels respectively. Now they were hers. She was astonished and—yes—crying again. "Thank you, Daddy. Everything is so beautiful. The box is stunning, and I love you for giving me something so special. I am overwhelmed. I have so many treasures today. Thank you." She kissed her father's cheek again as everyone clapped.

Roger rallied everyone, diffusing the emotional afternoon. "It's time to cut the cake, but not until Angilia extinguishes the sixteen candles." He quickly lit the candles as everyone circled the table and Angilia took her place of honor before the huge pink cake. Everyone collectively shouted "Happy Birthday" as she bent and took a deep breath. The candle flames were out in one blow.

Roger removed the candles and handed Angilia the cake knife to cut the first piece, which she slid onto a plate and handed to her father. "I am here because of you and Mommy, your love and devotion. Thank you for giving me life, Daddy."

"Oh, Angel, that is so beautiful. You really are the light of my life." He kissed her forehead. Susan and Roger passed slices of cake to everyone. Lemonade was served, as was ice cream to those who wanted some, and they settled comfortably for an evening of friendship, happiness, and laughter.

At 8:00, the chef, Antoine, appeared to announce that dinner was served, and everyone walked downstairs to the first-floor dining room. Angilia smiled at her father, truly happy and loved. The family and friends continued their camaraderie through dinner and desert, even after the plates had been cleared, until 10:30, when Christopher announced he must leave to be back at Wolfson College the next morning. "Thank you all for a wonderful afternoon and evening. This was amazing." He walked to Eric, who stood and shook his hand and thanked him for sharing Angilia's special day. "I wouldn't have missed it," Christopher said as he bent to kiss her cheek.

Christopher kissed Juanita's hand, shook Alejandro's, and said good night to Sam and the band members. "Daddy, I want to walk with Christopher to the garage, all right?" Eric nodded and smiled, and soon Angilia and Christopher were alone in the garage.

"Christopher, I need to talk with you for a moment."

He looked at her, puzzled, and asked if something was wrong. "No, not wrong. I've done a lot of praying and soul-searching over break, and . . . ." She stalled, finding it difficult to tell him her decision.

"You're staying in Valdavia." It was a statement, not a question.

She nodded, afraid to look at him. Christopher had done so much for her. He had guided her through her doctorate work and encouraged her to teach and share her expertise. She did not want to disappoint him, let him down.

"It's all right, Angilia. I understand. We've talked about this, remember? We knew you wouldn't and couldn't stay at Oxford for decades. Your life and your duty don't allow that. You have given us five years, Angilia, five glorious years. Like Daniel said, you are assuming more royal duties and obligations now. This is where you belong."

"Thank you. For everything. For teaching me, guiding me, mentoring me. For understanding now, when I couldn't find the courage to tell you. I will return, you know that. Oxford is far too important to me. I may not teach full time any longer, but I will return."

"Yes, you will," he smiled. "In early March. For the degree ceremony—you are still our keynote speaker, you know. That will not change. And then you have the scholarship ceremony. So, yes, you'll return soon."

"I will, and with Daddy. Thank you for making this less painful." She stood on her tiptoes and kissed his cheek.

"Happy birthday, Angilia." He got into his rented car and waved as he turned the corner to leave the palace grounds. She sighed in relief that he understood, since she had no intention of leaving her father now. She composed herself and rejoined everyone at the table, and soon Sam, John, Tim, Greg, and Joe said they would leave, too. They hugged and kissed her, and she reminded them about March in Oxford, when they would record the tracks for their next album.

Angilia, Eric, Juanita, and Alejandro leisurely walked back to the sitting room, and as they did, Juanita asked what was happening in March. Angilia began to explain the three events: the degree ceremony, the scholarship ceremony, and the recording session. When her grandfather asked how many songs she had written for the album, she smiled and said twelve, a mix of ballads and pop songs. "It's the perfect time to record the album, because the band will be with me at the scholarship ceremony the day before. It makes sense to go into my home studio the next day while everyone is already there. I'll send them the sheet music and demo tracks I did, they will learn the music, and we'll be set to record it all," she explained while they relaxed on the sofa together.

"Angilia is giving the keynote address at the degree ceremony in early March," Eric told his in-laws. "That will be five years since she earned her own Doctor of Philosophy from Oxford. Eleven years old. My little girl, the prodigy with the amazing memory. Five years as an Oxford professor, and she just turned sixteen today."

"She is very special, this one," Juanita said as she patted Angilia's arm. "Very special. She will do many more great things."

"Abuela, Daddy, come on. You'd think I was the only person who has ever done this."

Eric laughed. "I think you are! Royal duties, a recording career, and a professorship. All before your sixteenth birthday. I'd say that's pretty amazing. First record ten years ago, when you were six, doctorate five years ago at eleven. I don't think anyone's done those two before. One maybe, but not both."

"She was born to do these things. God created our Angilia this way for a purpose. And we are the ones God chose as her family. We are all very blessed, Eric," Alejandro reminded them.

"I know, Papa. I thank God every day for my Angel."

"What is this scholarship ceremony, mi nieta?" Juanita asked.

Angilia looked at her grandmother and told them. "Oxford proposed a music scholarship a year ago, in Daddy's name, and. . . ."

Eric leaned forward and interrupted. "It was supposed to be in her name, not mine. A music scholarship does not need my name attached."

"Stop it. It does, too. You filled my life with music since I was with Mommy. You played music, you sang to me, and I heard everything. I remember everything. You brought music into my life, Daddy. You. You are the reason for my music." She snuggled close to him and put her head against his shoulder.

"You give me far too much credit, Angel. But thank you. What do I have to do at the ceremony? Bestow the scholarship?"

"Yes, among other things."

"What things?"

"We each talk for a few minutes each at the start, and then have a question-and-answer session with the audience for a couple of hours. Most of the questions should probably be about music, though if I know the other Profs, they'll ask you about me, too. You know, about what you were talking about earlier."

"Your genius and prodigious beginning?"

"Funny. But yes. They ask me lots of questions anyway, like I'm a science experiment or an alien. They don't seem to have a handle on me really. I think they're scared of me. They don't like that I remember everything in detail. It freaks them out."

Eric laughed uproariously. "You scare me, too, baby."

"What?" She swatted his arm impishly.

"Seriously, how can someone as advanced as you be my daughter? You did not inherit any of that from me or my family."

"Of course I did, Daddy. From you and Mommy."

"Mi amada nieta, no. We are not geniuses. Marisol was a smart girl, but she was no genius. You do not get this from us. You must get this from God." Juanita shook her head in disagreement with her granddaughter.

"Well, I got it from someone. It doesn't just appear out of nowhere. And I say Daddy and Mommy and God. And since you all say I'm the genius, then I am right."

They all laughed, until she stunned Eric. "Oh, Daddy, after the Q and A session, my band and I will perform some songs, and then you'll sing our song."

"I'll what?" He nearly choked on his own words.

"Sing our song. You know the one. You've sung it to me since I was with Mommy. I want you to sing it at the ceremony."

"Oh no, baby, I am not singing in public. No."

"For me? Please?"

"Angel, I can't."

"Sure you can. You sing around here all the time. I love your singing, Daddy. Please! It's all I want. Please, Daddy? For me." She snuggled closer. "I love you more than anyone. And it's my birthday today. It will be the best gift ever."

Eric leaned his head back against the sofa and groaned. "How can I say no to her?"

"You cannot," Alejandro replied with a wink.

"No, I can't. All right, Angel, I'll do this for you. Just this once. I may never appear in public again afterwards, but I'll do it for you."

She climbed onto his lap with a large smile and hugged him. "Thank you, Daddy! Thank you!"

Angilia told them more about the upcoming Oxford events, until she noticed how tired her grandparents were. "Today has been a magical day. Thank you Daddy, Abuela, and Abuelo. I love you each." She stood and kissed her grandfather and grandmother and helped them to their feet. "It's also been a busy day, and it is late now. Why don't we get some rest?"

Eric stood, too, and the four of them climbed the stairs to the third floor. Angilia sent Susan to assist her grandmother again, and then kissed her father as they parted to enter their suites.

"Thank you for today, Daddy. You give me so much love and happiness. I love you."

"You give me so much, too, baby." He kissed her nose. "I love you. Good night, Angel. Pleasant dreams."

"Good night, Daddy."

§§§§§

Angilia slowly entered her suite. Pleasant dreams? Not tonight. Tonight she had to keep vigil, just in case. She never trusted Dr. Jamieson, and she knew he meant the threats, the threats that only she knew.

She showered, changed into her nightgown and robe, brushed her teeth, dried her hair, and turned off her bedroom lights. She peeked across the hall and saw her father's bedroom light beaming into his sitting room. He was still awake, she sighed.

She sat at her desk and looked at the small clock; it was 11:45. It was still her birthday, for a few more minutes. Angilia took her 2012 diary from the drawer. She turned to the next blank page, picked up her pen, and wrote:

3 January 2012

Today is my sixteenth birthday, and what a glorious day. Daddy— words fail when I think, talk or write about Daddy. I love him so very much, and I have for so very long. It seems like forever sometimes. I know human beings are not perfect, but Daddy is as close to perfect as any person can be. He is so full of love and light—his heart-glow I have always called it. He seems to glow from within. His soul is so loving, kind, compassionate, thoughtful, understanding, and yes fun-loving. We have lots of fun together, laughing, singing, dancing, watching old movies. I do love him. I hope he really does know how much love I have for him.

Abuelo and Abuela are amazing—such love, such devotion for all of their years together. Their eyes sparkle, sharing the happiness from within them. They have suffered their share of pain, yet they remain happy, strong, and faithful. If I can learn to be more like Abuelo and Abuela, then I will serve God, Daddy, and Valdavia well. I love them both. I am so happy they are here through February—I adore spending time with them and learning from them and hearing their stories about Mommy. Times like that are one reason I am so grateful for this memory I have—I want to remember everything, every detail, about them and their stories. Everything. I write their stories in a book, so that when I have children and grandchildren and all their future generations, they can read about their family—Daddy, Abuelo, Abuela, Mommy, Uncle Patrick, Grandmother, Grandfather, Great-Grandfather, Great-Grandmother, Great-Great-Grandfather, and Great-Great-Grandmother.

Sam, John, Tim, Greg, and Joe—more special people who bless my life. Tom is the only one who was not sitting with us, physically, in the room today. I can't believe it's been almost one year since the accident. I still wonder if I could have stopped it if I had been there. I would have been there if I had not had to return to Wolfson College. Tom hated to fly, especially alone, and if I had been there I could have changed his mind. I wish I could know the truth about that. Was that his destiny? And his gift—he must have bought that not long after my 15th birthday. He was saving it for today. Not Christmas 2011, but today. There was no card, because he thought he had more than enough time to get a card. He really was like a little boy in so many ways—he was insecure, afraid, yet full of fun many times. He reminded me of Uncle Patrick in many ways. I wonder if they have met in Heaven. They would be great friends.

Mommy was so present and palpable today. Not just in the gifts, although those are each remarkable—especially the cameo Daddy had made for me. How utterly gorgeous. Mommy's jewelry. Grandmother's jewelry. Now mine. I will wear their pieces with love and honor. These remarkable women are always with me, but wearing things of theirs carries them with me in tangible ways. I must have touched Mommy's cameo dozens of times today, as if she were physically present. That cameo is my favorite piece of jewelry, and I will wear it often. I do wish I could have met her. But she was not in my realm. Someday, though, when I die, I will meet her, and we will never part again. Mommy, Daddy, and I will be in Heaven, never separated. But not all three of us for a long time. I know that Daddy's destiny is to live past 100, though I was warned that our choices or things that others do to us can alter our destinies. That just cannot happen.

That's why Dr. Jamieson terrifies me so. I believe his threats, that he will kill Daddy if he thinks I've done or said anything. He would alter Daddy's destiny. I can never let that happen. I cannot let him hurt Daddy, never. That's why I told Christopher this evening that I am not returning to Oxford. I felt bad, because it was rather short notice, but Daddy is my priority.

I cannot and will not leave him here alone with that evil man again. I won't. Why did he come to the museum today? He paid just to taunt me and to terrify me? It worked. Daddy thinks I am afraid of the dark, clinically terrified of the dark. I have always let him think that. I can't ever tell him the truth—that is the one thing that Dr. Jamieson always threatens me never to do. If I tell anyone, he will kill Daddy. I believe him. I see the cruelty in his eyes when I have to visit him. I feel his brutality. He hurts me, but not in ways other people can really see. If I am cut or bruised, he just does things to the wounds—he never creates new wounds, because Daddy would notice and that would lead to his arrest and possibly worse. No, he is too clever to let it show. So am I. I never let it show, or at least I have tried not to let it show too much.

So tonight I will keep vigil in Daddy's room like I have done so many times. In the morning, he can think I am still afraid of the dark when he sees me there. As long as no one hurts my Daddy, I don't care. Daddy always comes first. I am going to wait for his light to go out, then guard him all night. If Dr. Jamieson or one of his thugs enters, I won't let them do anything to Daddy. God, I ask you to watch over Daddy always—do not let this evil man rewrite Daddy's history. Please. Amen.

Angilia tiptoed to Eric's suite door and saw that his bedroom light was still on; they never closed their doors at night. She quietly moved into the shadows near his bedroom door and sat on the floor, waiting for Eric to turn off the light. He had once told her that he'd never needed much sleep, but once he was tired and turned off the lights, he fell asleep rather quickly. She just needed to stay alert, watching and listening for anything or anyone. She would scream like a horror movie damsel if she heard or saw anything— the guards were close enough, and they would be there in seconds. When she had first left for her doctorate work at Oxford, she had told—not asked—the guards to keep watch at either end of the double staircases on the third floor. They were always posted there.

Finally, the light went out and she sat very quietly for several moments. After what felt like a short eternity, she stood and moved to the bedroom door. She peeked her head in, and in the soft moonlight, she could see her father curled on his bed. She took one cautious step inside his bedroom. He did not move. He was deep asleep.

She carefully tiptoed to the chair near his window and curled up for her night watch. She alternated between watching her father and watching his bedroom door. She was glad the chair was near the window, for anyone attempting to enter through it would be deterred at the sight of her sitting there. She was on high alert, and when she heard the guards moving on the landing at the far end of the hall, her heart skipped a few beats. She was grateful they were that close, though. Especially tonight.

§§§§§

"Daddy! No!" Angilia's screams shot through Eric at the exact moment he pushed back the sheets to get up. Panicked, he looked up just as she ran to him and fell to her knees at his feet. "Daddy, I heard something, and thought. . . . I'm sorry." She berated herself. She had fallen into her perpetual half-awake half-asleep state and her internal alarm went off when she heard her father move.

"Baby, everything's all right," he whispered as he lifted her onto his lap. "It's all right." She put her arms around his neck and held him close. Her deep, clinical fear of the dark tore him apart and saddened him. She had to deal with it alone when she was away from home. How awful that must feel for her.

"I'm sorry. I didn't mean to upset you."

"You haven't upset me, Angel. I just wish I could make this horrible fear go away." He gently brushed the hair from her tear-stained cheek. "I hate that you're so scared at night."

Yes, Eric once again thought she was terrified of the dark. She let him, as always. "I know. I hate it, too. I know I shouldn't be, but I am. I can't help it, Daddy."

"Shhh. It's okay. How long were you in that chair?"

"Since your light went off and you fell asleep. I didn't want to disturb you. I just felt safer in here tonight. Do you mind?"

"Have I ever, Angel? When you were little, you slept under my bed. Most tiny children climb in the bed, not under it. I just worry about you, that you aren't getting enough sleep. I don't want you to get sick over all of this."

"I'm all right, really, Daddy. I must have dozed off. I was half-awake half-asleep, and I heard you moving and panicked. That's all."

"Oh, sweetie, there aren't any monsters here. Even if they tried to, they couldn't get in here. The security surrounds the outside, and you had them guard the staircase landings, too. No monsters."

"I hope not," she whispered as she hugged him again. "I truly hope not."

"Here, you take the bed, Angel. Get some sleep."

"No, Daddy, you need to sleep, too. You're the one who has meetings tomorrow, I mean today. I'm not tired anyway."

"I'm not, either. I was going to get some water and then read for a while. So you snuggle down here, and I'll sit in the chair and read." He moved and helped her under the sheets. "We can turn the light on if it will help. You won't be alone or in the dark."

She sat up and hugged him, smelling the faint lilac scent of his pajamas as her head rested against his chest. His warmth, the soft cotton of his pajamas, and his comforting voice made everything all right. "Thank you, Daddy."

"Try to get some sleep. Okay?"

She nodded as she nestled against the pillows, but she had no intention of falling into a deep sleep. It was 3:17, and dawn was still a few hours away. Anything could happen still. She hated herself for lying to her father. She had never been afraid of the dark. But she could never tell him the truth, at least as long as Dr. Jamieson were alive. So she prayed to God for his forgiveness of her lies. She knew God understood why, and she prayed that he would forgive her.

She lay in her father's warm, soft bed and blinked away the sleep that tried to overtake her. At 4:45, Eric looked up and saw her watching him. She still had not fallen asleep. He placed his papers in the chair as he stood, and then walked to the bed and sat next to her. "Baby, you need to get some sleep."

"I'm not tired," she lied—again—to her precious father. She sat up and leaned against the carved mahogany headboard. "Daddy, I need to tell you something."

She sounded so serious that it concerned him. "What, Angel?"

"I decided not to return to Wolfson in a couple of weeks. I told Christopher last night when I walked him to his car. He understands everything. He knows that my real work is here, with you, in Valdavia. I want to stay here and assume more duties and responsibilities. I want to help you if I can. That's what makes me the happiest."

He smiled at her. "Are you sure?"

"Absolutely. I should have talked it over with you, I know that, and I'm sorry I didn't. Are you upset?"

"Upset? That my daughter wants to stay home with me? Of course not, Angel. Never. I miss you so very much when you aren't here. More than I have ever told you. I am so happy right now. You really are amazing."

She took his hand and looked at his long, strong fingers. "No, I'm not, Daddy. I feel so weak in every way right now. I feel like a little girl, and I want to stay with you." A tear slid down her cheek, and Eric gently pulled her into his arms and close to him. Her hands held his arms securely, as if afraid to let him go. She was afraid to let him go.

"You are so wise beyond your sixteen years, and you have accomplished so many great things. But you are a little girl—my little girl. You missed a lot of your childhood because of the schooling and recording and teaching. I often wonder if those were the right decisions."

"Daddy, no, don't. I've enjoyed my life, honestly, and you are the one who gave me the strength and courage to face and to do everything. I would never have done anything without you. I know I missed some things, but with every choice or decision in life we have to give up something else. No matter what I would have done or when, I would have had to give up on doing other things."

"Very wise, indeed, Angel. I am indeed blessed to be your father."

She echoed his sentiment as the first faint golden hues of sunrise intruded upon their private moment. She smiled, relieved and content. She was home to stay. It was now daylight, and her father was safe.

CHAPTER 2

Before breakfast, Angilia dressed in blue jeans and a t-shirt and ran to the stables. She greeted each horse with a kiss and a sugar cube, but was there to spend time with her beloved golden palomino. When she reached his stall, he nuzzled her cheek and neck, as if to kiss her, and she hugged his neck. "Good morning, Starlight, my beautiful boy. How about a ride this morning?" He whinnied and threw his head back, and she smiled as she tossed his blanket over his back, then lifted his saddle in place and secured its buckles. She took his bridle from its hook and put it on him, something she had done hundreds of times over the years.

She held the reins and led him to the paddock where she walked him for several minutes before their ride. She opened the gate and led him out of the paddock, closed the gate, and hugged his neck. "Ready, boy?" He nodded his head, and she mounted him and started him at a brisk walk. Soon they were at a full gallop, the wind whipping his mane and her long hair. Eric observed them from the watch tower telescope, and he smiled at their gracefulness. Starlight was devoted to Angilia, and the two of them shared love and trust.

He watched her dismount and lead him into the paddock for his cool down walk, during which she gradually loosened the girth until it was safe to remove his saddle. She rubbed his back with a towel, and walked him several more minutes. Angilia led him to the trough while she carried the saddle into the stable and put it away. After an hour with him, she checked his skin temperature and smiled at him. "You're just fine, Starlight boy. Time for your breakfast." She led him back to his stall, removed his bridle, and gave him some hay.

Joseph, the stable master, was feeding the other horses and smiled at her. "He is a good one, your Starlight. He likes it that you are here more now."

"So do I, Joseph. So do I. I'm going to miss him, though. We'll be gone almost a week." She hugged Starlight's neck and kissed him before she closed and latched his stall door.

"He will be fine. I'll take good care of him."

"I know you will, Joseph. Thank you." She hugged Joseph, too, as she rushed back to the house to shower and change before breakfast. She and Eric were leaving for Oxford in a few hours, just the two of them—and two security officers. She looked forward to getting away with her father and leaving everything else behind, the nightmare, the terror, the looming threat. Oxford had been her safe haven, and she prayed it would prove safe for her father over the next several days.

§§§§§

"I'm going to miss Abuela and Abuelo. I wish they could stay with us."

"I know. I miss them, too. They'll return in September for Independence Day, though. Maybe we can convince them to stay." Eric smiled at his daughter, knowing how difficult it must be to have such a small family, half of whom lived in another country.

"I hope so. It feels strange returning to Oxford, almost surreal, like I was never there. I do enjoy being home with you now." She patted his arm as their plane flew above the clouds. "Have you ever wondered what secrets the clouds hold?" she quietly asked as she looked out the window at the thick fluffy clouds.

"Secrets?"

"Sure. The realms where humans cannot venture are filled with secrets. I wonder if anyone else sees them."

"You're very philosophical today, Angel. What brought this up?"

"Looking at the clouds again just triggered a lot of memories, that's all. From a long time ago."

Eric giggled. "At your age, there is no long time ago. Unless you have what they call an old soul," he winked.

"Maybe," she vaguely replied, realizing she had said too much. "Are you ready for Monday, Daddy?"

"Monday? Oh, that. No. I don't think I'll ever be ready for that. But I promised you, so no matter how embarrassing or scandalous the whole thing becomes, I won't let you down."

"Stop it. You'll be perfect, just like you always are. You sing at home all the time."

"At home, not in front of a huge crowd. Big difference."

"Not really. The trick is not to look at the audience. Look above their heads. Focus on something in the distance, like a wall sconce or painting or something. Stare at that and you'll forget about the audience. That's what people with stage fright do. Or close your eyes. Lots of singers do that. Or look at me, and sing to me like you always do. I can stand near you with the guitar if you want."

"I do want," he smiled. "I like that. Look at you only. Sing to you. That will make it a lot easier. Thank you, baby."

"I know it's nerve-wracking the first time you perform in public, Daddy, but you'll be fine."

"You mean only time, right?"

Angilia giggled. "That's up to you. You might enjoy performing. You never know until you do it. But recording is much less stressful. You'll like that better."

"What?"

"I thought you could record your song while the band is in the studio. Just think about it please." She saw the reluctance on his face. "Think about it. Please? That's all I'm asking."

"All right."

"Thank you, Daddy. We'll be there soon."

The royal plane landed in the late morning; it took just under two hours to fly from Valmondois to Kidlington Airport in Oxford. They planned to stay for seven days, and since Angilia's Oxford house had not been cleared of her belongings yet, she had plenty of clothes there already and did not pack a suitcase. Eric brought one suitcase with suits and casual attire, as well as his travel case. Angilia made him wait until one of the two security officers exited first, then they exited down the stairs. The second officer followed, carrying Eric's suitcase and his own. The four of them greeted the airport steward, who escorted them to their waiting car. Within minutes, Angilia unlocked the gate to her house and they entered.

"Bedrooms are upstairs," she said, mostly to the officers, Mike and Tony, who had never been there before. She led the way, pointing them to rooms opposite hers and Eric's. After everyone freshened up, they walked to an old pub in the nearby village for a light lunch of sandwiches and tea, and then strolled casually for several blocks, enjoying the fresh air and sunshine. Oxford in early March was chillier than in Valdavia, so they started the walk home soon. As they walked, Eric pointed out a huge open field. "This looks perfect for a picnic. We should do that before we leave. What do you think?"

She beamed at her father. "That will be fun. We can order sandwiches and tea or lemonade from that pub, load up the basket, and just relax all day. That sounds wonderful, Daddy. Next Wednesday?"

"It's a date," he smiled.

§§§§§

On the afternoon of March 3, Angilia and Eric, with Mike and Tony, the two security officers, arrived at the historic

Sheldonian Theatre at the University of Oxford at 1:30. Christopher greeted them, and escorted them to the rooms where the faculty, administration, deans, and chancellors were preparing for the 2:30 degree ceremony. Angilia received warm welcomes from her former colleagues whom she had not seen since December 2011. While they chatted, Eric watched with paternal pride the respect shown to his young daughter. Soon, though, Angilia kissed his cheek before he and his officers were escorted to their seats in the theatre.

The tradition-filled ceremony began, and Angilia felt nostalgic as she remembered receiving her DPhil nearly five years earlier to the day. She understood how the 2012 graduands felt as they sat through the ceremony. Many of them had taken her courses, and she felt gratification and happiness in their achievements. The opening address concluded with the Vice-Chancellor's introduction of Christopher, who in turn introduced Angilia.

"Esteemed Vice-Chancellor, Regents, Registrar, faculty, graduands, families, and guests, it is my distinct honor to introduce today's keynote speaker. She herself earned her Doctor of Philosophy in literature and history in this theatre five years ago this week. She made history by doing so at the age of eleven. Most of you know her, as a firm yet compassionate professor, as a colleague, and as a friend. Some of you know this, but for those who do not, I offer this bittersweet announcement. She resigned her professorship on her sixteenth birthday on January 3, to devote her time and energies to her ever-increasing public duties, patronages, and charities. She returns today for the keynote address. Join me in welcoming Dr. Angilia DeBruce Martineau." Applause greeted her when she approached the podium. As she took her place, she looked at her father. Eric clapped fervently as tears shone in his turquoise blue eyes. She smiled at him as she began her address.

After thanking everyone for the warm welcome back, she congratulated the graduands. She spoke about their success, their determination to pursue their goals and their dreams, their skill, talent, and knowledge, all of which would prove beneficial to them in their future pursuits, as well as to the world they were forging for future generations. Then she spoke about the importance of their support systems, those family members and friends, who loved, encouraged, inspired, and believed in them.

"Can someone earn a degree from the University of Oxford without that support system? Of course. Many people have done just that. But those of us who are blessed with family and friends who offer that love, encouragement, and faith to us find our work and our lives less stressful. Our burden is lessened, because those who love us help us to carry that heavy load. Everyone who earns a degree makes sacrifices. So do our loved ones. I know that well. Five years ago, my father watched me receive my degree, as your loved ones watch you today. Please take a moment now to show them your love and appreciation." The graduands and Angilia applauded in honor of their families and friends, and she noticed the tears welling in her father's eyes as he sat watching her with a content smile.

"Graduands of 2012, I have been honored to know and to work with many of you in pursuit of your dreams. Although this part of your journey concludes, you begin the next phase of your life's excursion. As you undertake that adventure—for life itself is the greatest adventure of all—I leave you with my aspiration for you, stated in the ethereal poetry of Percy Bysshe Shelley:

> *Higher still and higher*
>
> *From the earth thou springest*
>
> *Like a cloud of fire;*
>
> *The blue deep thou wingest,*
>
> *And singing still dost soar, and soaring ever singest.*

"Like Shelley's skylark, now you must spread your wings and soar into the furthest reaches of the universe. Carry with you the undeniable truth that no one and nothing can stop you except yourself. Dream large and accomplish everything you feel compelled to accomplish."

Angilia received a standing ovation, begun by many of the graduands, who saluted her as she and they prepared to leave the University of Oxford behind. She thanked them and took a step away from the podium, but Christopher returned and held her arm to stop her. She looked at him, puzzled; they had not prepared anything further.

"Dr. DeBruce Martineau, we at the University of Oxford thank you for your five years of devotion and service. While I can personally state that we are sorry to lose you as a beloved colleague, your influence and shadow remain here forever." Christopher turned to address the audience. "I first met Angilia when she was nine years old and the youngest student in the history of the University. From that first day when I interviewed her as a prospective student, I was impressed, awed, and, yes, stunned.

"I knew any institution would desire her on their faculty, so five years ago when she earned her Doctor of Philosophy, I pulled her aside and asked her to please join my faculty team at Wolfson College. She accepted and made University history twice in the same day by becoming the youngest doctorate recipient and the youngest professor at the University. To have been even a small part of her life has been remarkable for too many reasons to declare here today.

"Dr. DeBruce Martineau, in appreciation and recognition of your service to and achievements at the University of Oxford, I am pleased to present you with this award." The audience once more stood, with Eric leading the applause loudly and proudly. Tears unabashedly trickled down his cheeks as he watched his little girl receive honors most people do not attain until much later in their lives. Christopher shook her hand as she stepped down to take her seat amongst her colleagues.

Angilia watched with smiles as the young men and women were awarded their respective degrees. After the degree ceremony, she was engulfed in a sea of graduands who hugged her and thanked her for teaching them. Several even asked her to autograph their programs. Eric could feel their love for his daughter while they talked with her, hugged her, posed for pictures with her, and endlessly thanked her. When the graduands and their families departed, her colleagues took turns congratulating her and wishing her well. As she told them, she would return from time to time, including Monday when her father's scholarship was awarded for the first time.

Finally, the crowds thinned, and Eric joined her and Christopher, who told them he had a ticket for the scholarship ceremony and would see them Monday. Christopher hugged and thanked her again, as her own life's journey took another avenue. She and Eric walked slowly to the car and she realized that could be the last time she attended a degree ceremony.

That evening, Eric ordered pizzas and breadsticks from a nearby pizza parlor. The four of them—Eric, Angilia, and the two security officers, Mike and Tony—sat in the living room watching DVDs as they ate dinner. She enjoyed times like this with her father. No, they were not truly alone, but the demands of his job were absent, and they could relax and have fun. If anything truly urgent occurred, Roger would call and Eric would be back in Valmondois in a couple of hours. Right then, she relished their relative quiet and freedom.

Later, she sat in bed and wrote in her 2012 diary about the day, as in the bedroom next door, Eric did the same. Each of them wrote about the same events, but from different perspectives. Angilia's entry focused on her love for her father and how he was the sole reason she had been able to accomplish everything. His love, his faith in her, his undying encouragement, and his tenderness made their separations bittersweet yet tolerable. Their closeness meant she could talk with him about anything (except Dr. Jamieson) at any time. Without that, she probably would have crumbled under the pressure. He remained her constant foundation and inspiration.

Eric's diary entry told of his never-ending and ever-increasing love for his daughter. She awed him, blew him away, with everything she had done so young and so easily. God had gifted her with talents, skills, memory, and intelligence beyond Eric's comprehension. God had gifted him with the most inspirational, loving, thoughtful, compassionate daughter known to earth. How and why Eric should be so blessed, he did not know, but he thanked God for Angilia every day. When he watched her that day, giving an unscripted speech and receiving so much love and respect, his heart swelled to the point he could feel it beating against his sternum, as if about to explode. How much joy and love did he deserve? He frequently asked why God had blessed him above all men with Angilia. Angilia was his rock, his comfort, and his love. Without her, his life had no real purpose.

§§§§§

"Good afternoon. Welcome. I am the Dean of Christ Church College, Kevin Lawrence, your host for the afternoon. Christ Church is but one of the colleges that offer degrees in music at the University of Oxford. Our faculty and students bring a wide range of musical skill and talent to the University, even some of them who are not in our music programs.

"Last year, the faculty and deans in the music programs proposed a music scholarship in Dr. Angilia DeBruce Martineau's name. As you know, she is herself a world-renowned singer, songwriter, and musician, and a former professor of literature at the University. While she was quite enthusiastic about the scholarship, she offered us a counter-proposal to create the scholarship in her father's name. We were all struck by her eloquent and heartfelt reasons, which she will share with you. In fact, Angilia was so enthusiastic about her father's scholarship, as she calls it, that she donated €2,000,000 to establish the inaugural scholarship for this year. It is my distinct honor to welcome to the stage Dr. Angilia DeBruce Martineau."

Eric stared at his daughter in complete bewilderment as she kissed his cheek and walked across the stage to a standing ovation. She waved to everyone, most of them familiar faces. She greeted Kevin with a hug, and whispered, "You were not supposed to mention the donation. Remember?"

"Sorry," he mumbled, and he handed her a microphone.

"Thank you for such a warm welcome and for coming this afternoon. As you know, one hundred percent of the ticket proceeds go into this scholarship fund, so thank you so much for helping future music students at the University of Oxford.

45

"Kevin mentioned my counter-proposal to the scholarship committee to establish the award in my father's name. The committee members, all of whom are in the front row, requested that I share with you the reasons I presented to them. I am truly honored to do so, because my father is my hero. Without him, I would not exist. You may find it rather sentimental if I say I was created in his heart, but that is true. My life is a fairy tale, but not for the obvious reasons. I am blessed, not because I was born a princess, but because I was born to my father, who gives me more love, devotion, support, instruction, inspiration, and friendship than I deserve.

"God blessed me with a man who guides me, encourages me, teaches me, and shows me what love, courage, dedication, commitment, honor, respect, and faith really are and look like. He does not just tell me, he shows me by his example. A better role model and hero does not exist. Without him, I would not stand before you today. Ladies and gentlemen, I am so very proud to introduce my father, Eric DeBruce Martineau."

Eric walked to his daughter with a full heart and a smile. He hugged her close and kissed her cheek, then turned to wave at the audience, who were again on their feet applauding. Angilia squeezed his hand as she passed him the microphone. "Thank you all. When Angilia first told me about this scholarship, I was stunned. I might understand political science or even history, but never music. A music scholarship does not belong in my name. That's what I told her that day and many days thereafter," Eric said to some laughter from the audience.

"I am one of those people who sing to the radio and around the house. I enjoy music, and I have always listened to various types of music. But that is as far as my musical expertise goes. My daughter owns the musical talent in the family, and I guarantee you she did not inherit that from me. She tried her best to convince me she had, but she failed for once in her life."

Angilia took the microphone from her father. "No, I did not. My father is also one of those people who do not recognize their own ability and talent. What I told him, and what I told the committee, is that without his influence, music would not have been such a huge factor in my life. Yes, he plays music—the radio, CDs—and he sings. I have heard him my entire life. He sang to me before I was born, and his was the first singing I heard. His voice surrounds me with beauty and love. I am serious when I do say that I would not be here today without my father's influence. He is the one who brought music into my life. He gave me the gift of music."

Eric then took the microphone from her. "She gives me far too much credit, but she also gives me so very much love, joy, and beauty. It's been an amazing journey to share her with the world and to watch others respond to her talents. I'm truly honored to be here today, and if having this scholarship in my name helps future students, that is all that matters."

They took their seats alongside Kevin, who briefly introduced the question-and-answer portion of the ceremony. The floor was opened, and the first question was posed to Eric: When did he know that Angilia was a musical prodigy?

Eric beamed and lifted the microphone and told them, "There is a really cool story about that, actually. When she was one year old, I turned on a Chopin CD and danced around the room with her, holding her in my arms. She smiled and giggled and held onto my shoulders as I danced. A while later, my assistant told me I had a visitor, so reluctantly I left Angilia with my father's helper, Susan, and went across the hall to the sitting room. After a few moments, I heard that same music and thought maybe I hadn't turned off the CD player, and went back to the music room to check. My friend went with me, and we both suddenly stopped in the doorway. Angilia was standing on the piano bench playing that Chopin piece! My friend looked at me and I looked at him, and neither of us knew what to think. I looked at Susan, and she said Angilia wanted up on the bench, so she lifted her, thinking she'd pound the keys like children do. Instead, Angilia played an entire Chopin waltz. She was 14 months old."

Angilia was smiling at him, but shaking her head. "What?" he asked her.

"That's only half of the story." Several giggles rippled through the audience from former colleagues well aware of her hyperthymesia, her unique autobiographical memory for minute details. "You left out the most important parts. Yes, it was Chopin, his Opus 64, number 2. This was on March 31, 1997, and the apple tree outside the music room window was blossoming. The windows were open, and the gold chiffon curtains fluttered in the light breeze. You were wearing black slacks, black socks, and black oxford shoes, a white button-down shirt, and a red cardigan. The vases on the tables were gold then, but one of them broke much later and you replaced them. You didn't just dance; you danced to the waltz, to the tempo. It was slower at the beginning, almost like a stroll during the tempo giusto. When it switched to più mosso, you galloped around the room, and then it moved into the più lento, and you actually waltzed. It went back to the tempo giusto and finally the più mosso. You followed Chopin's structure perfectly when you danced. That's why I was smiling so much that day. You made the music come alive for me. You made that waltz matter to me. You are the reason I paid attention and remembered it. You."

Laughter reverberated through the theater as Eric looked at her in stunned amazement. "This is why a music scholarship should never bear my name. I don't understand half of what she said."

"Yes, you do," she said and suddenly stood and walked to the piano that was set up for the band. She looked at Kevin. "May I?" Kevin nodded and everyone clapped their approval. Angilia sat and played the same waltz, and explained what each part of the tempo was: tempo giusto, più mosso, più lento, tempo giusto, più lento. Everyone applauded when she finished, and she waved them silent. "See? You know music instinctively, Daddy. You followed the changes in tempo perfectly, and you made the dance and Chopin's waltz memorable."

"I don't know about any of you, but I am constantly astounded by her memory of details. What I wore. The tree. The date. How?"

Christopher stood to make a comment and to ask a question. "She amazes and even scares some of us, Sir. No one could ever forget a detail when she was involved. I do want to ask Angilia what this prodigious life is like from her perspective."

"Normal. This is all I have ever known, Christopher. My earliest experiences and memories involve this, so to me this is nothing extraordinary, really. I don't say that in a sense of pomposity at all. To me, this is normal. The music opened many opportunities for me, and I have many wonderful friends as a result. I am neither the best nor the worst, but I do my personal best, which is all anyone can ever do. Music has been a huge piece of my world from the beginning, thanks to my father. For me, music is about creating art but more importantly about creating memories."

"What was it like working with Tom Greenfield, a former teen idol himself?"

"That's a multifaceted question, Sherice," Angilia said to one of the music professors. "Tom taught me a lot about performing, about connecting with an audience. He showed me how to remain comfortable and confident on stage. Tom never had a persona. He was always himself, and that is the most important lesson of all. Be honest, sincere, and true. Tom protected me, he believed in me, and he encouraged me to explore whatever came into my mind, to experiment, to take risks. He told me that others were wrong and that I was right, that all art had to project from the heart and soul of the artist or it was never authentic. If the artist did not exist in her work, the work was lifeless. We synced on that, and he let me know that it was all right to pour myself into my work and to make it personal."

The rest of the two-hour session was filled with more questions for both of them about different aspects of music and how their individual and shared lives had been impacted by her very young and sudden fame. Eric addressed that by saying that fame had not affected or changed Angilia except to make her more aware of how she was a role model for pre-teens and teens. She added that, like it or not, a performer's personal life could influence others, so she took that seriously. She had learned respect, faith, confidence, compassion, and courage from her father, and she tried to project those qualities in everything she did.

Kevin reclaimed the floor to announce that Angilia and her band would perform a short set before the scholarship was awarded. She moved the microphone stand to the front of the stage as she introduced her band: John Herbert on bass, Tim Hanley on electric guitar, Greg Smithson on piano, and Joe Arnold at the drums. She snapped the microphone onto the stand, then picked up her guitar and slipped the strap over her shoulder.

She actually played the first song solo, just her guitar and her voice. As soon as the first chords resonated through the theater, deafening applause erupted. She curtseyed in thanks as she began singing and as memories crowded her mind. When the song ended to more applause, she thanked them and remarked, "That song is one my father played often. He has a lot of records, several by Tom Greenfield. For some reason, I always heard that as a ballad, so that's how I was singing it that fateful day I met Tom and he led me on this journey. See, this really is due to my father." She turned and smiled at him, while he smiled in return, never before realizing the true impact he did have on her.

Angilia and the band performed four more songs from her ten-year career, songs she had written and composed. Her lyrics were sometimes confessional, often esoteric, and always spiritual. She explored her emotions, her philosophical questions, her memories, and her Christian beliefs in her lyrics and for some reason people responded to her work. She felt that God must have placed her on this path for a reason, and she strove to honor him as much as she could through her music.

"Thank you so much. We have one more song to perform, and now you get your proof that my father is magnificent." He joined her at the microphone, and whispered in her ear to stay close to him. She nodded, and he did turn to look at her, just as she had mentioned on the plane days earlier. Her guitar chords kicked off John Denver's "Sunshine on My Shoulders," and he felt everyone and everything else fade as he looked into his daughter's eyes, just as he always did when he sang to her at home. She smiled, often biting her lip to stop the tears. His performance was impeccable, she knew it and the audience knew it. When the last note was struck, they leapt to their feet in a standing ovation. She was filled with love and delight. "I told you, didn't I? Isn't he perfect?" The audience whistled and cheered their agreement.

After several minutes, Eric convinced them to stop and to please sit. "Thank you. My daughter talked me into this, and I appreciate your kindness. Truly, I do. Love has obviously blinded, I mean deafened, my daughter, though," he said to a few giggles and several shouts of disagreement. Angilia playfully swatted his arm and declared it most certainly had not.

As the jovial exchanges trickled into silence, Kevin handed Eric an envelope. "Ladies and gentlemen, we now proudly award the first annual Eric DeBruce Martineau Scholarship for Musical Excellence to Mr. Anthony Severson, a piano student at the University of Oxford," Angilia announced. Anthony walked up the stairs onto the stage and joined Eric and Angilia at the microphone. Eric handed Anthony the award certificate, shook his hand, and congratulated him.

Radiating with happiness, Anthony asked if he could kiss the Princess' hand, Eric gave his permission, and in a scene straight out of an Arthurian film, Anthony knelt on one knee and tenderly kissed her hand in reverence. Angilia thanked him, then offered her congratulations and the microphone to Anthony, who thanked them and the committee for granting him this honor and making it possible for him to pursue his dreams of becoming a concert pianist.

The three of them posed for photographs, and then greeted the guests, many of whom made further donations to the scholarship fund. Angilia felt elated that most people complimented her father on his performance, which she hoped would encourage him to record the song the next day.

Later that evening, as they relaxed in her library, she asked him if he had thought about recording the song. "I'm still not sure. People were very kind today, but the whole thing is a bit out of my comfort zone," Eric told her.

"You forgot anyone else was there. I could tell. In the studio downstairs, it will be even easier. There will be fewer people, and you already know them all anyway. And you can still look at me and forget everything else, like you did today." He hesitated. "You know all of my recording profits are donated to charities and foundations, right? And that I write a short essay about whichever charity or foundation receives that record's proceeds, right?" He nodded. "What if we donate this album's proceeds to your Open Heart Foundation? You can do the write-up, and even more people around the world will learn about Open Heart. The essay is always included, whether it's in a CD or with a download. When people download tracks, they get a PDF file of the essay. Sam also posts it to the web site permanently."

He grinned at her. "You're very tricky. But what if I don't like the way it sounds?"

"Daddy, you were flawless today, really. But if you really don't like the first take, you can do it again until you do like it."

"All right, Angel, I'll do this for you and for Open Heart." She kissed him on both cheeks and told him how wonderful he was.

§§§§§

Angilia awoke, showered, and dressed early the next morning, wanting to write an important letter before Sam and the band arrived and the day grew busy. She quickly brewed a cup of herbal tea and walked into her home office, to find Eric already sitting at the computer. Her smile lit up the room and she went to stand behind him. She kissed his head while he read aloud what he had typed:

"Open Heart Foundation began in 1993 to offer assistance and programs for our older population, as well as for their caregivers and families. Caring for older loved ones creates many concerns, stresses, and burdens, and Open Heart provides a strong support system for all of those involved.

Sometimes the caregivers' needs are overlooked, but not at Open Heart. Elder care often leads to burnout, fatigue, and depression, as well as relationship, emotional, and physical breakdowns. Open Heart delivers individual and family counseling services to offer moral support and to teach coping techniques that help to relieve the stresses of caregiving. Home care assistance is also provided at no charge, because at Open Heart we believe that we have an innate duty to care for those who first cared for us.

Caring for older family members and friends often involves making difficult, emotionally-charged decisions, and we are there to assist you in making those most challenging of life's decisions. Everyone at Open Heart honors the life and the dignity of each person, and we understand the complexities of caring for and meeting the needs of our older loved ones. We want to help you make this part of your life less painful and stressful. Life is a precious gift, and everyone deserves respect, compassion, and love."

"That's just right, Daddy. It's informative, emotional, and convincing. Open Heart should get a lot of donations after people read that. Thank you."

"It was your idea, Angel. I just need to save it to a flash drive for Sam." She opened a desk drawer and handed him one. He finished, then stood and picked up his coffee mug. He kissed her cheek and left to shower and dress. She sat at the computer and spent the next hour typing a letter, selecting her words thoughtfully. She printed it, signed and folded it, then addressed an envelope and readied it for mailing later that day. This was perhaps the most important letter she would ever write.

By the time she sealed and stamped the letter, Eric reappeared, clad in jeans and a short-sleeved polo shirt. He asked Mike, one of the security officers, to go to the market two blocks away for a variety of breakfast pastries, fruit, and orange juice. Mike took the rented car, and when he returned, Sam, the band, Eric, and Angilia were gathered around the kitchen island talking. They helped themselves to breakfast as they discussed the songs on the day's agenda.

Eric handed Sam the flash drive. "Here's the charitable foundation write-up. I can't believe she talked me into it."

"You'll be fine, just like yesterday. Which charity gets the honor this time?"

"The Open Heart Foundation. It was her idea."

"So was this the deal-maker? Or you just couldn't say no to her?"

"I tried to say no. But even if no one ever listens to my song, she'll sell millions of CDs and make hundreds of thousands euros for the Foundation."

"They'll listen, Daddy, believe me. You'll get more You Tube hits and downloads than Justin Bieber." Eric nearly spit out his juice.

When the giggles subsided, she led everyone to the basement recording studio. Sam took his seat at the control panels, Eric joined him in the booth, and John, Tim, Greg, and Joe went to their respective instruments. Angilia tuned her guitar, and soon they were running through ten of the eleven songs she had written and selected for the album. The band had rehearsed and learned the songs after she had sent them the sheet music and demo tapes in January.

Eric had watched her recording sessions before, and she never failed to impress him with her ease and naturalness. She preferred to record live, with no overdubs, splicing, or mechanical enhancements such as auto-tune, and almost always in one take. She was celebrated for her perfect pitch and five octave range. As he listened to her, he remembered the first time he had heard her sing. He had just helped her into her bed and was singing "their song" to her, and she started singing with him. He could feel again how his heart had trembled at the voice coming from his tiny little girl. Her voice held such maturity and skill. She did not sound like the two-year-old she was. Now she was sixteen and recording her tenth album.

Sam played back the first song and called it a done deal. The next nine songs followed suit, living up to her famous one-take formula. Her mix of ballads and more up-tempo pop songs, all of which she had written, blended to create an album built upon the themes of love, faith, and strength. The eleventh song was, in her heart, the most emotional and personal of the songs she had written.

That song used just her guitar for accompaniment, so the band mates joined Sam and Eric in the control booth. She closed her eyes and her fingers played the opening melody and harmony simultaneously in a style similar to Mother Maybelle Carter's celebrated finger picking. Soon the words of her song "The Gift of You" filled the room and her father's heart:

HEART-GLOW

You are the most beautiful man

This world has ever known,

Your heart filled with love

And your soul with such grace.

You take my breath away

With your truth and devotion.

How much more can my heart bear?

How much do I deserve?

What did I do so right

To be so blessed with the gift of you?

You are the most generous man

And my love for you has only grown.

My greatest desire is to honor you

And to please you for all of my days.

I love you. What more can I say?

To you I give my undying adoration.

To obey you is my fervent prayer.

You brought me from Heaven with your heart-glow so bright.

Your love brought me to life and brought me to you.

You take my breath away

With your truth and devotion.

How much more can my heart bear?

How much do I deserve?

What did I do so right

To be blessed with the gift of you?

I love you. What more can I say?

She looked at her father when she sang the last line, confirming that her words were about him. His hands were clasped over his heart.

Sam played the track, and everyone sat silent for a moment. Eric stood and walked toward her. She placed her guitar on its stand and rose to meet him in an embrace. Neither spoke, for words were unnecessary. Their hearts pounded in unison, saying all they needed to tell one another.

"Are you ready, Daddy?" she finally asked him.

"As ready as I can be. Listen, can we do this with just the two of us and your guitar? Just like we do at home?"

She nodded and looked at the band. They smiled and asked if they should leave. Eric shook his head. "No. We'll be fine."

Angilia placed Eric's stool across from hers and adjusted the microphone between them. She asked if he wanted to do a run-through, but he shook his head. Sam gave her the count, and like so many times before, her fingers played the familiar chords and he sang the poetic lyrics to his favorite John Denver song. He looked into her eyes. Soon they were done and Sam called it a take.

During the playback, Angilia felt tears falling from her eyes at the sound of her father's gentle, smooth voice, the voice with which she had fallen in love before she was born. Unanimously, the men called it done, but asked Eric what he thought. He shrugged and looked at Angilia. Through her tears, she declared it perfect. The record was complete. Eric quietly asked Sam for a copy of Angilia's song, and when he turned on his phone later, he found an MP3 file of "The Gift of You" awaiting him.

Everyone agreed on a dinner at the pub, where they could relax and talk. They freshened up and Angilia put the letter in her tote bag as they prepared to leave. After a day of studio work, they decided to walk in the fresh air, and when the group neared the pub, Angilia slid her letter through a postal box slot. She prayed to God for a positive response.

Before they left the pub, Eric asked the proprietor if they could have four sandwiches, four salads, and a gallon of chilled tea ready the next morning around 10:00. He said they would pick everything up themselves before they went to the open field for their picnic.

Angilia smiled the entire evening, and when she hugged Sam and her guys, as she affectionately called them, she thanked them for such a wonderful dream of a day. She promised to be in touch soon to start discussing the release date and to schedule a few shows. The men drove away amid shouts of good-bye and waves from Eric and Angilia.

Inside, she looked up at her father with a smile and tears in her eyes. "Happy tears, Daddy. Only happy tears today. You are amazing. Truly amazing."

They sat next to one another on the sofa for a long while. "You floored me with that last song, Angel. I have never heard a more beautiful song. I don't deserve anything so beautiful, but I have to echo you. I am so blessed by you. I love you so much. No father has ever been as blessed or as loved as I am, Angel." He clasped her shoulders with his hands and looked through her eyes into her soul. "I love you, my beautiful daughter Angilia."

An hour later, before she turned off her light, she wrote the March 6 entry in her diary. She described the recording session, emphasizing the last two songs: hers for and about her father and his inspired performance of "their song." She finished her joyous entry looking forward to their picnic:

Tomorrow will be equally or more glorious. Daddy and I (with Mike and Tony) are going on a picnic late tomorrow morning. I have passed that field dozens of times, but on Friday Daddy said it was the perfect place for a picnic. It is! We'll have so much fun, and I am so happy! I love Daddy so very much, and it has been a miracle to leave the nightmare behind for these few days in Oxford. I can't believe how blissful these days are. The next time I write will be tomorrow evening, when I recount the details of our fun picnic. I can only thank God for gifting me my Daddy and these perfectly idyllic and peaceful days with him. God has replaced the nightmare with a dream come true. ☺

CHAPTER 3

The next morning, the four of them arose early and dressed casually. Angilia paired her dark blue denim jeans with a white blouse and pink bolero sweater. Eric wore one of his white button-down dress shirts, untucked, with his blue jeans. Mike, one of Eric's longest-serving security officers, also wore jeans, shirt, and a sweater. Tony, the other officer, chose khaki slacks, a t-shirt, and a jacket. They all enjoyed their casual day. After a light breakfast of fruit and juice, they relaxed by watching an old Hollywood film on television. What a pleasant, relaxing Wednesday morning, certainly not typical of their weekday mornings.

Everyone freshened up and prepared to leave, and Angilia pulled a picnic basket from her kitchen pantry and placed flatware, napkins, condiments, plastic plates and cups, and straws inside. Eric tucked a battery-powered radio into the corner of the basket, and grabbed a couple of blankets from her linen closet. All they needed to do was pick up the food at the pub and enjoy the beautiful, cool, but sunny day. Angilia's happiness was obvious; she never stopped smiling, and Eric was relieved that her fears were abated.

During the brisk walk to the pub, even Mike and Tony commented on the carefree atmosphere. At the pub, the owner carefully placed the sandwiches and salads in the picnic basket, and handed the gallon of tea to Tony to carry. Eric carried the basket, and Angilia held the folded blankets. The pub owner smiled and wished them a lovely picnic. "Thank you, Mr. Kinney. Today is going to be a most perfect and happy day," she beamed. Eric put his hand on her shoulder, and soon they arrived at the field.

Eric selected the spot, and she spread the blankets. She placed the radio on the blanket and turned it on. She leaned back and watched the clouds floating far above. "I love watching clouds. They are so magical and mysterious." The four of them spent many minutes picking out shapes in the clouds, then Eric began emptying the basket and setting up the informal table.

While they enjoyed the salads, sandwiches, and tea, they talked, joked, laughed, and even sang along to the songs on the radio. She relished these moments with her father, away from the formalities and schedules his job demanded. Even with Mike and Tony there, the lunch was very casual, relaxed, and fun. She liked them, but for one second she wondered if Mike and Tony even needed to be there. After everyone finished eating, she placed the dirty dishes and wrappers in the basket. She lay back on the blanket, and smiled up at her father.

"How about a walk?" he asked her.

She nodded, and he helped her to her feet. Tony went with them, staying a few steps behind. No one could see the guns concealed by his jacket and Mike's sweater. They were always ready for anything. Tony scanned the area constantly as they walked, looking for anyone or anything out of the ordinary. Eric and Angilia slowly walked to the other side of the nearby pond and back, just enjoying their time together. When they returned to the picnic, Eric suddenly took hold of her and spun her into a dance to the song playing on the radio, an old Abba hit that had been one of his brother Patrick's favorites.

She giggled as they twirled, spun, and dipped, and when the song ended she held onto his arms to steady herself from her fit of the giggles. She looked up at him with a huge smile. "Thank you, Daddy. Today really is beautiful. I love you."

Suddenly, terror filled her, though, and her smile vanished as she saw the bright sun reflect off of silver metal behind a pile of rocks not far from them. Her father was in danger! She had to protect him. Everything happened so very quickly, though to her it seemed like the slowest motion. She pushed Eric backwards instinctively, just as a loud bang echoed through the air. He groaned when he hit the ground, his shoulder on fire. More loud bangs very quickly followed, and she felt something hot pierce her chest. A bullet. She had trouble breathing, but she had to shield her father. Someone was trying to kill her father!

Mike and Tony yelled for Eric to stay down and for Angilia to get down immediately. They were both shooting at the attacker, moving, running, circling him. The noise of the three guns was deafening. She saw Eric try to get up. "No, Daddy!" Quickly, she moved toward her father and felt something slice behind her right kneecap. She looked down at him, and he stared up at her in shock and disbelief. She was hurt. Abruptly another bullet hit her, in the center of her chest, and she felt weak. Eric watched in horror as blood gushed from her chest, and he moved to reach for her. She had to keep him down. She had to protect her father.

Bullets flew through the air, and Angilia flung herself on top of her father, covering his torso and head with her body and arms. "Don't move, Daddy," she whispered to him. He felt her warm, wet blood soaking him, his daughter's blood soaking him. Just as suddenly, everything was quiet, except for the sounds of Mike and Tony running toward the attacker and the radio still blaring. "He's dead," Tony said.

Immediately, Tony called the British emergency number, 999, and explained what had happened.   Mike rushed to Eric and Angilia just as Eric gently lifted her off of him and turned his daughter onto her back. Mike took off his sweater and folded it under her head. "You're hurt, Daddy. Oh God, you're hurt." All Eric saw was her blood, so much blood, and he grabbed a blanket to staunch her bleeding; she reached for it and tried to cover his shoulder wound. Eric pressed the blanket to her chest with all of his strength while she looked at him and put her hand over his left shoulder. She seemed distressed to see his blood trickling down his shirt sleeve. He was terrified and looked at Mike helplessly.

"I'm so sorry. I love you, Daddy," Angilia softly whispered as her hand slipped from his shoulder and her eyes closed. Eric could not feel her heart beating. He could not feel her breathing. Not her, not his precious daughter. "Angilia! Angilia, open your eyes, baby!" He screamed at her, he pleaded with her. "Angel, please!" He lifted her and held her limp body to him as he cried and screamed and pleaded. "Angel, please don't leave me." The ambulance arrived in less than one minute, and at the instant the cardiac surgeon reached her, Eric saw her eyes open and heard her gasp for air. He could barely hear her say "Mommy," but she was alive and that was all that mattered. His baby girl was alive.

The surgeon quickly lifted her onto the gurney and the medics rapidly loaded her into the ambulance. Eric jumped aboard and told her he loved her and was right there with her, while the cardiac surgeon explained he would prepare her for surgery in the ambulance so that he could rush her into the operating room as soon as they arrived at the hospital. Mike sat in the front seat with the driver, and Tony stayed behind to guard the scene and to talk to the police.

"I'm Matthew Taylor, dear, and I'm going to take very good care of you, I promise. I just need to do a few things right now so we can start to make you well. Okay?" Angilia nodded, looking at him and feeling oddly safe with him. Matthew explained she needed to remain still and calm so he could insert the endotracheal tube to help her breathe, and he kept talking to her in his soothing voice as he held her tongue down with the laryngoscope and carefully slid the tube into her trachea. He patted her shoulder. "You're doing great, sweetie. I need to unbutton your blouse now so I can insert a CVC to monitor the blood flow to your heart. This won't take very long, I promise." Eric watched in horror as his little girl was being prepped for emergency surgery. He saw her looking at him, and though she could not talk due to the breathing tube, she nodded at him, trying to reassure him. She was strong for him, and it crushed his soul.

"I love you, baby," Eric said to her as he struggled to control his tears and his distress. Matthew finished inserting the central venus catheter in her upper right chest. He looked over his shoulder at Eric and saw the fear in his eyes. "I'll take the best care of her, I promise. I won't let anything happen to her."

Matthew removed the ring from her left hand and handed it to Eric. "You hold onto that for her and you can put it back on her finger after we're finished." Eric clutched the ring, tears filling his eyes. How had this happened? Dear God, he prayed, please do not take her from me yet. Not yet. Please.

Matthew next told her he had to insert an IV in her arm for the saline solution and blood transfusion. He was gentle, knowing she was scared and in severe pain. He was amazed first that she was alive, second that she was conscious and lucid, and third that she was not in shock. He taped the IV in place after insertion, and she weakly squeezed his hand. He very gently squeezed hers in response, and attached the saline solution to the IV, then the type O negative blood they used in emergencies such as this. Quickly, he drew a vial of blood for type-matching. Just then, the ambulance pulled up to the John Radcliffe Hospital emergency entrance, and Matthew was informed that the surgical staff was waiting for them in the operating room. Police surrounded the entrance and the interior of the hospital and more officers surrounded the royal party as they wheeled Angilia inside. Mike walked alongside Eric, holding his arm.

"We have to take her to surgery now," Matthew quickly told Eric. Eric bent and kissed her cheek and told her how much he loved her and that he would see her soon. She nodded her head and barely squeezed his hand, and then the gurney was moving swiftly and she felt dizzy. Matthew's soothing voice sounded distant as they entered the bright operating room. "I'm going to scrub in and I will be right back, darling," he told her with a gentle squeeze of her shoulder. That was the last sound she heard before the world grew completely dark.

§§§§

Eric stood staring straight ahead, his brain reeling and trying to comprehend everything that had happened in the past few minutes. What had happened? How could it have happened? He felt numb and scared, more scared than he had ever thought he could feel. Mike was beside him, his arm around Eric, steadying him. Eric looked at him, and Mike saw the purest terror in the King's eyes.

A doctor came to Eric and introduced himself as Mitchell Taylor, Matthew's father. "Sir, believe me, your daughter is in the hands of the best cardiac surgeon in Oxfordshire. Matthew will treat her wounds expertly and take the absolute best care of her. Come with me, and we'll take care of you."

Mike and Dr. Taylor led Eric to a private examination room and helped him onto the exam table. Dr. Taylor washed his hands and pulled on latex gloves. He took two x-rays of Eric's shoulder and was relieved to see that the bullet was not deeply embedded and had not hit any major organs or any arteries. He explained this to Eric, who seemed oblivious. "Sir, we'll have your wound treated soon." He unbuttoned Eric's shirt and slid it down his arms.

"How is she?"

"I'm afraid it's too soon to know anything. But I will find out what I can as soon as I take care of you. I promise." Eric nodded, fear the only thing he felt. Dr. Taylor gave Eric a shot of local anesthetic, removed the bullet with surgical forceps, cleaned the wound, and then stitched it closed. The nurse dressed the wound carefully, while Dr. Taylor explained to Mike that Eric would have to wear a sling for several days. Eric refused to take off the blood-stained shirt, so Dr. Taylor pulled it back up and buttoned it. He and the nurse positioned the sling and situated Eric's arm. "You stay here for a while and relax in private. Police are outside, and Mike and Nurse Kara will stay. I'll suit up and get an update from Matthew and his team." Eric nodded.

Kara raised the head of the exam table so that Eric could recline. Mike helped him lay back, and Kara got a blanket from the cabinet and covered Eric. "You just rest some. She's going to need you strong and healthy when she wakes up after surgery."

Tears slid from Eric's eyes, and soon he was crying and moaning, almost wailing, unceasingly. Mike was not a close friend of Eric's, but he knew he was the only one there for him. He pulled the doctor's stool over and sat next to him, holding his hand and trying to comfort him. Fifteen minutes later, Dr. Taylor returned and removed the surgical mask and gown. Eric looked at him and sat up, tense and rigid. "How is she?"

Mike stood up and Dr. Taylor sat across from Eric and looked into his eyes. He saw the raw fear, but he had to be honest.

"It's serious, very serious. The bullet on the right side of her chest punctured her diaphragm, the breathing muscle. The most serious is the other chest wound. That bullet is lodged in her aorta. She's lost close to 40 percent of her blood, which is nearly fatal itself, but Matthew began the transfusions in the ambulance to counterbalance her blood loss. Matthew has performed a thoracotomy to access her heart. Right now, he has everything under control, but her wounds are extremely serious. I'm not going to sugar coat this. The wound to her aorta should have killed her instantly. But it didn't, and Matthew is taking care of her, Sir."

Eric turned gray and gasped for air. Dr. Taylor forced him to lean back and close his eyes, while the nurse placed an oxygen mask over his nose and mouth. Mike walked into the corner of the room and quietly called Roger and explained what had happened. Like everyone, Roger could not wrap his head around what he was told. He ran to find Daniel and Susan and tell them what he knew. Susan collapsed to her knees in tears. The men helped her up and explained they needed to hurry and pack so they could take one of the royal planes to Oxford as soon as possible. One of the security officers called the airport to have the plane ready for takeoff within minutes, making sure everyone understood the urgency.

Roger threw some clothes into a suitcase, as did Susan—who also grabbed a few things of Angilia's—while Daniel packed both his and Eric's bags. Ten security officers were told to accompany them to the hospital to guard the King and the Princess in addition to the local police. Soon the car was racing to the airport and the passengers were quickly boarded onto the King's plane. Two hours later they landed in Oxford and were driven to John Radcliffe hospital immediately. Word of the shooting had begun to spread through Oxford, and soon the news would reach the shaken and devastated citizens of Valdavia—and Angilia's maternal grandparents in Spain.

§§§§

Mike had alerted the police to expect Roger, Daniel, Susan and the security officers and to escort them immediately to the private exam room. The ten officers were put on detail near the operating room, where they would guard Angilia during surgery and her transport to recovery after surgery. Everyone was tense and vigilant, none of them ever expecting an attempted assassination. Some of the officers had worked for Eric's father, and had never used their guns for any reason. That the Princess was fighting for her life was incomprehensible to them.

Roger, Daniel, and Susan entered the exam room to a sight that haunted them for many years to follow: their friend pale, scared, his white shirt and blue jeans dyed red with Angilia's blood. Susan choked back her scream and tears and grasped Daniel's arm tightly. They had to be strong for Eric. Angilia was his life, and they knew how terrified he was; his fear was tangible.

Eric looked at them, his face taut, his eyes filled with tears and dread. Those tears fell down his cheeks, and Roger rushed to this man who was like a brother to him and held him in a strong hug. Eric grasped Roger with his right hand and unabashedly cried. Susan turned away, her hands covering her mouth, willing herself not to cry or to scream. This was not happening. That is all she could think. This was not real. It was all a bad dream.

Dr. Taylor said he would get another update from Matthew and his team, and Daniel nodded. After several minutes, Eric stood and went toward the door. "Something's wrong." Roger put his arm around Eric and tried to calm him. It did not work. "Something's wrong. I have to go to her."

The nurse stepped forward and gently took hold of his right hand. "She has the very best surgeons. Dr. Taylor will be back soon."

"I feel it. Something is horribly wrong." Susan could no longer fight her tears and fell against Daniel. Roger once more held Eric to him, his own heart sinking. After what felt like hours, Dr. Taylor returned. Eric rushed to him. "What's wrong? What happened to her? Tell me. Please tell me."

When the doctor told Eric to sit down, Susan gasped and fell to the floor, shaking and sobbing. Eric shook his head and looked into Dr. Taylor's eyes, his own pleading. Sighing, Dr. Taylor knew he had to tell Eric. "Angilia is stabilized now, but there was a complication. Her blood pressure plummeted, and that caused her heart to stop. Matthew knew exactly what to do, and he restored her heartbeat quickly. I stayed until I knew she was stable. She is now."

Eric's body went limp and weak, and Dr. Taylor grabbed him as he stumbled forward. He and Roger helped him onto the exam table, and the nurse placed a cold cloth on his forehead. Roger stood behind him, feeling sick and helpless. "Twice. My baby's heart stopped twice today. She can't leave me. She can't."

Dr. Taylor clasped Eric's right hand. "Matthew will not let that happen. He won't. Trust me. I saw my son in there, and he is not letting that happen. He knows what to do so that does not happen. And I saw her. She is not going to let it happen, either. She is strong and she is fighting. She's not ready to leave you. God is not ready to take her. There is a reason she survived what should have been fatal. This is not Angilia's time to die."

Eric squeezed the doctor's hand firmly. "Thank you," he hoarsely whispered.

Susan stood and dried her face with a tissue. She walked to Eric and bent to kiss his head and comfort him. He and his wife had hired her nearly seventeen years ago to be there as a father's helper to care for Angilia when Eric had to be away from home. He and Angilia were her family now. He held Susan's hand, and she rubbed his back with her other hand, in a maternal way that helped him to relax his tense muscles. He focused on what Dr. Taylor had said. Angilia survived. She was very seriously injured, but she survived. God was not ready to take her yet. It was not his daughter's time to die. She was fighting to stay with him. Their love was too strong and would keep them together. He kept praying to God as they waited several hours that felt like years.

Over an hour later, Eric reached into his front jeans pocket and pulled out his iPhone. Holding it in his right hand, he tapped the music icon with his thumb, and then tapped a song title. Everyone stood around Eric protectively as Angilia's voice reverberated through the room, singing the words to "The Gift of You" that he had watched her record nearly two days earlier. Everyone in the room knew that her lyrics were about her father, and they watched Eric apprehensively, his face registering the breadth of emotions he had experienced as the day replayed in his mind.

Hours earlier, she had been so alive, so happy, and now she fought to stay alive. He smiled as he saw her laughing, walking, dancing, pointing to clouds, and hugging him. The smile vanished suddenly as he saw bullets tear into her body and her blood pour from the holes in her chest. He felt her blood saturating him. He felt her lifeless and limp in his arms.

"How could everything change so drastically in just a few seconds? We were so very happy. She giggled as we danced. She told me she loves me, that she was happy. Then I watched bullets rip through her. She died in my arms just before the ambulance arrived.

"My baby risked her life for me. She saved my life. She was willing to die for me. I do not deserve her love. But I am so thankful she is mine. I love her so much. She is my heart, my soul, my life. And I am so very scared."

Susan and Daniel sat on either side of Eric, Roger stood behind him, and Mitchell sat in front of him. They comforted him, held onto him, and surrounded him with love. Eric bowed his head and whispered a tearful prayer. His friends and Mitchell bowed their heads in unison, casting their prayers to Heaven.

Angilia's so-called guardian angel watched the scene with love and tenderness and then resumed her vigil in the operating room. She knew that Angilia was not meant to die that day, and she made sure that the young Princess' destiny was not altered by another's evil actions. She forced Angilia's soul back into her body twice that day, and would do so as many times as necessary. Marisol refused to let her cherished daughter die before her predestined time.

§§§§

At nearly 2:00 in the morning, the door opened and Matthew entered. Eric was suddenly rigid again, though he fought to keep his panic under control. His blue eyes were bloodshot and tear-filled, and Matthew understood how scared he was. He stood in front of Eric and took hold of his right hand. "Angilia." Her name. That was all Eric had the courage to say at that moment.

"I just left her in her private recovery room. The surgery was long, complicated, and anxious, but I repaired the damage. Her body must rest and heal, which is not going to be quick or easy, but it will heal in time." Matthew sat next to Eric on the exam table and kept ahold of his hand.

"The orthopedic surgeon who repaired her knee will talk with you in a couple of days. She'll need physical therapy at some point, which will restore range of motion to her knee. That is the least serious of her wounds. The bullet wound to her diaphragm will also require physical therapy to help repair the muscle and to restore normal breathing function. That wound is going to complicate her recovery from the most serious procedure, though, since she needs immediate assistance with breathing. That's why we're keeping the breathing tube in place at least until tomorrow morning sometime. We just need to make sure she is breathing and getting oxygen to her heart, lungs, and brain, and the breathing tube does the work her body can't do right now at full capacity.

"The bullet wound to her aorta was and remains my priority. I'm not going to lie. It's very serious. It should have killed her, but it didn't. It tried to, but she didn't let it, I didn't let it, and her guardian angel didn't let it. Someone is watching out for her. My priority right now is to keep her stable, calm, and comfortable so that she can start to heal.

"Her body has suffered multiple traumas, and I have to tell you that she amazed me. She was calm and alert from the moment I arrived on the scene, and the fact that she was not in shock is a testament to her resolve and strength. She willed herself to that place where she remained present and with you the entire time. She didn't lose consciousness until we wheeled her into the operating room, which was perfect actually. We don't give heart trauma patients general anesthesia due to the high risks involved, and she did very well throughout most of the surgery.

"My father told you what happened?" Eric nodded. "We resolved that quickly, though. Like I said, between her determination to stay with you, her guardian angel, and my team, we all pulled her through. Tonight is going to be rough, on all of us. The next several days will be rough. She's going to be in tremendous pain, I need you to know that now. I had to perform a median sternotomy, and the post-op pain from that is very intense and brutal. Because of the damage to her heart, though, I have to be careful which narcotics we give her. Many of them can complicate heart issues, and that's a risk I just won't take. That means she has to learn to deal with the pain from the wounds and the surgeries. That is going to be very difficult. She's going to need you to keep her calm and keep her mind off of the pain. Okay?"

Eric closed his eyes and tears slid down his cheeks. Matthew squeezed his hand reassuringly. "That is going to tear you apart. I know that. You have to talk with her, sing to her, read to her, tell her stories, whatever it takes to keep her from thinking too much about the pain. When she knows that you are safe and all right, that will help. She's more concerned about you, I understand. So we just need to keep her calm, stable, and help her begin the healing and recovery process. I'll take you to her soon, but I don't think she needs to see you looking like this. How about you wash up and change first?"

Eric looked down at his formerly white shirt and blue jeans and moaned. Daniel picked up the suitcase containing Eric's clothes and walked his friend into the bathroom, where he and Mitchell helped Eric remove his blood-stained clothes and wash the blood from this skin. Daniel's heart broke for Eric; he knew what this had done to his best friend. He hated the people who had done this. How could anyone do this to Eric and Angilia? Eric sensed his friend's thoughts. "Thank you, Daniel."

He patted Eric's back, unable to speak due to the tears choking him. He helped Eric brush his teeth and comb his hair. Mitchell adjusted the sling and gave him a reassuring smile. "Do you need anything else?" he asked Eric.

"Just my daughter."

§§§§§

Matthew, Mitchell, and Eric were surrounded by security and police officers as they walked to the hospital's Cardiothoratic Critical Care Unit (CTCC). "Angilia is still unconscious," Matthew explained. "She is also hooked up to several tubes and machines, which can look frightening. You saw me start some of that in the ambulance. Her breathing tube is attached to a mechanical ventilator to assist her breathing. I placed flexible tubes in her chest to drain air, blood, and fluid, a Foley catheter in her bladder, and a nasogastric tube to decompress her stomach. The IV in her arm has the blood and the saline solution, which I began in the ambulance. The CVC is still in place in her upper chest to monitor the blood flow to her heart. We also have her hooked up to a heart monitor which reads her heart rate and blood pressure. The blood pressure cuff is on her left arm. It's all there to help us take care of her. Don't let it scare you."

Mitchell knew it would, though. He was a father, too, and he knew any father would be scared and upset to see his child in this condition. He put his arm around Eric to support him both physically and emotionally. Eric took a deep breath and closed his eyes in prayer when Matthew opened the door to her private recovery room. Several guards were in the hall, restricting access to the area and room, all of them rigid and highly alert.

Mitchell felt the muscles in Eric's back tighten when he entered the room, then felt Eric lurch at his first sight of Angilia in many hours. "Oh, God, no," he moaned and fell to his knees. Mitchell was beside him, holding Eric as he fought nausea. His whole world had been knocked off of its axis in just a few moments on what was supposed to be a fun, happy day with his little girl. How? Why?

Eric tried to wobble to his feet, and Mitchell and Matthew assisted him slowly. They helped him into the chair next to her bed, and he began crying when he looked at her. She was so small, so very pale, and he could see thick bandages covering her chest under the hospital gown and blankets. Her right knee was elevated and bandaged. She was so still and fragile looking that his heart felt crushed and bruised. How could someone do this to her?

He was almost afraid to touch her, but he very carefully slipped her right hand in his and leaned forward to tenderly kiss her cheek. She was so very cold to his touch, and Matthew explained that was due to the blood loss. Eric shut his eyes as he leaned close to her and prayed silently to God to protect her and to help her get well and strong. As he prayed, tears fell from his eyes onto her face. He felt her fingers feebly curl around his. "Angilia. Baby, it's Daddy. I'm right here, Angel. Everything's going to be all right."

At the sound of his voice, she began to open her eyes, blinking at the bright lights that stung her eyes. She tried to talk, but she could not. She saw her father, her precious father. She lifted her left hand and signed "I love you" with her fingers. Eric had never seen anything more beautiful. "I love you, too, Angel. I love you so much." He kissed her again, and she turned her face closer to his and lifted her right hand to his head to hold him close to her.

Matthew stepped closer and took her left hand. "Angilia, it is Matthew. Remember me?" She turned her head and nodded. "Sweetie, we're going to leave the breathing tube in overnight just as a precaution. If you remain stable, I'll remove it sometime tomorrow morning, okay?" She nodded again. "You need to get lots of sleep tonight so your body can begin to heal. Can you do that for us?" She looked at her father and clasped his neck with her right hand, as if to keep him with her. Matthew understood. "There's another bed right here for your father. We can move it next to yours, and the two of you can stay here together tonight. There are lots of security guards and police officers outside the room and throughout the hospital. Access is tightly restricted. Okay?" A tear slid down her face and she nodded.

Mitchell and Matthew rolled the other bed next to hers and told Eric to lie down and get some rest, too. When he hadn't moved after a few moments, she tickled his neck and pointed to the bed with her left hand, forcing the issue. He removed his shoes and lay on his right side facing her. She looked at him and became distraught at the sight of the sling holding his left arm. He leaned closer and held her left hand with his right hand, and told her he was all right. She shook her head, and her heartbeat grew erratic.

Mitchell came to her and took hold of her right hand. "Darling, I am Matthew's father, another Dr. Taylor. I took care of your father earlier. Believe me, Angilia, he wasn't seriously injured. Yes, he was shot in the left shoulder, but it is what people call a flesh wound. He's going to be just fine very soon, darling." She signed with her right hand. "I don't know sign language," he told Eric.

"She asked if you are telling her the truth," Eric translated.

"Absolutely. I was able to remove the bullet with surgical forceps. It wasn't very deep at all. It took just a few stitches to close the wound. If it were more serious than that, he would have been admitted. That's the absolute truth, dear. Okay?" She looked at her father, and Eric smiled at her in reassurance. She nodded and signed "I love you" to him again. "You get some sleep, Angilia. I know my son Matthew, and believe me. You don't want to listen to him lecture you about the importance of sleep." Mitchell winked at her and patted her hand.

"They're right, baby. You need to sleep. I'm staying right here beside you. I'm never leaving you. Close your eyes, Angel, please." He held her hand and leaned over to kiss her forehead. She shut her eyes and weakly gripped his hand as she let sleep take control. She did not want to upset her father any more than she already had.

§§§§

While Eric watched his daughter breathing with the help of a machine, Roger answered a call from Alejandro and Juanita. Their panicked voices and crying pushed him to the limits of what he could handle. He could not get Eric's blood-stained clothes and fear-laden eyes out of his memory, and now he had to try to comfort Angilia's grandparents by long distance. Susan saw his distress and took the cell phone from him. She told them Eric would be fine, but that Angilia was very seriously hurt. She explained that she and two security officers would come for them on one of the planes as soon as possible. She told them to pack a suitcase and she would call when the plane landed. She would have Eric's security arrange everything, including local Spanish police to drive them to the airport and stay with them. They were so worried, so scared, and she dreaded their questions, but she had to do this for them, for Eric, and for Angilia.

Roger and Daniel tried to get some sleep in the private waiting room where they were staying, while Susan and two guards headed to the airport. At 4:00 in the morning, Roger asked for an update at the nurses' station and was told that Angilia was still in CTCC recovery until the next day. He got a cup of strong coffee from the machine and stared out of a window trying to grasp everything that had happened. He was soon joined by Daniel, and they looked at one another with the same memory in their minds. They had stood beside Eric when the C-section was performed on Marisol's clinically-dead body and Angilia was born. Eric and Angilia loved each other from that first moment, and their bond was so tight. How could someone do this to Eric and Angilia? How and why?

"She has to be all right. She has to. It will destroy him if she's not." Daniel stared into his coffee, watching as tears splattered the dark liquid.

"Hey, don't. She will be. You heard the doctor. She survived. It's not her time to die. She'll be all right. He was right. She's fighting to stay. She knows what it will do to her dad if. . . . She'll be all right, Daniel." But Roger was scared, too.

Daniel looked at him and nodded. "I pray so," he whispered. Everyone was praying for her. At that moment, sunrise prayer vigils began in every church in Valdavia. Throngs of people waited for any word outside the hospital. She was well-respected and loved in Oxford, and everyone was shocked and saddened by the news of the shooting.

"We're all praying for her." Christopher was next to them, his own face betraying the fear and pain they all felt. "How is she? Please?"

They told Christopher what they knew, and the three men stood in solidarity for a few hours before a nurse informed them that Angilia would be moved to a private CTCC room that morning. Her room was ready, and as soon as Dr. Taylor determined she was stable enough, they would transport her. Eric and Mitchell Taylor would accompany her and Matthew, and security was alerted to be on standby for word of the move.

Angilia moaned and clasped her father's hand as she opened her eyes to the most excruciating pain. She didn't want to show her pain, though, and upset her father, so she clenched the blanket with her right hand while she signed "I love you" with her left hand. Matthew noticed, and unexpectedly felt tears stinging his eyes. Why did she get to him so much? It was like she had cast a spell over him with those remarkable blue eyes of hers. He turned away to compose himself.

"I love you, my beautiful daughter Angilia." Her father's familiar greeting felt like a soft blanket, and she touched his cheek with her left hand. He kissed her hand and smiled at her. He saw the pain in her eyes, and it took all of his tenacity not to cry at the sight. He had no idea how much pain she felt, how intense it was, but he saw the suffering exposed in her eyes. He knew she was trying to hide it from him, trying to be strong for him, and he felt such love and awe for his little girl. Even now, in the worst pain and fighting for her life, she placed him first.

Matthew caressed her right arm and smiled at her. "Angilia, I'm going to remove the breathing tube now. Don't try to talk yet. Your throat will be sore for a while, and we can give you some ice chips to help with the pain and dryness. Just relax, sweetie, and don't move. You'll probably feel like you need to cough, but don't. Just close your mouth and breathe through your nose for several minutes. Okay?" She nodded, and he delicately removed the endotracheal tube and reminded her not to cough. She closed her eyes and tried to relax, but she could not stop tears from falling.

Eric snuggled closer to her and softly talked to her and restrained his own tears. "You're doing fine, Angel. Just keep breathing. I know it hurts, baby, but you're doing fine. Everything's going to be okay." He kissed her head and stroked her hair with his right hand. "I love you, baby. I love you."

She could not stop the tears any longer. It hurt so much to cry, but she could not fight the tears anymore. Eric kept stroking her hair and telling her it was okay to cry. She crushed his heart, though, and he clenched his own eyes to keep his tears from falling. Eric literally felt his own heart aching from holding all of his horror and unshed tears. Matthew watched her vital signs on the heart monitor for several minutes, and then told the nurse to prepare four milligrams of morphine. "Sweetie, I'm going to give you a low dose of morphine for the pain. I can't give you too much this soon, but it will help take the edge off. Just keep breathing, though, and try to relax as much as possible." He slowly injected the morphine through the IV lumen and patted her hand when he finished.

Matthew explained that he needed to check her incisions and change the dressings. Mitchell asked Eric to go with him to the other side of the room so they could pull the curtain, and he would change Eric's bandage at the same time. Eric kissed her and for the first time in many hours, she kissed his cheek. "I love you, Daddy," she breathed, her first words since she had died in his arms. She smiled at him through the pain as Mitchell rolled Eric's bed away from hers, helped Eric to his feet, and pulled the curtain between them.

Angilia's face betrayed the full extent of her pain for the first time since the shooting, and Matthew felt his own heart fracture. He placed his hand over her cheek and she reached for his other hand. "I'm so sorry, darling. I'm so sorry. I know it hurts so much. But you really are doing fine. Your father is right. It's okay to cry. I wish I could do more for you right now. I'm so sorry I can't."

"It's okay," she hoarsely whispered.

Kara and Matthew removed and replaced her wound dressings, and both were so compassionate with her. She clenched the blanket as a wave of sharp pain hit her chest. The nurse placed a cool cloth on her forehead and Matthew kept talking to her in his soft voice. "Thank you," she whispered. "For being nice."

He was puzzled. Why wouldn't a doctor be nice to a trauma patient? "You make it easy, sweetie," he smiled at her as they finished and the nurse covered her with the blankets. Within minutes, security engulfed them as they took Angilia and Eric to a private CTCC room. The nurse attached her to the heart monitor in that room, adjusted the IVs, and made sure she was comfortable. A second bed was in the room for Eric, though he sat in a chair next to her bed and held her hand. He kissed her and told her to get some more sleep.

"Please don't leave." Her voice sounded small and wispy.

"I'm not going anywhere, baby. I promise. I'll be right here when you wake up."

She nodded, and whispered a weak "I love you" as her eyes closed.

§§§§§

Mitchell brought Daniel and Roger into the room, and both men felt nauseous at the sight of Angilia. They fought it back, though, because Eric needed their love and support. His face was haggard and strained, his eyes bloodshot and weary. "Hey, we brought some lunch," Daniel whispered and the nurse rolled the table close to Eric. He shook his head, but his friends unpacked the sandwich, fruit, and juice anyway.

"Come on, man, you have to eat. You know what she's going to say if she finds out you haven't eaten. Do it for her." Eric looked at Roger and sighed; his friend was right. He did not want to upset Angilia. He went through the motions of eating, but was otherwise oblivious to the food. The two men sat on either side of Eric.

"You haven't slept, either." Roger didn't ask, because he knew Eric had not slept. "You should, Eric. She doesn't want to see you like this. Besides, your in-laws will be here soon. Susan and a couple of guards went in the plane to get them."

"Oh, God, I didn't even think about them." Eric closed his eyes and leaned his head back in agony. Roger explained their call and how Susan had taken charge and gone for them. They would not want to see Eric so exhausted, either. They convinced him to at least take a nap. They, the doctors, and the nurse were there to watch Angilia. They noticed that he slipped his right hand under her left hand and leaned close to her, protectively, as he had done when she was a newborn and he lay with her and watched her sleep. Eric reached in his pocket and removed Angilia's ring. He gently slid it onto her left ring finger where she had worn it every day for five years. He kissed her hand and watched her, his body, soul, and brain overwhelmed and tired.

His body could no longer fight the exhaustion and heaviness, and within moments he was sleeping. His friends were relieved, until they saw her open her eyes. She had not been asleep; she had pretended for her father's benefit. She carefully turned her head to look at them, not wanting her movements to awaken her father. Her voice was so soft and strained that Daniel clenched his teeth to hide his agony.

"Thank you for taking care of Daddy." She tried to say more, but pain encircled her and she closed her eyes and grasped the blanket tightly. Daniel looked fearfully at Matthew, and he nodded and came to her bedside. He asked for another four milligram dose of morphine and slowly injected it through the IV lumen.

"I know it doesn't stop the pain, darling, but it's all I can give you. I'll give you another dose in four hours." She nodded, her eyes still closed to block the dizziness. At that moment, a guard knocked on the door and asked for Roger or Daniel. Daniel leapt from his chair to find Susan and Angilia's grandparents in the hallway. Their faces were drawn, their eyes wet, and Juanita grabbed Daniel's arm. He explained what he knew and saw Susan place an arm around each of them in support. Daniel quietly opened the door and motioned for Matthew.

The young doctor held Juanita's hand as she began to cry when he told them of Angilia's life-threatening injuries. He tried to reassure them, but he knew his words meant little. He prepared them for what they would see and escorted them in. Daniel and Susan waited in the hall, clutching one another. Roger stood and greeted them, telling them that Eric had just gone to sleep. He and Mitchell helped them into the chairs next to Angilia's bed, and Alejandro took her small hand between both of his. Juanita could not fight her tears, which wetted Angilia's cheek as she bent to kiss her granddaughter. "Dios mío," she murmured.

"Abuela. Abuelo. Te amo."

Alejandro never knew how he remained so composed that day as he saw his beloved granddaughter so weak, tiny, and hurt. His inner core of fortitude became the pillar which kept him standing during the worst living nightmare he would ever face. "Te amo, mi nieta hermosa. Te amo. Mi amada bonita, te amo." He raised her arm and kissed her hand, and she patted his soft cheek.

They would not let her talk much, and Alejandro stood and tucked the blankets around her. His strong hands on her shoulders, he told her to sleep. He kissed her forehead. "Sleep. Now. That's an order." He sat down and she turned her face toward her father and closed her eyes. When she was finally asleep, Alejandro covered his face with his hands and wept for a long while. Roger stood behind them, his hands on their shoulders. How could someone hurt them?

Ninety minutes later, Eric opened his eyes and lightly kissed Angilia's forehead, and then saw his in-laws sitting on the other side of her bed. He looked like a terror-stricken little boy to Juanita, who rose, walked to his hospital bed, and slid beside him. She held him, knowing his pain was worse than anyone's. "Mi querido muchacho. Yo amor, mi hijo."

"I love you both." His voice dropped to an almost inaudible whisper. "I am so very scared, Mamá, so very scared." Tears slid from the corners of his eyes and sliced through Juanita's heart as if they were razor blades. She rubbed her hands through his hair and whispered a prayer in Spanish. "I'd give anything if I could trade places with her." He felt Angilia's hand tighten on his and saw tears slide from her eyes as she opened them and looked at him.

"No, Daddy, never. Not you. Never you. I'm so sorry. It's all my fault."

Matthew motioned Eric to calm her down. They all heard the heart monitor's beeping grow more erratic. Eric snuggled closer to her, and slipped his right arm under her head, just as he had done when she was a very young girl. He kissed her head and very soothingly and slowly rocked her. He had calmed her fears of the dark that way.

"No, baby, it's not your fault. It's no one's fault. Let's just rest and get well. Close your eyes, Angel. I'm going to stay right here, just like I used to when you were scared of the dark. Everything's going to be all right."

She tried to cuddle closer to him, but she could not move. How could she ever tell him the truth, especially now, when Dr. Jamieson had followed through on his threats and hired someone to kill her father? It was her fault! Tony said the gunman was dead, but Dr. Jamieson would just hire someone else to finish the job. If she said anything, the police would question him and he would know she had talked. Then he would make sure her father was dead. She could never take that chance. She had to make sure no one hurt her father again.

The pain ravaged her, slashed through her, but she hid it, knowing the pain was worth it in exchange for her father's life. She could barely look at him; the guilt was stronger than the physical pain. Her father had been shot, and it was her fault. Matthew watched in near panic as her blood pressure dropped. Her heart rate had increased dramatically in her stress, and he had to get her calm quickly.

"Angilia, this was not your fault. Mike told us what happened, and how you saved your father's life. If you hadn't pushed him down when you did, this would have been very different. Your father is fine, and everyone in here is going to help you get well, too. And as long as you are my patient, I don't want any more of this blame game and guilt, neither of which does anyone any favors. End of discussion. Understood?"

She buried her face against her father's shoulder and ignored Matthew. Eric nudged her with his head. "Angilia, the only thing you did wrong was to risk your life. You have no idea how terrified I have been since this happened, baby, and I don't know how much more I can take. Please, Angel, you have to get well for me. Please." He hated to play the emotional trump card, but if that is what it took to make her focus on her recovery, then he had to go there. "I can't stand seeing you like this. You have to get well so we can go home. Please. For us. For me."

He was right. She had to get well. She could not protect him when she was confined to a hospital bed. She was the only one who knew the truth, and it had to stay that way for his safety. She lifted her left hand and lightly tickled his beard, like she had done when she was very young. She nodded. "I promise, Daddy. Anything for you. I love you too much."

Alejandro stood. "It's about time this is over. Now, you do what they tell you to, mi nieta, you hear?" He bent and kissed her temple and squeezed Eric's hand which cupped her right shoulder. "Come, Juanita, they must sleep now. We will come back tomorrow."

Juanita kissed Eric and walked over to kiss Angilia on her cheek and to whisper in her ear. "Yo amor, Angilia. Tú es mucho valiente, my darling girl. You must rest now and get well."

"I love you both." Her voice was weak. They left her, their hearts filled with fear, as Susan and two guards accompanied them to Angilia's Oxford house for the night. Angilia kissed her father's chin. "I love you so much, Daddy. But I'm not brave." He scarcely heard the last part, but he patted her shoulder and silently disagreed with her.

A light knock on the door brought another doctor into the room. He greeted Matthew and walked to Angilia's bed. "Hi, Angilia. You probably don't remember me, but I'm Andrew Hibbert, the doctor who worked on your knee. I came to check on you. Mind if I take a look at your knee?" She shook her head and he pulled on latex gloves. "I'm going to remove the bandages and just do a quick examination, nothing much."

Dr. Hibbert gingerly removed the blood-soaked gauze and cotton, and said the suture looked normal. He asked her to bend her knee, even a little. He supported her leg and she held her breath as she barely bent her knee. "Excellent. After you recover, we can begin some physical therapy and get you back to full range of motion." The nurse bandaged Angilia's knee while Dr. Hibbert talked more to Eric than to Angilia. "It's important that you flex your knee a couple of times a day, like you just did, to keep the muscles, cartilage, and fluid active. Do like you just did. Don't overdo things. Just keep the knee from getting stiff. Matthew will let me know when we're ready to begin physical therapy. You get well, and soon."

Eric thanked him and held Angilia in silence until she was asleep, and then he let the tears loose. How many times in twenty-four hours could she break his heart?

§§§§

The hospital room was quiet except for the beeping of the heart monitor. Roger slept in a chair, refusing to leave, while Matthew and Mitchell alternated napping and watching Angilia. Eric was too terrified to close his eyes. Mitchell sat on the other side of Angilia's bed and looked at Eric, father to father. "You have to take care of yourself. If you keep looking like a zombie, you aren't going to help her. She needs to see you as you always are, not sleep-deprived and starved. Go to sleep, Eric. For her."

"What if . . .?" Eric could not finish.

"That's what Matthew and I are here for. Get some sleep. Now."

"You have to wake me if. . . ."

"We will. I promise."

Eric nodded and took a deep breath. He kissed her head oh so tenderly and closed his eyes. Nurse Kara pulled the blanket over him, and soon he was asleep. Matthew awoke an hour later and checked her. She seemed to be sleeping well. Mitchell sent the nurse for some coffee for the three of them, and she returned from the cafeteria fifteen minutes later. Mitchell sipped his coffee and observed his son standing at the foot of Angilia's bed, looking at her like a lioness defends her young. Matthew had never fought so much to save a patient, had never become personally invested in a patient, and Mitchell was concerned, as a doctor and as a father. Was his son in love with a patient? With a princess? What would happen to Matthew?

Matthew breathed a sigh of relief for the peaceful night and hoped the drama was over. He slowly walked to the window and peeked through the slats in the blind at the night sky. He caught himself thinking a prayer, a prayer for Angilia's recovery. She was so young, so brave—her grandmother was right—and so filled with terror. She was not scared for herself. She was terrified for her father.

"No! Daddy, no! Not my Daddy!"

Her screams slashed through the quiet room, bringing Mitchell and Roger to their feet and Matthew racing to her bedside. Eric's heart lurched and he nudged her right shoulder with his left hand. "Baby, it's Daddy. I'm right here, Angel. I'm all right. Look at me, Angel."

She opened her eyes and reached for him with her right arm, her body moving to hold him. She screamed in pain just as Matthew grabbed her right arm. "Don't move, sweetie. Not yet." He carefully helped her onto her back while she winced and murmured an apology. "It's okay. You just had a bad dream. Just relax, and I'll give you some morphine for the pain. Your father is fine. See?"

He slid closer to her and leaned against her pillows next to her. He slipped his right arm under her neck again, his hand on her upper arm. She rested her head on his right shoulder and Matthew saw her vital signs stabilize almost immediately. Her father's warmth, his mere presence, made everything calmer. He was there, he was safe, and she could hear his heart beating as she rested against him.

"I'm sorry I woke you and scared you, Daddy." Her voice was frail.

"Shhh. It's okay, baby. Everything's okay. Go back to sleep. I'll be right here when you wake up in the morning." He kissed the top of her head, and she smiled up at him weakly. Her turquoise eyes hurt him, for they reflected not only her love for him, as always, but unimaginable terror and pain. He repeated his prayer that God ease her pain and fear. He knew her fear was for his safety, which hit him harder than any gut punch could.

§§§§§

Roger woke at 5:00 that morning, pleased to see both Eric and Angilia sleeping. Her breathing was labored, though, and Matthew lifted her right arm to feel her pulse. She tightened her fingers on his hand, and turned her head to look at him. Tears filled her eyes and skated across her cheeks. He nodded and told the nurse to prepare a syringe with seven milligrams of morphine. "I'm going to give you a bit more than before. We'll see how you do with that dosage today. I wish I could give you a full dose, sweetie, but I just can't."

She bit her lip, nodded, and signed to him. She didn't want to say anything and wake her father. Matthew smiled but shook his head; he did not know sign language. "She said, 'It's okay'."

"You're awake." She kissed her father's neck as she snuggled her head closer to him.

"Good morning, my beautiful daughter Angilia." He smiled at her, and for one second she almost tricked her mind into thinking they were home and everything was fine.

"I love you so much, Daddy. Roger, please take care of Daddy."

Eric smiled at her. "I can take care of myself, Angel."

"Then do it. Get up and do it. You haven't showered or shaved in forty-eight hours. You need to eat breakfast. Go."

Mitchell nodded and Eric slowly got out of the bed. Roger plopped Eric's suitcase on a chair and Eric selected a change of clothes and his toiletry bag. He blew her a kiss and closed the bathroom door behind him. When she heard the shower, she reached for Roger and he came to her side. He placed a hand on her cheek and told her everything would be all right.

She nodded. "Just please take care of him. He's the most important person in the world." Her tired eyes and voice made him want to cry.

He leaned down and kissed her forehead. "I will, Princess. I will. You just take care of yourself and get better. That's the best thing for everyone, especially your dad. You let me and Daniel take care of your dad, and you let the doctors take care of you. Deal?"

"Deal. Thank you. Please, can you get him some breakfast? You know what he likes." He nodded and left the room, almost literally running into Christopher. Roger opened the door and told her she had a visitor. "Hi, Christopher. You didn't have to come."

"Of course I did. My best student and professor, remember?" He lifted her hand and kissed it, then held up a bouquet of daisies. Nurse Kara took them, and Christopher sat next to her bed for several minutes. "Is there anything I can do to help? Anything at all?"

"Maybe. My grandparents are here, staying at my house with Susan. There's no food there."

"I'll take care of it as soon as I leave. Everyone's praying, you know. There are prayer vigils here and in Valdavia. Everyone loves you."

"Thank you."

Eric stepped out of the bathroom, freshly showered and shaven, refreshed, and smiling. Mitchell was right: Eric had to do this for her. It seemed to work, for she flashed him a smile and held out her arm to him. He made a 360° turn and smiled back at her. "How do I look?"

"Handsome."

He went to her and kissed her nose, then greeted Christopher. The men talked until Roger returned with Eric's breakfast. Christopher kissed her and said he would go to her house and check on her grandparents. Eric sat next to her and forced himself to eat. Every time he looked at her his stomach heaved at the sight of her so weak, pale, and in pain.

When Eric finished, Matthew said he needed to change her bandages and examine her wounds. Roger stepped into the hall, but she panicked at the mention of her father leaving the room. Eric moaned at her distress and fear. Mitchell calmed her by taking Eric into the bathroom to check his bandage.

While the nurse and Matthew gently removed the wound dressings, she grabbed his arm. "It hurts so much. It hurts to breathe, to move, to cry. I don't know how much longer I can hide it from him."

"Oh, God, I'm so sorry, sweetie. We need to see how you respond to the increased dosage of morphine today before we do anything else. There's only so much I can do or give you. The damage to your heart is my priority and that determines what I can give you. The wrong thing can either weaken or stimulate your heart, which would cause far too many complications. I really wish I could make it go away, I really do. It kills me that I can't," he said, his amber eyes stunning her with their pools of concern.

"I understand. It's okay, really." She felt so defeated, tired, and weak.

"One thing might help you feel better. You need some food, too. How about some vegetable broth? It's got to be better than ice chips, right?" She grimaced. "Just a few sips to start. We'll take it easy for now and build up to more. Fair?" She nodded, and when they finished dressing her wounds, the nurse went for a cup of broth. Matthew adjusted her bed and pillows to make her more comfortable, and told their fathers they could rejoin them.

"Tell her." Eric winked at her, hoping to boost her spirits.

"Your father doesn't need the sling anymore. He's doing very well."

Eric smiled at her, but was astonished by her question. "When can we go home?" He looked at her in shock, then at Matthew.

"Not for a few weeks, baby. You need to recover and get strong again. I don't want anything else to happen to you, Angel. You just work on getting well so we can go home." He stroked her hair and looked at Matthew again.

"You'll be here at least six weeks, Angilia. These first two weeks are all about beginning to recover from the surgeries. After that, we have to begin physical therapy to retrain your body and make it stronger again. These were major surgical procedures, and you're not even getting out of this bed until at least the end of next week. If you tried, the surgical incisions could rupture. You just need to sleep as much as possible while your body begins to heal."

That wasn't what she wanted to hear, but she knew she could not change things. She had to buck up and make the best of the situation. Her priority was getting well so she could stay beside her father and protect him the best she could. She nodded in resignation. "If I have to."

The nurse returned with the broth, and Eric took it and helped her take small sips until her stomach got used to food again. She drank it all, though, for him, and leaned back against the pillows just as her grandparents and Susan entered the room. Susan had not seen Angilia since the morning Eric and his daughter had left for Oxford. She forced a smile when she saw how pale and tortured Angilia looked, and bent to kiss Angilia's cheek.

"Hi, darling. I brought someone for you." Susan pulled a teddy bear from a bag. Angilia smiled and reached for it. She held it on her lap and clapped its front paws together playfully. "I know how special he is to you. I also brought some of your other things for later, when you can wear your own pajamas. You just hurry and get better so we can get you out of those hospital gowns and play dress up again."

"I will. Thank you." She smiled at her father. "You gave me Little Bear the first time I was in the hospital, with Mommy. You sat him on the bed near me. He's been with me ever since." She heard her grandmother gasp, and reached for her. "Abuela, lo siento. No quiero lastimarte. Lo siento."

"No, mi nieta. You do not hurt me. But how do you remember any of that? It was before you were born, my Angel."

"I remember all of it, Abuela. If you have any questions about any of it, you can ask me. But only if you want to and you're sure nothing will upset you. I do remember everything."

"Someday, yes. Not today. I need to think. You are too much for me, mi nieta, just too much for my brain to handle."

"Now you know how I feel every day," Eric teased. Angilia swatted his leg with the bear and he beamed at her. She was his beautiful daughter Angilia all right.

"What?" she asked, perplexed by his huge smile.

"I love you." He leaned over and kissed her nose and she put her left hand on his neck and held him close.

"I love you, Daddy. I love you." She realized that their happiness, their future, and his safety were her responsibilities. Her duty was to get well so they could return home to their lives and she could remain ever vigilant. She would ignore the pain, she would do what Matthew told her to do, and she would resume her vigil.

Another knock on the door brought Mike, the security officer, who came to check on Eric and Angilia. He stayed long enough to greet them, tell them everyone was praying for them, and present a huge bouquet of roses for Angilia. He also delivered a large burlap sack filled with telegrams, letters, and cards that had been sent to her Oxford house.

Angilia motioned him to her, and when he leaned down, she kissed his cheek. "You stayed with Daddy. Thank you." He patted her cheek and kissed her hand.

Eric stood and walked to Mike, who extended his hand. Eric ignored the hand and hugged Mike. "Thank you." Mike nodded in response, not used to emotional exchanges. Mitchell and Mike had stayed with Eric during the darkest moments of his life. Mike left, telling Eric to call him for any reason and with a lump in his throat.

"Let me see my little girl," Alejandro suddenly said. He leaned down and kissed her forehead, chin, right cheek, and left cheek. She smiled at him and kissed him, holding his hands. He felt how weak she was and saw her pain. "It's my turn to cuddle her," he smiled at Eric as he tenderly slid next to her on the bed. He put his left arm around her shoulders and she rested her head against his chest. Eric asked for another blanket and covered her as he kissed her and whispered in her ear.

"I love you, too, Daddy. I love you all." Soon she was asleep, and Juanita tucked Eric into the other bed and kissed him in a maternal way he missed. He watched Angilia breathing, cradled in her grandfather's arms, and for the first time since the shooting he felt that they were safe. He finally let himself fall asleep, surrounded by his family, closest friends, and father-son doctors who truly cared about his little girl. Yes, they were safe, at least in this room with these people.

§§§§§

Angilia's sleep was short-lived. Her agonizing moans and tears were stronger than her resolve, and she could no longer try to hide or fight the pain. Alejandro stood up and Matthew sat next to her on the bed, listening to her heart and taking her temperature. He gave her seven milligrams of morphine, though the small doses barely made any difference. He stood and told the nurse to keep a cold cloth on Angilia's forehead. Then he motioned Eric and her grandparents into the corner where they could talk.

"This is it, the most brutal days. Her pain is off the charts and she has a fever, but I can't give her too much. It's too dangerous. You all have to be strong for her, you need to keep her still and calm. You have to take her mind off of the pain. Talk to her, tell her stories, read to her. Do anything to distract her mind. She needs to sleep, but that's difficult when she's in this much pain." Matthew saw their grim faces, Eric's terror back in his eyes. "It's okay if she tells us it hurts. But she has to stay calm and still or the sutures could rupture. You're the ones who matter most to her. You have to do this no matter how much it hurts you. Understood?"

Eric closed his eyes and took a deep breath. "Yes." He hugged Juanita and grabbed a large handful of letters and telegrams from the sack Mike had brought. He gently slid next to Angilia and cuddled her as he read the letters and telegrams to her. Everyone wrote that they were praying for her, loved her, and just wanted her to get well soon. Some of the letters were from former students, colleagues, neighbors, and many were from strangers. Telegrams from the Queen of Great Britain, the Presidents of the United States and France, the Prime Ministers of Canada and England, and from several entertainers were sent.

Eric asked for more letters, and Susan handed him another stack. Angilia pulled one from the pile and asked him to open it. There was a crayon heart drawn on the envelope, and she smiled. Eric read the letter aloud, hand written in crayon by a young child. *"Dear Princess, I am so sorry you are hurt. I pray to God every day that you are well soon. I have all of your CDs. You are my favorite singer. My mom told me we can go to your concert next time. I hope that is soon. You are very special. I love you. xoxo Marilyn"* He handed her a drawing that was folded in the envelope.

She smiled at the crayon drawing of her with a guitar and a tiara. "How sweet. Susan, will you write Marilyn a letter for me? I'll sign it." Susan nodded and took the letter. She pulled a tablet of paper from her tote bag and hand wrote a letter, explaining that the Princess read the letter and adored the picture. She mentioned that Angilia appreciated the prayers and hoped to meet Marilyn one day. Angilia signed at the bottom, and Susan addressed an envelope. Kara took it to the mail for them.

Juanita and Alejandro took turns reading some of the letters to her, and she leaned against her father's shoulder. She was so sick and in so much pain, but if strangers cared enough to write to her, then she could be stronger and stop complaining. Susan, Roger, Daniel, even Juanita and Alejandro wrote replies to many of the letters for her, and she signed each one.

After a few hours, she snuggled closer to Eric and was soon asleep. Susan collected the letters and cards, clearing the bed, and they all sat silently observing her sleep. Kara kept a cold cloth on her forehead to offset the temperature. Eric could feel how hot she was, but Matthew assured them the temperature should break within twenty-four hours. Until then, they had to keep her still and relaxed, sleeping as much as possible.

The next several days were similar, with letter answering sessions, lots of naps throughout the days, and tremendous pain.

After her fever broke, she was able to start eating soft fruits and drinking juices. The food made her nauseous at first, but after her body readjusted to eating solid foods, she began to regain some color. Alejandro left her each evening with his tough-love lectures, and Eric stayed beside her constantly.

One week after the surgery, Angilia sat up with Matthew's assistance, and the nurse raised the head of the bed. Susan brushed her hair and braided it, tying it with a pink satin ribbon. "I hear you'll get to ditch the hospital gowns next week." She smiled at Angilia, grateful to just talk with her.

Juanita brought a photo album and told stories about Marisol and Eduardo. Angilia gently fingered the photographs. She had never met her uncle, though she prayed fervently that she would soon. Vividly she recalled her mother. "I remember Mommy's voice so clearly. She always trilled her Rs so prettily. But I only saw her once, very briefly." Eric leaned forward, his brow furrowed. How? Marisol had died three months before Angilia was born, kept alive by machines until the Caesarian delivery. There was no way Angilia could have seen Marisol except in pictures. Juanita glanced at Eric, alarmed. Was the child hallucinating? Angilia looked at them and smiled.

"I did see Mommy. You were holding me, Daddy. She was dressed in white, and her dark wavy hair was long and loose around her face. Her eyes were closed. You placed a white rose across her chest, Daddy. But I recollect her mouth the most. Her dark pink lips seemed to be smiling. I remember her smile most of all. You were all there," Angilia said as she looked at Daniel, Roger, Susan, and her grandparents.

Juanita's hand covered her mouth, and Angilia put her right arm around her grandmother. She slipped her left arm around her father and kissed his cheek. "I didn't mean to make you sad, Daddy, Abuela, and Abuelo. She was so beautiful, and I see her smile whenever I think of her. I'm never sad when I think of her."

Alejandro leaned across his wife and clasped Angilia's shoulders. "You should not be sad, mi nieta. Never sad. Your mother was happy. You have the most beautiful memory of her."

Eric buried his face against his daughter's neck, reliving the day which Angilia conjured. "Yes, you do, Angel. Mommy smiled a lot. Her smile lit the universe. Thank you, baby. Thank you."

Susan grabbed a tissue, reminiscing about the woman who had spent days talking with her, making sure she was the right woman to help care for her baby daughter. Marisol knew she would die soon, and all she cared about was her baby and her husband. Marisol was buried the day after Angilia's birth, and Susan, Roger, Daniel, and Marisol's parents stood in the church while she was placed in her tomb and Reverend Hutchins prayed. Eric held their newborn daughter as he bent to place a white rose over Marisol's heart. Angilia remembered her mother's burial. How bittersweet and beautiful.

§§§§§

Angilia slept snuggled against Eric, her left hand clutching her teddy bear. She looked so young, sweet, and angelic. "Ten days. It's been ten days. Everything changed in just a few seconds. We were laughing and then seconds later she was on top of me bleeding. Why her? She's never done anything wrong. She's never hurt anyone. He kept shooting her. I was out of his range. But he kept shooting her. Why?" His voice was a choked whisper.

"Who was he? Why did he do this? Why? If he wanted to kill me, why did he shoot her? None of it makes any sense to me. If they hadn't killed him, I would have. I would have ripped his head off. What kind of monster does this to a girl?"

Roger sat close to Eric and spoke softly. "The police are trying to find that out. They're going through everything in his apartment, his postal box, his bank accounts, everything. They're checking everything and everyone connected to him. They said they have some leads, and they're working around the clock with INTERPOL. They'll find out, Eric. They will."

"This is worse than any nightmare. Nightmares aren't real. This is very real. I am so scared, Roger. I watch her breathing just to know she's alive. I nearly lost her twice in the same day. I never knew what terror was until this happened. God help me. I am terrified to let go of her."

"I know. You don't have to let go, Eric. You don't ever have to let go."

§§§§

Angilia awoke early and realized it was March 21—exactly two weeks since the picnic, the shooting, and the surgery. She looked at her father, who was watching her, and she smiled at him. She kissed his cheek and sat up. She flexed her knee a few times, as Dr. Hibbert had told her to do, and took a few deep breaths. Breathing felt atrociously hideous, but she had to get stronger.

Susan and her grandparents arrived, with homemade breakfast for Eric and Angilia. She obediently ate fresh cantaloupe and strawberries and drank freshly-squeezed orange juice. Her father dined on ham, eggs, and toast with his juice. When they finished, she looked at Matthew expectantly, her eyes reflecting a mixture of pain, hope, trepidation, and eagerness.

He and Nurse Kara unhooked her IV bags, removed the heart monitor electrodes, and slowly helped her stand for the first time in two weeks. They kept their arms around her while she regained her equilibrium after two weeks in bed. Kara slipped a pink robe Susan handed her onto Angilia while Matthew supported her. "Just take one step at a time to start. It's been a while since you've stood or walked, so let's take it slow and easy. Don't put too much weight on your right leg. Just keep your arms around us and let us support you."

"Okay." She took a feeble, painful step, then another, and gasped for breath. Matthew made her stop after each step, explaining that her diaphragm and heart had to get used to working harder again. She had to take it slow, he reminded her. Eric bit his finger as he watched her struggling, and Alejandro held him, restraining him from running to her. Eric groaned when he heard her moan in pain, and Juanita held his arm. They understood his instinct was to run to her and pick her up. They knew he could not do that.

After the longest thirty minutes, Matthew and Kara had helped her to walk across the room. When she turned, with their help, she appeared exhausted, sweat beading her forehead, but smiled at her father. She prayed silently, asking God to make her healthy soon so that she and her father could return home. She hated putting him through this torture.

Another agonizing thirty minutes later, Matthew and Kara helped her into bed. Matthew listened to her heart and took her pulse as she closed her eyes to erase the dizziness. He replaced the saline solution into the IV lumen, and gave her seven milligrams of morphine. "You did great, darling. This is very rough at the beginning. We can do some more walking tomorrow, just to get your body used to this again. You need to rest now."

Angilia had never been so drained. Matthew said she did very well, but she was dejected. It took one hour to walk across the hospital room and back. How pathetic. Eric saw her face and knew what she was thinking. He sat next to her and caressed her shoulder.

"I'm so happy right now, Angel, so very happy. Two weeks ago I nearly lost you. Just to watch you doing anything after what you've been through is a miracle. You are my miracle, Angel, you always have been. I love you so much."

"I love you, Daddy. I just want to go home, home with you, forever. That's all I want."

"A few more weeks, baby. You just rest now like Matthew said, and keep getting stronger." She nodded and kissed his neck as she snuggled into him. For the first time in two weeks, she bent her knees and slightly curled her body. She slipped her left arm under her father and her right arm over him. She fell asleep holding him, her soft breath blowing against his neck. Nothing else could feel so wonderful at that moment. He smiled at his in-laws, truly happy. She would be all right. His little girl would be all right.

§§§§§

Matthew and Angilia returned to her room from their morning walk up and down the hallway, surrounded by a dozen guards. Two weeks of walking and mild exercises had made her stronger. They both knew she had a lot of grueling work ahead, though, to regain her muscle strength.

Angilia bypassed the bed and walked to her father, slipping her arms around his neck as she sat on his lap. She smiled at him, but he could see and feel her labored breathing. She was working so hard to get well. "I get to relax with you for a while before Matthew and I go to the PT room." She laid her head on his right shoulder and signed to him. Eric smiled at her.

Matthew leaned against the wall watching. "I don't trust that. I never know what she's saying and if it's about me," he said with a smile.

"Don't flatter yourself," she jokingly sneered in reply.

Eric giggled. "She said, 'I adore sitting with my favorite man'." And she did just that for a couple of hours, talking with him, before she fell asleep. Eric gently stood with her cradled in his arms and placed her on the bed. He covered her, kissed her, and quietly asked Matthew how she was.

"She's doing well. Yes, this is tough and brutal on her. It hurts a lot. But she can't fully recover unless she gets strong again, from the inside out. I'm not letting her push too hard. But it won't help her if we're too soft on her, either. I monitor her very frequently. I won't let her keep going if she's distressed at all. I promise."

Eric thanked him and watched her sleep for a few hours. When she awoke, Eric ate lunch with her and afterward Susan helped her freshen up a bit. Angilia washed her face, brushed her teeth, and let Susan braid her hair. She stepped out of the bathroom with a smile, wearing grey cotton track pants and button-up shirt. The sneakers on her feet felt heavy; she had to get used to everything again.

"I suppose we ought to get busy now," she said to Matthew. "I'll be back in a little while, Daddy." She kissed him and left with Matthew and a small army of guards. In the PT room, she began with mild stretching exercises, and then the treadmill, which forced her to regulate her breathing to try to control the chest pain as she strengthened her heart and diaphragm. Matthew stopped her after fifteen minutes and checked her heart rate, pulse, and blood pressure.

She drank some water, and Matthew helped her on the stationary bicycle and reminded her to start slowly. She grimaced at the pain but focused on her breathing. Dr. Hibbert came in just in time to check her knee while Matthew took her vital signs. "You're doing much better than I thought you would, Angilia. You're amazing."

She shook her head. "I have to do this. I want my father to get his life back, and he can't until I get out of the hospital. I have to get well so I can protect him."

Dr. Hibbert gave Matthew a quizzical look, but smiled at her as he left. Matthew told her to continue on the bike for a little while. "Angilia, Mike and Tony killed the shooter. He's dead. He's not a threat anymore."

"Yes, I know he's dead. That doesn't change anything."

He asked what she meant, but she refused to elaborate. He noticed the panic on her face and he changed the subject. "Do you ever regret going through graduate school so young? Do you feel you missed out on some things?"

"Regret? No. Do you mean missing things like making friends my age and going to dances? I don't feel like I missed anything, but that I did other things instead. I have some wonderful friends, but they aren't sixteen years old. Do you regret it?"

"Sometimes. I feel torn. I love my work, I do, but there are other things I want to do and experience. I just rushed from school to career with no time or space for anything or anyone else."

"What do you want to do?"

He smiled sadly. "I've been thinking about that a lot the past couple of weeks, actually. I'd like to leave the hospital and go to France and study art."

She stopped peddling and got off of the bike. "Really? You want to leave here? What did your father say?"

"I haven't told anyone else, just you. I really want to leave. It may or may not be forever. I don't know. But my heart is telling me to leave."

"You're sure?"

"That I want to leave? Yeah. I tried to ignore that idea at first, but then it just kept pounding in my head. I'm sure. Why?"

"Well, it just got me thinking of something. Just hear me out, okay?" He was puzzled, but nodded. They walked around the room as they talked, trying to keep the guards from overhearing their conversation. "Well, Valdavia borders France, you know. And I need a doctor, someone I trust and like. I hate my doctor." She shivered and crossed her arms across her chest. "Would you come to Valmondois and be my personal doctor? Once I recover from this, I won't need you all the time. So you will have time to go to France, visit museums, and study art."

He stopped walking and looked at her. "Me? Your personal physician? Live in Valmondois?"

She nodded. "In the palace. There's plenty of room. I'll be your only patient, and when I'm well you won't have a whole lot to do."

He started walking slowly, silently, and she watched him anxiously, afraid he would decline the offer. She would never trust another doctor. She couldn't. Without Matthew, she would be despondent and with no one she would trust. After several minutes of quiet, she was certain he didn't want to go. "It's okay. I understand." She turned, motioned for the guards, and left the PT room.

Matthew realized she had left just as she pushed the elevator button, and he ran to her. "Wait. Come here." She limped into the room with him, the guards behind. "You're sure about this?" he asked her. She nodded. "All right. You have yourself a personal doctor." She smiled, relieved and elated. They returned to the hospital room and told their fathers, both of whom were surprised.

Eric was pleased, knowing his daughter trusted Matthew. Eric appreciated Matthew's gentleness with and compassion for Angilia from the first moment. No other doctor would have stayed with her every moment for weeks and given her such devoted attention. And affection. Eric suspected more to Matthew's feelings than a doctor's concern.

Mitchell was shocked, though he, too, had noticed and had wondered about his son's affections and intentions. Before either man could speak, Matthew sped through his speech. "I was planning to leave the hospital soon anyway, Dad, and she's right. I'll still get to do medicine but I'll also be close to France and can take weekend trips to museums, galleries, and universities. It's what I really want to do." Mitchell knew he could not change his son's mind, but reminded him that his mother would need more convincing.

Mitchell called his wife, Katherine, and asked her to come to the hospital. She was perplexed when he greeted her at the entrance and told her that Matthew needed to tell her something important. She was even more stunned when she was ushered into the Princess' tightly-secured private room.

Matthew introduced his mother to Eric, who stood and shook her hand with a smile. "Your Majesty," she said as she curtseyed.

"Please call me Eric. This is my daughter Angilia." Angilia stood, but became dizzy and grabbed for her father.

Mrs. Taylor watched in horror as Eric lifted Angilia onto the bed and Matthew rushed to her. He listened to her heart, took her pulse, and demanded seven milligrams of morphine immediately. He slowly injected it into the IV lumen as he listened to her heart. Her heart was unaccustomed to the work and rigor she had endured that day. "She'll be okay. It's just too much excitement in one day. A walk, a workout, and hiring a personal physician in one day are a bit much, after all."

Matthew winked at Angilia. "I guess I better tell her," he said as he turned to his mother and launched into a soliloquy. "Mom, when Angilia is released from the hospital, I'm going with them. She asked me to be her doctor today, and I accepted. I was going to leave the hospital anyway and go to France, so this is perfect." He kept talking, preventing his mother from saying anything. "I can still practice medicine and be close to France. When she recovers, she won't need me there constantly, so I can take short visits to France to study art. This is perfect."

Katherine looked at her son, her husband, Angilia, and Eric, openmouthed and astonished. "Study art? When did this come up? Did you know about this?"

"I presume that last question is for me," Mitchell said. "Not until a few minutes before I called you. I had no idea. But he's a grown man, and this is what he wants to do. She does need a doctor, and he is closer to France."

"Mom, I'm going. I want to. I need to. I'll resign from the hospital regardless, so I might as well do something that makes me happy when I do leave. This will make me happy."

"But so far away?"

"Two hours by plane, Mom. It's not that far."

Katherine observed Angilia, weak and in pain, her son sitting next to her holding her hand so tenderly. Then she looked at her husband, her face asking the questions they both thought: Was Matthew in love with Angilia? Was that the reason he longed to go with her? Mitchell's expression seemed to answer in the affirmative. If that were true, then they really could not persuade him to stay in Oxford. "You're sure, Matthew? This is a huge decision, son."

"I'm positive. I told you, I had already decided to resign. I was waiting until she was released before I handed in my resignation letter."

Angilia blinked in disbelief and moved to sit up. Matthew's hands were on her shoulders, gently pushing her back onto the pillows. "What do you mean you were waiting on me? You stayed at a job you don't want just because of me? That's absurd."

"No, it's not. You're my patient. I'm not going to turn you over to just anyone." She was bewildered. Were most doctors this caring and concerned? The only doctor she had known was the cruelest and most evil man.

Katherine and Mitchell looked at Eric, the three parents fully aware of Matthew's unspoken message. Daniel, Roger, and Susan were just as aghast and aware of the implications of Matthew's words. Everyone in that room except for Angilia recognized the truth at that moment: Matthew loved Angilia.

§§§§§

Mitchell answered a knock on Angilia's door and saw five men standing there, men he did not recognize. Angilia heard their voices. "Sam! My guys! Oh my gosh, come here!" Mitchell stood aside and they entered, with sunglasses, leather jackets, and long hair.

"We were on a plane back to the States when we learned what happened. We wanted to come back right away, but we decided to wait a bit. You don't know how wonderful it is to see you, Angel," John said as he sat on the edge of her bed.

"Come here, Sam," she said, her arm outstretched. Big, muscular Sam was crying, leaning against Tim. Sam walked to her, drying his eyes with the back of his hand, and gingerly hugged her. "I love you, all of you. You are my guys, and I love you. I'm all right now. Really."

Joe reached over and kissed her forehead, cleared his throat, and said, "I love you, too, Little One." Greg and Tim followed suit, and the five of them sat talking with her for an hour. They had been so scared.

"Listen, Angel, we have a lot more music to make together. You get well so we can keep rockin' and rollin'," John told her, while he held up his palm for a high five from her. She complied, and kissed them each before they left and told her they would visit her at the palace when she was home again.

§§§§§

Angilia, Matthew, and the dozen guards took the elevator to the PT room, where she began with warm-up stretching as always. They rotated her routines, and that day she began on the leg press, working her knee. After ten minutes, Matthew stopped her and checked her vital signs. He handed her a bottle of water and she took a few sips before moving to the elliptical trainer.

Seven minutes later she stopped and closed her eyes. "Matthew." Her voice was strained, and he carried her to a chair. "It hurts too much." Tears squeezed out of her clenched eyes. "I can't do this. I'm sorry."

"You don't have to. Where does it hurt?" She hesitated. "Angilia?"

"My head. I never get headaches. I tried to ignore it, but everything makes it worse." She leaned her head on his shoulder and moaned. "I feel sick."

"Let's have my father take a look. He has a lot of migraine patients, so he'll know what to do for a headache like this. You're doing well, you know. We don't have to do this today. Our target release date is one week from today. We can continue therapy after we leave here, you know. We will."

She leaned on him as they entered the hospital room, and Eric ran to her in panic. "I'm okay. I just have a sick headache. I have to throw up." Eric helped her into the bathroom, and she winced as her chest constricted when she vomited. He wiped her mouth and carried her to the bed.

Mitchell asked her a few questions and shone a light into her eyes. She closed her eyes and covered them with her hands immediately. "It appears to be a migraine. I can't give her what I normally would, though, because those drugs all cause irregular heartbeats. Why don't we try nine milligrams of morphine?" Matthew nodded and prepared the syringe. Mitchell slowly injected it into the IV lumen, and told Nurse Kara to turn off all of the lights in the room. She also pulled the curtain across the middle of the room to block the light from the window.

Mitchell placed a cold cloth over her forehead and covered her as she lay curled on her side, obviously fighting the pain and queasiness. "You just lie still, dear. Try to sleep through it if you can."

"Okay." Her hand covered her eyes, and she felt her father curl behind her and put his arm around her. "You did this when I had food poisoning once, remember? You also sang to me, Daddy."

"Did I?" She heard the smile in his voice, then his voice softly singing in her ear. She smiled through the pain, and fell asleep for a while. While she slept, Mitchell warned them that migraines and similar headaches lasted several hours, sometimes days. Nausea was common, but he and Matthew agreed that they could not give her much of anything for the pain. The morphine might help take off the sharpness, but it was a waiting game. In answer to Eric's question, Mitchell explained that stress was a common cause, and in her case understandable.

"The closer we get to leaving the hospital, the more anxious she seems," Matthew told them. "She's afraid someone will try to hurt you again." Eric groaned and closed his eyes. "We just need to keep her calm and assure her that you are safe. Until we make the transition to her house, she will struggle with this. She's so afraid there's another attacker waiting when you leave."

"My poor baby. How can I erase this nightmare from her life?"

"You just have to make her see that everything is all right, especially outside these four walls. It's safe here, it's secure here, and you are not in any danger as long as you are here. She has to see that it's the same out there," Mitchell firmly said.

Eric nodded. "That will be the worst part of all for her. I know that."

§§§§

The following week, Angilia was back on the elliptical machine, this time for fifteen minutes. Matthew and she walked several laps around the room before she did fifteen minutes of leg presses. He forced her to take a fifteen minute break, gave her a bottle of water, checked her vital signs, and sat talking with her.

"We're leaving the hospital tomorrow, Angilia. It's been seven weeks tomorrow since you were hurt, and you are so much stronger. This is what you've waited for. Are you excited?"

"I don't know. I'm terrified of what will happen out there. I'm so scared of who is out there. Another assassin. I'm so scared, Matthew."

"I know. But you'll both be completely surrounded by guards and officers. No one will get close to either of you. We won't let them. You know, everyone is going to be gathered near the front of the hospital, like every day, and no one knows that you two are leaving here tomorrow. No one except me, my dad, Kara, the security people, and your friends know your release date. No one.

"That means we can trick our way to the east exit tomorrow. We'll tell everyone we need to take you for an MRI and we need the area secure. No one else will be in the area. We'll say your dad is going with you to the MRI to keep you calm, and the entire security team is guarding you both. No one will know that we'll veer off and exit on the east side, where the car will be waiting. My dad and I worked it all out with the security leads. Don't worry about anything.

"People see the car come and go from your house daily, with Susan and your grandparents. They won't think anything of Susan getting out to open the gates to let the car in. Daniel and Roger will bring all of the suitcases and things to the house separately. It's all planned, Angilia. We won't let anything happen. I promise."

She looked at him with tears of gratitude in her eyes. "Thank you. You have no idea how this makes me feel." She leaned over and kissed his cheek.

His heart fluttered, but he composed himself and smiled in return. "I'm glad. I want to do anything I can to help you. You're a very special girl, you know."

CHAPTER 4

"**M**i nieta bonita!"

Angilia limped to her grandmother and hugged her. "Te amo, Abuela. Te amo, Abuelo." She stepped to her grandfather, and he put his arms around her gingerly, tears shining in his eyes.

"Welcome home, Angel. Welcome home. My heart is so happy to see you here, you have no idea," Alejandro said with a broad smile.

"I do, Papa. I do." Eric joined his daughter and father-in-law in an embrace. "I prayed for this moment every second of the past seven weeks."

Angilia put her arms around her father and leaned against him. "I love you, Daddy." She stood on the toes of her left leg and reached up to whisper in his ear. "You are the love of my life, Daddy, my first love and my greatest love." She kissed his cheek, relishing the familiar feel of his close-shaven beard and the smell of his cologne.

Eric bowed his head onto hers and kissed her. "I love you more than life, Angel. You are my life." He lifted her into his arms, smiled at her, and carried her into the small sitting room, where he sat her on the chaise lounge and adjusted pillows under her head and neck. He kissed her forehead and walked toward the hall.

"Daddy, where are you going?" Her panic-stricken voice stopped him, and he turned to look at her. "Please don't leave. Don't leave."

"I'm just going to the kitchen to get us some juice. I'll be right back." He walked out of the room, and she stood and followed him, limping to keep up with him. He looked at her and forced a smile, not saying anything while he got glasses from the cabinet and poured the juice. Mitchell had advised him to behave normally as much as possible so she would see that he was safe. She followed him back to the sitting room, and Eric looked at Mike, his face showing his sadness at her persistent fear.

Mike stood and walked into the sitting room before Eric. Angilia looked up at him with a woeful expression. "Stay with my father at all times. Please." Mike nodded his head and stood in the sitting room doorway.

Eric sat facing her. "Angilia, we're safe now. Everything's all right. I wish you could let go of this fear, baby." She shook her head, but she couldn't say much without jeopardizing his life.

"Daddy, please, you have to be extremely cautious. You have to. You can never be alone. Please." Tears filled her eyes and seared his heart. "You can't take anything for granted. That's what the security is for, to protect you. They have to protect you. They have to. This can't happen again."

Eric sidled next to her and she put her arms around him. "All right, Angel. You're right, that's what Mike and the other officers are supposed to do." He prayed that her fear would ease when she realized—soon—that he was safe. The gunman was dead. He was safe.

§§§§§

That afternoon, Angilia very slowly limped up the stairs to her room and got her journal off of her night stand, where she had put it seven weeks earlier. Eric leaned in her doorway watching her, his arms and legs crossed casually in a James Dean stance. She smiled and looked at him with those turquoise eyes so full of love. "I have a lot of catching up to do," she said as she picked up the diary and a pen. He looked down at the sight of her diary. "Don't be sad, Daddy." She walked to him and hugged him. "Don't be sad. I remember everything anyway, and I may as well write it in the diary. Isn't the point to record everything that happens, to write our individual histories?" She smiled at him, but he frowned.

"I don't want to remember it, Angel. None of it." He looked and sounded like a little boy. The past seven weeks had brutalized and battered him completely.

She hugged him and walked with him to an oversized sofa in her room. She sat and pulled him down to her, his head resting on her chest as he curled his legs on the sofa. Angilia held her father as he cried, kissing his head and stroking his back. What had she done to him? How could she have let this happen to her beautiful father? She vowed to God and to herself that it would never happen again. She would do whatever she had to do in order to protect him from the demon who threatened him. She was the only one who knew the truth, and she was the only one who could truly safeguard her father. From that moment, his safety became her sole life's mission.

Angilia could never tell anyone about any of this. She had to keep it all between God and herself. Her father's life depended on her. She would resume her vigils that night, sitting in his room as he slept. He was too vulnerable in Oxford. Her house there was not nearly as secure as the palace. They were flying home to Valmondois on May 1, thirteen days later. She had to forget her pain and focus on her duty.

Mitchell stood outside her doorway quietly watching them while Eric cried himself to sleep in his daughter's arms. He read the emotions and determination as they exposed themselves on her face. He knew Angilia feared for her father's life and blamed herself—for some reason—for the shooting. She looked up, sensing someone there, and he saw her lean over Eric as if to shield him. He stepped forward and smiled at her, though he felt like crying. She visibly relaxed when she saw Dr. Taylor.

He walked to her, and she put a finger over her mouth as a signal that Eric was asleep. Mitchell nodded as he knelt next to her. What would convince her that her father was safe? She looked at him and very quietly said, in answer to his unspoken question, "There's nothing you can do except to take care of him, make sure he's all right. Please?" He stroked her hair and nodded, his paternal side jolted into full gear. He stood and got a blanket from her bed and covered them. Then he moved her desk chair next to the sofa and sat with them. Maybe if she knew everyone was protecting Eric she would let go of her fear.

She looked at him with such an expression of bewilderment. "Thank you for being so nice to us. Both of you. I've never known a doc—anyone like you and Matthew." Her whisper was barely audible. "You don't have to stay in here."

"I want to. Do you mind?" She shook her head. Matthew had shared something Angilia had said when she asked him to be her doctor—that she hated her doctor. She was hiding something, what he did not know, but Mitchell knew she held onto a secret involving her doctor. What had that man done to make her feel this way? Mitchell's suspicion sent cold chills through his body: abuse.

Mitchell placed his hand on her shoulder protectively and reassuringly, and she smiled at him in gratitude. "Dr. Taylor, I feel safe with you and Matthew."

"I'm flattered, Angilia." He also felt heartbroken and angry. He determined to find out what that other doctor had done to her and to make sure he never did it to her again.

§§§§§

Angilia limped into Eric's room after the light was off, and moved toward the chair. "Come here, Angel." Her father's voice surprised her, and she stopped. He cringed as he watched her limp to the bed, and he pulled the sheets back for her. He helped her onto the bed and covered her as she curled on her side next to him.

"I'm sorry I woke you, Daddy."

"You didn't, baby. You're scared to be alone again? You've been in that hospital room with all of us around you for six weeks. Being home is going to take a bit of getting used to, isn't it?"

"Yes. I just don't want to be alone tonight. Are you angry?"

Eric turned and faced her. "Of course not, Angel. But how did you cope with this when you were here alone?"

"I called you all the time. Remember?" She reached for his hand and held it between both of hers. "I'm so sorry, Daddy. I made your life completely miserable." Tears trickled from the corners of her eyes, and he pulled her closer to him.

"No, you did not. Never. I just wish I could have been with you. I did miss you so, baby. I lived for our visits and phone calls. Always. You are my light and my life. I love you, my beautiful daughter Angilia. And I'm sorry for this afternoon. I didn't mean for that to happen, baby. I should never subject you to that. I'm so sorry."

She ran her finger over his cheek. "Oh, Daddy, don't. I want to take care of you. I want to protect you. I love you. You are my universe. I'm so sorry for all this this."

Eric kissed her nose. "I really do not deserve such a blessing as you, Angel. Now, let's get some sleep. Okay?"

She nodded and closed her eyes, pretending to fall asleep until she heard his soft, rhythmic breathing. Angilia opened her eyes and watched her father sleeping throughout the night. He never moved and neither did she. She felt so very tired, but she dared not close her eyes and risk falling asleep. When the faint golden hues of sun shone through the curtains, she thanked God, literally, for keeping her father safe.

When he opened his eyes several minutes later, she was staring at him, wide awake. "Good morning, my beautiful daughter Angilia." He kissed her forehead. "How long have you been awake?"

"Not long," she lied and prayed—again—for God's forgiveness. "I love you, Daddy." She kissed his cheek.

§§§§

Later that day, Matthew checked on Angilia to find her napping on the living room sofa, her head on Eric's lap while he watched the midday news. "She did very well this morning. Stairs are demanding for her, but she's getting a bit stronger every day. The knee brace seems to help, too. I'll be back to check on her in a little while."

"Thank you, Matthew. For everything. She awes me. I know I could never do what she's done. Her strength, her courage, her selflessness. I don't know where she gets it all, I really don't. I have seen grown men crumble under less, and my little girl never surrendered."

"It's all because of you, you do know that. She's quite fierce when it comes to you. Everyone needs a reason, motivation, and you are hers. I've got to admit that she impressed me from the beginning. And there's something almost supernatural about her that's difficult to explain."

"Supernatural? As in paranormal?"

"More like ethereal, otherworldly, spiritual, celestial." Eric's brow furrowed, and Matthew felt awkward. How could he explain without seeming foolish? "Divine. Heavenly."

"Angelic? I chose my daughter's name before my wife even knew she was pregnant. I knew it first, don't ask me how, and I knew the baby was my daughter Angilia. Her name means "Angel," you know. She is my angel. Heavenly? Yes, I felt that in her from the beginning. Michel Remais commented on that when her portrait was unveiled. He called her 'ethereal', too. There is a quality in her. And she often says the most esoteric things or refers to long-ago memories, then catches herself like she's said something she shouldn't have. Maybe she really is an angel." Eric stroked her hair and smiled.

Matthew returned the smile and strolled to the back yard, wondering what had possessed his mind. He had never thought or said such things. It all began during her surgery, when he felt this thing he called her guardian angel. He had always been so level-headed and logical, and now he was talking about art and angels. What had happened to him?

§§§§

Mitchell made two cups of coffee and joined his son in the back yard. Handing Matthew a cup, he launched immediately into his misgivings. "What do you know about Angilia's Valdavian doctor?"

"Nothing, really. She doesn't like him or trust him. I don't even know his name. Why?

"She told me something yesterday, or rather she let it almost slip before she self-corrected. She thanked us again for being so nice to her and, I'm quoting, 'I've never known a doc—anyone like you and Matthew.' She started to say she's never known a nice doctor. The most bone-chilling terror flashed in her eyes when she said that. Then she told me she feels safe with us. Something is very wrong, Matthew. Very wrong."

"Like what?"

"What would make a young girl terrified of her doctor, make her hate him?"

Matthew pondered his father's question for a moment, until suddenly his face registered revulsion. "Dad, you think he. . . . You think he. . . . Oh, dear God."

"I suspect he abused her, yes. I do. Eric knows nothing. He would have slaughtered the pig if he knew anything. Whatever happened, she has kept it to herself. I intend to uncover her secrets."

"How?"

"I'm not sure yet. You have to help me. If we can learn his name, that's a start. Don't ask her or Eric, though. Ask Susan, or Daniel, or Roger. If I have his name, I can get his records from the medical board. If there were complaints or accusations, those will be in the records. That's a start."

"I'll get his name. All I have to do is tell one of them I need her files transferred from that doctor since I'm now her personal doctor. That part's easy. I'll talk to Roger this afternoon." Mitchell nodded. "What are you going to do if—if he did something to her?"

"Make sure he never does it again." Mitchell's furor startled Matthew, who prayed his father's suspicions proved incorrect. Mitchell would kill the bastard if he had done anything to hurt Angilia.

Two hours later, Matthew texted his father the name: Gregor Jamieson. Mitchell stepped outside, to the furthest corner of the back yard, and telephoned the Valdavian L'Ordre National des Médecins, the medical board which maintained transcripts, job histories, malpractice suits, complaints, criminal records, and other pertinent information for every doctor in Valdavia. Mitchell explained that he was one of two doctors treating and caring for the Princess and he needed a copy of their complete file on her former physician. After nearly one hour of answering questions and verifying his identity, Mitchell was told he would receive the file electronically in approximately one week. He was rather disappointed, but one week was not too long to wait.

Mitchell texted his son this information. Both of them had to wait patiently and keep this secret in the meantime. Until they had proof, they could not mention this to anyone, especially Eric. Mitchell hoped he was wrong, though his instinct told him he was right. That overwhelmed him, as a human, a doctor, and a father. How would he tell Eric?

§§§§

Angilia opened her 2012 diary and reread her last entry from the night of March 6. Her pen sped across the next page as she let the thoughts and feelings pour through her onto the page. While she wrote, she prayed for God's forgiveness. And for her father's.

19 April 2012

I have not written in several weeks. So much happened. Where do I begin? How do I begin? Where I left off, I suppose. The day of the picnic began as a dream and ended in a nightmare. Someone—that demon—tried to kill Daddy. How could I have been so stupid? I let my defenses down and fooled myself into thinking he was safe here in Oxford. I saw my father get shot. Someone tried to kill him.

Dear God, I am so ashamed. I let this happen. I was selfish. I enjoyed our days here, and I talked myself into believing he was safe. Daddy was nearly killed because of me. I always believed Dr. Jamieson's threats and that is why I never told Daddy anything. I never told him the truth. You know, God, how I lied to him all these years, and you know how I hated that. I had to lie to Daddy. I know you understand why. Dr. Jamieson always warned me that if I ever said one word, he would kill Daddy. That's why I lied. And I never have told Daddy any of the truth. Never. So why did he hire someone to shoot Daddy? Why? I don't understand that, and it terrifies me more than words can express. He wants to kill Daddy no matter what I say or do. God, please, please help me to protect Daddy and keep him safe. I am so very scared. So scared. Please help me. Please keep Daddy safe. Please.

She placed the diary in her downstairs office desk drawer and, for the first time, locked the drawer. She could never risk her father reading it, simply because the information was lethal to him. More than ever, she had to remain attentive and vigilant. Vigil became her personal mantra. Her duty was to shield her father.

§§§§

Matthew was waiting for her when Angilia came out of her room dressed in a pink track suit, her long hair in braids, looking much younger than her sixteen years. They did some warm-up stretches, and then walked down the stairs. She turned and he kept his arm poised behind her, ready to grab her if she stumbled, and they slowly climbed the stairs. The pain was evident in her eyes no matter how much she attempted to disguise it from him.

Angilia did five repetitions before Matthew checked her heart rate, pulse, and blood pressure. She drank some water and did five more repetitions, walking up and down the stairs. Finished, she limped into the living room to find her father and Mike sitting on the sofa. Eric patted the seat next to him with a smile. She slipped her sneakers off, curled up beside him, and rested her head on his shoulder.

Juanita entered from the kitchen, wiping her hands on an apron, and bent to kiss her granddaughter and son-in-law. "No snacking this afternoon. I am making a wonderful dinner of stuffed green peppers with my grandmother's recipe. For you, mi nieta, I use couscous instead of meat. There is plenty, so everyone needs to be hungry tonight."

"Abuela, you shouldn't do all of that work."

"Angel, it is not work when you enjoy what you do. I like to cook, especially for people I love."

"Thank you, Mamá. It smells delicious. I'm already hungry," Eric smiled up at her. She patted his arm and returned to the kitchen.

Before long, Angilia's eyes closed and she was asleep. Eric turned off the television and picked up a book he had selected from her office. He read several chapters, engrossed in the story, as he kept his right arm around his daughter. Mike solved the crossword puzzle in the morning newspaper and kept his promised guard duty near Eric. Except for the sounds from the kitchen, the house was remarkably quiet, Eric thought, especially with so many people staying there.

Eric dropped the book, though, when Angilia's frantic screams lacerated the quiet. She threw herself across her father, screaming and crying and holding him tightly. "Angilia, it's all right, baby. Look at me. It's all right. Angilia."

Gasping for air, she stopped screaming and looked at him. Half a dozen other security officers raced into the room, as did Matthew, Mitchell, Roger, Daniel, Susan, Katherine, and Juanita. Alejandro ran in from the back patio and frantically asked, "What is wrong? What happened?"

"She had another bad dream," Eric replied, and stared into her eyes. "Baby, look at me. Look around. I'm all right. Everything's fine. We're safe, Angel. We're safe."

She nodded her head and apologized, though she knew that he was never safe as long as Dr. Jamieson lived. However, she forced herself to appear relaxed, and he picked up the book and smiled at her. Susan brought her a glass of orange juice. Mitchell gave his son a resolute, knowing look and marched upstairs. Alejandro escorted Juanita to the kitchen, where she wilted against him and cried. How long would her sweet nieta suffer so horribly?

$$\S\S\S\S$$

That night, the house was dark; the security officers stood at their posts, and most of the residents slept. Angilia, as usual, stayed awake and crept into her father's room. There, she sat in the chair and kept her diligent watch, more petrified than ever that an assassin would strike at any moment. She was back to keeping her diary current, while simultaneously updating it with details from the past seven weeks. She took short naps during the days and kept her vigils at night.

Matthew had peered into the hallway, watching her sneak into Eric's room again. He had seen her the previous night, too. He texted his father and told him, wondering if there was more to all of this than they realized. Mitchell quietly got out of bed, crept into the hallway, and motioned for his son to follow him downstairs. They went into the office, closed the door, and talked softly.

"Dad, it's not normal for someone to be that afraid, especially with all of these guards here. Why doesn't she just tell some of them to stand lookout in her father's room? She sat in there all last night, not sleeping, watching him sleep. Apparently, she did this same thing Wednesday night. Three nights in a row. I get it that she's scared because someone tried to kill him. I do. But this?"

"I know. I wondered the same thing this afternoon. But how do we prove this is all connected somehow? If they are connected."

"I'm not sure, dad. I just see too much fear and guilt in her. She's terrified for her father's life. She's guilty about the shooting. She's terrified of her doctor and doesn't feel safe around him. I don't know. Angilia is afraid, guilty, and insecure. They seem to fit together."

"Eric thinks she's terrified of the dark. He told me she used to crawl under his bed at night when she was very young. When she was a bit older she started sitting in the chair in his room. He said she did that on her birthday this year and screamed in horror when she dozed off and heard him moving," Mitchell shared.

"Dad, if she were afraid of the dark, wouldn't she crawl into the bed under the covers? She's sitting in there refusing to sleep, watching him sleep. Why? I'm worried. Something is wrong."

"I know. Just talk to her like you always do. She has a tendency to let things slip around us. Maybe you can find out more until that file arrives from the medical board."

§§§§§

Juanita and Katherine made a grand breakfast Sunday morning, and everyone gathered at the table. Angilia sat between her father and grandmother, while Matthew positioned himself across from Angilia. Her grandparents were flying home to Spain that afternoon. In nine days she and her father would fly home to Valmondois. She smiled at her father at the thought of him being home in the more secure palace. Her smile comforted his heart more than she knew.

"After we eat, we need to get ready for church, Angel."

"What? No. We can't." Her smile vanished, replaced by sheer terror. Everyone stopped eating, looking at her instead.

"Why not, baby?" Eric leaned close to her, more worried than ever.

"It's too dangerous. There are too many people there."

"Mi nieta, no one will hurt you in a church." Juanita put her arm around her granddaughter.

"Not me, Abuela. Daddy. And a church won't stop them." Angilia stumbled out of the chair and limped upstairs. Eric ran after her, and his shoulders sank when he saw her lying across her bed crying. She clutched her hands over her heart and curled into a fetal position. Crying was so intensely painful.

Eric went to her and held her, attempting to soothe her and stop her tears. After several minutes of trying and failing, he called for Matthew, who bounded up the stairs, ran for his medical bag, and rushed to her. "Can you leave us for a few moments, please?" Matthew asked Eric.

Angilia reached for her father and pleaded with him not to leave. "Angilia, nothing is going to happen in the hallway. I need to examine you," Matthew said. Mitchell entered the room, took hold of Eric, and walked him to the hall, shutting her bedroom door.

Matthew took out the stethoscope and listened to her heart, which was beating rapidly and irregularly. He scowled at her. "What's going on, Angilia?"

"I thought you understood. He can't go anywhere. There is danger everywhere. He can't. They will try again, Matthew."

"Who? Who will try again?"

"The people who tried to kill my father. They will try again."

He had never seen anyone more horrified than she. "Angilia, the gunman is dead. There is no one else waiting out there."

Her breathing was labored as her panic increased. "Yes, there is. Just because that assassin is dead doesn't mean they won't hire another one."

"How do you know that? Who did this?"

"I won't let him go. He is not going." She grabbed his arm, dizzy and afraid.

"You have to calm down now. No one is going anywhere. You're making yourself sick." He leaned her back on the pillows, placed an oxygen mask over her nose and mouth, despite her protests, and prepared a syringe with five milligrams of morphine. "Be still. I'm giving you a little morphine for the pain. You need to breathe. When you're stable, I'll let your father in again."

She looked at the door and willed herself to relax. Despite the pain, she took deep breaths and regulated her heart rate. Matthew listened to her heart and when it was relatively normal, he put his things away. "Angilia, please. Your grandparents leave this afternoon, and you don't want them to worry about you now, do you?"

"No. I'm just so afraid, Matthew. If they want him dead, they will keep trying. Anywhere, anyone, any time. That's the terrifying part—I don't know where, when, or by whom. It could be anyone, even someone sitting in that church. That's how they plan these things. When and where the person least expects it to happen, it does happen. Just like the day of the picnic." She looked at him with such sadness and tears fell from her eyes.

She seemed so forlorn, like a lost little girl, and he held her for a moment. "I'm sorry. I'm so sorry. I didn't mean to be so harsh. Please relax. I'll leave now, so your father can come in and sit with you."

"Thank you." He nodded, and opened the door. Matthew quickly explained that he gave her some morphine for the pain and told her to rest for a while before her grandparents left. Eric thanked him and sat next to her on the bed, rocking her gently in his arms.

§§§§§

Alejandro and Juanita joined Eric and Angilia in her room, simultaneously surprised and delighted at the sight that greeted them. Angilia wore a pale blue dress, Eric a suit and tie, and they sat on the sofa together as she read aloud from the Psalms. She held the white Bible her grandparents had given her on her fifth birthday. Angilia smiled up at them and they sat with her and Eric on the sofa.

The four of them took turns reading from the Bible for nearly one hour. Then they sat and talked for a couple of hours, sharing stories and memories. Juanita told Angilia about the night Marisol and Eric had met. "Marisol attended a charity dinner at the Grand Hotel. This was in the summer of 1989. I do not remember what it was for. But she went, even though she did not want to go at all. She found these dinners boring. She found the people boring. She was 38 years old, mi nieta, she was no child. She had been to lots of dinners and parties and she never met anyone interesting. Until that night.

"Your father gave a speech, and as I understand it they talked most of time after the speech. She came to the house after the dinner, very late, you understand. I had to get out of bed and let her sit me on the sofa and talk at me until morning. I did not say one word. She did not stop talking, and so fast she talked. She made me dizzy.

"She said she had done it. What did she do now? That is all I thought. She was always doing something, that one. Well, she said to me that she was going to be married. I asked her when, to whom. This was so sudden. She stood and told me she did not know when, but he was a Prince and his name was Eric. She turned and walked out of the house and left. Almost two years later she did just that."

Angilia smiled at her father over her grandmother's head. She had heard her father's version of the story many times. They had met at the Maria Sabine Cancer Foundation fundraising dinner on July 9, 1989. Angilia wanted to remember her grandmother's version just as vividly and write it in the family memoir she maintained. She adored her grandmother and her stories, the way she phrased sentences and the sound of her voice.

"Abuela, that is the most romantic story, just like a fairy tale." She leaned close to her grandmother and whispered a question in her ear. "Was it love at first sight?"

"It most certainly was, at least for your mother." She patted Angilia's hand and whispered to her granddaughter. "And for your father, too, I believe." Angilia smiled at her and kissed her soft cheek.

A while later, Susan knocked on the door and said it was almost time to go to the airport. Angilia looked at her grandparents and felt tears forming. She loved them dearly and wished they lived closer. She pulled her grandmother into a hug.

"I love you, Abuela. I will miss you terribly."

"Yo amo mi nieta. Yo amo tú. I will miss you so very much." She turned to Eric and held him tightly. "You must take care of yourself, mi hijo. And of our little girl. I love you so much, Eric."

"I love you, Mamá. So much."

Alejandro clasped Angilia to him, his tender side more than evident. His tears wet her hair as he held her close. "You are my special girl, you know that, Angilia. You are meant to do many more things. You will. I love you, little one." He kissed her forehead.

She put her arms around him and kissed his cheek. "I love you, Abuelo. I wish you could both stay."

"We will return in September, yes? For the Independence Day. It will be here before we know time has passed." She kissed him again.

Alejandro hugged Eric, now his only son, and whispered to him that he stay strong and healthy for his daughter. Eric patted his back and promised he would. The four of them shared a family hug and Angilia bowed her head. "Dear God, Thank you for our family and our love. Amen." Eric, Juanita, and Alejandro echoed her "Amen" and soon Eric and Angilia were alone again.

§§§§§

Angilia sat curled in a chair in her home office, writing in her diary. She was tired after sitting awake in her father's room all night, but wanted to get her diary up to date. After writing more entries for the week of the shooting, she turned to that day's page and expressed her innermost thoughts and feelings.

23 April 2012

Abuela and Abuelo returned to Spain yesterday afternoon. Abuela shared the most beautiful story of the night Mommy and Daddy met. I so loved hearing her tell the story. She has such a lovely way of telling stories. I did not tell her that Daddy has told me his version of that night many times. How wonderful to see Mommy as she was that night, alive through Abuela's story. I have written the story, as she told it, for my family history book. I miss Abuela and Abuelo so much. September is so far away it seems. I pray for an answer to my letter. Not for me. For Abuela and Abuelo.

How long must this living nightmare endure, God? Forgive me. I know when it will end—when Dr. Jamieson dies. As long as he lives, Daddy remains in danger. But when will Dr. Jamieson die? How long must Daddy live under this threat that he does not even know exists? Forgive me, please, God. I should not wish for another's death. But he has tried to kill Daddy once. He will try again. His death is the only sure end to this nightmare.

Meanwhile, Mitchell received an email containing the medical board's file on Dr. Gregor Jamieson. He took his iPad to the office so he could read the documents in private. Mitchell was anxious to learn what the file contained. He turned off the tablet when he saw Angilia sitting there writing.

She smiled at him and he sat near her on the sofa. She looked exhausted. She had not slept the night before, he and Matthew knew that. "Your exercises must have taken a toll. You look tired, Angilia. Why don't you take a nap soon?"

"I will as soon as I finish this entry. I am tired, Dr. Taylor." She did not have to lie about that at least. She closed the diary and locked it in the desk drawer. "I'm going to the living room. You can use the computer any time, you know."

"Thank you. I'll check on you later." He had no intention of opening that file on her computer and leaving its footprint there. He turned on the iPad and took a deep breath before he clicked on the file. What would it reveal?

Gregor Jamieson was born in Perth, Scotland on August 6, 1948, making him 64 years old. He had attended Perth High School, then the University of Aberdeen in the history program, before taking a job at a Scottish museum. A museum? There, Jamieson had worked in the conservation room, helping to restore and preserve national artifacts. Mitchell wondered what had prompted the man to enter medicine if his interests were in history.

Jamieson left that job suddenly after two years to enter the University of Aberdeen School of Medicine for their six year course of study and internship. A copy of his application letter indicated an interest in helping children more than he desired to do anything else. Jamieson knew his calling was to be a pediatrician, and he wanted to dedicate his life to making sure no child suffered. His life's purpose was to ease their pain.

Jamieson graduated in 1981, after which he moved to Valdavia and applied to lease an office in the King Gerard IV Public Hospital, which was approved. That office opened in 1983 and he had been there ever since, obtaining clients steadily over the years. Many of his earliest patients now brought their children to him. So far nothing seemed unusual.

The file contained copies of Jamieson's transcripts, recommendations, licenses, and degrees. There were no complaints or lawsuits. Nothing untoward was included in the file. Nothing indicated Jamieson had done anything unethical or illegal. Former patients brought their children to him, one of the highest compliments a doctor could receive, Mitchell believed.

Admittedly, Mitchell was relieved, for that could mean his suspicions were unfounded. However, he also knew this actually neither proved nor disproved his suspicions. What if Angilia were the only patient he had abused? She had never said anything to anyone, so there would be no complaints on file. Mitchell felt frustrated. He had little more information than he had the week before. Now what?

$$\SS\SS\SS$$

After her morning exercises with Matthew, Angilia joined her father on the living room sofa. The previous night's sleepless vigil and the exercises left her weary. Mike sat, as usual, on the other end of the sofa guarding Eric, per her insistence. She kissed her father and told him she and Matthew had increased her workout to ninety minutes.

"I don't want you to overdo this, Angilia. How is your pain?"

"It's not too bad. How is yours, Daddy?"

"Mine?" Eric gave Mike a baffled look. "Honey, I'm fine." She looked at his left shoulder, tears filling her eyes. "Angilia, I'm fine, really. Mitchell told you the night of your surgery that I wasn't seriously hurt. Believe me?"

She nodded and lay down on her back, her head on his lap. She was exhausted. Within minutes, she slept. Mike stood, straightened her legs, and covered her with a blanket. He sat in a nearby chair, while Eric continued reading a book. He prayed she would very soon eliminate her debilitating fear for him. He saw the toll it took on her and how it affected her physical and psychological recovery. Eric smiled, though, when he looked at her sleeping peacefully, and consoled himself with the thought that her psychological healing would occur—someday.

After two hours, Eric gently lifted her head and stood to get a snack from the kitchen. Mike followed, though Eric told him that was unnecessary. "I know, but if she wakes up and sees you gone and me there, she will panic. You know that."

"I know. I just wish she wouldn't. That tears me apart," Eric said as he took a plate from the cabinet. It shattered on the floor when they heard her scream for him in terror. Eric and Mike sped to her side, and she grabbed her father tightly, crying against his chest. "What happened, Angel? What's wrong?"

"I'm sorry. I was so scared."

"Another nightmare?" She nodded. What could he do to make them stop?

"Don't leave me today, Daddy, please. I just have this sick feeling that something is going to happen today. I'm so very scared." She refused to let him go, and he knew the only way to calm her was to stay in her sight. He carried her to the sitting room chaise lounge and held her until she fell asleep. He looked at Mike, who stood in the door, his expression asking when this would end.

§§§§

Tony entered the sitting room and announced that Oxford police officers and an INTERPOL official needed to speak with

Eric and Angilia. "Police? INTERPOL? Did they say why? What's wrong?" Eric's heart pounded furiously as he struggled to think why police and INTERPOL officers would need to talk to them both.

"No, they didn't say anything except that it was urgent they speak with both of you immediately."

Angilia awoke, feeling her father's frantic heartbeat. "What's wrong?" she whispered, afraid of the answer.

"I don't know, Angel. We'll find out soon. Bring them in, Tony."

Eric stood when six Oxford police officers and the INTERPOL official entered the sitting room. Angilia, too, stood and held her father's arm, feeling her own heart racing and making her lightheaded. What happened?

"Do you know this man?" an officer asked Eric and Angilia and held out a picture. Angilia gasped and stepped in front of her father.

"Yes. He's Angilia's doctor. He has been since she was born. Dr. Jamieson. Why?"

"Is this him, Your Highness?" he persisted. Angilia turned pale and nodded.

"We need both of you to please come to the Oxford police station. Gregor Jamieson was arrested last night and charged with murder-for-hire. We traced the gunman who shot you to Jamieson. The evidence is substantial and conclusive."

Eric stood rigid for a few moments, disbelief and shock encircling him, while Angilia began crying. "No. My father can't. It's too dangerous. Far too dangerous."

"Your Highness, Jamieson is securely held at the jail in Valmondois. He cannot do anything to either of you."

"Yes, he can. He will hire someone else. This will happen again. I won't let it."

Eric turned Angilia to face him, his hands grasping her shoulders. "What are you talking about, Angilia? What is going on?"

She shook her head. "This will happen again. You can't leave this house. You can't." She held him tightly, and he looked in desperation at the police officers.

"Her doctor hired that gunman? Is that what you're telling me?"

"Yes, Your Majesty. Jamieson hired and paid the hit man, Paul Whitman. Jamieson remains under tight restraint and guard. He actually wants to make a formal confession, and we need the both of you to come to the station please. Since he is confessing, there is no need for further action except for formal sentencing, which we understand is under your jurisdiction, Your Majesty."

"No! Daddy, you can't. You cannot get involved. That will cause him to do this again. You can't."

"We need to go over some documents with you both. What you decide to do or not do in terms of his sentencing is certainly your decision. You are quite safe, I assure you. We have several police cars here and several officers to guard you, in addition to your personal security officers. This will be over this afternoon."

"No, it won't. It will get worse now." Angilia had never looked more terrified or defeated. This would mean her father's death.

Matthew and Mitchell watched and listened from the hall, both more stunned than ever. "Dear God. Her pediatrician hired the assassin. Why?"

"I have no idea, Matthew. I think we should go with them just in case the shock of this causes her to have some heart complications. Get your medical bag." Matthew nodded and rushed upstairs and back.

Eric insisted on going to the station, his muddled brain attempting to grasp what the police had said. Why would Dr.

Jamieson hire a hit man to kill him? The two men had few interactions except for her infrequent visits to his office. They never socialized. What did Jamieson think Eric had done to him? Why would he jeopardize Angilia if Eric was the intended target? None of it made any sense.

Angilia demanded that the officers cocoon her father as they walked to the car, and they did. She held his arm tightly as they sat in the police car, officers on either side of them. Matthew, Mitchell, Mike, Tony, Roger, and Eric's security officers, traveled in police cars that drove on either side of the car that carried Eric and Angilia to the station. When the cars stopped at the station, security exited first and completely surrounded and engulfed Eric and Angilia until they were in a private room.

The large screen computer was on and the web cam showed an interrogation room at the Valmondois police station. Angilia recognized the officers in the room, one of whom spoke to them. "Your Majesty, Your Highness, I know this is difficult to comprehend and will be difficult to watch. But Gregor Jamieson told us this morning that he wants to make a formal confession. He is tightly bound, with his hands cuffed behind him and his ankles cuffed as well. We have him surrounded by armed officers who are instructed to shoot to kill if he attempts anything. He will be brought in shortly. He does not know that you are watching his confession. Once he is returned to solitary confinement, the Oxford officers need to explain some of the evidence to the two of you."

"I still don't understand any of this. Why did he do this?" Eric asked.

"That is actually in the evidence the officers need to go over with you, Sir. They're transporting him here now."

Angilia gasped and turned extremely pale at her first sight of Jamieson since January 3, when he had taunted her in the museum. She instinctively moved in front of Eric, shielding him. "It's okay, Angel. He can't do anything," he softly said and held her protectively close while the Valmondois officers seated and guarded the doctor. Eric felt his daughter's heart beat rapidly, and he looked at Matthew in concern.

Gregor Jamieson stated his name and profession for the record and then launched into his formal confession. "Yes, I hired a professional hit man, Paul Whitman, to assassinate Princess Angilia." That first statement stunned everyone, particularly Eric, who felt queasy. Relishing the reaction he knew his statement generated, Jamieson continued. "My plan all along was to gain trust and credibility as a doctor in Valmondois so that I would be the pediatrician to the King's children. To exact my revenge for what his ancestor did to my family, I needed to hurt him in the only way possible, by hurting his beloved children."

Eric held Angilia close and tight, their roles now reversed. He struggled to process what the monster said. Revenge? For what? Angilia, too, found it difficult to grasp the truth, that her father was not the intended target. She was. They had intended to kill her. Why did that man shoot her father then? Why?

"I wanted to make him suffer as my family has suffered. This would have been perfect. She was supposed to be killed while he watched. That would cause him the greatest of pain, and I savored the image of watching him agonize over her murder for years. Then I would have him killed. The kingdom of Valdavia would cease at that moment with no heir. This should have been perfect.

"Everything I did led me to that moment when Whitman pulled the trigger. I instructed him not to kill her with the first shot, but to make her death long and torturous. The thought of that thrilled me. But the fool botched everything. If he had not been killed that day, I would have killed him myself for ruining my perfect plot for revenge. He was never supposed to shoot Eric, only her. It all went wrong, although I prayed she would die from her wounds.

"All of these stupid people with their prayer services and anger and sadness, what utter nonsense. While they prayed for her recovery, I prayed for her death. At least that would fulfill the revenge and make their beloved King suffer. They would bury their Princess. Oh, that would have been the most joyous day for me, to watch him at her funeral. But it all went so terribly wrong.

"That fool Whitman trapped me, tricked me, and took me down with him. But I can testify that I have no regrets. I did my utmost best to achieve the revenge. For my ancestors who have been labeled as villains in Scottish history, when it was their ancestors who were the true villains. I lived my life for that revenge, and it was so close, so very close."

Eric was pale and slumped into the chair, feeling as if he had been beaten and left for dead. Angilia held him to her and rested his head on her shoulder. This was all because of her. She had put her father through so much suffering, just as the demon wanted. She truly hated that evil man for everything he had done to her father.

Suddenly, Angilia stood, again shielding her father. Something was horribly wrong. Confused, Eric stood behind her and put his arms around her. Gregor Jamieson looked directly at her and sneered evilly, just as he had done on her birthday. Eric felt her tense, felt her tremble, and he kissed the top of her head reassuringly. They watched Jamieson, both nauseated and afraid.

The doctor bit down on something in his mouth, the whole time staring at them, and then he collapsed onto the wooden table in the interrogation room. What had happened? Officers felt his pulse and checked for breathing. Another doctor rushed in and quickly checked Jamieson's vital signs. "He is dead," Dr. Portland announced to a very shocked group. An Oxford officer asked for verification of the death and Portland confirmed that Jamieson was dead. "There is no pulse and no breathing. No vital signs of life. He is quite dead."

Many people in the room were talking, asking questions and trying to comprehend everything that had just occurred. Angilia abruptly felt the fear leave her. "It is over." She turned and looked up at her father. "You are finally safe, Daddy. It's all over forever. I just wrote in my diary that, God forgive me, this nightmare would never end until he was dead. He is. The nightmare is over." She felt so changed somehow, lighter, freer, more peaceful. She smiled at her father and hugged him, not in fear, but in happiness.

$$\S\S\S\S$$

The officers brought water and tea to Eric, Angilia, and the members of their group, while they all struggled to understand Jamieson's confession and its implications. Angilia sat at a table next to Eric, who was shell-shocked—and looked it. "Daddy, I'm so sorry for lying to you all these years. Please forgive me. I hated that I had to lie to you."

"You lied to me? About what?"

"I've never been afraid of the dark. I had to let you believe that, though, and I hated myself for lying to you. You put up with me all those years, with my intrusions and fears, and I had to lie to you. Please forgive me." Tears slid from her eyes.

"What do you mean you had to, baby? Why did you think you had to lie to me? You know you can tell me anything."

She shook her head. "Not that. Never. I couldn't tell you any of that or he would have killed you. I had to lie so he wouldn't kill you."

"Jamieson? Angilia, what happened? Tell me." Matthew and Mitchell looked at each other, now knowing that Mitchell's suspicions were indeed correct. That man had abused her.

"He threatened me each time I went that if I ever said even one word to anyone about what he did, he would come to your room while you slept and slash your throat and kill you. I always believed him. He would have killed you, Daddy, and it would have been my fault. I could never let that happen. I couldn't let him kill you."

Eric's stomach lurched as his brain registered what his daughter had said. He felt anger and sickness rising in him and he clasped his hands in an effort to control himself. "What did he do?" Dear God, what would she tell him?

"He hurt me. He never did anything you or anyone else would see, though. He just did things no one could see." The fear and pain on her father's face saddened her, but she needed to tell him and stop lying to him and keeping secrets from him. She held up her left forearm and exposed a scar there. "Do you remember this, Daddy?"

He nodded and ran his finger along the scar. "Yes. You fell and cut your arm when we were playing."

"In the backyard. It was in June of 2001 when I was five. You grabbed me, wrapped my arm in a kitchen towel and rushed to the hospital, to his office. He always made you wait outside in the hall. You thought it was so you wouldn't get sick or something, but it was so you would never see what he did." Eric clutched the chair and clenched his teeth to keep from either screaming or vomiting.

"That day he sat me on the counter next to the sink and held my arm over the sink. He never gave me local anesthetic. He took a scalpel from the drawer and made the cut deeper. Then he poured a bottle of rubbing alcohol over it to make it sting. He let it bleed for a few minutes, and then he stitched it. He wrapped it in gauze. The whole time, I gripped the edge of the counter with my other hand and clenched my teeth. I could not cry or scream, or you would have heard me and rushed in. And he would have killed you right then. He would have. When he finished, he put his face right in front of mine and repeated the threat he always made. If I told anyone about anything, he would come at night and slash your throat.

"I never told you. I never told anyone. I wrote everything in my diary and I prayed to God, but that's it. I kept it all inside of me. I had to, Daddy. So when he first said he would come at night and kill you, I started coming in your room at night. I wasn't scared of the dark. I was terrified that he would make good on his threat and kill you. I'm so sorry for lying to you."

Eric stood and leaned against the wall, pounding it with his fist while he cried. He was angry, she knew. "I'm so sorry. I've never lied to you about anything else, I swear. Please, Daddy, can you forgive me?"

Eric turned and fell to his knees in front of his little girl, hugging her to him, his tears falling onto her shoulder. "There is nothing to forgive, Angel, nothing. You never did anything wrong, darling. Oh, God, I am so sorry. How did I not see any of this?"

She kissed his cheek and hugged him, telling him she did not want him to see anything as long as Jamieson were alive. She reminded him that he was safe now and their nightmare was finally over.

Matthew, too, felt sick to his stomach. His father put an arm around him. "What a bastard. How could he do this to a little girl?"

"I don't know, son. She carried the weight of this all alone for so many years. Now Eric will have to suffer through his guilt. Jamieson may not have killed her, but he has made them suffer. If he hadn't killed himself, I would have killed him with my bare hands," Mitchell whispered through gritted teeth.

§§§§

An hour later, the police brought a box into the room. Eric, Angilia, and the others had spent the previous hour processing what they had learned. Roger remained at Eric's side, adding his reassurances to Angilia's and trying to convince Eric that he had not done anything wrong. No one had suspected anything for all of those years, none of them. The only person to blame was Jamieson, and he was now dead.

Mitchell and Matthew sat near Angilia and Eric, as well, knowing that facing the evidence would be emotionally disturbing for both of them. Matthew noted that Angilia looked transformed, relaxed and fearless. Her blue eyes no longer mirrored internal fear. Eric, though, appeared brutalized. Everyone had presumed he was the target of the assassination attempt, not the teenaged princess.

"When the Valmondois officers discovered the documents and recordings that Paul Whitman had placed in a bank safe deposit box, proving that Jamieson had hired him, they arrested Jamieson and obtained search warrants for Jamieson's home, office, and other locations he kept property. He knew he had left evidence of his own guilt, and he knew he would not escape punishment. That's why he offered his confession, we suspect. He likely committed suicide to avoid the punishment you would order, Your Majesty. He was actually proud of what he did, and he wanted to proclaim his twisted sense of honor before he took his own life.

"He kept notebooks for years that detailed his plot for revenge. Your Highness, your history background will help in our understanding of some of this. See, Jamieson himself earned a history degree and worked in a Scottish museum to learn more about this prior to moving to his medical degree and career. He did carefully plan his every move. He prepared for this, as he said."

The officer opened one of the notebooks and flipped to a bookmarked page. "Here he writes about the ancestor he mentioned in the confession. Jamieson was a direct descendant of John Comyn, Lord of Badenoch." He watched Angilia's face and saw the clarity and incredulity shown there.

"That was in 1306, and no one knows what really happened. My father was nearly killed over something that happened 706 years ago?"

"Who is John Comyn?" Eric asked, more baffled than ever.

Angilia shared what she knew of the long-ago events. "He and his family were competitors for the throne of Scotland against Robert the Bruce. His mother was John de Balliol's daughter Eleanor. So Comyn believed that he had a right to the throne due to his dual royal descent from both the Comyn and Balliol lines. He even married William de Valence's daughter Joan just so he would have a link with England's King Edward I. William was Edward's uncle."

Eric's head was spinning. What did this have to do with them? "The Comyn family hated the Bruce family. All of this occurred during the rise of William Wallace and Edward I's battle for the throne of Scotland. Robert the Bruce became an ally of Wallace's, and that meant that Wallace by association became an enemy of the Comyn family, too. So John Comyn agreed to help capture Wallace and turn him over to Edward I for execution," she continued.

"What is known is that Robert called a meeting with John on February 10, 1306 at the Greyfriars Church in Dumfries. There were no witnesses to what actually happened, but the folklore says that Robert stabbed John and that Robert the Bruce's friend Robert de Kirkpatrick ran into the church to finish the job and kill John.

No one will ever know what really happened, but descendants of Comyn believe that Robert killed John to prevent him from becoming King and that they still have a right to the throne of Scotland. Some of them are still pleading their cases and trying to prove their rights to the kingdom. Robert is my eighteenth great-grandfather. We are direct descendants of Robert the Bruce, which in Jamieson's mind means our family stole the throne of Scotland from his family."

"God help me, I can't believe he would want to hurt you over this. What would that accomplish?" Eric visibly struggled to comprehend the twisted revenge minutely plotted throughout Jamieson's life. "His whole life was spent planning this revenge, and for what? There is no throne of Scotland, and if there were, we do not have any jurisdiction over that anyway."

"Your Majesty, Jamieson wrote about that in his notebook, too. In his confession, he mentioned that the kingdom of Valdavia would cease to exist after your murders. In reality, he planned to take that kingdom as restitution for the murder of Comyn."

Eric and Angilia read the notebook entries themselves, an act of closure they needed. "I actually pity him," Angilia softly said.

"Pity him? For what?" Eric was taken aback.

"His life was spent in anger and hatred. Anything good he might have done was for the sole purpose of fulfilling his revenge. He wasted his entire life engulfed in hatred and sin. How sad."

Eric looked at her and smiled for the first time that afternoon. "You really are amazing, Angel. After everything that monster did to you, you still find compassion for him in your heart. I love you so much, Angilia." He kissed her cheek and she smiled up at him.

They walked out of the Oxford police station into the bright sunlight, not surrounded by officers and guards, but hand in hand. An officer drove them home while they sat alone on the back seat of the car. Angilia looked out the window and waved to a group of teenagers walking along the side of the road. "Daddy, can we all walk to the pub for dinner tonight?"

Eric smiled, realizing that the nightmare was over for her. She no longer lived in fear for him. "Of course we can. Do you realize we will be home in Valmondois one week from today?"

"I know. I'm so happy, too, Daddy. So happy."

§§§§

The next morning, Eric awoke alone in the room. Angilia was not sitting in the chair guarding him as she had done every night since her release from the hospital. He showered, shaved, brushed his teeth, and dressed, then looked in her room and smiled. She slept soundly, curled on her side. He silently thanked God that her fear had ended. She was free. Was he? He blamed himself for failing to recognize the signs of what that man had done to her. Would he ever be able to forgive himself?

During breakfast, everyone noticed the change in Angilia. She seemed relaxed and truly happy. She was. Katherine observed her with maternal concern, still sickened by what her husband and son had shared with her the previous night. She could not fathom what the child had endured most of her life, living under the umbrella of that evil man's threats. No wonder the poor girl had nightmares and stayed awake guarding her father. Who could blame her?

"Daddy, Matthew and I are going to walk to the campus today for my exercise. Do you want to come with us?"

"Yes, I'd like that. If we time it just right, we can have lunch at one of the pizza parlors nearby. How does that sound?"

"Wonderful."

"What time are you leaving?" Mike asked her.

She smiled at him. "You don't have to come. But you can if you want to join us for lunch."

Mike smiled at Eric, realizing that her fear and paranoia were erased, as if by magic. Mitchell smiled, too, and asked if he could walk with them. Susan echoed the question, elated that Angilia felt so safe. Angilia responded that anyone who wanted to could join them.

At 11:00 Angilia, Eric, Matthew, Mitchell, Katherine, Susan, Daniel, and Roger walked to the University, where she went up to visit Christopher in his office. After his initial shock, she asked him to join them for lunch. The nine of them sat at a large table in a nearly pizza parlor and enjoyed a laughter-filled lunch. Several patrons stopped at their table to wish Eric and Angilia well and to ask for her autograph. Someone put money in the jukebox and selected one of her songs before turning around and seeing her sitting there. She smiled at him, and he stopped to tell her he loved her music.

On the walk home, Angilia pulled her father away from the group. "Daddy, I know what yesterday did to you. You did nothing wrong. None of what happened is your fault. Don't feel guilty because you didn't know. I went out of my way to make sure you never knew anything. I went to a lot of trouble to hide it all from you. Don't do this to yourself. Please. I did what I had to do, and I don't regret any of it. I am sorry I lied to you, but I had reasons. The only one who is guilty is Jamieson, and he's dead now. We are free, Daddy."

He breathed deeply and looked at the fluffy clouds. "You know the last time I watched the clouds float in the sky was at our picnic that day. It was a wonderful day, wasn't it? Until that Whitman fired his gun. I want to remember the fun, the laughter, and the happiness of that day. I don't want to let Jamieson take that from me. That would give him the victory, wouldn't it? Let's remember the love and happiness. Can we do that, Angel?"

"Yes, Daddy, always. Besides, what happened that day has made us even closer. We already made something ugly and hateful into something beautiful and loving. Everything ugly and hateful and fearful died with Jamieson."

Eric smiled at her and they caught up with their friends for the rest of the walk home. Angilia's neighbor was working in her flower garden and called to her. She cut a yellow rose from a bush, removed its thorns, and handed it to Angilia with a hug. Everyone seemed happier.

§§§§

Saturday morning, Angilia brewed a cup of herbal tea and walked into the back yard. She sat on a tree swing and enjoyed the fresh air and sunshine and the light breeze that blew her long hair. She thought of Starlight and how she missed riding him. Had he forgotten her, given up on her? The morning she left, she promised him she would return the following week. Nearly two months had passed.

"You look very pensive, Angilia."

"Oh, Dr. Taylor, good morning. I was thinking about Starlight, my horse. I miss him."

"You'll see him in a few days, dear. You must be excited."

"I am. Dr. Taylor, may I ask you something?" He nodded as he sipped his coffee. "Daddy and I trust you and Matthew. Would you consider being our doctor, too? I mean, Matthew is my doctor, but he's a cardiologist. We need someone like you, though, a family doctor. I'd really like it if you would be Daddy's doctor. It's not that his doctor is horrid, but you've taken care of him since the shooting. Will you think about it please?"

"I'm flattered, Angilia. I promise I'll talk it over with Katherine and we will consider it carefully. However, if I do accept, I would need time to prepare my practice for the transition to another doctor. I need to notify my patients and make a lot of arrangements. That would take a little while."

"Thank you," she smiled and leapt from the swing to hug him.

§§§§

Angilia rose early the next morning and was dressed and sitting at the kitchen island with a cup of tea when Katherine came down. "You look pretty, Angilia."

"Thank you. Daddy and I are going to church this morning."

"Good morning, my beautiful daughter Angilia. What's this? Which church are we attending this morning?"

"I thought we would go to University Church of St. Mary the Virgin. That's where I usually attended church when I was here."

"Sounds nice. What time does the service begin?"

"10:30. It's a beautiful church."

Eric smiled broadly at Katherine, and he thanked God for healing them. Everyone was equally thrilled, and they all prepared for the morning service. They walked, which was exercise for Angilia, and enjoyed the company and nice spring weather. The congregation greeted them fondly, most of them welcoming Angilia back after her ordeal.

The sermon, the hymns, and the fellowship mingled to create a fuller sense of peace and happiness deep within Angilia. Most of her life had been lived in fear and guilt, and this freedom was alien to her. She enjoyed her newfound freedom. She radiated joy throughout the service, and Eric found it contagious. His own soul lightened under the influence of hers, and he felt his guilt slipping away.

Eric recognized that neither of them had done anything sinful, that they were not to blame for Jamieson's actions. No, he had not correctly interpreted the signs and clues, but that was not his fault. She did what she felt she had to do in order to protect him, and for her self-sacrifice he felt such tremendous love, gratitude, and respect for his God-given daughter. No man was as loved and blessed as he was, of that Eric was certain.

§§§§

Angilia pulled her suitcase from the closet and opened it on her bed. She began packing some of the clothes from the closet, clothes she had kept there for her work and life in Oxford. What she could not fit would get packed with the rest of her belongings over the next several days. Everything in the house would be packed and her personal things shipped to the palace in Valmondois. Everything else—furniture, appliances, utensils—would be donated to local charities. She smiled, thinking about her life in Valmondois with her father and how gloriously content they were now.

"Someone's happy to go home," Susan said as she came in to help Angilia pack the things she would take with her on the plane the next morning. Susan had known Angilia since her birth, and she had never seen her so joyful and carefree.

"Oh, Susan, I am, more than you know. We're going home, without fear and trepidation. Do you know what that's like for me, Susan?"

"Honey, I have no idea what it was like for you all those years living with the fear and pain. But I see the peace and joy in your eyes and face now, and I know what that must feel like." Susan hugged the girl she had watched grow into a lovely, intelligent, brave young lady, and her heart filled with love.

"Can I join you?" Katherine asked from the doorway. Angilia held out her arm, and Katherine hugged her. "I'm going to miss you, you know." She and Mitchell would return to their home in Oxford, not that far away, the following day.

"Thank you for helping us, Mrs. Taylor. You are all so wonderfully kind to us. I'll miss you, too."

"Mitchell told me about your conversation, that you asked him to be your family doctor. We've talked about it, dear, and I shouldn't say anything, but. . . ."

"I thought I told you not to say anything just yet," Mitchell interrupted his wife. "Angilia, I spoke with your father yesterday after church. I have several things to do first, but I am honored to accept."

Angilia reached up and hugged him, then Katherine again, and thanked them. "I know you are both giving up a lot for this. I can never thank you enough."

"It's my pleasure, dear. We'll need to sell our house here and buy one in Valmondois before we can move, though. During that process, I'll transfer my practice and patients to another doctor. I'll miss my patients here, but I'm gaining two very special patients in exchange."

"You don't have to buy a house in Valmondois. There is a house on the palace grounds. My grandmother lived there after my grandfather died. I used to visit her there all the time. It's a gorgeous house. You can live there if you like it and don't mind."

"Angilia, that is awfully sweet of you, but what does your father say about that? He may not want us underfoot constantly," Katherine responded.

"He says it's perfectly fine. Angilia and I have already talked about this. The house is yours if you want to live there. We're thrilled to have you there." Eric joined them and shook Mitchell's hand when he said they would be delighted. Angilia beamed with pure happiness. Having the Taylors there would be a lot like having family with them.

§§§§

30 April 2012

I shall write tomorrow evening's diary entry in my beautiful bedroom at home. We have been in Oxford for nearly two months. When I left Valmondois, I was happy just to get Daddy away from Dr. Jamieson for a few days. I return completely free of terror and guilt.

God, thank you for your blessings and for protecting my father throughout this ghastly nightmare that is now over forever. Our lives and our futures hold many unknowns, but I do know they hold love, happiness, gratitude, peace, and light.

We face our futures with hope, anticipation, faith, love, and the bond that has united us for so very long. Someday I shall reveal my past to Daddy. I have so much to tell him, and even though I was told then that I would not remember any of it, I do—you know that, God, because you gifted me this memory. You must have intended for me to remember. Thank you.

CHAPTER 5

Angilia unlocked the front gate and was greeted by several dozen well-wishers on the sidewalk outside her house. Surprised, she accepted bouquets and stuffed animals and she signed autographs. Eric joined her and greeted everyone. Eric and Angilia posed for pictures and thanked them for taking time to come and for thinking of them. Matthew watched from the driveway, relieved for them that their lives were returning to normal. Mitchell and Katherine stood with their son, smiling at Angilia's comfort in public.

A taxi arrived for Mitchell and Katherine, who hugged their son once more. They also hugged and kissed Angilia and she told them she looked forward to their arrival in Valmondois. "So do we, dear. You've become very special to us. I'll miss you until we move," Katherine replied, on the verge of tears. Eric hugged Katherine, shook Mitchell's hand, and thanked them both for everything, especially their concern for and care of Angilia.

Soon, the taxi drove away, and the two Rolls Royce cars prepared to leave for Kidlington Airport. Eric, Angilia, Matthew, Daniel, Roger, Susan, Mike, and Tony rode in one car, while the remaining security officers rode in the second car. The two groups boarded Eric's two planes and the security officers' plane departed first. Angilia watched the first plane ascend higher into the sky, looking forward to their return home. While Eric thanked the airport staff and security, Angilia simply enjoyed the fresh air and sunshine.

Finally Eric and Angilia settled into their seats, followed by Matthew, who sat across from her. She smiled at her friends as the plane prepared for takeoff. She and her father had flown to Oxford just under two months earlier on March 2. At last they were flying home on May 1. She treasured the sound of that word and what it meant—home. "Daddy, we're really going home. I feel like Dorothy Gale, because there really is no place like home."

"No, Angel, there isn't. Today is a miracle. I can never tell you how happy I am today."

"You don't have to. I see your happiness in your eyes, and that makes me happy." Soon the plane soared into the sky. She wrote in her diary for a while, recording the morning's memories. Tonight, she would have so many more memories from this glorious day that she would write. She breathed deeply, still awed at the freedom and joy that now filled her being.

She looked out of the window and smiled when she saw they were up among the clouds, surrounded by their softness. Angilia wondered if those whom she had known were watching them at that moment. They were so close, she knew, yet none of the others aboard the plane were aware of that. For a while, this would remain her secret. When the time was right—she would know when—she would reveal everything to her father. Did he know anything? Did he remember their encounter on that tragic day long ago?

$$\S\S\S\S\S$$

Just over two hours after takeoff their plane landed at the Valmondois National Airport. Angilia smiled at her father and held his hand in anticipation. Mike received a briefing from a member of the ground security and came to relay that information to Eric, Angilia, Matthew, and the others prior to debarking. Thousands of people had come to welcome them at the airport and along the route to the palace. Police had tried to barricade the crowds to no avail; their excitement and fervor were out of control.

Both Eric and Angilia had seen huge crowds at official events, and honestly expected people to greet them. People always did. Eric seriously doubted, though, that "thousands" of people clogged the streets. Angilia smiled at him. "They love you, Daddy. Don't be surprised."

Tony exited the plane first, followed by Daniel, Roger, and Susan. Angilia linked her arm through her father's and they stepped onto the top stair, saluted with deafening cheers from thousands of their fellow Valdavians. Both stood, momentarily stunned, taking in the sights and sounds. People held aloft signs welcoming them home, as well as bouquets and gifts. Matthew stood behind them, his eyes wide. He had viewed similar scenes on television, but seeing and hearing it all in person left him feeling amazed and stunned.

Eric raised his left arm and waved at everyone, and Angilia followed suit. Flashbulbs blinded them as dozens of press photographers took hundreds of pictures. Mike leaned forward and told Eric that if he wanted to make a brief statement, there was a podium and microphone set up. Eric nodded his head and slowly walked down the steps with Angilia, one step at a time. Matthew followed behind her, his hands poised to grab her if she slipped. Mike exited last.

Eric took a deep breath and walked with her to the podium. "Thank you. Wow." His simple first words to the people in two months sent them into rapturous cheers, which took several moments to subdue. "Thank you so very much. Angilia and I looked forward to today for so long, and we are both thrilled to return home. We never expected such a magnificent homecoming. This means more to us than we can tell you with words." The roar of the crowd escalated again, and then they began to chant her name.

Eric smiled at her and leaned over closer to her ear. "They want to hear from you, Angel." He beamed, and she nodded and stepped in front of the microphone. When they saw her there, ready to speak, the crowd suddenly grew very quiet, anxious to hear their adored Princess. "I don't know what to say. Thank you seems inadequate at this moment, but I do thank you. If the past two months was a race, then this is the finish line—coming home. You have no idea how much we waited for today. Seeing all of you is warmer than the sunshine. Thank you. I love you." She blew them a kiss and turned her head to ask Matthew if they could do a walkabout. He shook his head, saying it would be too strenuous.

Eric returned to the podium and they hushed to hear their King. "We are so grateful to you all, truly we are. Angilia would love to greet you, but right now that just is not feasible. I am sorry to disappoint you, but her doctor advises against a walkabout today."

One of the reporters shouted a question to Eric. "Can we get a statement from the Princess' doctor please?" Eric hesitated and then looked at Matthew and explained that he did not have to say anything, and if he did to make it brief and general. Matthew had never anticipated this, and he was admittedly nervous.

Angilia took his hand and stepped to the podium. "Ladies and gentlemen, thank you for your support and concern. My father and I received hundreds of cards and letters, and we remain so touched by all of them. My doctor is with us today, actually, Dr. Matthew Taylor. As you can see, though, I am doing well. Dr. Taylor?"

"The Princess is right. She is doing remarkably well considering the severity of her wounds. Declining the walkabout was my call, simply because I feel it imprudent for her to stand and walk for that length of time. I know her practice is to talk with as many people as possible, sometimes for hours, and I feel that would be too taxing at this moment. Thank you."

Eric and Angilia waved to the thousands of people who continued to cheer them, and then entered Eric's Rolls Royce convertible. Matthew and Eric assisted her into the left side and made sure she was comfortable. Eric sat next to her, Matthew across from them, and Mike in the front passenger seat. Eric smiled at her. "We'll be home in about half an hour, Angel." She smiled and waved again at the screaming throngs who had waited to welcome them home.

The Rolls Royce turned out of the airport and onto the street that would take them straight to the palace. Eric's expression caught Matthew's attention, and he turned his head to see what was wrong. "Whoa! How many people live in this country? I think they're all here today."

Angilia giggled. "Not quite. We have just over 83,000 citizens. Eventually, you'll see the whole country if you accompany me when I travel. Plus, we sometimes spend a couple of weeks in the summer at the country house." Her voice was very quickly drowned by the screams and shouts of thousands of people who did in fact line both sides of the street five or more deep, from the airport to the palace.

People approached the car as it passed, and the driver had no choice but to move extremely slowly. Eric and Angilia were besieged by people handing them flowers, cards, gifts, and stuffed animals. Some even reached over the car doors to hug them. Many people cried, emotional upon seeing their beloved King and Princess alive and home after two long months.

Matthew watched in amazement while the car was bombarded, people even throwing themselves onto the car in their excitement. The car barely moved, creeping like the proverbial snail millimeter by millimeter along the street. Mike remained attentive and scanned the crowd for anything or anyone suspicious, though he doubted anything would happen. During his many years as a security officer for the royal family, nothing untoward had ever happened. Although today's frenzy was unprecedented, Mike understood that it was a manifestation of the peoples' elation in welcoming home Eric and Angilia.

That frenzy persisted, and two hours after they had left the airport they were merely halfway to the palace. Angilia smiled at her father and leaned close to his ear so he could hear her. "This is staggering. Everyone loves and respects you so, Daddy."

"I don't think they came just to see me, Angel. They are here mostly for you," he beamed in reply.

Suddenly Angilia heard a familiar voice. "Princess darling!" She turned and shouted for the driver to stop.

"Billy!" She opened the door and he stepped forward and kissed her hand. "Oh, Billy, I've missed you."

"I missed you, too, Princess darling. I missed you a lot." Angilia hugged him and wiped tears from his cheeks. "Here," he said with a sniffle and handed her a red rose. "And I want you to have this to keep you safe." He held up a teddy bear in a soldier uniform.

"Thank you, Billy. He's perfect." She held the bear and kissed the top of Billy's head. He kissed her cheek, saluted Eric, and closed the car door. "Dad, he is the sweetest, isn't he?"

"Yes, he is, and he's very smitten with you."

"Billy asks the guards at the gates at least once a week what he has to do to become a royal guard," Mike turned to tell them. "He's quite intent on slaying the dragons for you, Princess."

"There aren't any more dragons," she replied with a smile. She waved to and greeted people as the car continued to creep along the street. She spotted someone in the crowd and told the driver to stop again.

"Daddy, it's the man who spoke to us outside the museum." She discreetly pointed to the elderly man in the wheelchair. "Remember? He has lived through four kings."

"Yes, I do," Eric said just as she opened her car door and got out. Eric slid across the seat quickly and followed her. "What are you doing?"

"I just want to thank him, that's all," she said over her shoulder. She bent and told the gentleman she and Eric remembered him and thanked him for coming to welcome them home.

He took their hands in his and kissed hers with tears in his eyes. "My dear Princess, how wonderful to see you. We were all so worried about you."

"Thank you so much," she said and kissed his cheek. Eric thanked him, too, and the man pulled Eric into a hug. Angilia smiled and reminded him, "People love you, Daddy. You have so much love and respect."

They returned to the car, and after another ninety minutes they saw the palace gates. They were almost home. The car was filled with flowers, cards, and gifts by the time the car entered the gate to the courtyard. "So much for getting home in thirty minutes," Eric grinned. He asked Mike how long the drive had taken. Eric groaned at the answer: four hours and thirty minutes, four hours longer than usual. "Well, we're here now, Angel."

The mall outside the palace was filled with what looked like thousands more people, all screaming and chanting for them. The car stopped near the front entrance to the palace. Mike exited the car first, then Matthew, and finally Eric, who told Angilia to wait. When Eric opened his door and stood, the screams grew deafening. He smiled and waved at them for a moment, then walked around the car.

Eric opened the car door and helped Angilia stand. She slipped her arm through his and they walked—she limped—around the car again so everyone could see them both. At their first sight of the Princess, people became hysterical, crowding to get a glimpse of Angilia. She smiled at them, waved, and looked up at her father with happiness in her eyes. They finally walked to the door, followed by Matthew, and turned to wave again before they entered their home for the first time in two months.

§§§§§

Eric and Angilia stepped into the foyer to another surprise greeting. The entire palace staff stood there, smiling, many crying, and ecstatic to welcome home King Eric and Princess Angilia. Angilia limped to them and hugged each person, and Eric followed suit and thanked each of them for the touching homecoming. When Angilia reached Joseph, she hugged him and asked about Starlight.

"He is well, Princess. He misses you, but I made sure he got exercise and ate right. I talked to him every day about you."

"Thank you, Joseph. I missed him so much. I can't wait to see him. And to ride him." She turned to her father excitedly. "Daddy, can I change and go ride Starlight now?"

Eric was flabbergasted. "No, Angilia. You know you can't." He looked at Matthew for help.

"Angilia, it's still far too early for anything that rigorous. You can walk him, which will be good exercise for both of you, but you cannot ride him anytime in the near future," Matthew told her firmly.

She felt and looked disappointed, but she realized he was right. If she wanted to become fully recovered and healthy, she had to abide by his instructions. "All right. I'll be a good girl."

"Speaking of which, you look tired, Angel. Sitting in the airplane for two hours and that car for four and a half hours was a bit much for all of us. You need to rest for a while before dinner," Eric said as he looked at her, exhaustion evident on her face. He could tell she was on the verge of protesting, so he picked her up and carried her up the stairs to the third floor.

He walked into her suite, and she looked around with an expression of childlike wonder. "We really are home," she whispered. He carried her to the bed and gently propped her against the pillows. He slipped off her shoes and covered her with a blanket. He handed her Angel Bear, as she had named it, a stuffed bear with angel wings and halo that a British aristocrat, Lady Connie, had given Angilia on her fourth birthday. Eric had worked with Lady Connie on a charity board in the late 1990s. She had kept Angel Bear on her bed ever since. Angilia smiled at her pretty Angel Bear and snuggled it close to her. Angel Bear had a secret, just as did Angilia.

Matthew knocked on the door and entered with his medical bag. He smiled at her and said he just wanted to do a quick check after the long, emotional homecoming. He listened to her heart and lungs, checked her pulse, and commented that under the circumstances she was doing well. He saw pain in her eyes, and he knew sitting in the same position for over six hours had been grueling for her. He prepared a hypodermic needle with a typically small dose of morphine and said, "I'm going to give you a bit of morphine for the pain. That will help you rest." He injected it in her arm and put a bandage over the spot. He stepped into the hallway and found Roger waiting to show him to his new suite in the palace.

Eric sat on the edge of the bed and smiled at her. "What are you thinking?"

"We are home, Daddy. I'm in my beautiful room, in my bed, and we are all here like always. I'm never leaving again. This is my home, with you, and I'm never leaving you again. My heart and my happiness are here with you, Daddy, always and forever." She smiled at him, with the truest and purest happiness she had ever felt.

Soon, her eyes closed and she slept peacefully. Eric kissed her forehead and went to his suite to change clothes. He saw himself smiling when he looked in the mirror, and he bowed his head and said a silent prayer of thanks that Angilia was alive and getting well, that they were finally home, and that their menacing nightmare really was a thing of the past.

§§§§

That evening after dinner, Angilia sat on the window seat in her sitting room, writing in her diary. She paused occasionally to look out of the window at the gloriously familiar landscape, her entire being overflowing with feelings to which she was still adapting. She had literally transformed at the moment of Jamieson's suicide, for he had been the terror and threat that had imprisoned her most of her young life.

1 May 2012

As I write this, I sit in my room—my room in our home! We are home, and we are so very happy. Getting home took most of the day, which actually made me even happier. Thousands of people waited for us at the airport, and they were ecstatic to see Daddy again, and when he spoke their cheers were incredibly boisterous. They love and respect him so very much! But I've always seen and known that.

The street from the airport to our home was so crowded with thousands more people. I loved seeing our friends and neighbors again. Little Billy was there! He is so sweet. And the gentleman who spoke to Daddy on my birthday—the gentleman who has lived through four Kings of Valdavia. How

149

incredible! Mike said it took us 4.5 hours to drive home. Matthew drove with us, and I suppose he will go everywhere with me for at least a while.

This is difficult to explain. I am still me, but I have changed. All of the fear left me immediately when Dr. Jamieson killed himself. Poof. Gone. Most of my life was lived with that fear surrounding me, dictating to me, and it just vanished. I've been happy before, of course I have, but not like this. Now my happiness is constant and merged with an internal peace which is new to me. I never knew peace at all until the moment Jamieson died. I feel so free. And I no longer worry about Daddy, not like I always did when I feared Jamieson would kill him. The threat died with Jamieson. Daddy is safe now, and we are both free.

I will never lie to Daddy about anything, no matter what it is or how difficult it may be to tell him. I hated lying to him, and I hated myself for lying to him. I will never lie to or hurt him again. Nothing is worth that.

When I wake up tomorrow, I will be in my room, and I am so grateful for that. My life, my work, and my duty are here. I belong here. This is the place of love and joy. I will never leave here again, not like I did in the past, to live and work somewhere else. My heart and soul are here.

§§§§§

Wednesday morning, Angilia awoke to bright spring sun shining through her curtains and she smiled as she stood. Her knee was stiff, so she gently flexed it several times to loosen it. After a soothing shower, she dressed in a comfortable track suit and sneakers. Susan came in and styled her long hair in a pretty French braid. "It feels so wonderful having you home, Angilia," Susan told her with a wide smile. Nearly two months after the shooting, it was a miracle to have Angilia.

Angilia stood, hugging Susan as she said, "It feels wonderful being home." Susan helped her slowly walk down the three flights of stairs, and Angilia limped into the dining room. She greeted her father with a kiss, and soon they were joined by Daniel and Roger. Angilia looked around, realizing that Matthew was not at the table. Soon he came dashing in through the kitchen and explained he had gone for a jog.

"What are we doing today?" Angilia asked him.

"I thought we'd begin with a walk around the grounds, just to get some fresh air and sunshine, too. Walking is the best exercise you can do right now, anyway," he explained. She nodded and said she wanted to visit Starlight that day, too. Eric assured her they would, and she could walk him around the paddock for a while, too. She smiled, which proved contagious. Everyone and everything did seem different now, in the most marvelous way, she thought.

After breakfast, she walked—slowly—to his fourth floor office with Eric. He flipped the light switch, and she walked in and looked up at the carved ceiling with a huge smile. Eric smiled at her happiness, relishing the joy of watching her walk and smile. He could almost forget that she had nearly died. Almost.

He sat at his desk, turned on the computer and picked up the stacks of official mail waiting for his attention. Angilia pulled her cell phone from her pocket and snapped a picture of her father, much to his amusement. Eric pushed an intercom button on his telephone. "Carol, can you please come in my office for a moment?" Eric asked the Press Secretary, whose office was across the hall. She entered with a smile and Eric handed her his iPhone and motioned for Angilia to sit on his lap. "I'd like you to take a picture of us at my desk." She snapped the picture and returned the phone.

"Sir, I need to talk with you at some point about a few things. Nothing is urgent. Is there anything you need?" Carol asked.

"Yes, actually. Angilia and I would like to issue a joint statement thanking everyone for their prayers, cards, letters, gifts, and that amazing welcome home yesterday. We'll write something up and I'll message it to you for release."

"Absolutely. As soon as I receive it, I will issue the statement to all of the media venues and syndicates," Carol assured Eric. She returned to her office with a smile and Eric typed their statement on his computer as he and Angilia agreed on what it should say. They kept it relatively brief, but felt it important to make a formal statement. They knew people were concerned and curious.

Within ten minutes, the file was delivered to Carol's computer. She prepared it on Eric's formal electronic stationery and forwarded it to the Valdavian media and the global news syndicates for immediate release. A few moments later, Angilia received a text from Matthew asking if she was ready for their walk. She kissed her father's cheek and very slowly navigated the stairs. By the time she reached the first floor, her chest hurt from the effort, but she closed her eyes, took a few deep breaths and joined Matthew on the back patio.

The fresh air and sunshine did feel heavenly—literally—and she ignored the pain while she enjoyed seeing everything for the first time in what felt like a very long time. She mentioned some more rugged walking paths to the west, where the terrain was hilly, but Matthew sternly forbade them for the foreseeable future. She walked him toward the north, pointing to a gazebo far in the distance. "How many acres is this?" Matthew asked her.

"Twenty-five thousand acres total."

"We're not walking that much," he replied with a groan. "They'd have to send a rescue squad for both of us if we tried that." She giggled, and he truly enjoyed her happiness. "Let's turn back now. We've covered a lot of territory already. We can see that gazebo another day, when we have a golf cart, perhaps." She nodded with a giggle, and they began their walk back to the palace.

She looked up at the watch tower, though she could not see much as far away as she was. "Daddy's probably watching us." He looked puzzled and asked how. "From the watch tower telescope." She pointed to the east side of the castle, to the tall tower in the front corner. "That's where the soldiers used to stand, with their cannons and guns, when this still belonged to the French monarchy. The telescope was installed by my tenth great-grandfather, Leon II, in 1580. He married Muriel Darrell, a direct descendant of Robert the Bruce, and formally took the surname DeBruce Martineau at his coronation in 1579." She winked at him.

Matthew was fully aware of the importance of Leon's marriage, for it brought the Bruce bloodline into the Martineau dynasty and was at the heart of Gregor Jamieson's twisted plot for revenge. "It's okay, Matthew. None of my ancestors had anything to do with what happed in March. The only one to blame for that is Dr. Jamieson, and he will face whatever divine judgment God decides upon for him. That will be far worse than anything he would have faced here."

"I suppose," Matthew said, astonished at her mindset. They walked the rest of the way in comfortable silence, entering through the same patio door to find Eric waiting for them. Matthew was a bit surprised, but not Angilia. "Hi, Daddy. We walked a lot this morning."

"I know. I saw you," he smiled at her.

"I told you," she smiled at Matthew. "I said you were watching us from the telescope in the watch tower. I even told him about Leon and Muriel," she winked to her father, who slightly grimaced.

"This place is amazing and huge. I'm exhausted," Matthew admitted and excused himself to wash up before lunch. Angilia went to the kitchen, grabbed a bottle of water from the refrigerator and walked to the chapel in the east wing. She sat on a pew and bowed her head in prayer, thanking God for bringing her father and her safely home.

§§§§§

After lunch, Eric, Matthew, and Angilia walked to the stables to visit the horses, especially her beloved Starlight. Eric linked his arm with hers to prevent her from rushing and injuring her knee. Her bright smile delighted him; she was so excited to see her horse. Eric had taken Angilia to a horse ranch on her tenth birthday, already intending to purchase the Palomino colt for her present. When she saw that horse, she had rushed to him and they had an instant rapport.

Starlight's first sight of Angilia in two months excited him, and when she approached his stall, he nuzzled her cheek. She kissed his nose and unlatched the stall, slipped on his reigns, and walked him to the paddock. Starlight sensed she was hurt and he gently rubbed her arm with his nose, kissed her cheek, and rested his head on her shoulder. Matthew was impressed at how gentle and affectionate the horse was with her. Joseph joined them from the stable and smiled.

"I told him you were coming this afternoon. He waited patiently, but he was excited. He has missed you, Princess," Joseph told her.

"Thank you. I've missed my boy, too. Yes, I did," she said softly to Starlight and hugged his neck.

Matthew looked at Starlight's face as Angilia hugged him. "Is that horse crying?" he asked incredulously.

"Probably," Eric said. "They communicate with one another in a way I don't understand. It's fascinating to watch them together. It's been that way from the first moment they met six years ago."

"So she's a horse whisperer," Matthew smiled.

"In a way, I suppose," Eric agreed.

The three men watched her walk Starlight around the paddock, something she did regularly, especially before a ride. She usually let him trot, but he intuitively refrained and kept at a moderate walking pace, not putting any stress or exertion onto Angilia. She walked him to Eric, Starlight raised his front right hoof for a handshake, and Eric obliged.

"Daddy, since I can't ride him yet, will you? Just for a little while?" Her blue eyes convinced him and Eric nodded. She handed him the reigns and went to the stable for Starlight's saddle and blanket. Joseph ran ahead of her and lifted the heavy saddle, reminding her not to do such things yet. She grabbed the blanket, threw it over Starlight's back, and let Joseph put on the saddle.

Eric mounted and Starlight nuzzled her neck while Joseph opened the paddock gate. Angilia and Matthew watched Eric and Starlight, and her delight was palpable. She grabbed Matthew's arm and looked at him with such elation that he felt his heart flutter. "Aren't they magnificent?" she asked him.

"They certainly are," he said, staring into her amazing turquoise eyes. He leaned closer to her, on the verge of kissing her pink lips, but regained his composure at the last second. Eric noticed and sped to them, stopping Starlight right in front of Matthew. She smiled up at her father and rubbed Starlight's ears. Matthew cleared his throat nervously, and Eric asked him to open the paddock gate.

Eric walked Starlight into the paddock, dismounted, and handed the reins to Angilia for the cool-down. Eric shot Matthew a knowing look, and leaned against the fence looking very much like a Western hero in his blue jeans and white shirt. The only thing missing was the sheriff's badge. Matthew felt uncomfortable, not knowing what he should say or do.

After the longest awkward silence of his life, Matthew was relieved when Angilia returned Starlight to his stall. The walk back to the palace was just as unnerving for him, though. Eric had seen. Eric knew. Angilia appeared oblivious. Matthew thanked God for that. She was still so young. At times he felt like he committed a mortal sin just for looking at her. He could no longer deny the truth to himself, however: he loved Angilia. God help him, he loved her.

§§§§

"Sam!" Angilia saw him on the back patio waiting for them as they returned from the stable. He hugged her gently, afraid of hurting her, and then hugged Eric.

"How is my favorite person in the whole world?" Sam asked as he put his arm around her shoulders. "You look wonderful, Angilia."

"Thank you. I'm doing much better. Right, Matthew?"

"Yes, you are," he said with a forced smile. "It's nice to meet you. Excuse me, though, while I go shower and change."

Eric excused himself long enough to fetch a pitcher of lemonade and some glasses. He served Sam, then Angilia, and poured himself a glass. They relaxed in the light breeze and talked for a while before Sam mentioned the reason for his visit.

"Angilia, Eric, I'm here really to finalize the release date and plans for the album you recorded in March. Are you sure you want to release it now, Angilia? We can wait as long as you want."

"Now is fine with me, Sam. Whatever interest there might be will help Open Heart. The sooner it's released, the sooner Open Heart receives the funds."

"Well, if you're sure, we'll release the album next Tuesday, May 8. How does that sound?" Sam looked at Eric.

"She won't have to do anything too strenuous, will she? It's still too soon."

"No, of course not. She doesn't have to do anything. I'll actually handle everything next week, the press, the interviews, everything. I don't normally do any of that, but I am this time. I'm tightly restricting what she does and access to her." He looked at Angilia. "You're not doing any press junkets, no touring, nothing. Honestly, the songs sell themselves. I'm not even doing much, simply because I don't feel it's necessary."

Eric nodded. "Thank you. I understand that people are interested, but I just don't want her out there for a while."

"Neither do I. The morning DJ here, Dave Rodan, wants to debut it live on his show next Tuesday, and I will talk with him on air during the debut. Let me know what you want people to know about the songs, and I'll stick to that. This is going to be all about the music. Dave knows not to bring up anything else. He won't. Both of you just leave all of the press to me."

"Which song are you releasing first?" Angilia asked Sam.

"Well, I have my choice, but I wanted to ask you about that, too. What do you think?" Sam handed her a piece of paper.

She smiled at him. "I like that, a lot." She returned the paper.

"Good. I had a feeling you'd be okay with that selection." Sam winked at her. "You know how your fans get when new music is released. There's going to be interest, know that. But I want to talk with Carol, too, about forwarding all requests she gets to me. She doesn't even have to deal with anything. I'll take care of everything."

"Can I at least write something for the web site? Just a short message?"

"Of course, Angilia. There's a message board on there, and you can post it there, for fans to respond. I have to say, they've been posting on there since we set it up a few years ago, and we've never had anything negative happen. I also want to tell you that everything on there for the past two months has been about their concern for you. They care, and all they want is for you to get well. So, they are fantastic, Angilia."

She smiled at her father. "Maybe you should post something, too, Daddy."

"I could, but why would they want to hear from me?"

"Because your song is on the album. You'll have your own fans soon."

"I seriously doubt that. But, sure, I'll post something if you think I should."

They finalized the plans, and Eric walked Sam to Carol's office so Sam could alert her and arrange to have all media requests related to the album forwarded to him. "Of course," Carol stated. "In fact, we can issue a press release next Tuesday to all of the media outlets that all requests should be directed to Sam. If you want, that can be ready to release early that morning. We will forward anything we receive to your office, Sam."

"That sounds great," Sam said, and Eric agreed. "Everything's in place, then, for another hit album. Your daughter is Stone Canyon's best-selling artist ever, you know."

Eric smiled as the men walked downstairs. "She takes my breath away, Sam, she really does. I've seen her writing in her music notebook over the past couple of weeks, too. I think her next album is taking shape already. I don't know where it all comes from."

"I don't either. It's been this way since I met her ten years ago. She always has far more songs written than we could ever record. She may have to record more in the future. She doesn't have to tour. A few concerts a year, maybe, but no tours like when she was working with Tom. Her fan base is strong enough that her work sells itself. A huge promotion is really unnecessary. She considers recording part of her charity work, you know."

"I know. I'm so proud of her. That was totally her idea from the beginning. She told me she wanted to donate one hundred percent of the proceeds to charity, because she did not need the money anyway and it could help others."

Sam put his arm around Eric. "That blew me away, too. Plus, she will be the first monarch with a multi-million-selling recording career. Angilia keeps making history."

Eric smiled in return and said, "She'll continue to make history for a very long time, Sam."

§§§§§

The following morning, Carol met with Eric in his office to discuss the overwhelming requests for interviews the Press Office had received in the past two months. "We began receiving requests the moment the news broke. We never expected that. I did issue a statement informing all media outlets that neither you nor the Princess was available in the near future. That didn't stop the requests from coming, but we refused to further respond," Carol explained.

Eric was stunned. "They sure didn't waste any time. They all want to be the first to ask, as if that will impress me. My daughter was fighting for her life, and they only think of a ratings coup. How disgusting." Eric flipped through the pile of requests. "Is there anyone who did not jump on the bandwagon?"

158

"Actually, yes. Franklin Sydney sent a condolence message, but he never requested anything. He even asked if there was anything he could do to assist us."

"That does not surprise me, Carol. Franklin has always been a man of integrity. Call him and ask him if he would like to conduct the only interview we will do." Eric turned his desk phone toward Carol and she dialed his direct number. She explained the reason for her call and he seemed reluctant, saying he did not want to take advantage of the tragedy. Carol whispered this to Eric, who reached for the handset.

"Franklin, this is Eric. If we are going to do this, I prefer to do this with you. I have no desire to deal with those other people. I understand that people are concerned and anxious to see us and hear us, especially Angilia. But I refuse to line the pockets of those ambulance chasers. You are my only choice, Franklin."

"I am honored, Sir. When do you want to do this?" Franklin asked.

"Tomorrow, in my office at the palace. Thank you. Carol will work out the details with you. She will call you again in a short while." Eric hung up and told Carol his demands. "I know Franklin would never ask anything inappropriate, but I still want a written agreement." Carol nodded and jotted notes as Eric spoke. "He cannot ask about the shooting or her health. Those topics are strictly forbidden. Everything relating to them is strictly forbidden, including the gunman, the details, her injuries, her current doctor. Nothing at all about any of that. He can ask about the scholarship, her new album, our future plans, anything along those lines. Have him send you the questions this afternoon so you can review them just in case something is in there that I would not want asked."

"Absolutely. I shall call him now and arrange everything. The camera and lighting crews will need to set up in here prior to the interview, and we will make sure that interferes with your work as little as possible. As soon as I receive the questions, I will forward them to you, as well." Carol knew from years of experience how to handle the press, and she knew how to remain firm in making sure they understood any guidelines or restrictions.

Eric thanked her and walked to Angilia's suite one floor below. She stepped out of her dressing room/wardrobe seconds later, her hair still damp from the shower. She smiled at him and told him, "Matthew and I finished my exercises a little while ago. I used some of your equipment in the workout room. I did some leg presses and the elliptical machine today."

"How do you feel, Angel?"

"A bit tired, but okay. You look serious. Is something wrong?"

"No, nothing is wrong. I just need to go over something with you." He led her to the oversized couch, where she sat sideways looking at him. "Lots—hundreds—of reporters bombarded Carol's office with interview requests as soon as the news broke of what happened. Stupid, I know. I don't want to deal with any of them, to be honest. But I do understand that people are curious and concerned. They want to see you. They want to hear from us, especially you, Angilia. They need to know that you are getting better. I thought it might be all right if we do one interview only, that can be exclusive and yet broadcast worldwide if syndicates want to do that."

"With whom?"

"Franklin Sydney. He never asked for anything from us. Carol said he even offered to help her office. I trust him, Angel. I always have. But Carol is writing up a formal agreement of topics not allowed at all. She's also requesting a list of his questions so we can make sure there's nothing in there that should not be there. What do you think?"

"If you want to, I don't mind. When?"

"Tomorrow in my office. Is that too soon?"

She shook her head. "No. I don't have anything else to do," she smiled.

§§§§

Two cameras and some lights were set up in Eric's office while he and Angilia sat in the chapel. They prayed, and then talked quietly about being home, their contentment, and looking forward to Dr. and Mrs. Taylor's impending arrival. "I really like them, Daddy. Both of them are so kind and compassionate. Matthew is, too. He actually stunned me right away, in the ambulance. He was so gentle. I'm glad it was him."

Eric looked at her face carefully. "You like him?"

"Well, yes. He is nice, and gentle, and he's also fun. Plus he is the first person I've met who has a similar academic experience. He understands what it's like to do that. I trusted him immediately. There is something very familiar about him that I find comforting, too."

She was unaware of Matthew's romantic feelings for her. "I'm glad. I trust him, too, as your doctor. We best head to the office, Angel. Are you ready?"

She nodded, and they left the chapel. Eric put his arm around her and supported her as she climbed the four flights of stairs slowly. Carol and Roger stood in Eric's office, both there to monitor the interview, ready to stop it for any reason if necessary. Franklin Sydney bowed to Eric and Angilia, and asked if there were any concerns. Eric assured him there were not, and Eric motioned to the selected seats.

He and Angilia sat next to one another on the sofa, while Franklin sat across from them in the matching chair. Angilia was remarkably calm and smiled at her father, knowing he would generate far more attention than this the following week when his song was released. Franklin briefly explained the general order of topics they would discuss while the lights were adjusted one last time. "The interview will air live, and then repeat a few times throughout the weekend. News syndicates who purchase rights will broadcast the interview, unedited in any form, next week. All syndicate proceeds will be donated to the music scholarship at the University of Oxford," Franklin announced.

Angilia beamed at him and actually stood to hug him in thanks. "Thank you so much. That is so generous, and I know the students appreciate this." Franklin actually blushed, and fought to regain his composure minutes before they began. The cameraman gave them the three minute warning, the two minute warning, and then counted down the last ten seconds. The red light signaled they were now broadcast live to the local network and homes across Valdavia.

"Good afternoon and welcome to a special broadcast of the midday news live from the Palais Royale de Valdavia. We are extremely honored to have as our very special guests, His Majesty King Eric de Valdavia and Her Royal Highness Princess Angilia, Duchesse de Valmondois. Thank you both for welcoming us into your home."

"We are both delighted to have you here," Eric said.

"Your Majesty, Your Royal Highness, you returned home on Tuesday, to several thousand people greeting you at the airport and along the route to the palace. What was that day like for both of you, from your perspective?"

"We were stunned, Franklin. Neither of us ever expected a homecoming as grand as that one. The entire day was filled with love and warmth, which made coming home all the more emotional," Eric replied, looking at Angilia as he finished.

"Happy is the one word that keeps recurring in my mind. I am so very happy to be home, and seeing our friends and neighbors just made the day happier, sweeter. I have always seen how much love and respect people have for my father, just never to such a massive degree at one time before. That makes me happiest of all, honestly," Angilia said, and smiled up at her father.

"Your Royal Highness, no one can deny the outpouring of respect and love everyone in Valdavia feels for His Majesty. I dare say, though, that the expressions were directed toward you, as well. You have earned the admiration, love, and adoration of everyone in this country and around the world. Some people in the media have proclaimed you the new People's Princess for your charitable work and compassion. You are known for donating one hundred percent of your recording proceeds to charities and foundations."

"You are very kind, Franklin. I am deeply honored to be even remotely compared to Diana, Princess of Wales. She is an inspirational figure to so many people, including me. However, I could never attempt to, nor do I want to, fill the void she has left in this world. Like all people, Diana is irreplaceable, particularly to her family and friends."

"Your Royal Highness, we understand that your new album will be released on May 8. Are there any details you can share? Which charity receives the proceeds from this album?"

Angilia quickly smiled at her father. "The charity we selected this time is The Open Heart Foundation, for which my father wrote an excellent piece that will be included with the CD and downloads and available on the web site. The album contains twelve songs and is titled <u>Heart-Glow</u>." She again smiled at Eric, who was hearing this for the first time.

"Your Royal Highness, did you write all of the songs on the album, as you usually do?"

"There is one I did not write, Franklin, and I predict that song will become the runaway hit from the album."

"May I ask who did write that song?"

"You may, but I do not want to say anything else just yet and spoil the wonderful surprise everyone will get when they hear the song for the first time. I will tell you that I am very excited about that song, more excited than I have ever been about a song." She could not stop smiling.

"Your Majesty, have you heard this mysterious song? What are your thoughts?"

"Oh, yes, I have heard that song. I shall refrain from commenting just yet." Eric squeezed her hand, knowing she was having fun.

"Did you have a hand in selecting The Open Heart Foundation as the beneficiary, Your Majesty?"

"No. That was entirely Angilia's idea and engineering. I am thrilled, and I know the Open Heart board members are as well. Their work is tireless, and they deserve all of the support they can receive."

"Your Royal Highness, the University of Oxford made two announcements in early March that we would like to hear your thoughts about. The first is your resignation from the faculty there. What prompted that decision?"

"My life and my work are here, in Valdavia. That was actually the easiest decision I have ever made. My duties are here, alongside my father, and I want to become more actively involved with my charities and patronages," Angilia stated, omitting the core reason, which Eric now knew. He patted her hand in support.

"Angilia will always be the most valuable asset Valdavia possesses. I am elated that she is remaining here, and I look forward to watching her be the dynamo she is and charge into her role with the enthusiasm and passion which she brings to everything she does," Eric proudly declared.

"We look forward to that, as well, Your Majesty. Your Royal Highness, the other announcement from early March was the official inauguration of the annual Eric DeBruce Martineau Scholarship for Musical Excellence established at the University of Oxford. Could you tell everyone about the scholarship and how it came into creation?"

"Of course. The music faculty, deans, and scholarship committee approached me over one year ago proposing to establish the scholarship, and of course I am overjoyed to have a music scholarship in my father's name. Once each year, the committee, with our input, selects one incoming music student to receive the scholarship, which pays their tuition for four years."

"I understand anyone can donate by going to the University of Oxford web site."

"That's correct, Franklin. There are many scholarships at the University to which people can donate."

"Your Majesty, what is it like for you to have a scholarship in your name at Oxford?"

"It is a tremendous honor, but I have to say that the scholarship was not proposed in my name. It was proposed in my daughter's name, and she convinced them to establish it in my name. It is for a wonderful cause, though, and that is all that really matters." Eric smiled at her and she winked in reply.

"Your Majesty, Your Royal Highness, in our remaining moments, is there anything in particular you would like to say to everyone?"

"Thank you. Thank you for your support and concern. The love and compassion you have shown us both means more than my words can tell you. Despite what we often see and hear in the news, I know that most people are benevolent and welcoming. Everywhere I travel, I meet people who give me nothing but kindness and a warm welcome. And to my fellow Valdavians, thank you for making ours the most peaceful, stable, and secure country and home. I love Valdavia and everyone here. Also, in the coming months I will make an important formal announcement," Eric proclaimed with his boyishly dimpled smile.

Angilia looked at her father, wondering about his cryptic message. She turned her attention back to Franklin, though, and shared her thoughts. "I want to thank you all, too. Thank you for helping to make my life so wonderful. You inspire me more than you know. Thank you for all of the support and prayers. Thank you for loving and respecting my father, even though he makes that so very easy. Thank you for proving Anne Frank correct: '*In spite of everything I still believe that people are really good at heart.*'"

"Your Majesty, Your Royal Highness, thank you for such inspiring words. Thank you for sharing this hour with us and for such an enjoyable conversation."

"Thank you, Franklin. It was my pleasure," Eric said.

"Thank you for everything," Angilia concluded the interview.

§§§§§

Although the next day was Saturday, Eric wanted to answer some of the official mail that had arrived during the past two months. He and Roger worked in Eric's office that morning answering the most important correspondence, the open windows letting in the fresh spring air. The outside noise also infiltrated the office, breaking Eric's thought process. He finally tossed his pen on the desk in weariness.

"It's impossible to work today. What is going on out there anyway? Doesn't it sound like they are calling Angilia's name?" Roger shrugged his shoulders. Eric stood and walked to the window and leaned out. "They are. Come here." Roger put down the papers and joined Eric at the window. Hundreds of people were outside the gates on the mall.

"Come on," Eric said and rushed to the fifth floor. He opened the heavy drapes in front of the formal balcony, and heard the screams grow louder when he opened the double doors. He stepped out and was greeted with a plea for Angilia. "They don't want me," he called to Roger over his shoulder. "Where is Angilia?"

"She was in her room writing the last I knew," Roger answered as he peeked through a crack in the blinds. Eric rushed two floors down and startled Angilia when he dashed into her room.

"What's wrong?"

"Nothing's wrong. Come with me." He picked her up and ran up to the balcony. He told her to stay out of view for a moment, and he went back out. He was bombarded with shouts and questions demanding Angilia. She looked at Roger, who was staying out of sight, wondering what all the noise was about. Eric motioned for her and she stepped out and took his hand. The screams below became deafening, and suddenly dozens more screaming teenagers filled the mall.

"Wave, Angel. They wanted only you." Eric beamed with love, and she dutifully waved.

166

"Just wait until next week, Daddy. Just wait," she forewarned him. She noticed several people motioning her to come down. "I think they want me to come down there."

"Are you sure that's a good idea?"

"Why not? Susan can go with me. There are guards out at the gate if we need them, though we won't. We'll be fine."

Roger called Susan and told her to meet Angilia at the main entrance. Eric carried her down the five flights and ran back to the fifth floor so he could watch her from the balcony. Roger plugged his ears with his fingers and stood next to Eric watching Angilia.

She shook hands, talked to people, accepted cards and gifts, signed autographs, posed for pictures, and comforted those who cried when they saw her. One teen girl became so distraught that she cried hysterically, and Angilia asked the guard to open the gate. Angilia stepped to the girl and hugged her, which somehow made her more hysterical. After talking to the girl and signing the CD she clutched, Angilia managed to calm her. She asked one of the guards to get the girl some water, which he did from the small room at the bottom of the tower where they kept supplies.

"My daughter is amazing, Roger. She is down there comforting and reassuring them, putting them first. Angilia is going to be one remarkable queen." Roger smiled at his best friend. "I love her so much, Roger. So very much."

"I know, Eric. She loves you more than anyone has ever loved."

§§§§

The following morning, Angilia, Eric, Matthew, Roger, Daniel, Susan, and Mike walked to Christ Church Valmondois. Crowds joined and followed them, with more joining them every step of the two-block trek. Billy suddenly appeared beside Angilia and held her hand, escorting his adored Princess darling into the church, her first service there since February 26, the Sunday before she and Eric had gone to Oxford.

167

Reverend Samuel Hutchins stood at the entrance to welcome the congregation, utterly amazed to witness more than half of the congregation following Eric and Angilia, as if they were Pied Pipers. Reverend Hutchins bowed to Eric and Angilia, and she greeted him with a smile and a kiss on the cheek. "I have missed you, Reverend Hutchins," she told him.

"We missed both of you, Angilia. What a blessing to have you here today."

Eric walked with her to their pew, Billy escorting her, followed by Matthew and the rest of the royal party. Eric and Matthew sat on either side of Angilia, and she kissed Billy's cheek in thanks for his escort. He kissed her hand, bowed to Eric, and joined his parents in the next aisle. "He really does like you," Matthew commented. "How old is he?"

"Billy is ten. I've known him his entire life. He truly is a very sweet boy."

Soon the pews were filled with people, all there to welcome home their King and Princess. The choir sang a hymn, followed by Reverend Hutchins' invocation thanking God for his divine intercession in bringing the King and the Princess home. His sermon of thanksgiving for Eric and Angilia was drawn from King David's Psalm 145. "In verses eight and nine, David reminds us that '*The Lord is gracious, and full of compassion; slow to anger, and of great mercy. The Lord is good to all: and his tender mercies are over all his works.*' We gather today to praise and to thank God for his healing and compassion for King Eric and Princess Angilia. As we know, Satan can never triumph over God's will, and we are truly grateful that God's will brought our beloved King and Princess home to Valmondois."

Reverend Hutchins' sermon concluded with his reminder that each person honor and praise God for the mercies he shows to them all. The choir sang another hymn, during which the congregation stood and sang, too. They remained standing for the Reverend's benediction. An impromptu greeting line formed near the pulpit, with Reverend Hutchins, Eric, and Angilia thanking each member for attending and for their prayers.

Finally, the royal party began their walk home. No one had known the topic of the service—at least no one in the royal household—and each was deeply touched. Angilia smiled up at the clouds and suddenly knew the perfect day to share her past with her father. She winked at the clouds, a silent, secret message between her and another.

"'*In order for light to shine so brightly, the darkness must be present*,'" Angilia suddenly said.

Eric looked at her, about to ask where that was from, when Matthew added, "Francis Bacon wrote that."

"You read that, too?" She smiled at him. He nodded, and Eric squeezed her hand, offering his own silent prayer of thanksgiving.

§§§§

That afternoon, Eric and Angilia walked with Matthew to the smaller house on the palace grounds where his parents would live. He had not noticed it, snuggled as it was behind a line of lush trees. His eyes boggled. Small? Compared to the palace, of course it was small, but on its own it was a mansion. Eric unlocked the door and motioned for Matthew to enter first.

"It's kept clean and orderly, just in case we need it for visitors. Everything is working—lights, water, heating and cooling, appliances—but let me know if there is anything your parents need." Eric opened the blinds to reveal valuable antique furniture, elegant wall coverings, and rich carpets. What could his parents need?

"I come here once in a while just to sit where my grandmother lived. I've written a lot of songs in this house," Angilia softly said. "This house has been lonesome for eleven years."

Matthew looked at her quizzically. She often said the oddest things. Eric snapped Matthew out of his reverie by suggesting he take pictures of each room to send to his parents. If they wanted anything changed or needed something, Eric would make sure it was ready by their arrival. Although he did not think this necessary,

Matthew obliged and took dozens of pictures on his cell phone and texted them to his parents.

Dr. and Mrs. Taylor called him, with Katherine doing most of the excited talking. After a few moments, Matthew passed his phone to Eric, saying his mother wanted to talk with him. "This is too much. Really. I don't know what I thought when Angilia said smaller house, but this is far too grand, Eric. It's extremely gorgeous, there's no denying that. But. . . ."

Eric jumped in when he found the chance. "Nonsense. We want you to live here. The house has not been lived in for eleven years. It's empty. You may as well use it. I insist." She finally relented, said the house was perfect, profusely thanked him, and said goodbye to Eric and then to Matthew.

"That's settled, then," Eric declared, and the trio returned to the palace. Matthew felt more thunderstruck than ever. He and his parents living at a royal palace, he and his father the official royal physicians, and he in love with a real life princess. He would have never dreamed or imagined this more than two months earlier. Never.

§§§§§

Monday morning, Angilia awoke very early and very aware of the day's significance. She quickly showered and dressed, then quietly and slowly walked downstairs to the chapel. Sitting on a front pew, she bowed her head and prayed to God, thanking him for protecting her father and bringing them both home to the greatest love and contentment. Eric came down the staircase as she left the chapel, and he walked with her to the dining room for breakfast.

Roger, Daniel, Susan, and Matthew joined them, all of them also aware of the date. Other than good morning greetings, they sat quietly. Eric, however, appeared extraordinarily different than he had two months earlier. His broad smile was for his daughter only.

"Angilia, what do you think of us spending the day together, just the two of us?" Eric asked her.

Her smile seemed to fill the room. "I think that sounds like Heaven on earth, Daddy."

"Wonderful. We'll head out in my car after breakfast and spend the whole day together, with no agenda. We'll do whatever we decide and want to do."

Matthew smiled, too, vividly recalling his first sight of Angilia and Eric two months earlier to the day, both of them drenched in her blood. That insane Jamieson had damn near killed her, he thought. Matthew truly did enjoy watching her living so joyous and carefree. She deserved a day of fun with her father after everything they had endured and conquered.

She finished eating and asked if she could be excused to go upstairs to change from her dress to something more casual. Eric nodded, she kissed his cheek, and she ignored the pain in her knee as she climbed the stairs. Susan came to style her hair in a herringbone braid, Angilia's signature hairstyle. "You have fun, dear," she smiled while Angilia hugged her and waited in the hall for her father. He came from his suite a few minutes later, and together they walked to the garage and pulled out in his two-seated convertible. Mike followed in another car, at his insistence.

Eric drove for a while and asked her what they should do first. "I don't really care. I just love being with you."

"Let's spend some money," he said as he pulled in front of a small shop. Inside were shelves of cute items, and Angilia fingered a porcelain figurine of the Archangel Michael. She tenderly ran her finger along his sword, her mind swirling with memories and images. She smiled and turned to another shelf, where she saw a book about the history of Valdavia. She flipped through it, seeing portraits and pictures of her ancestors. She held the book, deciding to purchase it. She found an art book and picked it up, too.

Angilia joined her father at the register, just as the cashier handed him a bag. She placed her books on the counter and reached in her small bag for money, but he paid before she knew what was happening. She handed him €50, but he refused it, saying he wanted to treat her. "That's what daddies like to do, you know," he grinned and ruffled her hair. She hugged him and they walked back to the car, where he put their bags in the trunk.

A few miles later, Eric pulled into the parking lot of an antique store. The bell on the door announced their arrival, and the owner welcomed them with curtseys, stunned to see the King and Princess in her shop. Angilia was overwhelmed with the thousands of items lining the walls and shelves. She walked toward the back of the store and found herself suddenly staring at a framed portrait of her great-grandfather King Stefan. She audibly gasped, and the owner rushed to her in concern.

"May I see that portrait, please?" Angilia asked her. The woman told her she certainly could and stood on a stepladder to remove it from the hook. She handed it to Angilia, who smiled in complete wonder at her Great-grandfather's kind face, a face she cherished. "I have to buy this, please. I want to keep it in my room," she said softly.

"I'll hold it at the counter for you, Your Royal Highness."

"Please, call me Angilia. Thank you." She browsed and located a cookie tin commemorating her great-great grandfather King Gerard III's June 15, 1895 coronation. She ran her fingers over it tenderly, smiling at his image depicted on the front. She held it cradled in her arm, and soon added a plate commemorating her parents' 1991 royal wedding. Her eyes filled with tears as she looked at their engagement portrait in the center of the plate, encircled by their names and the date.

Angilia asked the owner if there were other similar items in the shop, and the woman immediately walked to a jewelry case. "There is this," she said, and handed Angilia a pair of cufflinks celebrating her grandfather's 1963 coronation. Her eyes lit up. "I have to get these for my father. Please don't let him see these. I want to surprise him." The owner nodded and smiled at Angilia. How sweet, she thought. "Can I pay now, before he sees anything?"

Angilia walked to the register with the woman, who carefully wrapped and packaged the royal souvenirs. She handed two bags to Angilia. "How much do I owe you, Ma'am?"

The woman shook her head and came around the counter. "These are yours, dear. They belong with you. I want you to have them."

"But, I can't. . . ." The woman gently waved a finger in front of Angilia, shushing her.

"You can. This is your family, and I want you to have these. Consider them welcome home gifts." Angilia set the bags on the floor and hugged the woman. Eric approached the counter at that moment.

"What did you do, Angilia? I told you I want to treat you today."

"You'll see." She picked up the bags and took them outside to Mike. "Can you put these in your car, please? They're very fragile." He placed them on the floor of the front passenger seat, smiling at her happiness. Angilia rushed back inside and picked up an old blank ledger and took it to the counter. Eric forced it from her hand and paid for it with his few things.

He turned away, and Angilia pulled €200 from her purse and slipped it on the counter to pay for the family souvenirs. She followed her father as quickly as she could and soon they were far away from the shop. At lunch time, Eric stopped at a restaurant and raised the convertible top of the car, locking it securely. He motioned Mike to join them, and they entered to incredulous faces and sat at an empty booth.

Their lunch was interrupted occasionally by well-wishers and autograph requests, but relaxed and fun. Angilia did not care where they were or what they did—she simply adored spending the day with her dad. He relished the day, as well, realizing that they would both write about the same things in their diaries that evening. Mike smiled, contrasting today with the horrific day exactly two months earlier. Today felt like a veritable miracle.

After lunch, Eric drove nowhere in particular for a few hours before he turned to drive home. He stopped for ice cream cones on the return drive, and they stood next to the car giggling as they licked the melting ice cream as quickly as they could. When they finished, she walked to Mike's car, pulled a small box from one of the bags and handed it to her father.

He looked at her, his eyes asking her what it was. "Open it, Daddy." He did, and smiled at his father's profile on the onyx and gold cufflinks. "I had to get them for you. I didn't want you to see them back at the store. That would have spoiled the surprise."

He pulled her to him, hugging her close, tears now filling his eyes. "Thank you, Angel. I will treasure them." He kissed her head. "Thank you."

§§§§§

Angilia opened her eyes the next morning, feeling happier than she thought anyone could feel. She showered, dressed, and walked through her suite, stopping suddenly when she saw the Michael figurine on her desk. Her fingers touched his wings, and she felt her eyes fill with tears. Across the hall, Eric had just finished dressing and was turning to leave his suite when Angilia grabbed him in a hug.

"Thank you, Daddy. He's beautiful."

"I saw you looking at him, so he seemed like the perfect surprise. I'm glad you like him."

"I do. Michael is quite magnificent and beautiful. Thank you so much for him." They walked down the stairs to breakfast. "I can hardly wait to see him again."

Eric giggled. "He's not going anywhere, Angel. He'll be on your desk after breakfast."

"I know. It's just that he's a very special angel. Michael is the only Archangel, after all, and God's supreme warrior." Until she shared everything with him, she had to be more aware of what she said, she berated herself.

§§§§§

The radio was on in the dining room, Dave Rodan reminding his audience that Angilia's new album debuted in ten minutes at the top of the hour. She had forgotten after yesterday's wonderfully happy day. Dave introduced Sam, who explained when the songs were recorded, in one day, the day after the scholarship ceremony in Oxford. He mentioned that Angilia had written eleven of the twelve songs, and, yes, they were recorded in one take each.

The first song Dave played was a ballad in which the character dreamed about the most beautiful, peaceful, loving place, only to awake from her sleep to find herself in Heaven. Dave commented that it reminded him of many of the Old Testament's Psalms. Angilia smiled; King David's psalms were important and inspirational to her. Dave played a few other songs, including an up-tempo pop song declaring the speaker's refusal to allow her oppressor to defeat her. Sam and Dave discussed the theme of independence, while everyone at the dining room table looked at Angilia with the truth blazing in their brains. Eric placed his hand over hers protectively, his eyes hinting at sadness.

The day she recorded that song, the day before the shooting, he did not know what Jamieson had done to her. Not all of her songs were autobiographical, so Eric did not presume that song was, either. Now he knew that his daughter was speaking to Jamieson through that song, saying with music what she could not say to his face. She saw his angst. "It's all right, Daddy. I was never going to let him win. God was not going to let him win. Other than my diaries, that was the safest way to express myself. But he's gone forever, and that song is not about him anymore."

Eric smiled and hugged her, once more amazed at her strength and faith. Angilia was right. That monster was gone forever, and they were happy. He turned the radio up a notch as Dave and Sam played a few more songs and discussed them. Finally, Dave asked Sam what he knew about the next song, and Sam told everyone that it was Angilia's most heart-felt and honest song. Dave advised everybody to listen to the lyrics and played "The Gift of You." Matthew was the only one in the room who had not heard that song. Daniel, Roger, and Susan had. Eric had played it on his iPhone while Angilia was in surgery. They knew the song was about Eric.

Eric sat with his hands clasped over his mouth, tears trickling from his eyes. When the song ended, Dave's voice came over the radio declaring that the telephones were ringing off the hooks and that emails were pouring in by the hundreds in response to that song. Dave read a few of the emails and took some listener calls live on air. One woman was obviously crying when she told Dave that was the most beautiful tribute to a father she had ever heard. Everyone knew how much the Princess loved her father, but that song touched them deeply. Another caller said his father had died the previous year, and he wished he could have said those words to his own father to let him know how much he was loved. Sam, with Angilia's blessing, confirmed that the song was indeed about King Eric, and that this was released as a single that day.

Angilia smiled, knowing what Sam would reveal next. "We are actually releasing two singles from the album today. The twelfth song on the album, and the only one Angilia did not write, is the second single. This is my pick for runaway hit from the album." Sam had asked Dave not to reveal any details prior to playing the song, so without another word, Dave played Eric's recording of "Sunshine on My Shoulders."

Eric looked at her, stunned, unaware that his song would get this kind of attention. She beamed at him, thrilled that the whole world would hear the beauty and magic she had heard since before her birth. Roger dropped his fork when he heard Eric's voice instead of Angilia's, Susan dabbed tears from her eyes, and Daniel sat open-mouthed that his friend had actually agreed to do this. Matthew sat shocked by the entire morning, from her defiant lyrics about that Jamieson, to her tribute to her father, to hearing Eric sing for the first time.

Eric closed his eyes, uncomfortable hearing himself, slightly embarrassed that everyone in the country was potentially listening to him sing at that moment, and overwhelmed by his daughter's love for him. "You really like this?" he asked her.

She nodded, her smile never fading, and proclaimed, "Of course I do. I always have. You know that. I love you, Daddy, and I love your song. I'm so happy. Thank you for doing this for me."

He smiled at her and said, "That's all that matters, then. I did it just for you, Angel. Only you." He squeezed her shoulder as the song ended, and Dave's voice filled the room again.

"Ladies and gentlemen, our email inboxes are filled to capacity, our phones have thousands of calls coming in, and we are inundated with requests to play His Majesty's song again. So here it is."

Angilia leapt from her chair and hugged her father, who looked as stunned as he felt. "I knew it. I told you people will love it, Daddy. How could they not?"

"Wow. Eric is a rock star," Roger declared with a smile.

"I am not, Roger. It's just a novelty for people. Come with me to the office. We have some work to do." Eric kissed Angilia's nose. "Thank you, baby. I'm glad it makes you happy. That's all that matters to me. But I have to get some work done this morning. We'll go out for lunch today, though, I promise."

"Okay. I'll like that." She stood and watched him walk out of the room. "He's going to get mobbed when he goes out, I hope he knows that."

"You didn't tell us," Susan said. "I mean, I've heard him sing that to you before, but I never expected to hear him on the radio."

Daniel giggled. "Neither did I. Even in college, no one could get him to do stuff like that. Eric was more serious then. Patrick, yeah, he'd sing, dance, act silly, but never Eric. How did you talk him into that?" he asked Angilia.

"I simply asked him to do it for me, and he did," she smiled and left the dining room.

§§§§

Angilia sat at her desk most of the morning, writing in her diary and listening to the radio. Songs from <u>Heart-Glow</u> played almost constantly throughout the morning, especially her father's song, and she felt such warmth and happiness. She truly never tired of hearing him. She glanced at her Michael often, too, realizing that in over two months she would reveal everything to her father.

Angilia called one of the staff to her room to help her hang the portrait of her Great-grandfather she had found at the antique shop the day before. She wanted him above her desk, where she could see him while she wrote. She cleaned the glass and frame, and soon King Stefan looked down upon her. She loved him so much, and knew they would meet again when she died and her soul returned to Heaven.

She resumed writing, and at noon she heard her father's footsteps on the stairs. She smiled, understanding he would gain a new level and type of fame and admiration now that his song was so very popular. She turned off the radio, knowing they were leaving for lunch very soon. He came to her desk and noticed his grandfather's picture hanging above her. "Where did you get that? I've never seen it here before."

Her eyes sparkled up at him. "I walked right to him in that antique shop yesterday. Great-grandfather's portrait is the first thing I really noticed. I had to get him. He's very special to me." Eric knew how much his daughter enjoyed researching her family and how she felt connected to each of her ancestors. "I also found a couple of other items there."

Angilia pointed to the white bookcase which coordinated with her other furniture, each piece hand painted with delicate pink roses and vines. On the top, held in place by small art stands, were the tin and the plate. Eric lifted the plate with a smile, looking at his and Marisol's engagement portrait that was released on May 21, 1990 when their engagement was officially announced. "I have not seen one of these in a long time. This was in an antique shop?" he asked with a giggle. "So I'm an antique now?"

"Don't be silly, Daddy, of course not. The owner had just the four items, and I bought them. Great-grandfather's portrait, yours and Mommy's plate, great-great-grandfather's tin, and grandfather's cufflinks. I just had to get them." She picked up the history book she had bought at the first shop. "This was one of the two books I got at the gift shop. Your picture is on page 557," she smiled.

"I'm a historical antique," he grinned, and Angilia giggled in response.

Eric carefully returned the plate to its stand and picked up the tin. "1895. Wow. That was ninety-nine years before your birth, Angel. And I love the cufflinks. I'd never seen those before, either. I was nine years old when Father was coronated. Everyone loved and respected him, Angilia. I wish he would have lived to meet you."

"I know, but he will meet me someday, you know. We'll all meet ancestors we have read about and heard about. I want to meet Mommy first, though."

Eric kissed the top of her head, always comforted by her absolute belief and faith, as if she knew as fact things that theologians and philosophers had contemplated and questioned for centuries. Her talk of destiny, eternal life, the splendors of Heaven, and of certain ancestors would seem incredulous if he did not know his daughter so very well. What would make him doubt another's sanity somehow encouraged him when she spoke. Her eyes held such incredible depth and honesty that he believed Angilia.

He snapped back to the present. "Let's go get some lunch now. Why don't we ask Matthew to come with us, too?" She nodded and walked down the hall to his suite. The door was open, and she saw him. He sat on the window seat sketching the landscape outside. She gasped, unexpectedly finding herself transported back to another place and life, where she had observed that scene frequently. He looked up, surprised to see her there, the light from the windows creating a halo effect around her.

"Daddy and I are going out for lunch, and we want you to come with us," she told him. He smiled, nodded, put down his sketch pad, and walked to the first floor with Eric and Angilia. "Daddy, I think you should ask Mike and Tony to come with us, too."

"Angilia, we don't need them just to go to lunch. We're not in any danger. I thought we'd walk to the coffee shop right across from the mall."

"I know, but you do need them, believe me. Besides, they have to eat lunch, too." She texted them before he could protest, and within minutes, both security officers joined them. When Matthew opened the front door for Angilia, the crowd at the gate began screaming for her and Eric. "I told you, Daddy," she said as people pleaded for them to sign autographs.

"You've got to be kidding," Eric remarked, honestly taken by surprise. Angilia took his hand and led him to the gate to greet his adoring fans. The guards at the gate kept black markers nearby for such moments—Angilia had been dealing with this sort of attention for ten years—and handed Eric and Angilia each a marker. Eric obliged, smiling and thanking everyone, and signed their newspapers, pictures, and newly-bought copies of the <u>Heart-Glow</u> CD. Nearly one hour later, they began their walk to the coffee shop.

Even though it was a relatively short walk, Eric and Angilia were stopped multiple times and asked to sign the CD. Several fans asked to have their pictures taken with them, one woman all but swooning when she met Eric. Angilia smiled up at her father, her expression reflecting her love and happiness. "I told you everyone will love your song." She linked her arm though his and enjoyed the adoration he received.

Angilia noticed that her favorite outdoor table was empty, and she excitedly claimed the seat she preferred every time she came to the coffee shop. It seemed so long ago that she had last gone there for herbal tea and lemon cookies. Eric and Matthew sat on either side of her, with Mike on Eric's other side and Tony between Mike and Matthew. They glanced at the menus, deciding on their orders before the waitress came to the table.

"Oh my stars, darling, I am so happy to see you again. You two are the talk of the town today, you know." The waitress had known Angilia her entire life and adored her. Angilia stood as Cheryl rushed to her.

"I've missed you, too, Cheryl." They hugged, though Cheryl refrained from the big hug she wanted to give her little girl, as she called Angilia. She introduced Matthew to Cheryl, and he stood to shake her hand. The radio played in the background as Cheryl took their orders, and they heard Angilia's songs. Cheryl brought their drinks moments later, the radio suddenly turned louder by one of the patrons inside.

Other patrons and passers-by approached Angilia for autographs, and several ran to Eric begging for his, as well. The elderly gentleman in the wheelchair was being pushed by his nurse, and he told her to take him to the King's table. Angilia stood when she saw him and bent to kiss his cheek. She asked him to join them, and he was delighted. Matthew and Tony pulled another chair to the table for his nurse, and Matthew moved closer to Tony so that the man could sit beside Angilia.

He patted her hand, and smiled at Eric. "I must say, I have lived through a lot of history in my 96 years, but never anything like today. You, Sir, are the first King to have a hit song, yes you are." He told the nurse to hand him something from the bag hanging from the wheelchair handle. "I will be honored if you would sign this for me, Sir." He held a copy of <u>Heart-Glow</u>, and Angilia handed it to her father with a huge smile illuminating her face.

Eric signed it unquestioningly and Angilia passed it to Mr. Brennan, who told her she must sign it, too. She wrote a special message to him and signed it with her familiar xoxo. He leaned over and kissed her cheek, and Eric smiled. Suddenly, a small army of screaming teenagers saw Eric and besieged him with protestations of love, sobbing, and shrieks. Cameras flashed as paparazzi spotted Eric and Angilia.

Cheryl brought the sandwiches and salads they had ordered, though she could not reach the table for the throngs of screaming teenagers. Matthew watched the veritable mob scene in horror, his amber eyes huge. This was surreal, to say the least. Eric's song blared from the radio, which incited more frenzied screams and tears from the girls who shouted for his attention.

Matthew's cell phone rang, and he answered a call from his parents. "We called to tell you we'll be arriving in Valmondois next week, on May 15. Our flight arrives at 11:15 that morning," Mitchell informed his son. "I'll text you the flight number and other details."

"Matthew, are you all right? What is all of that screaming and noise?" Katherine sounded panicked. "What's wrong?"

"I'm fine, Mom. Eric, Angilia, and I are at a coffee shop for lunch, and he's being mobbed by screaming, crying, and fawning high school girls."

"He's what?"

"Yeah. Angilia's CD was released today, and Eric recorded a song for it, and now he's like some rock star. It's crazy over here."

"Eric? A rock star? I'm so out of the loop. I've been doing laundry and packing all day. I have to turn on the radio. Where is his security?"

"They're here. Call me later. I can barely hear you." Matthew hung up, and much to his relief, the hysterical teens were finally shooed away by Mike, Tony, and extra officers who raced to the coffee shop to help manage the crowds. Finally, the noise abated, and they could eat with fewer intrusions now that the table was surrounded by guards.

"I told you that you will be bigger than Bieber," Angilia reminded her father, referencing her comment from the morning of the recording session.

"Not likely. This is just a novelty, Angel. No one will care after a few days."

"Don't count on it, Daddy. You've already made those girls replace their Bieber posters with your picture, I guarantee you. I think you need to do an entire solo album."

Eric covered his mouth with his napkin, nearly choking on his sandwich. "I don't think so, Angilia. This was my one foray outside my comfort zone."

"Look at all the money you would make for your charities, though, millions and millions of euros."

"Nice try, Angel. This is your thing, not mine."

She smiled, knowing she would convince him eventually. When they finished eating, Mr. Brennan and his nurse thanked them for lunch, and he kissed her hand. "I think the Princess is onto something, Sir. You should record an album. You sing much better than most of those other people who try to sing these days."

"Thank you, sir. You are too kind," Eric said and shook the man's hand.

The trio walked back to the palace, surrounded by security, not because they feared an assassin but to protect them from over-zealous fans. "That was insane," Matthew commented. "My parents called while you were being mauled by those teenagers," Matthew grinned to Eric. "They're arriving next Wednesday."

"Wonderful. It will be nice to have them here," Eric replied with a smile.

§§§§

"Good heavens, this is magnificent," Katherine pronounced when the Rolls Royce approached the palace and drove through the gate. She tried to take in every detail as Tony drove into the massive garage and as she and Mitchell followed Matthew to the back patio. She smiled to see Eric and Angilia waiting there for them. Katherine gently hugged Angilia, and said, "How wonderful to see you again, dear. You look splendid." She turned to Eric, grabbed his arms, and embarrassed him by saying, "And you, a rock star now."

"Not likely," Eric disagreed. "Welcome, Katherine. Mitchell."

Mitchell clasped Eric's hand, amazed at how truly happy he and Angilia appeared. "It's lovely here. This is some country you have." He held out his arms, smiled, and asked Angilia, "Do I get a hug, too?" She stepped to him and he, too, gingerly hugged her.

183

"You do look wonderful. I guess you were right. Home has done wonders for you."

Eric motioned for them to sit and he rang for tea and finger sandwiches. Angilia had specifically asked the chef to prepare a British tea for the Taylors' arrival. The five of them enjoyed the cool breeze, the refreshments, and one another's company as they caught up. Mitchell asked about local golf courses, and Matthew rolled his eyes. "You know I like to golf, son. You didn't think I would leave my clubs behind, did you?" He winked, knowing his son liked to tease him about the cliché that doctors and golf are inseparable.

"I followed your example, dear, and donated most of our things to charities. I even went through my closets and donated a lot of clothes, as well. There is a group that provides suits to women who need them for job interviews, and that seemed like the perfect solution. I told Mitchell I want to look into volunteer opportunities here, something as simple as visiting long-term health care patients and reading to them or talking to them."

"I told her that is perfect for her," Mitchell replied with a smile. Katherine swatted his arm.

"Ignore him. I'd like to talk with you about charities or organizations with which I can get involved," Katherine told Angilia. "Maybe one of your patronages."

Angilia smiled and said that would be delightful if they could work together sometimes. She glanced at her father's watch, startled to realize they had been sitting and talking for more than two and one half hours. Eric noticed, too, and suggested they show the Taylors to their new home.

Katherine linked her arm with Angilia's and walked with her as she continued to take in the majestic palace and grounds. "This place is really breathtaking, Angilia. How old is the palace?"

"It was begun by King Pepin in 755 and completed by his son Charlemagne in 800. King Philippe VI created the kingdom of Valdavia for my seventeenth great-grandfather Christophe Alexandre Martineau and declared him our first King on September

16, 1331. Christophe was coronated on November 17, 1331, 623 years to the day before my father was born."

"Charlemagne? The Charlemagne? As in the Holy Roman Emperor?" Katherine asked, growing more amazed by the moment. Angilia smiled and nodded. "This place isn't just gorgeous, it's living history. And a kingdom created for your ancestor. This is more fantastical than any fairytale. You have got to tell me more sometime."

"I'd love to, Mrs. Taylor. History is my truest passion, if I am honest. I love the stories about the people involved, the personal aspects that often remain unacknowledged or neglected. It doesn't get any more personal than learning about my family."

"Unless you want to be her captive for hours at a stretch, I advise you to withhold your history questions around my daughter," Eric teased Katherine. "She has uncovered a tremendous amount of documents and information. The library contains hundreds of books, by the way. Feel free to borrow anything."

"Thank you. Oh! Matthew wasn't exaggerating at all. This is a mansion. Are you really sure about this, Eric?"

"Absolutely, Katherine." He opened the door for her and she reached for Mitchell, both of them speechless.

"This is magnificent, Eric," Mitchell said as he looked at the carved ceilings, antiques, and spiral staircase.

"Let me know if you need anything," Eric said as he showed them the downstairs rooms, and then led them upstairs. "The entire house is yours, and we can change anything." Eric paused outside a bedroom on the second floor, and Angilia put her arm around him. "There is only one room I keep locked and do not want to change. Call me sentimental, but it was Mother's room, and everything is just as she left it eleven years ago. I hope you don't mind."

Katherine took a tissue from her purse and wiped her tears from her face as she sobbed. "Of course not, Eric," Mitchell said for both of them. "Are you sure you don't mind us being here?"

"Of course I don't. It's just this one room. Angilia visited her grandmother here very frequently, and she even came here after Mother died. A few times I discovered her in Mother's bedroom, sitting in the chair writing." He smiled down at his daughter, and she smiled in return.

Katherine sniffled. "I hope you'll visit us here, too, dear. And you can go in her room whenever you want to. A house needs people and love or it starts to die. Help me keep it alive and well, Angilia. Promise?"

"I promise," Angilia whispered as she and Katherine hugged.

CHAPTER 6

Angilia cut a bouquet of freesias and lilies from the garden and tied it with a green satin ribbon. Dr. and Mrs. Taylor entered the patio just as she finished, and she smiled at them. "You look beautiful, dear. And that cameo—I have never seen anything like that," Katherine said.

"Thank you, Mrs. Taylor. She's my mother. Daddy had it made for my birthday this year. Today is the anniversary of her birth. Daddy and I always celebrate her life on this date. These are her favorite flowers."

"They are heavenly, Angilia."

"So is Mommy, Mrs. Taylor," Angilia replied with a smile.

Eric joined them, smiling at his daughter, and told the Taylors to make themselves at home. Angilia put an arm around him, and they left to walk to the church, just the two of them. They stood in front of the altar and prayed, then went to Marisol's tomb in the royal vault. Angilia felt her father breathe deeply, and she slightly tightened her arm around his waist. He squeezed her shoulder and smiled at her, tears shining in his eyes.

Angilia handed him the flowers and whispered, "I'll leave you alone with her." He shook his head and held her hand. He wanted her with him, with them. The three of them were eternally bound.

"I love her so, Angel. I always will. I knew the night we met that she was the woman God predestined me to marry. She knew it, too. Our time together was short but extremely loving and blissful. I am blessed to have had in her my life for the time I did."

Angilia could never comprehend how her father truly felt. Soon he would commemorate his 21st wedding anniversary alone. He and Marisol were together as husband and wife only four years. She held his left hand, her thumb tenderly caressing the gold wedding band he still wore. She admired his devotion to his wife, a devotion not cloaked in grief but in love. He wore his wedding band as a symbol of his undying love for his wife.

Angilia slid a tiny slip of paper under the plaque on the tomb's lid, something she did every year, starting when she was three. Thirteen slips of paper, all with the same message: "Mommy, I love you." Eric placed the bouquet on the lid and bowed his head. Tears stung Angilia's eyes and she felt her chest ache. Her hand automatically covered the top of her thoracotomy scar.

Unexpectedly, a warm breeze blew around them, which roused Eric from his prayer. The vault was closed, with a few tiny stained glass windows. From where did the breeze come? "Angilia, what's wrong?" he asked her, noticing her pain. The warm air swirled around her, gently embracing her, and soon her pain eased. She felt the warm air leave, and she knew. She had felt her mother force her soul back into her body after she was shot. Her mother had saved her life that day. Her mother had just soothed her pain.

Angilia smiled at her father, hugged him tightly, and just as she did after the shooting, after she came back to life in her father's arms, she whispered, "Mommy." Eric held his daughter close to him and looked at his wife's tomb. Angilia was right. Marisol had made her presence known to her husband and daughter on what would have been her 61st birthday, May 21, 2012.

§§§§

Angilia handed her father the May 25 morning newspaper when he stepped out of his suite to go downstairs to breakfast. The front page headline took Eric off guard: Devoted Public Requests 20th Jubilee to Honor King Eric. "Is this for real?" Eric asked.

"Of course it is. Isn't this wonderful?"

188

He smiled at her. "I'm truly flattered, Angel, but we can't do this. I need to write a statement in response after breakfast. Come on."

An hour later, she followed him to his office, knowing her father and that he would never condone using public funds for a jubilee. She understood why he felt this way, for he always put what was best for the people over his needs. She admired his benevolence. He sent the message to Carol for immediate release.

Angilia helped him with correspondence and paperwork, sitting at the end of his desk. Soon Carol knocked on the open door and entered with a huge stack of telephone messages and emails. "Eric, your statement is not getting the desired response. Take a look at these." Carol handed him the messages from Valdavians, all essentially making the same point: they loved Eric even more for refusing a jubilee to celebrate and honor him, which made them want to have the jubilee even more. Angilia read over his shoulder and hugged him. "A group of people want to form a committee to plan the jubilee, Eric. They await your approval," Carol added.

"They are too kind. I'm honored, really I am, but I cannot allow this." Carol nodded, telling him the staff would respond accordingly. "Thank you, Carol. I need to work on this proposal for the elementary school annex. The board meets next week."

Angilia kissed him and told him, "You are so very loved, Daddy. I think a jubilee is a brilliant idea. Great Britain celebrates the Queen's Diamond Jubilee all this year."

"I know, Angel. The Queen deserves the honor for her sixty years of dedicated service to Great Britain. But I cannot justify spending public funds on a jubilee."

"I know, and I understand why. It is still a wonderful idea," she smiled and waved as she left his office and walked across the hall to the Press Office.

Angilia asked Carol for the committee information, but made Carol promise to never tell Eric. "I promise. By the way, I think it's a wonderful idea, too. Let me know if I can help," Carol whispered with a wink as Angilia thanked her and left.

Angilia called each of the newly-christened Jubilee Committee members and asked them to meet her at the coffee shop. She went alone, not wanting anyone to know what she was doing, her portfolio tucked under her arm. At her favorite table, she discussed the dates and agenda for the week-long jubilee with the three men and women. They agreed upon the week of August 19-25, 2012, with special events planned for each day.

"How do we conduct fundraising without King Eric knowing?" asked Joshua Forte, who owned the nearby bakery.

Angilia smiled. "We don't. Are we in agreement that Mr. Forte be the treasurer for the committee?" Everyone approved, and Angilia pulled her checkbook from her portfolio, filled out a check, and handed it to Mr. Forte. "That should get us started. If anything arises that the available funds do not cover, please let me know. I will take care of everything."

"Your Highness, this is too much. We never expected you to pay for the jubilee," Mimi Baldwin, who owned an interior design business, declared.

"I agree. This is far too much. €2 million. You should not pay for your father's jubilee, Your Highness," added Jessica Campbell, whose family owned a florist shop.

"Who better? I want to do this. You make the arrangements. Let me know if there is anything I can do to help." She stood, and the astounded Jubilee Committee quickly stood, bowed or curtseyed, and shook her hand. "Thank you, all of you, for wanting to honor my father. He deserves this more than anyone does."

§§§§

"Eric, the Israeli Military Secretary is here to see you," Roger announced while Eric sat at his desk drafting a proposal for upgrades to the national water filtration system.

"Did he say why?" Roger shook his head. "Show him in, Roger."

Eric stood and greeted his guest, who introduced himself as Gil Saidoff. "Your Majesty, I am honored to meet you. However, my mission is to deliver this letter to Her Royal Highness The Princess Angilia."

"Angilia? May I ask what this is about?"

"The letter must be delivered only to Her Royal Highness, Sir. Is Her Royal Highness available?"

"Roger, please inform Angilia that she has a visitor in my office," Eric instructed, his mind whirling. What could the Israeli Military Secretary have for Angilia? Eric saw Roger and his daughter in the doorway and motioned her inside. "Angilia, Mr. Gil Saidoff came from Israel to meet with you."

Angilia's heart jumped and she felt momentarily faint. Was this about her letter? "Mr. Saidoff, it is a pleasure to meet you." He bowed to her and asked if he could speak with her in private. She looked at her father and asked if they could use his office.

"Of course," Eric replied. He and Roger left, but stood in the hall, both more bemused than ever. While they speculated and waited, Angilia sat on the sofa with the Prime Minister's Military Secretary.

"Your Royal Highness, I give you this official letter from the Prime Minister. His Excellency is most pleased to offer this to you, and I am pleased to deliver it on his behalf. He requested that you read this in my presence so that I may relay your response to him upon my return to Israel."

Angilia took the letter, her hand shaking. She walked to her father's desk and used his letter opener to slit the flap of the envelope. She removed a thick parchment sheet with the Prime Minister's seal embossed at the top. She closed her eyes, prayed, and read the letter. Angilia stared at the letter in disbelief and reread it to verify its contents. God had answered her prayer. Angilia closed her eyes and thanked God for this miracle.

She turned to Mr. Saidoff, tears in her eyes. "Thank you. Thank you so much. This means more to my family than my words can say to you."

"The Prime Minister is happy to help in this endeavor. He was quite impressed and touched by your letter."

"Would it be appropriate if I write a thank you letter to His Excellency?"

"Of course, Your Royal Highness."

Angilia sat at her father's desk, used a sheet of his official stationery, and hand wrote a heartfelt reply to Israel's Prime Minister. She sealed it in an envelope, addressed it, and handed it to Mr. Saidoff.

He bowed, placed it in his briefcase, and removed a small package. He handed it to her and thanked her for meeting with him. She held the precious letter and the package while she escorted Mr. Saidoff to the main entrance. She watched his car pull out of the courtyard before she returned to the foyer and closed the door.

Eric and Roger stood there waiting for her. She saw the questions in her father's eyes and smiled at him. Angilia walked to him, handed him the letter, and told him to read it. He did, his brain doubting the words he read. "Angilia? You did this?"

"All I did was write to him asking if he could help. That's all."

"That's all? Do you realize that every President, Prime Minister, and Monarch has tried to do this for twenty-two years? None of us succeeded, not my father, none of us. With one letter, my teenage daughter accomplishes the impossible. When? When did you do this?"

"March 6, the day we recorded the album. I wrote the letter that morning after you wrote the Open Heart essay. I mailed it when we went to the pub that evening for dinner."

"I don't know what to say, Angel. We all feared the worst after so long. No one has heard anything about the hostages in twenty years. We could never get any information. You are remarkable."

"The Prime Minister did everything. Daddy, I don't think we should tell Abuela and Abuelo until Mr. Saidoff confirms Uncle Eduardo's arrival date."

"We won't." Eric put his hands on her shoulders. "You will meet your mother's brother, your uncle. He does not even know about you. He was captured before Mommy's and my wedding, and I cannot wrap my head around this yet. My brother-in-law is coming home." He pulled her into a hug, tears filling his eyes. Roger listened in astonishment, remembering the news of Eduardo's capture in 1990 while he covered the Gulf War for Spain's major magazine. He and King Gerard had written hundreds of letters and e-mails and made hundreds of telephone calls, to no avail.

"I prayed for this so much, Daddy. I wanted this for Uncle Eduardo. I cannot fathom what he has been through. I wanted this for Abuela and Abuelo mostly. I had to try, Daddy. I had to. The Prime Minister is such a good, kind man, and I knew if anyone in the Middle East could help, he could. I am so grateful to him."

"You really are remarkable. I can only imagine what you will accomplish as queen." He looked at her in awe, knowing in his heart that his daughter was ordained by God. "What is that?" he asked, nodding toward the small package she held.

"Mr. Saidoff handed it to me before he left." She removed the wrapping to reveal a small prayer book. Inside the front cover was a handwritten inscription that she showed Eric: *Angilia, you are an angel on earth. The world is blessed to have you. God's Blessings, Bibi.*

§§§§

The following Monday morning, Angilia knocked on her father's office door. Eric smiled and told her, "You don't have to knock, Angilia. Come here."

"This is official business."

"Official business? How may I help you, Your Royal Highness?"

"You may please sign this proclamation," she replied and placed a formal royal proclamation on his desk.

"I may?" His eyes twinkled and his voice betrayed a hint of a laugh.

"Yes, please, Your Majesty."

Eric read the proclamation, unprepared for its contents. "Angilia, when did you write this? I had no idea. How did you manage to keep this a secret?"

"I never told anyone about this. I did not want you to know until now. I got a piece of the parchment from the Press Office late Friday and worked on this in my room over the weekend."

"In your room? You actually did this by hand?" She nodded. "This is beautiful. It looks like an ancient illuminated manuscript. What can you not do, Angilia?"

"Thank you, Daddy. One thing I cannot do is sign that and make it official. Only you can. Please."

"Come here, Angel. This is amazing in every way. Both of us will sign this, Angilia." Eric signed and dated the proclamation, wrote "On behalf of" underneath his signature, and Angilia signed below that.

"Thank you, Daddy." She kissed his cheek.

"I am having this original framed. I need to have Carol make a copy of this one for official release." He stood, went to Carol's office, where she scanned the original, released it to the press and public, and within the hour the country had two new holidays. The citizens of Valdavia were surprised and excited, officially having the opportunity to honor the people most important to many of them.

Royal Proclamation

Whereas we are instructed to honor our parents;

Whereas the bond between parents and children is forged from birth and strengthened over their lifetimes;

Whereas it is our duty and privilege to celebrate fatherhood, motherhood, and parenting,

Therefore we sanctify the following dates annually to show our love, appreciation, and respect for and to our parents:

The second Sunday in June is henceforth declared Father's Day, beginning in 2012.

The fourth Sunday in June is henceforth declared Mother's Day, beginning in 2012.

Signed: Eric R

on behalf of

Angilia DeBruce Martineau

Dated: 4 June 2012

§§§§§

"Good morning, and welcome to a special edition of the news on this very extraordinary Sunday morning. I am Franklin Sydney."

"And I am Laurie Dougray. Welcome, indeed, to our coverage of Valdavia's first annual Father's Day celebration. We will broadcast the entire Father's Day Service live from Christ Church Valmondois to those of you at home and to every church in Valdavia."

"That's right, Laurie. In moments we will cut to the church to see the arrival of King Eric and Princess Angilia. The Princess wrote the proclamation declaring the second Sunday in June as Father's Day and the fourth Sunday in June as Mother's Day perpetually in Valdavia."

"Isn't this amazing, Franklin? What a perfect year to initiate Father's Day in Valdavia than 2012, the 20th anniversary of King Eric's sovereignty."

"Yes, and I know that must have occurred to Her Royal Highness, as well. We are going to Christ Church Valmondois live. The King and the Princess are arriving with their party."

Eric and Angilia, with the Taylors, Roger, Daniel, Susan, and Mike, greeted Reverend Hutchins at the entrance to the church and followed him inside. The rest of the congregation was seated, anticipating the inaugural Father's Day Service. Eric, Angilia, Matthew, Katherine, Mitchell, Roger, Susan, Daniel, and Mike filled the royal family's pew. The congregation stood for Reverend Hutchins' invocation, in which he praised God as the ultimate father, the Heavenly Father. His opening sermon followed that theme, illustrating the multiple blessings bestowed upon all people by the Heavenly Father and why his children should honor and praise God for his blessings.

Reverend Hutchins transitioned into a discussion of earthly fathers and the honor they, too, deserve. He cited Joseph, Jesus' father in the truest sense of the word, as a prime example of what male parenting should be: loving, compassionate, didactic, and hard-working. The choir then sang a version of Ecclesiastes 3, written many centuries earlier by King Solomon, which Angilia had set to music for the service.

When the hymn concluded, Angilia squeezed her father's hand and walked to the pulpit. Eric had not known in advance the program for the service and that Angilia would deliver the main sermon. He noticed she had no notes. She would not read her message but rather speak from her heart.

"Proverbs 23:22. *Hearken unto thy father that begat thee, and despise not thy mother when she is old.* King Solomon of Israel wrote that verse about his parents, King David and Bathsheba. Solomon was king for forty years, three of those years jointly with his father, King David. Solomon has always been known and noted for his incredible wisdom, which he inherited from God and from David.

"I have a special affinity for Solomon. God blessed him greatly, ordaining David as his father, and thereby placing Solomon in the direct lineage of Jesus Christ. Like Solomon, God blessed me immensely by gifting me to my beautiful father. Like Solomon, I have been taught well by both God and my father.

"Words fail to impart my love for you both, Daddy, but you both know, you and God, how very much I love you both. My prayer is that everyone feels as blessed and loved by your fathers as Solomon did and as I do. Please join me in a prayer." The congregation stood and bowed their heads in unison.

"Dear God, Thank you for blessing our lives and our souls with our beloved fathers. Bless all of the fathers in the world, protect them, and comfort them. Let them see and feel how very much we love them and how very much you love them. Amen."

"Amen," echoed the congregation before they sat.

"I want to conclude with Proverbs 4:1-13, Solomon's words to us all. *'Hear, ye children, the instruction of a father, and attend to know understanding. For I give you good doctrine, forsake ye not my law. For I was my father's son, tender and only beloved in the sight of my mother. He taught me also, and said unto me, Let thine heart retain my words: keep my commandments and live. Get wisdom, get understanding: forget it not; neither decline from the words of my mouth. Forsake her not, and she shall preserve thee. Wisdom is the principal thing; therefore get wisdom: and with all thy getting get understanding. Exalt her, and she shall promote thee: she shall bring thee to honour, when thou dost embrace her. She shall give to thine head an ornament of grace: a crown of glory shall she deliver to thee. Hear, O my son, and receive my sayings; and the years of thy life shall be many. I have taught thee in the way of wisdom; I have led thee in the right paths. When thou goest, thy steps shall not be straitened; and when thou runnest, thou shalt not stumble. Take fast hold of instruction; let her not go: keep her; for she is thy life.'*"

Angilia returned to her seat next to Eric, and he clasped her hand. Reverend Hutchins returned to the pulpit to offer the benediction, and the congregation stood and bowed their heads. Eric took that moment to thank God for his precious daughter. The congregation remained standing for the closing hymn and sang with the choir.

At the conclusion of the service, Reverend Hutchins motioned for Eric and Angilia to join him in a receiving line. Each member of the congregation greeted them, praising Angilia not only for initiating the holiday but for her sermon. She wished each father a Happy Father's Day, and when Dr. Taylor reached her, she hugged him and wished him a very wonderful Father's Day. Most of the parishioners commended Eric for his parenting of Angilia and they all wished him a very blessed Father's Day.

"Ladies and gentlemen, that was quite an inaugural Father's Day Service. No one knew the Princess would deliver the bulk of the sermon, did they Franklin?" Laurie Dougray asked her co-host when the broadcast returned to the studio.

"No, we did not. I really enjoyed the split screen so we were able to view King Eric during his daughter's sermon. I know how much love he must feel."

"It was very emotional, indeed, especially for His Majesty. I know she politely disagreed with your comparison during the interview last month, Franklin, but the Princess is a hybrid, if you will, of Mother Theresa, the Virgin Mary, and Diana, Princess of Wales. She is compassionate, giving, pure and righteous, and also very beautiful and stylish."

"She is all of that, Laurie. You mentioned righteous. I dare say, Her Royal Highness will be a Queen of Valdavia in the mold of King David: righteous, wise, loyal, and stunningly beautiful. We are blessed to have Eric and Angilia."

"We are. Thank you all for joining us for this special Father's Day broadcast," Laurie concluded the newscast.

In the meantime, Eric and Angilia told their party to go on ahead, that they wanted to remain at the church for a while. After everyone left, Eric opened the door to the royal vault and they walked to his father's tomb. Father and daughter bowed their heads in prayer, and Angilia saw him wipe a tear from his eye. He placed his hand on his father's tomb and said a tear-choked "Happy Father's Day." Angilia slid a slip of paper under the plaque, which had the same message written upon it, with the date on the reverse.

She walked to her Great-grandfather's tomb, slid a letter under the plaque, and bowed her head in prayer. Eric joined her, slipping his arm around her waist. She smiled up at him, and they left the church hand-in-hand. "I love you, Daddy." He smiled at her, happier than he had felt in a long while.

The service was repeated on television during lunch, and Angilia giggled at the concluding comments. "I cannot be David, Daddy. You are my David, my wise, righteous, beautiful father."

He smiled and retorted, "Then you are my Solomon, my beloved, wise, righteous, beautiful child."

They hugged, and excused themselves from the others to spend the afternoon together. Angilia asked him to meet her in the watch tower. She slipped into her room and snuck a gift up to the tower. Eric joined her a moment later. They sat at the small iron table, enjoying the view and the breeze.

"The service was incredibly beautiful. I feel so loved, Angilia. So very loved."

"You are." Angilia handed him Valdavia's first Father's Day card, one which she made, illustrated, and wrote just for her father. Inside, in calligraphy, was a Petrarchan sonnet she wrote for him:

God's Gift

If I were to search this universe wide,

Nowhere could I find any to compare.

None who can match your heart and soul so rare,

None who in my loving heart could reside,

None who could take my life on this joyride,

None who could ever answer my soul's prayer,

None for whom I could ever be the heir,

Not of riches but of love rarified.

Among the billions you remain the best,

The world's sole recipient of my heart.

You alone were chosen for me by God,

Who knew with you my life will remain blessed.

Through eternity we shall never part.

Jointly in Heaven we shall e'er trod.

Eric read the poem four times, tears blurring the words. A lone tear fell onto the card, smearing the ink of her "xoxo" at the end of the poem. Angilia smiled at him. "A love blot," she called the tear stain. He kissed her cheek, letting tears fall, knowing he truly was the most loved man alive.

"You are spoiling me, Angel," he said as he cleared his throat.

Angilia smiled and handed him a gold-wrapped gift. "More?" he asked. He removed the lid and lifted out an exquisite book. "You made this? For me?" She nodded. He flipped through the book, realizing she had illustrated, hand lettered, and hand bound the entire book. "Angilia. This is the most beautiful gift anyone has ever given me. It is the most magnificent book I have ever seen. This looks like handmade paper even."

"Thank you, Daddy. It is. Read it?" It was about them, their blessed life together from her in utero time during her mother's pregnancy to the present, emphasizing their eternal bond and his now-famous heart-glow, as she called it. She had written it in the style of a fairy-tale, with alternating pages of text and illustration. She watched his face as he read, slowly, dabbing tears with his knuckle a few times.

Eric turned to the inside front cover and reread her inscription: *"Beloved Daddy—My love for you lived in my soul long before I saw you or came to you, when we danced in dreams. You are the love of my life. You are my life. xoxo Your Angilia"* He closed the book and placed it back in the box. For a few moments he clasped his hands in front of his mouth, tears choking him, rendering him speechless.

He looked at her, opened his arms, and she slid onto his lap, hugging him. Eric laid his head on his daughter's shoulder, crying, his emotions overflowing. "Happy Father's Day. I love you, Daddy," she softly said against his neck.

"I love you, Angel. I love you."

$$\S\S\S\S$$

Three days later, on June 13, Eric's office telephone rang. When he answered, Mr. Saidoff asked to speak with Her Royal Highness. Eric called her to his office, and she spoke with Mr. Saidoff for almost ten minutes, telling him her cell phone number. Eric watched her face intently, anxious to know what the Military Secretary told her. He prayed it was positive news.

"Daddy, you need to call Abuela and Abuelo now, so they can prepare for their trip here. Mr. Saidoff will escort Uncle Eduardo to Valmondois on June 20." Eric stood from his chair and hugged her.

"He's safe? He's well?"

"Yes, they are all alive, all ten of the hostages. Each one will be escorted home by military personnel. They were all taken to Bathesda, Maryland, to the Walter Reed National Military Medical Center for examinations and any treatment they needed. Mr. Saidoff said they were somewhat malnourished, but overall in good health. Two are still in the Medical Center, but the other eight are returning home soon, including Uncle Eduardo."

"Thank God. All right, I won't tell them about their son yet, though. I'll tell them the truth, in part, that we want them to spend the summer with us. I'll send a plane for them, with Susan and a guard." Angilia agreed, and Eric dialed his in-laws' home telephone number. Juanita answered, and told Alejandro to pick up the extension so they both could talk to Eric. Eric put the call on speaker phone so that Angilia could hear and talk to them as well.

"Angilia and I really want the two of you to spend the summer with us, Mamá and Papa. Please don't say no. Angilia especially misses you both. Just pack a couple of suitcases and I can send the plane for you on Friday morning. You could be here in time for lunch with us."

"Mi hijo, we will love to see you, but we do not want to intrude upon you for so long," Juanita said.

"Nonsense, Abuela. I love you. Daddy loves you. Both of you. Family is never an intrusion. Please say yes. For me, please."

"Yes, we will come. For you, anything, mi nieta bonita," Alejandro said to her. "We miss you, our Angel."

"Wonderful. The plane will arrive around nine that morning, but Susan and Tony will pick you up at your house. Susan will call you when the plane lands so that you can be ready when she and Tony arrive. We love you." Eric hung up the telephone and smiled at his daughter.

"Come on. We need to prepare their suites, Daddy." She grabbed his hand and marched to the stairs with him in tow. She still took the stairs slowly, which sent a pang through Eric. His instinct was to pick her up and carry her, but both Matthew and Mitchell had warned him about such pampering. She had to completely heal and become stronger. She may have a slight limp for the rest of her life, but only time would reveal that.

Angilia selected the suite next to hers for her grandparents, across from Matthew's, so that they would be closer to her. She smiled at the thought of that. The suite on the other side of theirs would be Eduardo's. Eric agreed, and they looked around and decided what needed to be done to make the suites ready in less than 48 hours. Angilia opened the curtains and windows to let in fresh air and sunshine. No one had used those suites during her lifetime. With the help of two housekeepers and Katherine the suites were vacuumed, polished, redressed, and stocked by Thursday evening.

Angilia barely slept that night, excited to see her grandparents again, and also anxious to share the news of Eduardo's homecoming with them. She had asked Matthew and Dr. Taylor to please be there when her grandparents learned that their son was alive and coming home. After twenty-two years, the shock may be too much for them. She prayed that night for God to please safeguard Eduardo on his journey home, and to protect Abuela and Abuelo during their flight and especially during the conversation that would change their lives forever.

§§§§

Susan texted Angilia as the Rolls Royce approached the palace. "They're here," Angilia announced excitedly. Eric grabbed her hand to prevent her from trying to run to the garage, and walked with her to greet them. The Taylors heard her shrieks of delight, and Katherine smiled. Matthew recalled his first meeting with the Martínezes in the hospital after Angilia's surgery, having to face their heartbreak and fear.

Now Angilia walked back to the patio between her grandparents, all of them smiling broadly. "It does feel nice to be here again, mi hijo," Juanita said to Eric.

"Angilia wants me to persuade you to stay, just so you know. I would enjoy that myself. You both remember Dr. and Mrs. Taylor and Matthew." Mitchell, Katherine, and Matthew stood to welcome Alejandro and Juanita.

Juanita walked to Matthew and hugged him, much to his surprise. "Dear boy, I will never forget you. Never. You saved my nieta's life. Thank you." She cupped his face in her hands, her eyes brimming with love. "After everything, after losing our two children, we would not have survived losing our precious Angel."

Angilia gasped and grabbed her father's arm just as she fainted. Eric caught her, while Juanita screamed and Matthew held her. What had just happened? Eric placed Angilia on a nearby chaise chair, and Matthew motioned for his father to take care of Juanita. Matthew rushed to Angilia, and she moaned and opened her eyes. She tried to sit up, but Matthew told her to stay still for a moment. He raced to the third floor, grabbed his medical bag, and breathlessly returned.

"I'm fine, really. I just fainted," she insisted, but Matthew forced her to be still while he listened to her heart. Her pulse was a bit fast, but her vital signs were not alarming. Eric handed her a glass of water, and she dutifully drank some. "I really am all right." She saw her grandmother, hands over her heart, supported by Mitchell and Abuelo. "I'm sorry, Abuela."

"She is really all right, Dr. Matthew?" Juanita asked him.

"She is. Just a bit too much excitement, that's all," Matthew assured her.

Juanita went to her granddaughter and sat facing her, holding her hands. "I should never say such things, mi nieta. My words upset you, yes?"

Angilia looked at her father, both of them aware that this was true. Juanita's comment about Marisol and Eduardo had stunned him, and with Angilia's concern for her grandparents heightened, her stress had peaked. "It just took us by surprise, Mamá, that's all. This is a very emotional day," Eric said, thinking that it truly would be. He and Angilia wanted to share the news with Alejandro and Juanita after dinner.

§§§§

That evening, Eric, Alejandro, Juanita, Mitchell, Matthew, and Katherine went to the sitting room and settled on the overstuffed sofas and chairs. Angilia joined them a few moments later, clutching her portfolio in her arms. Her father and grandparents sat together on one sofa, Mitchell and Katherine on the other sofa, and Matthew sat in a chair near her grandparents. Angilia selected the chair near her father, and placed the portfolio in her lap, gripping it tightly.

Alejandro was describing an annual festival, and although she adored listening to him, at that moment Angilia was extraordinarily nervous. Eric knew this, and when Alejandro finished, Eric smiled at him. "Papa, Mamá, Angilia and I asked you to come for a very important reason. We have something to tell you. Actually, Angilia has something to tell you." He looked at her, and she took a deep breath.

Angilia opened the portfolio and removed the letter from the Israeli Prime Minister and handed it to her grandfather. "Please read this." Her hands shook, and her grandparents looked both scared and confused, staring at her without speaking. "Please."

Alejandro put on his reading glasses, and held the letter so that both he and Juanita could read it together. At times their brows furrowed, they frowned, they smiled, and they appeared frightened. They looked at one another, tears filling their eyes simultaneously. "Please, Eric, tell us this is real, not a cruel joke," Alejandro pleaded.

Eric held his father-in-law's hands and looked in his eyes. "This is very real, Papa. The Prime Minister's Military Secretary delivered this personally to Angilia."

"Our son, our Eduardo, he is coming home? He is alive?" Juanita asked in a tear-filled whisper.

"Yes, Mamá, Eduardo is coming home. Very soon. Angilia has more to share with you."

"Mr. Saidoff, the Military Secretary, called me two days ago, and after his call Daddy called both of you so that you would be here in plenty of time. Mr. Saidoff is escorting Uncle Eduardo to the palace on June 20, in five days."

Juanita covered her face with her hands and wept tears of relief and joy after a very long twenty-two years. Alejandro held his wife of sixty-four years and cried with her. After many moments of unleashing their pent-up emotions, they dried their eyes and turned to Eric. "How did you do this, mi hijo? After so many attempts, how did you do this now?" Juanita asked him.

"I did not do anything. Angilia did. See? The Prime Minister's letter is addressed to her." Eric held up the letter. "Our Angilia did it all on her own, without telling anyone."

"Mi nieta, you did this? How? So many important people have tried for so long and nothing. How did you do this?" Alejandro asked, questions swirling through his mind.

"I wrote to the Prime Minister and asked him if he could help. That's all I did. He did everything. He located Eduardo and the other hostages. He negotiated their release."

"What did you write in this letter? You caused a miracle, mi nieta, a true miracle. What did she write?" Juanita asked Eric.

"I don't know. Angilia?" Eric turned to his daughter. She pulled a sheet of paper from the portfolio and handed it to her father. He read a copy of the letter she had mailed the day before she was nearly killed. He passed it to Alejandro, who read it aloud to Juanita—and everyone else. Angilia wrote that although she had never met her uncle and dearly wanted to, she was really writing on behalf of her grandparents. Their only other child, her mother, had died before she was born. Her grandparents needed to know the truth about their son, and if he were alive they needed him home with them. They should not be denied their son and be forced to lose both of their children. Angilia prayed that her grandparents be reunited with their beloved son. All ten families deserved that. She appealed to him to please do what he could to help or to counsel her on what more she could do to ease the families' suffering and release the ten hostages.

Juanita cried again, her head against her husband's shoulder. Alejandro looked at his granddaughter, this sixteen-year-old girl, who had brought his son home. He handed the letters to Eric and held his arms open, beckoning Angilia. She went to him and he held her close to him, a look of unadulterated joy on his face that brought tears to Eric. "I have said this before, but God has preordained you just as he did David and Solomon."

She looked over her shoulder at her father. Katherine grabbed Mitchell's arm. Five days earlier, Angilia's Father's Day sermon had focused on David and Solomon. Eric smiled, placed the letters in Angilia's portfolio, and stood. "Are you both ready for another surprise?"

"Another surprise? What more is there?" Juanita asked, drying her eyes with her handkerchief.

"Oh, just a program. Why don't I turn on the television and start the DVR? You will enjoy this, I promise." Eric began the program and rejoined his parents-in-law on the sofa.

"You recorded this?" Angilia asked her father.

"Of course I did. Franklin also sent me a DVD of the program," he smiled at her. Angilia watched her father as he viewed the Father's Day Service—again—and smiled. Alejandro placed his hand over his chest when he heard his granddaughter speak about David and Solomon and how God had ordained them. Juanita cried with love and pride, her heart too full on this evening of blessings.

When it ended, Eric turned off the television. "Pretty amazing, isn't it?" Eric asked with a smile as he looked at Alejandro. "Guess who made Father's Day and Mother's Day official holidays in Valdavia?"

"Mi nieta?" Juanita replied. "I have said since her birth that she will do many great things, yes? We are blessed to have you, Angel." Juanita went to Angilia and pulled her into a hug. "I start to wonder if you really are an angel, mi nieta." Angilia hugged her grandmother, holding tight to her secret for a few more weeks.

§§§§

Angilia awoke at 3:00 the following Wednesday morning, slipped on her robe, and walked downstairs to the chapel. Bowing her head, she prayed for her uncle's safe arrival and for her grandparents. As joyous as their reunion with Eduardo would be, they would still feel stress. So would Eduardo, free after so many years, seeing the world again, talking with people other than his nine fellow hostages, going where and when he desired. So much had changed in twenty-two years, so very much. Most of all, his sister had died nearly seventeen years earlier. She prayed for him, that the shock of everything would not be too much for him to tolerate.

Angilia slowly returned to her suite, sat at her desk, and took her diary from her desk drawer. Like most days in recent weeks, this one would burst with moments and memories. Until the day was over and her family reunified, she would feel uneasy. She picked up her pen and wrote her early-morning thoughts on this historic day.

20 June 2012

Today Mr. Saidoff brings Uncle Eduardo home. I trust and believe him and His Excellency, but until Eduardo is actually here with Abuela and Abuelo, I will remain anxious. I pray for his safe return nearly every moment, and I know God's protection covers him. Still, after so many years under an evil regime, he is not safe until he is here. More than ever, I know what those who seek vengeance can and will do.

I wrote to the Prime Minister so that Abuela and Abuelo might have their son returned to them. However many years they have left on this earth should be shared with Eduardo, their son. The three of them need and want each other. I am eternally grateful to His Excellency for his efforts to cause this miracle, for bringing all ten hostages home to their families. My heart soars for Abuela, Abuelo, and Uncle Eduardo. I know the joy they shall share for the rest of their earthly lives. In a few short hours, the miracle will bear fruit.

She closed her diary, returned it to the drawer, and walked to her sitting room balcony to watch the golden sunrise. She heard her father's footsteps on her carpet and smiled. Eric joined her on the carved stone Juliet balcony, still clad in his pajamas and robe. He placed his hands on the rail and breathed deeply, squinting at her as the sun's rays shone in his eyes.

"You couldn't sleep either?" he asked her. She shook her head. "My brain knows this is true, yet I'm having a hard time processing this. Twenty-two years is a long time to hear nothing and then everything. He will be here soon, Angel. In just a few hours, Mommy's brother will be home."

"I know. I keep praying. Until he is here, with Abuela and Abuelo, I cannot relax. I know Uncle Eduardo is in God's hands. Is it wrong of me to worry until he arrives safely?"

"No, Angel, of course not. It's normal to worry about our loved ones, especially in a situation such as this one. Terrorists held him hostage for more than two decades. That is never easy to forget. I was lying awake thinking about all of this when I heard you go downstairs. To the chapel?" Angilia nodded. "You have brought Eduardo this far. Your prayers will carry him the rest of the journey."

§§§§

Angilia returned to her suite after breakfast and sat at her desk reading. Occasionally she looked up at her Great-grandfather's portrait and wished she could hear his firm yet encouraging voice and feel his strong yet comforting embrace. He had the kindest eyes, slate blue like Uncle Patrick's eyes. She closed her eyes, remembering everything so distinctly.

Her cell phone rang, snapping Angilia back to reality. Mr. Saidoff's name and telephone number appeared in her caller identification. Her heart raced. She answered, talked with him briefly, and hung up. Her heart was pounding against her chest, hurting, and she tried to breathe deeply.

She texted her father a short, life-altering message: Mr. Saidoff's plane would land in Valmondois within half an hour. A car was waiting to drive him and Uncle Eduardo to the palace. Eric excused himself and left the others, who were nervously waiting in the sitting room, and bounded up the stairs to Angilia's suite.

Eric knelt before her and looked into her eyes. "This is real. Just a few more minutes."

Angilia grasped his hands, her own shaking. "Mr. Saidoff will call me again when they land and are in the car on their way here. Stay with me please, Daddy. Stay with me until he calls, until we know that Uncle Eduardo is really, truly here."

He pulled her to him, feeling her heart pounding. Eric stood, took her hand, picked up her cell phone, and walked to the sofa. She curled up next to him, clutching the phone, waiting and praying. Eric gently rocked her, realizing that she must have wondered and prayed about the Prime Minister's response to her letter during her hospital stay. They sat quietly, both of them waiting for that telephone call and praying.

Angilia closed her eyes and leaned her head against her father's shoulder, hearing his heart beating strongly, as well. What were Abuela and Abuelo thinking and feeling as they waited for their son, now 55 years old? What was her uncle thinking and feeling? She could never begin to comprehend what Eduardo must be experiencing at that moment, minutes away from seeing his parents again. Had he thought them dead? Her heart ached for what he had endured, yet rejoiced at his freedom. Angilia understood freedom. She had recently gained her own.

She gasped, nearly jumped, and Eric's hand tightened on her shoulder. Her phone was ringing. Angilia took a deep breath and answered. She spoke briefly, thanked Mr. Saidoff, hung up, and looked at her father. "Their car is leaving the airport now," she whispered.

Eric smiled, kissed her forehead, and stood. He reached for her hand. "I will be there soon. I want to stay here for a few moments, Daddy." He realized how stressful this had been for her. This had been yet another major life event that she had borne independently, not wanting to cause him or her grandparents further stress or heartbreak until she knew her uncle's fate. Eric touched her cheek and nodded, knowing she wanted to pray.

Eric returned to the sitting room with a huge smile. "Mamá. Papa. Mr. Saidoff and Eduardo are in the car on the way to the palace now. Let's go to the foyer and greet them." Juanita and Alejandro stood, hugged, praised God, and linked their arms with Eric to walk down the flight of stairs. Katherine motioned for Mitchell and Matthew to follow, just in case the stress of the reunion was too much for any of them. The father and son doctors did, but stood in the shadows of an arch, not wanting to intrude on the family's personal moments.

Eric walked to the front entrance, opened the door, and stepped into the courtyard to watch the gate open and the car pull close to him. He breathed deeply. He had met Eduardo a handful of times, never getting the opportunity to know him well. That was about to change. The car door opened, Mr. Saidoff exited, greeted Eric, and motioned to the man exiting the passenger side of the car. Eric watched in wonder as Eduardo turned, saw him, and smiled.

Eric went to him, grabbed him in a hug, and knew this was no dream. This was happening. "Eduardo. God knows how wonderful it is to see you again. Welcome home." Eduardo appeared too overwhelmed and emotional to speak. He held onto Eric's arms for a moment, struggling to assimilate each second as his senses were bombarded with sights, sounds, smells, emotions, and people.

"Mi familia?" Eduardo managed to ask.

Eric's heart sank, knowing that Eduardo had not been told that his sister had died. Now was not the time to tell him, although Eric knew Eduardo would very soon ask for her. He dreaded that moment. "Come inside." Eric kept his arm around his brother-in-law, supporting him as he faced the most poignant moment of the past twenty-two years.

Juanita's hands covered her face as Alejandro held her. "Mi hijo! Mi Eduardo! Alabado sea Dios!" Juanita exclaimed through her tears of utmost joy. Alejandro wept, unable to speak, his face reflecting his happiness. Eduardo, too, cried, seeing his parents, older yet so much the same, after years earlier accepting that he would probably never see them again.

After a few minutes, Eduardo rushed to his parents and gathered them both into a strong hug. They held him, kissed him, cried with him, for many moments. Mitchell and Matthew smiled at one another, elated for the Martínez family, for Eric, and for Angilia. Both were also aware that they were witnesses to history, as well, with the homecoming of a Gulf War hostage. Mr. Saidoff smiled as he, too, witnessed the spectacular reunion.

Juanita motioned for Eric to join them, and he shared the hugs and happiness. Eduardo admitted to them that he was not always certain what day, month, or year it was, since the hostages rarely received any information. He had kept a makeshift calendar on a piece of paper, making tick marks for each sunrise that indicated a new day, which helped him maintain a sense of time. "Sometimes, I even forgot how old I was, which may or may not be such a bad thing," he joked with them. "But I did not ever forget you," he smiled to his parents. "You were always in here," he pointed to his head, "and in here," he placed his hand over his heart.

"There is so much to learn and to relearn, you know. There are many things I must get, too. I saw my first cell phone when Mr. Saidoff and his officers took us to a hotel before we left Iraq. Apparently, nearly everyone has one. And a hand-held computer. I have so much to learn about," Eduardo told his family with a huge smile.

"Right now, though, I just want to be with my family, my wonderful family." Eduardo looked around the foyer, and Eric's heart lurched. If he asked for his sister, what would happen? How could they tell him so soon after his arrival? "Where is mi hermana, my sister?" Juanita turned away, sobbing. Alejandro's face changed from joyous to crestfallen. Eric could not leave this to them. He had to tell Eduardo. No one saw Angilia peering from the shadows on the staircase landing above, tears falling down her cheeks.

"Come with me, Eduardo," Eric said softly and led him to the chapel. Mitchell went to Alejandro and Juanita, putting his arms around them as he led them to a settee. While he comforted them, Eric sat on a pew and explained everything that had happened to Marisol: her leukemia diagnosis, the treatments, the warning that she had one and one half years at the most to live, the pregnancy that so delighted them both, the minute arrangements to keep her organs alive until Angilia's birth, her death, her being kept alive by machines, the C-section delivery of Angilia, and Marisol's burial. "We loved each other so much, Eduardo. We had four glorious years together. And we had Angilia."

Eduardo stood, walked to the altar, bowed his head, and cried. For more than thirty minutes he cried and grieved his sister, almost seventeen years after her death. He cried until he could cry no more tears. Finally, he wiped his face and turned to Eric. "I feared perhaps my parents would be dead by now. Never my sister. Strange, is it not, how fate decides the order of events?" He reached for Eric's hand, clasping it. "I am sorry, Eric. She loved you. The two of you should have lived many long years together. A husband's loss is much different from a brother's loss, yet we both loved her and we both grieve her."

Eric stood, pulling Eduardo to him in a tearful embrace as they shared their love and grief for Marisol. Eric knew that the full impact of the loss had not yet affected Eduardo. He had been through so many shocking moments and emotions over the past several days that his brain had not yet fully subsumed the loss. When it did, Eduardo would begin the grieving process in earnest and need his family's love and support.

"Let us return to our parents, Eric." Eric smiled at that—our parents. They were a family, the only five members of the family. Angilia called them a small but love-filled family. They were indeed. Today their number had increased by one again, and for that Eric thanked God. The two men reentered the foyer, smiling. Alejandro and Juanita smiled, too, and met them in another hug. Eduardo kissed his parents and told them that he loved them dearly.

He looked around the foyer again, the smile fading from his face after several seconds. He searched the shadows of the arches, the corners, apparently disappointed. He kept turning his head, seeking, examining, wondering. He looked upward and suddenly radiated with happiness. "There is my Angel," he proclaimed and sprinted up the staircase to her. Eduardo stared into her turquoise eyes as she looked into his brown eyes. A tear slid down her cheek. Eduardo embraced his niece, his sister's daughter, his savior. She was his Angel.

§§§§

"Eric, the requests keep pouring in by the hundreds, even with your statements and her refusals. They all want to talk to Angilia, and they just don't want to hear no. We keep telling them that she isn't speaking to anyone, that she isn't granting interviews, but they persist. We can keep doing this; that is not the issue. We can handle this on our end. That is not what concerns me," Carol said to Eric in his office two days later.

"I know. My fear is that they are going to stalk her every move now. The paparazzi are already staked out everywhere with their long lenses spying on her. I want them to leave her alone. I do not want them to do anything to her," Eric replied with a hint of anger in his voice.

"That's my fear, too. They want something from her. They are going to write and publish their stories with or without her consent or input. We know that. What if she wrote a statement? She can write whatever she wants, and we will release it to all of the media outlets and syndicates worldwide. That will give them something from her at least. They can have their quotes and fill their quota," Carol suggested.

Eric sighed. "Do you think that will really be enough? It won't, but it's all they are getting. I'll talk to her about it, Carol. Thank you." Eric stood, understanding public interest in the people involved in the hostage release. Angilia did, too, but she did not want to become the focus, the center, of this event. She did not want to shine a spotlight on what she said was her simple act of writing a letter. Eric appreciated her lack of narcissism. Angilia had not written to the Prime Minister to gain public attention. She had written so that the hostages would be freed and reunited with their families.

Eric walked downstairs and onto the back patio. Angilia and Eduardo had spent much of the past two days together, talking, listening to music, getting to know one another. He saw them in the distance, walking together in the summer sunshine. He headed toward them and after several minutes caught up with them. "You have replaced Matthew as Angilia's walking buddy," he smiled to Eduardo.

"I am trying to wrap my head around everything I am learning about my niece. A few days ago, I didn't know about her, and now I am amazed by her. But she does not like to talk about herself much, so I have to pull it out of her. She makes me use my journalism techniques," Eduardo commented with a teasing smile.

"It's actually ironic you say that. I want to talk with you about something, Angilia. The press is relentless. They want to hear from you. What if you issue a statement, your only public comment about this? Say whatever you feel is right. I know you do not want any of this to be about you, and I love you more for that. I do think if you give them something they will at least be pacified for now."

Angilia stood silent for a couple of minutes, forced to deal with the one effect of the hostage release she had never anticipated. She should have, she realized now, but she never imagined the intensity of the press attention. Helicopters flew day and night over the palace grounds, hoping for pictures. One buzzed nearby at that moment, but she and Eduardo had decided to behave as if it were not there. They would not let the paparazzi dictate their actions.

Her father believed a statement would ease some of this scrutiny. She trusted his judgment.

"All right. Let's get it done, then, and maybe they will leave us in peace," she finally said. The three of them returned to Eric's office, where she typed a statement and showed it to her father and uncle for their approval.

23 June 2012

I want to publicly thank His Excellency the Prime Minister of Israel for locating the ten Gulf War hostages and negotiating their release. I remain eternally grateful to His Excellency for his commitment and compassion in reuniting our families.

My family is exceptionally blessed to have my uncle with us again. He and I are enjoying getting to know one another. My family is complete. Our prayers have been answered in the most glorious way. Thank you for your concern and your kindness in providing us much-needed privacy during this joyous and emotional time.

"I like that last sentence especially," Eduardo said. "Thanking them for doing what they are not doing but should do is a clever tactic that should guilt them into backing off."

"Whatever you want to say is fine with me, Angel. Send it to Carol so she can release it immediately," Eric advised her. Angilia did so, and soon the press was buzzing, rushing to be the first to publish a story about the Princess' involvement using her exact words.

§§§§§

The following morning after breakfast, the royal family and the Taylors, with Daniel, Roger, Susan, Mike, and Tony, walked to Christ Church Valmondois for the first Mother's Day Service. Like the recent Father's Day Service, it too was broadcast live to every church in the country and via television for those who could not attend church. Reverend Hutchins greeted and blessed Eric, Angilia, Alejandro, Juanita, and Eduardo as they arrived, and the group followed him to the royal pews.

This morning they needed two of their front row pews, with Eric, Angilia, Eduardo, Juanita, Alejandro, and Mike taking one. Mitchell, Katherine, Matthew, Daniel, Roger, Susan, and Tony sat on the middle pew. Reverend Hutchins offered the benediction, followed by a hymn sung by the choir. The Reverend's sermon spoke about the anointed place and role of mothers throughout Christianity, beginning with Eve, the first wife and mother, to the Virgin Mary, to those mothers present that day in the churches of Valdavia.

At the conclusion of his sermon, Reverend Hutchins bowed to Angilia and stepped away from the podium. She squeezed her father's and uncle's hands and kissed their cheeks before she approached the podium. Eric noticed his daughter's unspoken tribute to her mother. Even the newscasters, Franklin and Laurie, commented on the Princess' striking appearance in their post-service commentary. Angilia wore an emerald-green dress printed with lilies-of-the-valley—the color of Marisol's birthstone and her birth month flower. Around her neck was the pearl necklace Alejandro had first given Marisol and then gifted Angilia earlier that year, the emerald clasp turned to the front. Pinned above her heart was the green agate cameo of Marisol that Eric had made for their daughter. Eduardo, too, recognized the significance of his niece's attire.

"Father's Day and Mother's Day are holidays that remind us what we should do each day, as commanded to us in the Bible. God set forth the Ten Commandments for his people to obey, the fifth stated clearly in Exodus 20:12. *'Honour thy father and thy mother: that thy days may be long upon the land which the Lord thy God giveth thee.'* Because some argue that the Old Testament was negated by the New Testament, we have Ephesians 6:1-3 to reiterate this commandment's importance. *'Children, obey your parents in the Lord: for this is right. Honour thy father and thy mother; which is the first commandment with promise; That it may be well with thee, and thou mayest live long on the earth.'*

"The Ten Commandments are God's laws that tell us how we should live. The first four commandments teach us how to love, respect, and obey God, who is or should be first in our lives above all others. The remaining six commandments teach us how to love and respect our fellow humankind. The placement of the fifth commandment remains significant, for we are instructed to honor our parents over all other people. In the hierarchy of the Ten Commandments, our parents come just after God in our lives, as they should.

"As Reverend Hutchins so eloquently stated, mothers are anointed by God. Their roles extend far beyond the obvious acts of giving birth, feeding, or soothing scraped knees. Our mothers show us love from our first spark of life. A mother's love, like God's, is eternal. Even when she is no longer with you physically, she is with you in all of the ways that matter most.

"I know that well, as many of you know, too. My mother's love was and still is tenacious and unyielding. All women make some sacrifices to become mothers, some more than others, but they all must give up part of their lives for their children. That alone merits the love, honor, and obedience God commands us to have for our mothers.

"Mothers are given special honor in the Bible, by none other than Solomon, in Proverbs 31:10-31. *'Who can find a virtuous woman? for her price is far above rubies. The heart of her husband doth safely trust in her, so that he shall have no need of spoil. She will do him good and not evil all the days of her life. She seeketh wool, and flax, and worketh willingly with her hands. She is like the merchants' ships; she bringeth her food from afar. She riseth also while it is yet night, and giveth meat to her household, and a portion to her maidens. She considereth a field, and buyeth it: with the fruit of her hands she planteth a vineyard. She girdeth her loins with strength, and strenghteneth her arms. She perceiveth that her merchandise is good: her candle goeth not out by night. She layeth her hands to the spindle, and her hands hold the distaff. She stretcheth out her hand to the poor; yea, she reacheth forth her hands to the needy. She is not afraid of the snow for her household: for all her household are clothed with scarlet. She maketh herself coverings of tapestry; her clothing is silk and purple. Her husband is known in the gates, where he sitteth among the elders of the land. She maketh fine linen, and selleth it; and delivereth girdles unto the merchant. Strength and honour are her clothing; and she shall rejoice in time to come. She openeth her mouth with wisdom; and in her tongue is the law of kindness. She looketh well to the ways of her household, and eateth not the bread of idleness. Her children arise up, and call her blessed; her husband also, and he praiseth her. Many daughters have done virtuously, but thou excellest them all. Favour is deceitful, and beauty is vain: but a woman that feareth the Lord, she shall be praised. Give her the fruit of her hands; and let her own works praise her in the gates.'*

"Solomon was blessed by God with a wise, kind, loving father and with a loving, protective, compassionate mother in David and Bathsheba, just as I am blessed by God with my amazing father and glorious mother. All of us have been blessed with parents who love, care for, and teach us. Please join me in a prayer for our beloved mothers."

The members of the congregation stood in unison and bowed their heads. Billy held his mother's hand. Matthew held Katherine's hand. Eduardo's right arm was around his mother. His left hand reached out for Eric's, a symbol of the woman they both loved and who bound them together forever, Marisol. Eric thought of his own mother who had died eleven years earlier and of his beautiful wife who had died before she could see her baby.

"Dear God: Thank you for your special gift of mothers and your eternal example of absolute love that they share with us, their children. Our mothers' love is a precious gift to us. In every way, our mothers devote and give their lives to us. Their influence and impact on us extends throughout the whole of our lives. Your divine blessings and love shelter our mothers infinitely. Our love and respect for our mothers are boundless. Please help them see and feel our love and your love for them. Amen."

The congregation repeated Angilia's amen and remained standing for the closing hymn, "Christ is Made the Sure Foundation." Eric and Eduardo held Angilia's hands during the hymn, and she sent a silent prayer of praise to God for making their family whole again. She knew her mother's spirit was in the church with them that day. She felt her mother just as if Marisol were tangibly holding her hand.

The receiving line after the service included Reverend Hutchins, Eric, Angilia, Alejandro, Juanita, and Eduardo. Many people told Angilia how much they remembered her mother and how proud Marisol was of her as she looked down from Heaven. They commended Eric, they welcomed Eduardo, and they blessed Alejandro and Juanita. When Katherine came through the line,

Angilia embraced her and wished her a joyful Mother's Day. Matthew shook Angilia's hand and slipped a note in her palm unbeknownst to and unseen by everyone.

The parishioners trickled out, leaving Reverend Hutchins and the royal party. Eric had already told the Reverend that they planned to stay for a while, so he blessed them and left them. Roger, Daniel, Susan, and the Taylors left and walked back to the palace, leaving the small family to pay their respects to Marisol and Eric's mother. Mike and Tony respectfully waited near the pews while Eric opened the vault door and turned on the light.

Eduardo held tightly to Angilia's hand as they followed Eric to Marisol's tomb. Though they all loved and missed her, Eduardo had just days before learned of her death and was just now grieving her. Angilia kissed his cheek and gently pulled her hand from his, leaving him alone with his sister. Juanita and Alejandro went to their son, crying with him, more for his pain than theirs.

After several minutes, Alejandro and Juanita quietly turned and told Eric they would return to the palace now. Eduardo needed to be alone with his sister's spirit now. Eric motioned for Tony to escort them home, and to call for the car if necessary. Angilia walked to her uncle, hugged him, and slipped a note under the plaque on her mother's tomb.

Eric joined her and they walked to his mother's tomb. Eric prayed, Angilia held his hand, and they smiled through their tear-filled eyes. They left the vault and walked outside to the churchyard. They stopped in front of his brother Patrick's grave and sat on a marble bench there. Eric looked at his brother's name and dates carved into the granite: *Patrick Alain David DeBruce Martineau, 6 January 1958 – 19 July 1977*. Nineteen years. Patrick's life had been only nineteen years in length. He had died far too young and far too soon. As if sensing his thoughts, Angilia put her arm around her father.

"Uncle Patrick lived his life to its fullest every moment with no regrets," she softly said without thinking first.

Eric looked at her, puzzled. He had never talked about his brother much for some reason. "What do you mean, Angel? How do you know this?"

Angilia took a deep breath and scolded herself silently. Soon. Not yet, but soon. Keep quiet until July 19. "Oh, I just feel it, that's all," she said, not lying. She did feel that and so much more. She would tell her father everything on July 19. Until then, she had to be very careful.

"You are right about one thing. He did live life to the fullest. He loved life and living. Some people exist, and some people live. Patrick lived. You would have liked each other, you and Patrick. You are like the proverbial oil and water, you two, different in many ways yet similar. You and he would have been great friends, Angilia. He was the sportsman and jokester to your academic and thoughtful nature. Yet he often had his introspective moments, what Mother called his dark moments. And you have your playful side. You and Patrick would have complemented each other perfectly. I so wish you could have met," Eric said with a half-smile as a tear fell from his eye.

Angilia brushed it from his cheek tenderly and had to force herself to wait just a few more weeks. If only her father knew. What would he think of the truth, of how much he instinctively seemed to know? She would find out soon enough. "I do, too, Daddy." That was true, too, of course. Patrick had died long before Angilia was born, and he was no longer living on earth then. Like her mother, Uncle Patrick lived in Heaven when Angilia was born.

Thirty minutes later Eduardo joined them on the bench. "I know I cannot undo or change the past. I do wish things had been different, I really do. To not know of this for seventeen years, to never expect this to happen, has been the most unnerving part of this experience. I am so very grateful to be free, to be with my family. I just wish I could have had a chance to see her again. But God planned things differently," Eduardo sighed. "You have made me so very happy, Angilia. Truly happy."

"I think I have something that will make you all happy," Eric said with a smile as he stood. "Come. Let's return home so I can share my surprise with everyone." Eric locked the vault and the three of them walked slowly back home, followed by Mike.

Eric leaned down and asked Angilia, "What did that boy give you?"

"What boy? Oh, you mean Matthew. I don't know." She pulled it from her purse and unfolded the piece of paper. "Just a note," she said and handed it to her father.

Eric handed it back to her and rolled his eyes. "I thought he was a bit more mature than to write notes during church."

"He wrote a love note to her during church? She is just a child," Eduardo said with a touch of anger in his voice.

"What? Good grief, Uncle Eduardo, no. The note says the service was sweet and charming."

"Sweet and charming? What man writes that?" Eduardo asked. "Sounds like a love note in disguise, if you ask me." Eric took a deep breath. God help me, he silently prayed. Everyone, even Eduardo, saw it plainly except for Angilia. Matthew better slow it down, Eric thought. Way down.

§§§§

Everyone gathered in the dining room for lunch, and when they finished, Eric announced his afternoon plan. "All right, everyone, let's change into casual clothes and meet in the media room. I have something very special to share with you, and today is the perfect day."

Eric changed into jeans and a shirt, then went to his office and locked the door. He unlocked a cabinet built into the bookcase, and then opened the safe. He reached into a small box and removed a DVD. He locked everything and went to the basement (what centuries earlier was the dungeon) media room, a private theatre where he and Angilia watched films together.

Everyone settled into upholstered chairs, Eduardo choosing to sit next to Angilia. His parents sat next to him, and the Taylors sat behind Eric, Angilia, and Eduardo. Roger, Daniel, and Susan sat near the Taylors. No one knew what Eric wanted to show them, and they waited for him to begin. Eric prepared the equipment and had the DVD ready to play, the remote control firmly in his hand.

"No one has seen these. I have not watched them since they were made. I had several backup copies made many years ago, and one copy will belong to Eduardo and his—our—parents." Eric looked at his daughter. "These were made especially for you, my beautiful daughter Angilia, gifts of love from your mother and me. Today really is the absolute perfect day to give them to you."

Eric sat next to Angilia, holding her close to him. He knew she would treasure these, but that this would be extremely emotional for her. She had talked about many of these events or moments, though this would complete her memories, adding dimension to her auditory memories. She heard everything when she was in utero, and she remembered it all vividly. She obviously never saw anything then, though that was about to change.

Eric smiled at her, took a deep breath, and pushed the remote's play button. The screen showed a wall in Eric's suite, and Marisol's voice was heard. "Eric, you really mean to record my entire pregnancy? I am not the first woman to have a baby, you know. Can you at least wait for me to freshen up before you aim that camera at me?"

"Mommy," Angilia whispered. "The day of her pregnancy test." Eduardo gasped when he heard his sister's voice, and again when he heard his niece's comment. Eric smiled at him and nodded, as if to tell him that Angilia was right.

Marisol appeared, in full view, smiling at her husband, who held the camcorder. Her black hair cascaded to her shoulders in soft waves, and her brown eyes shone and sparkled. Eric's hand was seen waving at his wife while she giggled and waved back. Eric's hand touched Marisol's slender belly, and he said—for the first time—"Hello my beautiful daughter Angilia." Angilia remembered how warm she felt when she heard him say that for the first time. He knew her. Her father knew her. Angilia smiled and kissed Eric's cheek, snuggling closer to him.

"I just had the pregnancy test and you already know our baby is a girl. And you have already named her. What if you are wrong?"

"I'm not. I know her." His voice was soft, tender, and full of love.

"She is much loved," Marisol replied. The video showed them kiss, and then the screen went dark for a moment. Eduardo smiled at Eric, grateful to see moments of his sister's life, moments he had missed, moments of love and happiness.

More scenes followed, showing Eric and Marisol shopping for baby clothes, nursery furniture, bedroom furniture, toys, books, movies, anything and everything. The couple was shown decorating her suite, supervising wallpaper hangers, painters, carpet installers, and arranging furniture. Everyone watching recognized the suite, for it was still the same. Angilia had the same custom made furniture, the same wallpaper, the same curtains, everything still the same. Apparently, the suite they created for her really did suit her taste.

Other scenes showed Marisol at doctor appointments, including the ultrasound. The nurse was heard asking if they wanted to confirm that the baby was a girl, and they said no. "She is so tiny and perfect," Eric said in awe as the camcorder zoomed into the ultrasound screen. "I love you, Angilia."

Angilia smiled at her father, knowing what everyone would see next. Sure enough, they were amazed by what they saw. "Did she . . . ? Play that part again, Eric, please. Mitchell, have you ever seen that happen before?" Katherine asked her husband, who reminded her he was not an OB-GYN. Juanita and Alejandro were not sure they had seen what they thought they saw.

Eric smiled and replayed that scene. "Unbelievable. She did wave at you. Everyone else saw that, right?" Katherine asked, looking from person to person. Juanita was sobbing, Eduardo was staring at his niece, and Matthew was dumbfounded. "Is this normal?" Katherine asked her husband and son.

"I don't know, Mom, I'm a cardiologist." Normal for Angilia was not the normal assigned to most people, Matthew realized.

"Keep watching," Eric said and hit the play button again. Marisol was heard excitedly describing what they had just seen, and the nurse tried to explain it as normal reflexes. Marisol argued, disagreeing with the nurse, saying that she felt her baby respond to Eric all the time.

At her silent urging, Eric talked to Angilia, telling her how much he loved her, how much he looked forward to holding her. Both tiny arms reached for him, in his direction, and Marisol said she could feel her daughter pushing on her as if trying to break free. No one watching could deny that Angilia did indeed recognize and respond to her father's voice. Juanita, Alejandro, Katherine, and Susan were crying. So was Eric, tears trickling down his cheeks.

Other similar moments were captured, of Eric reading to Angilia while Marisol sat in a chair, and her commenting on how their daughter was very active when she heard Eric's voice, pushing against Marisol and trying to get to him. Every time it happened, Marisol was amazed, saying that there was already a very special love and bond between her husband and her daughter. Once, she remarked that none of the pregnancy and childbirth books she had read mentioned anything like this. Eric laughed and said, "That's because there is no one else like our Angilia." Everyone in the room agreed with Eric, particularly her grandparents.

The following segment showed Marisol in bed early one morning, her voice a whisper. "Good morning, Angilia. Usually your Daddy has this camera glued to his hand and I can never record anything." People laughed at that, knowing how true it was. "I just want to tell you how very happy I am to have you here with me. I love you so much. Your Daddy loves you, you already know that," Marisol softly said as the camera turned from her face to show Eric asleep. His head was on her right shoulder, his hand on her belly. "He is holding you. See," she whispered, and showed Eric's hand on her belly, now in the sixth month of her pregnancy. The camera returned to Eric's face.

"Angilia, we are both so very happy, happy because of you. You make us happier than we ever thought we could feel. I want to tell you that I love you, my baby girl, and I will always live in your heart. Where you are, so will I be. Always and forever."

Eric woke up, sleepily smiled at the camera and waved. "Good morning, beautiful wife," he said and then kissed her. Marisol kept the camera on him as he said, "Good morning, my Angel," and kissed her belly, kissed Angilia. "I love you both, Marisol and Angilia. I am the most blessed man who ever lived."

Eduardo held Angilia's hand, crying, and Juanita hugged him through her own tears. Everyone was crying, even the men, seeing the love so vibrant it was practically tangible. Angilia remembered hearing her mother's soft-spoken words that morning, and her father's, but seeing them and their love was the most precious gift. She hugged her father, wondering if she would be so blessed to find a love as true and lasting as her parents' love.

Eric pulled his daughter closer, knowing what they would see next. The camera was now on a tripod and the first sight was of Eric taking his seat next to a hospital bed. The entire day, Eric stayed in that room, the sound of machines in the background, machines that kept his wife's organs functioning. Marisol had died the previous day and her explicit plan put into motion immediately. She had insisted that their baby be delivered at full term to avoid any potential problems or complications. Now Eric visited his baby in a private hospital room.

Throughout the remainder of the pregnancy, the final trimester, his days were similar to that day for the most part. "Good morning, my beautiful daughter Angilia. I love you." Those watching saw his hand gently caress Marisol's stomach, and a smile spread across Eric's face when he felt her move at the sound of his voice.

Angilia looked at the screen and smiled, tears shining in her eyes. "This is when you gave me Little Bear," she said.

Eric squeezed her shoulder, while on the screen he took a teddy bear from the bag he had brought. "Angel, Daddy brought you a special friend who will stay with you forever, even when I cannot be here. Little Bear will stay right here beside you, baby." Eric patted Marisol's stomach with the bear's paw and then sat it beside her near Angilia.

Eric read <u>Winnie-the-Pooh</u> to her, his voice full of inflections and emotions. When he finished, they heard him say, "Perhaps Little Bear will become your Pooh Bear. I love you so very much, Angilia. Somehow I feel I have known and loved you for so long. You are my life, my love, my sunshine."

Angilia gasped audibly and beamed at her father. "This is why, Daddy. This moment." She nudged her uncle's elbow and moved closer to her father. Within seconds everyone knew why she was so excited. On the video, Eric softly sang "Sunshine on My Shoulders" to his baby girl for the first time. Angilia had heard him sing to her, and she loved him, she knew that even then. But now she saw him in that moment nearly seventeen years earlier. She leaned her head on his shoulder and cried tears of true happiness. Juanita, Katherine, and Susan were crying again, too, which they did frequently that afternoon.

They all watched Eric on the screen, and when the song ended he said, "I love you, Angel," leaned over, and kissed Marisol's stomach. They saw him smile as he leaned over his wife, pressing his face to her stomach. They noticed a tear fall from his eye. "I feel you, Angel. I can feel your tiny hands, baby, yes I can. Daddy loves you." Juanita sobbed, leaning against her son, overcome with emotions.

Angilia smiled at her father and reached her hand up to his cheek. "That is what I was doing, Daddy. I felt you and you felt me. I knew that. I love you, Daddy." He kissed her nose, something he had often done, and smiled. Most of the days that followed were very similar, eliciting oohs and aahs and tears.

Eric suddenly paused the DVD, aware of what was next. Angilia sensed it, and said, "It's all right, Daddy. It happened. But I'm right here." She leaned across him and pushed the play button. That day's segment began like most, with Eric greeting her, reading to her, and singing to her. They heard him talking to her and then, as he did, saw him jump when the monitors in the room signaled a problem.

Matthew sat bolt upright and uttered, "Oh, no." He knew that sound and what it meant. He watched in disbelief as nurses and doctors rushed in, a nurse getting Angilia's image on the ultrasound, a doctor demanding a syringe of epinephrine immediately. He saw Eric, hands pressed to his face, crying, moaning, terrified. He heard Eric's frantic pleas to his baby to not leave him—just as he had heard Eric plead with her as he ran to them that day in March.

Eric moaned as he watched. Mitchell did, too. Matthew muttered. Angilia held her father close to her. Dr. Jamieson took the syringe and viciously stabbed Angilia directly in the heart with the needle. The force was cruel and painful, Matthew thought. Now Eric could see the man's hatred.

They breathlessly watched Eric's hands cover his baby, Marisol's stomach, and heard the heart monitor stabilize. They heard Eric's sobs. They heard Dr. Jamieson grunt and saw him rush from the room with no concern for Eric or his baby. They were enthralled when Eric's tears turned to a smile as he pressed his hands over his baby. "Hello my beautiful daughter Angilia. I feel you again, baby. I love you more than you will ever know."

As that scene ended there, Angilia leaned close to her father and said, "I do know, Daddy. I have always known."

Two more weeks' worth of typical days in the hospital room, with songs, books, toys, and talks followed before the climactic day when Angilia was born, January 3, 1996. Susan held the camcorder that day, while Eric stood next to Marisol, Roger and Daniel on either side of him for moral support. Marisol's OB-GYN performed a Caesarian section, and everyone noticed that Eric held his wife's hand during the procedure. Juanita and Eduardo cried softly as they watched, even more so when Eric said, "Soon, Angilia, very soon, we will meet."

Dr. Jamieson positioned himself and grabbed Angilia immediately after she was cleaned. When she was born, his was the first face she saw; his was the first voice she heard. Jamieson looked at her and said, "Welcome to the world, Valdavia's new princess."

She began screaming and crying, not as newborns cry, but in terror. Her arms and legs flailed as if she were trying to get away. The baby they saw looked distressed, and now most of them knew why.

Angilia smiled at her father, though, remembering what happened next. Everyone was amazed to see Eric reach over and gently take her from Jamieson. He cradled her in his hands, her tiny body not much bigger than his two hands. Eric smiled at her and said, "Hello my beautiful daughter Angilia." She instantly stopped crying and screaming. She recognized her father.

The camera captured newborn Angilia smile at her father and reach a tiny hand to his cheek, as she had tried to do for many months from the womb. Eric kissed her forehead, both of her cheeks, and her nose. He held her tenderly against the warmth of his chest. Angilia put both of her hands on his face and smiled up at him.

Roger and Daniel, everyone saw, were stunned by her reaction to her father. "It's like she knows you already," Roger said. "Do newborns usually have that much hair?" he asked no one in particular. Everyone watching giggled. They all saw her golden curls. Susan was sobbing, they could hear, just as she was as she watched the birth for the first time in over sixteen years.

"Her eyes," Daniel said. "She has your eyes, Eric."

Eric smiled, never looking at anyone except his daughter. "I know. She is my little Angel. And I love her more than life." Eric's tears fell as he looked at his precious baby, knowing that the next day they would bury Marisol.

The next scene was of Alejandro and Juanita with their newborn granddaughter, who was dressed in a pink onesie. They and Eric marveled at her beauty, with her thick golden curls, fair skin, turquoise eyes, and pink lips. Alejandro kissed her cheek and she giggled. "Your mustache tickles her. Stop that," Juanita told him. Her first afternoon was spent in the arms of her small, love-filled family.

Eric took her home the next morning, as she was in perfect health, and fed her as he sat on the chair in her bedroom. A short time later, he dressed her in a white gown for her mother's burial. As he dressed her, Eric told her that her mother loved her very much. He wrapped her in a white angora blanket and carried her to the church accompanied by Alejandro, Juanita, Roger, Daniel, and Susan. The burial service was not recorded, although Angilia had described it when she was in the hospital.

When they returned home, he fed her again, holding her cradled in his arm. He talked to her for a while, and then placed her in the center of her canopy bed for a nap. He curled up beside her, encircling her with his body and arms, shielding her, protecting her. Baby Angilia stared into his eyes until she fell asleep. Matthew's breath caught in his throat. That is how she had looked at her father while she was in the hospital after her surgery. She had stared at him until her exhausted body fell asleep.

The camera recorded Eric watching her sleep, smiling, kissing her head a few times. Katherine sobbed when they saw Angilia's tiny hand wrap around one of Eric's fingers and hold it the entire time she slept. She slept peacefully, never moving or fussing. After close to two hours, she woke up and rubbed her face with her other hand, never letting go of Eric's finger. Eric smiled and said, "Hello my beautiful daughter Angilia." Those watching gushed when they saw her open her eyes, smile at him, and put her hands on his cheeks. She made a sound, which Mitchell swore sounded like "Daddy," although he kept that to himself. Newborn babies do not talk, he scolded himself. Eric leaned over and kissed her nose, Angilia cooed and clapped her hands, and Eric laughed.

Despite the highly-charged emotional day, he was joyous and so full of love. "I love you so much, Angel, my miracle, my sunshine," he told his baby. Sixteen year old Angilia smiled, because her Daddy sang "Sunshine on My Shoulders" to her that day. Everyone in the media room truly understood why she had asked Eric to record that song in March.

The home movies ended, and each person felt the love and bond between father and daughter more than ever. Eduardo smiled at Eric and thanked him. "My sister was very happy and much loved. Her life with you was all about love. I will always miss her, as you will, but I am not sad any longer. Thank you, Eric." Eric pulled his brother-in-law into a hug and patted his back.

Eduardo looked at Angilia, his eyes betraying his astonishment. "You are very special. There is something otherworldly about you. You truly have what they call an old soul. I saw it in the home movies. You have never been like other people. Your father called you a miracle, and he is right."

Matthew had said something similar to Eric when they were in Oxford. Angilia was special, different, and otherworldly. There was something quite hauntingly familiar about her that excited and scared him. She was so wise in many ways, so mature, yet so inexperienced and unaware in other ways and such a child. Angilia was an enigma, and Matthew was fascinated by her.

§§§§

On Tuesday morning, Eric awoke to find a card and three flowers on the chair in his bedroom. He picked up the flowers that were tied together with a white ribbon. One lily, Marisol's birth month flower; one chrysanthemum, Eric's birth month flower; and one rose, the June flower. All three were white, symbolizing pure, true love. He smiled and opened the card.

'*Happy Anniversary, Mommy and Daddy*' was inscribed on the front, as was the date of their wedding, 26 June 1991. Inside was a note from their daughter. Eric held it to his chest and walked to the balcony, looked toward Heaven, and smiled. "Our little girl is remarkable, Marisol. I love her, you always knew that. I know how much you love her, too. She loves us both. I hope you feel her love. She feels yours. Happy 21st anniversary, dear. I love you for all eternity."

CHAPTER 7

"Happy birthday, Abuela!!" Angilia proclaimed when she entered the sitting room where everyone else was already seated. She hugged her grandmother while the chef placed a cake on the table.

"What is this, mi nieta? A surprise party at my age?"

"Of course, Mamá," Eric said. "We love you. Happy birthday." He kissed her cheek as Eduardo smiled and approached his mother.

"I have waited so long to say this to you again, Mamá. Happy birthday. I love you so much," Eduardo told her while he hugged her tightly. He handed his mother a gift, his first in twenty-two years. Juanita opened the box to find a mother's ring with four stones: emerald, citrine, aquamarine, and garnet.

"My children and granddaughter. How beautiful, mi hijo. I treasure this always." She kissed her beloved son, tears falling down both of their faces.

Alejandro gave his wife a bracelet that matched her new ring. "Mi marido y mi hijo, gracias. Muchas gracias. These are very special. I have my dear family with me always. I look at this and see each of you."

Eric smiled. Juanita was 82 years old now. Angilia had wanted her grandparents' remaining years to contain as much peace and happiness as possible, and with Eduardo's return that was assured. Whatever years God still planned for Juanita would be happy and love-filled. He picked up a wrapped present and handed it to his mother-in-law with a loving kiss on both cheeks.

"I am getting spoiled today, mi hijo," she smiled.

"You deserve to be spoiled, Mamá," Eric assured her.

She gasped when she saw a fine porcelain figurine nestled in protective foam inside the gold box. "Oh! Never have I seen anything so beautiful, mi hijo! She is so beautiful. Thank you. You know I love her." She grabbed Eric in a hug, her eyes shining with tears. "My hands are shaking too much, I am afraid to touch her. Will you take her out please?" She handed the box to Eric and he carefully removed the figurine and stood it on the table between the sofas.

"Oh my gosh! She is so lifelike. She looks just like the portrait in the museum," Katherine said. "That looks like a Lladró. Oh, it's gorgeous."

"I bought three of them. Now I can display mine in the bookcase in my office," Eric smiled at his daughter, who was blushing. "It is Lladró. I like her," he winked, which made Angilia blush more. The figurine depicted her in the gown and pose from her 16th birthday portrait.

"I like her, too, mi hijo," Juanita said and hugged Angilia. "You do not look that way, so embarrassed, mi nieta. This is a great honor, and the first of many. I just want to live long enough to get your bridal figurine," she smiled.

Matthew nearly turned over his tea cup, tea spilling into the saucer. Mitchell looked at his son, wondering how long this would linger. Eric cleared his throat and decided to change the subject. "Speaking of Angilia, she has something for you, too, Mamá. Don't you, Angel?"

Angilia nodded, picked up her gift, and handed it to her grandmother, her face displaying her nervousness. What if her gift somehow offended or hurt Abuela? Maybe she should not have done this. It was too late, though, for Juanita was tearing the wrapping paper. Angilia clasped her father's arm and stood behind him. He felt her heart pounding and put his arm around her. Why was she so anxious?

Juanita's hands covered her face, tears fell from her eyes, and she whispered her daughter's name. Eric was confused and concerned, especially when Angilia's grip tightened and she sobbed a whispered, "I'm so sorry." Eric looked from his daughter to his mother-in-law. Juanita clutched the large box to her chest and cried inconsolably. Alejandro and Eduardo sat on either side of her, trying to comfort her. Eric walked to her, leaned over the back of the sofa, and asked her what was wrong. He did not see Angilia leave the room.

"I am sorry. This is so beautiful and wonderful. I am overcome with happiness is all. I cannot believe mi nieta made something this beautiful." She held the box so that Alejandro, Eduardo, and Eric could see what Angilia had given to her. Eduardo gasped and took the box. He ran his finger along his sister's face and smiled.

"She is just like Marisol, exactly like Marisol," Eduardo said through tears. "This is beautiful, Mamá." Alejandro smiled and agreed with his wife and son.

Eric was staggered and reached for the box. Inside, resting on white tissue paper, was a framed oil paint portrait of Marisol on an 11 inch by 14 inch canvas. In the lower right corner, Eric saw a small *Angilia 2012*. She had not copied a picture of her mother, but had painted from her memories and sense of her mother to capture Marisol beautifully and perfectly. Eric noticed the glint in his wife's eyes, the same glint that had drawn him to her that long-ago evening at the cancer benefit. "This is stunning, Mamá. I had not seen this before. You kept this well-hidden from us all, Angilia," Eric said and turned to his daughter, only to find her gone.

"Where is she? Angilia?" Eric appeared confused and concerned. Juanita turned, disappointed that her granddaughter had left the party. Eric handed the portrait back to Juanita and patted her shoulder. "I'll go check on her and we'll be back in a moment to continue your party, Mamá."

Eric rushed to Angilia's suite, and was slightly puzzled that she was not there. What had happened? She had seemed upset after she handed her grandmother the present. Why? Eric stood, hands on his hips, trying to figure out where Angilia could have gone. He rushed up the east staircase to the watch tower, a place she enjoyed. She was not there, either. Eric ran downstairs to the chapel, her other favorite place, but no one was there.

Finally he knew. He remembered what she had said several years earlier when he had looked in every room for her. She had been in the last room he had searched, the last place he had expected to find her. She had called it her Thoughtful Place. Eric ran back to the third floor, to the east wing, and saw his brother Patrick's suite door halfway open.

Eric peeked in and saw her sitting in Patrick's large brown chair, her head bowed. "Can I join you?" he softly asked her. She nodded, and he sat beside her. "What upset you?"

"It was wrong."

"What? Your portrait of Mommy?"

Angilia nodded. "It hurt Abuela. I should have never done it. I never considered how it would affect her. My vanity overrode my common sense and my concern for Abuela. Vanity is a mortal sin, and I let it take control of me. It's like I flaunted what I did and never once thought about Abuela."

"Why did you paint it in the first place?" Eric asked her, knowing the truth. "Did you do it intending to hurt Abuela?"

"No. But I did."

"No, you did not. She was crying because she was overcome with joy when she saw the portrait of her daughter. Isn't that why you painted Mommy? To make Abuela happy?" Angilia nodded. "You did. Eduardo, Abuelo, and I love it, too, really we do. It's the most beautiful portrait of my wife I have ever seen. She is just as I remember her, vibrant, full of spark, and lovely."

"Abuela is not upset?"

"No one is upset. Let's go back to the party, Angel." They walked down to the second floor and returned to the sitting room.

Juanita stood and went to her granddaughter, embraced her, and whispered in her ear. "Mi Marisol is as beautiful as I remember her, mi nieta. You have given me the most wonderful gift I have ever received. Muchas gracias."

Angilia smiled at her grandmother, kissed her cheek, and whispered to her. "That is how I see her, Abuela. I love her so much, and I love you very much. Always and forever, I love you both."

§§§§§

3 July 2012

Today Abuela celebrated her 82nd birthday. I love her so very much, and I am so grateful that Uncle Eduardo is with her and Abuelo now. They love each other dearly, and they are so happy. I feel blessed just watching them together. However, I am ashamed of my behavior during her surprise party. I was rude and selfish. I panicked and thought the painting of Mommy would cause them pain. I ran away like an insolent little girl. Daddy had to leave the party just to find me and take me back to the party. Regardless of their reaction, I should have stayed and dealt with whatever happened. I have so very much to learn and much to change within myself.

Friday, I want to talk with Daddy about the two of us going to the country house soon. I want and need to share everything with him, and I think we need to be alone, away from everyone else for a few days. There is so much to reveal to him, and I know it will not be easy for anyone to accept. I hope his calendar is open for those few days so that we can do this on the perfect date.

§§§§§

Angilia stepped into her father's office Friday morning as she had planned. "Daddy? Do you have a few minutes?"

Eric smiled up at her. "For you, always. You look serious."

She sat in the chair next to his desk. "I just want to ask what your schedule is like the week of the 16th."

Eric opened his calendar on his computer and looked at the week of July 16. "Nothing important necessarily. Why? What are you planning?"

"I thought we could go to the country house for a few days that week, just the two of us." Angilia looked at him, her eyes telling Eric how important this was to her.

"Just the two of us? That means you won't be here on the 19th."

"I know. I go there at least once a week, though, early in the morning before anyone else is awake."

"You really want to go that week?" She nodded. "We can leave late on the afternoon of the 17th and return on the afternoon of the 22nd. How does that sound?"

Angilia smiled, and Eric saw the hint of tears in her eyes. "That sounds wonderful." She stood and hugged him. "Thank you, Daddy."

§§§§§

The sunrise news the following Monday stunned Eric as he listened while shaving. "A group of local citizens calling themselves the Jubilee Committee issued a press release this morning. The 20th Jubilee for King Eric will take place the week of August 19 through August 25, with special events planned and scheduled for each of the seven days. A detailed agenda is forthcoming, and the Committee promises that the week-long festivities to honor His Majesty will be exciting, fun, and full of surprises." Eric quickly finished, dressed, and texted Carol. She was still eating breakfast at her house, she replied, and had just heard the news herself. She was equally surprised, she told Eric.

Roger rushed to Eric and asked him what was going on, since Eric had said an emphatic no to the jubilee. "I don't know, Roger. I'm flattered that they want to do this, but they don't need to spend their own money on this, either. Heck, I'll pay for a party if it will make them happy, but this is a bit much." Angilia listened from her doorway, and quickly joined her father and Roger as they walked downstairs to breakfast.

"Oh, let them, Daddy. They want to do this. What can it hurt?" Angilia smiled up at him.

"Maybe they did some fundraising or took donations in their businesses or something. Or maybe they have a wealthy donor," Roger added.

"Maybe," Angilia agreed, never wanting her father to know she had donated. She wanted to do this, and he deserved this. "Just let them do this for you. They obviously want to, Daddy, and they are determined to have the Jubilee."

"All right, Angel. I still say it's a waste of money, though." Angilia smiled, knowing the Jubilee would be incredible. She looked forward to the week of celebrations to publicly honor her father across the country. She had told the Committee members that no one deserved this honor more than her father did, and she meant that. They had informed her of their plans and progress at least once each week, and she had known the announcement was coming this morning.

Angilia smiled throughout breakfast, elated that her father would have a week-long celebration, whether he felt it necessary or not. His lack of ego made her love him even more, if that were possible. He truly was as close to perfect as any man could get. She had loved him far longer than he realized, although that would soon change.

§§§§

Tuesday afternoon, Eric packed a suitcase with Daniel's assistance. Roger came in, too. "Are you sure you don't want at least one security officer to follow in another car? I mean, after everything, do you think it's wise to go without security?"

Eric smiled at his friend. "I'm sure. We're fine now. Angilia is the one who said she wanted us to go alone. She isn't afraid anymore. We need a few days to ourselves." Eric picked up his suitcase. "Don't call my cell phone unless it is absolutely urgent.

We'll come back Sunday afternoon." His friends smiled and wished him a relaxing, wonderful week with his daughter.

Angilia had a suitcase and small carryall waiting in the hallway outside her suite. Matthew handed her a tiny bottle with a few pain pills in case she needed them. She smiled and put them in her tote bag. Would she ever share with him what she would reveal to her father in a couple of days? Time would tell.

Eric picked up her suitcase and lifted the carryall. "What have you got in here? Do you need all of these books for just a few days?"

"Yes. They are very important. I can carry them."

Matthew took the carryall from Eric. "I will," he said and walked with them to the garage. Eric unlocked the Aston Martin's trunk and placed the suitcases inside, and then Matthew sat the carryall in. "Remember, if you have any pain, take one of the pills I gave you. Call me if you need anything."

"I will. Thank you." Angilia slid into the passenger seat; Eric closed her door, and then got behind the wheel. They waved at Matthew and were soon on their way to their country house. Once they were out of the city proper, they were surrounded by lush hills and trees. The convertible top was down, and Angilia breathed in the fresh air.

"Thank you, Daddy. The next few days are going to be very special for us."

Eric smiled at her, his turquoise eyes hidden behind dark sunglasses. He knew she had something planned, but did not want to ask her any questions about it and spoil her surprise. "Yes, they will, Angel. Just you and me, completely free to do whatever we want to do. I don't remember the last time we went away together, just the two of us. You do, though," he giggled.

"I do. Five years ago after I graduated, we went to Spain for a couple of weeks to visit Abuela and Abuelo. We didn't take anyone else with us. That was wonderful."

"Oh, yes, I remember now. It's been five years? We're long overdue for some alone time. I'm glad you brought it up."

For the next few hours, they enjoyed the breeze as the car twisted and turned along the highway through the countryside. Eric turned on the radio, and soon the sound of his voice filled the air. He groaned and reached for the dial, but Angilia grabbed his hand. "Please don't turn it off." He looked at her, leaning back against the seat looking at him with that smile that always melted his heart. He shrugged and let the song play. It was the least he could do for her.

At dusk, Eric lowered the convertible top. They were almost at their house. "What do we want for dinner?" he asked her. "If everything's the same as it was last time we came, there is a Chinese restaurant, a steakhouse, a diner, and a pizza parlor in the area. What about some take-out so we can sit at home together and eat?" She nodded, and they decided on pizza. Eric pulled into the pizza parlor's parking lot, and came out twenty minutes later with a pizza, some breadsticks, and some sodas. Angilia held the food on her lap for the short drive to their house.

Soon they were there, safely locked behind their iron gate, and settling in. Eric got their bags and drinks from the trunk while Angilia got plates, cups, and napkins from the kitchen and set an informal table in the living room. They watched old Hollywood films on the movie channel while they ate, enjoying the freedom and informality that most people took for granted. There was always someone else around, whether a security officer or a staff member. They understood the need for that, but treasured their very rare times truly alone.

As the day neared its end, Angilia pulled her 2012 diary and a pen from her tote bag and wrote the day's entry while curled up on the sofa next to her father. Her heart trembled when she wrote that early Thursday morning she would begin her revelation. Her father would know everything about her, some of which she suspected he knew or remembered, even if it was latent at the moment. If the memories were there, they would resurface, and he would understand so much more about her and about them.

§§§§

Eric and Angilia spent Wednesday doing things they enjoyed, driving to a market for a few things for meals, strolling through the woods that bordered their property, playing old board games, and talking. Eric plugged in his old turntable and played records that afternoon, and they sang along to the songs. They collapsed into a giggling heap on the floor. Angilia picked up a piece of paper from the notepad on the telephone table and sketched her father quickly, capturing his brilliant smile and happy eyes with a pencil.

Eric glanced at the sketch as she finished, and smiled at her. "You used to draw all the time when we came here. I don't know how many sketch pads you must have filled. What happened to them?"

"They are in the toy box in the play room. That's where I always put them when we packed and got ready to leave here," she told him.

"I haven't been in that playroom since you went to university," he said and then laughed. "That sounds so bizarre. You should still be in high school at your age. You are so wise and mature in many ways, but you are still my little girl. Come on. Let's go in the play room for a while."

He took her hand and led her to the play room next to his bedroom at the back of the house. Her doll house, the stuffed animals, everything so neat and in its place, brought back so many memories of them sitting on the carpeted floor playing. Eric and Marisol had designed the house as a private sanctuary for their impending family, and the architect had just completed the house weeks before Marisol's death. Eric had brought his daughter there every summer of her life.

Eric kneeled on the floor in front of the toy box and lifted the lid. Angilia sat next to him and reached inside for some sketch books. "Which one is your first one?" he asked her. She flipped through them and found one with the year 1999 written inside the cover in pink crayon. She handed it to her father with a smile.

"What are you looking for?"

"Nothing in particular. I just want to see them again. We had so much fun here." He smiled as he slowly turned the pages. She had started drawing young, and he relished reliving the world as his three-year-old daughter had seen it. He stopped at a page filled with bright sunshine and flowers, butterflies and birds. Her world was filled with beauty, even though Jamieson was mistreating and threatening her at the time. She may have feared for Eric's life, but she never let that monster destroy how she saw the world. For that, Eric was immensely grateful, and Angilia saw pure happiness in his eyes.

"I want these. I want to look at them, I want to enjoy them, and I want to keep them with me." He looked at her. "May I have them?"

"Of course you can, if you want them. I haven't looked at them in years. They are just filled with my perspective of the world, nothing earth-shattering."

"Oh, yes, they are. To me they are. To me they are part of you. And they mean so much more now, because they show me that you really do see beauty even when there is darkness and ugliness. You saw a beautiful world even during all of those years you lived with the fear and terror of that evil man. There is no reflection of that in these sketchbooks. There is only beauty and peace. You are truly remarkable and breathtaking, Angilia. As much as you refer to Anne Frank's diary and her hopefulness and belief in goodness, you are just as much a beacon."

Angilia smiled at her father. He did not recognize the connection at all. "You don't see it. All that time they were hiding, she had one person who constantly believed in her, encouraged her, taught her about love, and showed her love. Otto Frank, her father. I have you. You are the light, the hope, and the love that always helps me through whatever happens. With you, there is no ugliness, not really. She and I share that, just as Solomon and I do. Our fathers."

Eric did not even attempt to stop his tears. He and Angilia held each other, sharing the truest, purest, most blessed love they would ever know. "I love you so much, Angel. I do not know why

God blessed me with you, but he did. There are many times when I feel like I have known you far longer than you know. Far longer. Maybe you have been part of me for my entire life."

"I love you more than you know, Daddy." You will remember just how long we have been together, and you will learn all about me, tomorrow. It all began for us on that date, she thought. Eric would learn and remember everything on the anniversary of his brother's death.

§§§§§

19 July 2012

Today Daddy learns everything about me. Whatever he knows will either come out or be awakened. Thirty-five years ago today, Uncle Patrick died. Daddy has to remember that day, even though he never has talked about it. I know how painful that day was for him, and it breaks my heart to remember him hurting so. I also know he did not forget one moment of that day. He could never forget. He will wake up soon, and I will put it all before him. No more secrets.

§§§§§

"Good morning, my beautiful daughter Angilia," Eric said with a smile when he stepped into the kitchen. He kissed her cheek as she sat at the island sipping chamomile tea.

"Good morning, Daddy." He made a cup of coffee, got a croissant, and sat across from her. "Daddy, may I ask you something?" He nodded as he chewed a bite of his pastry. "You have said that to me since the day of Mommy's pregnancy test. How did you know?"

"Know what?"

"That I was a girl, that I was Angilia, that I was me. You had not seen me yet, so you had no idea what I looked like. How did you know it was me?"

Eric took a deep breath, unprepared for her question. What could he say to her? How had he known? He knew the answer, but

242

he never liked to revisit that day in his memories. It was still too painful. "I just knew, Angel. I just knew it was you."

"How? What made you one hundred percent sure?"

She persisted, and he realized he needed to tell her. "I have said before that I feel that we have known each other for far longer than seventeen years. I've never told anyone about this, about the day Patrick died. People would think I was crazy if I did."

Angilia's heart pounded. He did remember! "What about that day? I want to know, Daddy."

"I watched my brother die. I saw his boat crash. I swam out and helped bring him to shore. The doctors told me that Patrick was dead, but I made them do CPR. I would not let them stop. I just stood there praying, crying, screaming. Patrick was only nineteen. He was so young and full of life. It felt so wrong that my little brother was suddenly dead. So very wrong.

"Finally, the doctors stopped. I felt hollow. I stood next to him, crying and looking up at Heaven, thinking how wrong it all was. I saw a girl, a beautiful, teenaged girl with long ash-blonde hair and with my eyes, step out of the clouds. She walked down an invisible staircase and stood across from me next to Patrick. She was so beautiful.

"I stared at her. She had my eyes, these turquoise eyes that no one else in the family had. And she was crying as she looked at me in a way that stunned me then but is so familiar to me now. I wrote in my diary that night that I thought she was an ancestor who had come back for Patrick. I was wrong. Wasn't I?"

Angilia looked at Eric, her eyes so full of love, and a single tear slid down her cheek. Eric's hand covered his mouth, tears filling his eyes. She looked just as she had thirty-five years earlier when she had come to him. "I knew you remembered," Angilia told him. "I knew you could never forget anything about that day. I did come for Uncle Patrick. I also came for you. You broke my heart that day. I wanted to stay with you then, but I could not do that. It was not my time yet. I had to wait for the pre-destined date of my birth. The whole time I was with Mommy, I knew it was coming soon, and I was so anxious to be with you."

Eric was crying, his body heaving, his heart pounding, his pulse surging. He had known, but he had pushed it all to the furthest recesses of his brain. He had buried everything about that horrific day, to the extent of rarely talking about his brother. Angilia walked around the island and stood next to him, holding him close to her.

"I saw everything, too, Daddy, from the third Sphere. I saw you and Roger standing on the shore, with the crew and doctors there as well. I saw Uncle Patrick in the boat, speeding atop the water of the lake. I saw the boat hit something and capsize, and you and others rushing to him. But I knew. It was his pre-destined time, and I knew. I did not want it to happen, but no one could have stopped it, Daddy. I was Uncle Patrick's Spirit Guide into Heaven. I had to come for his soul.

"I also came for you. We never felt pain or sadness in the Spheres, but I did that day. I watched you in agony, and I felt pain and heartbreak for the first time. I cried for the first time. You did break my heart, Daddy. I wanted to make it all go away, I wanted to undo it all, but I could not do that. It was beyond my power and control. Time does not exist in the Spheres, so I do not know how long I cried, but I did cry for a long time. For you. Uncle Patrick stayed with me while I cried, something that I was not supposed to be able to do in the Sphere."

Eric looked into her eyes. "This is true. It really happened. I saw you thirty-five years ago. You saw me. I wrote it in my diary then, that I loved you from that first moment. Somehow I knew it was you, even before I really knew."

Angilia smiled and nodded. "You did. I waited for the perfect day to tell you everything about me, Daddy. Today is that day. There is so much I need and want you to know about me, about us. We were always meant to be father and daughter, from earliest time. We just had to wait for the pre-ordained dates for us to come together on earth, in life."

"I chose your name because it means Angel and because you are my miracle," Eric whispered. "Years later, when I realized it was you who came to me that day, I wrote in my diary that you really are my Angel. You are, aren't you? An angel?"

"Do you want to know everything, Daddy?"

"I do. Of course I do."

"Come with me, then," Angilia said, and took his hand. She led him to the sofa in the living room, and sat beside him. Her diaries were stacked on the coffee table. "Everything about me is in my diaries. I want you to read them. You gave me my first one the Christmas before I turned five, but I used blank books to write out everything from my life and existence before 2001. My earliest memories, all of my memories, are in these diaries. Everything. Please read them."

Angilia handed him a book with the number one inscribed on the spine. She smiled, stood, and kissed his cheek. "I'll make you some fresh coffee. You have a lot of reading to do."

Eric felt elated, calm, and overwhelmed simultaneously. His little girl really was the angel who had come for Patrick's soul. He saw her nineteen years before she was born. He had known that truth, yet had tried to bury it within his mind. She was real. He was real. July 19, 1977 was real. It had all happened just as he had written in his own diary that night thirty-five years ago. He opened Angilia's first diary just as she placed his mug on the table, patted his arm, and walked softly upstairs to the loft.

§§§§§

1 February 2001

This diary contains my earliest memories. I remember everything vividly and clearly, including all that happened to and around me before I was actually born five years ago. Someday Daddy will read this, and many years from now other people may read this. I write this for them, mainly Daddy. There are times I want to tell Daddy everything, but I never do. I will know when the time is right, and then I will hand him this diary to read. If you are reading this now, Daddy, please know that everything I write in this book is true for me and about me.

The best place to begin is at the beginning, as Glinda tells Dorothy when she and Toto start their journey down the yellow brick road. My life has been a lot like Dorothy's journey—filled with many people, events, and probably highly unbelievable to those who hear it or who read it. Nonetheless, here is my story from my first memory onwards.

I need to explain that where I was before I came to earth is very different. There is no time there. I can place certain memories in a time frame now based on what I have learned here on earth. So I refer to time only in the context of earthly events.

My first memory is of standing in a place, a huge place, which looks like the finest white marble, like the Greek temples only far more beautiful. Michael, the Archangel, told me I was in the Unborn Children Sphere, where we are manifestations of our souls waiting for our appointed times to be born to our parents on earth. Hundreds of other children of all ages are there, all of them happy and healthy. I remember watching them, not in fear or worry, but in wonder. I walked slowly around the place, watching the other children doing whatever they desired, whether it was chemistry or reading or music or anything at all.

Everyone was so friendly and welcomed me, telling me how glorious it was to be there. Being there, they said, was such fun. There were walls lined with books, musical instruments of all types scattered about, podiums for orators to practice their speaking skills, laboratories for scientists to conduct their experiments. Everyone was free to do and to be whatever he or she wanted.

I remember running my hand over a shelf of books, fascinated by the titles and authors' names. I took a book of poetry and held it while I kept walking, meeting so many other children. There was no fighting, no name-calling, no bullying. There was just friendship, happiness, and peace. It was so lovely there.

I kept walking up the spiral staircase and stopped at the top, in what looked like the tower of a castle (much like our watch tower, Daddy). There was only one boy there, and he smiled at me when I came up. He was sitting cross-legged on the floor, drawing in a sketch pad. His first words to me were, "You are new here. Welcome. I will be your friend." His smile made me feel— what? I do not know which word is correct. Not safe, because there was no fear there. I do not know the right word for what I felt, but it was like knowing I had found someone I could trust.

I sat next to him, and watched him draw. We talked a lot during our time there. In earthly terms, he was what we would call my best friend. We shared everything we thought, felt, wondered about, and how we envisioned our lives on earth. He wanted nothing except his art. He just wanted to draw and paint, like he did there. We could not figure out what I would probably do, since I was either reading, writing, or playing the piano. One day, he laughed and said I could just do all three.

I remember my friend so clearly, the sound of his voice, how he looked, his mannerisms. Rather than describe him, I will try to draw him here.

Eric smiled as he read, charmed and comforted by Angilia's first diary entry. Michael, the Archangel. No wonder she had said she looked forward to seeing him again. She had not meant the figurine he had given her. She had meant the real Michael. She had often said things that startled him and never truly made sense to him, and he knew why now. On the flight to Oxford, she had talked about the clouds holding mysteries. Boy, did they ever, Eric thought.

He looked at the color pencil drawing of her best friend and could not breathe for a moment. He actually flipped back to the date at the top of the diary entry to confirm that Angilia had drawn this when she was five years old, eleven years earlier. Eric stared in disbelief. Underneath the sketch she had written his name: *Matthew.* "Angilia," Eric called to her.

She came to the loft railing and looked down at him. "Yes?"

"Please come here, Angel. I need to talk with you." She limped down the stairs and sat on the floor beside his seat. "I know I just started reading, and I am only on the first entry. But. . . ." Eric paused.

"The boy?"

"Yes. You drew this in 2001. How can this be him?"

Angilia smiled at him. "He was there, too. I do not think he remembers anything, though. We were each told we would never remember anything about the Unborn Children Sphere."

"But you do. You remember everything. This is really him. It all makes perfect sense. He never thought of resigning from the hospital until you became his patient. He had never mentioned art to Mitchell or Katherine until that day in the hospital when he told them he was coming to Valmondois. Remember, Katherine asked Mitchell when all of this had started. You become his patient, and he suddenly wants to quit medicine and study art."

Angilia picked up her 2012 diary and turned to one of the entries she had written in retrospect after her release from the hospital. She handed it to Eric and he read, everything becoming clearer.

26 April 2012

One of the most surreal moments of the past several weeks occurred when I was lifted into the ambulance. The surgeon who sat next to me and started preparing me for surgery was my best friend in the Unborn Children Sphere. Before he inserted the breathing tube, I should have said something to him, but I was stunned. What was he doing there? He had wanted to be an artist, not a doctor. I did not understand at all. It was him, I know that. His name is Matthew, the name he told me to call him so long ago in the Sphere.

I felt so safe with him, even though I never thought I would trust another doctor. I know Matthew, though, and I do trust him with my life and my soul. I do not know what happened to his art or why he became a cardiologist, but I strongly suspect God planned it this way. God brought us back together on earth. If I was going to need a doctor, then God made sure it was one I could trust and never fear.

I had to really fight myself from saying anything the day he told me he wanted to resign from the hospital and study art. He told me he felt he had to do that. Of course he does! He was meant to be an artist. Serendipity. God planned everything so brilliantly.

"Do you think seeing you triggered his memories?"

"I don't know, Daddy. Someday, I will bring this up with him, but not yet. It is still far too soon. Keep reading the first diary, though," Angilia said with a mischievous grin. Eric helped her stand, and she ruffled his hair and walked to her bedroom.

Eric smiled, sipped his coffee, and turned the page. Most people would think them crazy, he thought, her for writing all of this and claiming it true and him for believing it all. He did not care. He had instinctively known. All of his references to his daughter being ordained by God, being unique, being his Angel—somewhere deep inside Eric had known the truth. He knew beyond doubt on her eleventh birthday in 2007 that his little girl was the angel who had come for Patrick. What more would she reveal to him as he read?

2 February 2001

I do not know how long I stayed in the Unborn Children Sphere, but I left long before I was born to Mommy and Daddy. Everyone stays in the Sphere until they are born to their parents. I remember my leaving, though, and will try to describe everything as it happened.

Matthew and I were always together in the Sphere. He would draw or paint, and often I would either read poetry aloud or play the piano while he worked. Sometimes, though, we would talk, mostly about what we thought our lives on earth would be like. We could not observe earth or the people on earth, and it was for the most part a huge mystery to us. He kept saying he wanted to make his art, that art was his purpose. Most of the unborn children had a clear purpose already, regardless of what it was. I was the oddball, for there was not one thing that defined who I was. I admit that I wondered why I was so different. Matthew always smiled whenever I said that aloud, and he told me that I must have been created different and not to worry about that. He had a way of making everything seem all right, even though I should not have wondered about why I was that way.

Once when we were in the tower together, Michael came. He is so beautiful, more beautiful than I could ever describe or depict. God's supreme angel, the only Archangel, God's warrior. Michael rarely came to the Unborn Children Sphere. I remember looking at Matthew, presuming he was to be born that day and would leave the Sphere. Michael read my thoughts, my unspoken words, which he has the power to do, and told me he had not come for Matthew. He had come for me, but not because I was being born.

He read my thoughts again, and said I would never see Matthew again unless it was on earth after we both had been born. We were not sad, not as we feel sadness on earth. But we said goodbye to each other and hugged. Michael took my hand and we left that Sphere and sat atop what he told me was the Third Sphere of the Angel Realm. Each Realm contains three Orders of Choirs, and I would be in the third Choir of the Third Sphere. Michael was in the second Choir of the Third Sphere.

Michael told me that Overseers were in the first Choir of the Third Sphere. The first Choir is for the Principalities, who are much like kings. Michael explained that my Overseer had actually been a King during his life on earth, as well, and that he was not just my Overseer but my ancestor. I had learned about that from the books I had read. The easiest way to explain my Overseer is to say he was my teacher—and my Great-grandfather.

Michael was in the second Choir, the Archangel Choir, in the Third Sphere, between my Sphere and Great-grandfather's Sphere. Granted, Michael is the only Archangel, and a soldier of God. Gabriel is also there, along with a few others, although Michael is referred to by God as "The" Archangel.

I was in the third Choir of the Third Sphere, the Angels Choir. I should explain our purpose so that what I must write soon makes more sense. Angels are messengers of God who are sent to mankind. We are like the link between God and humans. We are often sent to earth to interact with or to help people. I hope that makes some sense, because it will be crucial in understanding why Michael was instructed by God to take me from the Unborn Children Sphere to the Angels Choir.

The utter beauty—words can never do justice to the unimaginable beauties of Heaven. The Spheres are part of Heaven, although not everyone enters or sees the Spheres. I will always remember the glorious light and peace there. No one should ever fear death, because if they have lived a life under God, they will spend all of eternity in the absolutely most perfect and gorgeous place ever created, Heaven. God knows how long each of our lives will last, and he has known for all time. We may not know, but there is a time assigned for each of us to be born and for each of us to die.

What scares me most is that other people can change that pre-destined time. They can do things to alter God's plans for us. Like murder. I am not afraid of death at all, but I am terrified of someone else changing what God pre-destined, not for me but for the person I love most.

Eric closed his eyes and stopped reading. He knew now exactly what Angilia meant when she wrote that at the age of five. More than ever, he understood why she had always been so protective of him. His little girl had kept so much to herself for so long, alone in the world in so many ways. Eric knew why she never shared any of this with him while Jamieson was alive, but he wished she had not been forced to endure it all alone.

"Daddy, I was not alone really," Angilia softly said from her bedroom door. "I talked with God every day. I always have had the winning team on my side."

Eric smiled up at her. "Can you tell me why God chose to bless me this much by ordaining you as my daughter?"

Angilia smiled, a hint of mischief in her eyes. "I am not going to argue with you about which of us is most blessed. I can't answer that, but someday, a very long time from now, you can ask God that question. I am sure he will tell you. It is a beautiful, loving place, and death as we know it really is not scary at all." She turned and left him to the diaries again.

Eric knew he would read about the day Patrick died, soon, and although he dreaded that, he also knew that doing so would help to finally heal and close the wound that had remained within his heart for so long. Angilia knew he had to do this, and in her wisdom had declared the anniversary to share her entire story with him. He resumed his reading, learning more about the three Choirs in the Third Sphere before reading about his grandfather, the man whose portrait now hung above Angilia's desk.

3 February 2001

After Michael explained the three Choirs, he led me into the Angels Choir, which is so full of light and beauty. The other angels welcomed me with such warmth. Michael took me away from the other angels and told me I would meet my Overseer, who came down from the first Choir. He looked like a king, wearing a gold crown and carrying a gold scepter. He told me so much to prepare me for my role or purpose.

He explained that on earth he is called my Great-grandfather, although he had died and been reborn in eternity as I now knew him. He told me that his two grandsons were teenagers and that one of them was my father. I asked Great-grandfather when I could see you or meet you, Daddy, and he told me I probably would not until I was born.

Over time, although I do not know how much time, Great-grandfather taught me many things. While I was an angel, I could go to earth, but not at my own will. God had to send forth the order first. If I breached that and went without God's permission, I could be restricted from ever going and thus derail my purpose for being in the Angels Choir.

Great-grandfather said God had sent Michael for me so that I could prepare for my purpose. I learned about Spirit Guides, those angels who return to earth when someone dies. Spirit Guides greet the person, now in spirit or soul manifestation, and escort them into Heaven. Usually Spirit Guides are connected or related to the people they escort. Great-grandfather told me that God appointed me as the Spirit Guide for one of my relatives. I would go to earth and greet him and then I would take him to Heaven. I remember how Great-grandfather looked at me, and if I had to compare it to anything familiar, it would be a rather stern look. He warned me with his steel blue eyes.

He told me that when I went to earth as a Spirit Guide, no one else would see me, no one else would know I was there, and that I should not do anything to change that. He kept looking at me, and he said he knew that I would want to do things I should not do. He told me that I could not change what had to happen, no matter how much I might want to do that. Many times over, Great-grandfather drilled all of this into me, making sure I understood my parameters. I thought I did.

Eric paused again, knowing where this was leading. July 19, 1977. He had lived through that day. He walked to the kitchen and brewed another cup of coffee, steeling himself for what he would next read. His grandfather had known how difficult that day would be for Angilia, an angel who did not fear death. He had warned her not to interfere with destiny. She had told him early that morning that she had wanted to do that. Even then, as an angel, she felt the pain of that day. Eric took a deep breath, returned to the living room, and picked up his daughter's diary.

4 February 2001

In many ways I dread writing this and knowing you are reading this, Daddy. I am so very sorry. I was selected by God to be part of the worst day of your life. In Heaven, there is no sadness, no grief, no tears. Except that day. I know what you felt, because I felt it, too. I felt your pain. I should not have, I was not supposed to, but I did.

In fact, you were not supposed to see me, but you did. I did not make that happen. I do not know how you did, but you saw me, Daddy. No one else did, not Roger or the crew members or the doctors. No one except for you. Great-grandfather must have known how I would feel, what it would be like for me. I wanted to rush to you. I wanted to stay with you. I wanted so much to undo what had happened so that you would not hurt so much. I could not.

I could not speak to you, as much as I wanted to. I could do nothing to help you. I learned later that God had allowed you to see me that day, Daddy. He thought it would help you somehow if you did. I have no idea how, but that is what Michael told me. For the longest time, it seems, I remained inconsolable when we returned to Heaven. I could not forget you. Uncle Patrick even sneaked away to earth and returned with an angel teddy bear for me. The bear's wing got torn on Patrick's escape from the toy store, and an angel mended it for me. I loved Patrick for that, and I love Angel Bear! (I do not know how he made his way to Lady Connie, but I think she was the one chosen to bring Angel Bear back to me.) Still, I cried for so long. No one could make me stop, so Michael finally relayed God's message. You were allowed to see me, you would know who I was, and our love was already sealed. We would be together forevermore, even before the pre-destined date of my birth. Michael said I would help to take away your pain, although I did not understand how.

That day, though, my purpose was to escort Uncle Patrick to Heaven. He kept looking back at you while we walked into Heaven. So did I. Neither one of us wanted to leave you. He was not sad. I was. Ironic that the angel, who had never known sadness and pain, felt them so strongly. The man who had known them felt only peace and joy. You changed me forever. I loved you from that very first moment.

Uncle Patrick told me so much about you, Grandfather, Grandmother, the palace, Valdavia, life on earth. He knew that I wanted nothing except to go to you. I know—we all know—that we first saw one another on 19 July 1977. In earthly time, it was several years later that I came to you, on Christmas 1994. 17 years I waited in the Angels Choir. Now that I know and understand time, I know how long I waited. In the scheme of infinite eternity, 17 years is nothing, but to me, waiting for that one moment, it was longer than eternity. I should not say or think or feel that, but I do. I lived then only to be reborn to you on earth.

Gabriel even visited me and played his glorious music for me. None of the other angels knew quite what to do with me or for me. I was different even there. Great-grandfather told me that he had not wanted me to be Patrick's Spirit Guide for this very reason. He knew I would love you instantly and that it would be difficult for me to return to the Sphere as if nothing had happened. I remember him sighing heavily, telling me that we had to wait, you and I. He did not know my pre-destined birth date. Those who did know—God and Michael—never told anyone else, and said it would not mean anything even if they did. Time does not exist there, they reminded me. It sure felt like it did. Michael kept reminding me, too, that I would never remember anything about my life in the Spheres. My life, he kept saying, would begin when my mother became pregnant.

Uncle Patrick was perpetually happy. And doing things he probably should not have done. He is the only angel I met who played pranks and told jokes. And I met thousands of angels. Great-grandfather often wore a purple robe. Once he could not find his robe, which was puzzling, because things do not get lost or go missing in Heaven. He and I looked throughout our two Choirs for his robe, never finding it. Other angels joined our search. Several hundred angels looked through the entire third Sphere. Michael even joined us at one point. Only one angel did not search.

I knew he had hidden the robe, and when I asked him about it, he laughed. He said he was very clever. He put his grandfather's robe in the most unlikely place. He kept laughing and said none of us would find it in the third sphere. I asked him where he put it, and told him to please go get it. "Oh, no, I am never going back there," he laughed. "I almost got caught, and I am not going again. You go if you want to." He finally told me where, and I made him go with me. I grabbed his arm and pulled him, until we were almost there.

At that moment, he was like the Cowardly Lion facing the Great and Powerful Oz. He stopped laughing. Michael stood before us and told Uncle Patrick to follow him. Michael looked at me and told me to return to my Choir. I did, but I did not want to. Later, Uncle Patrick returned with the robe and apologized to Great-grandfather for hiding it. His punishment was to write a thirty-page paper about the virtues of honesty and kindness. He winked at me, and Michael made him go to the Archangel Choir to write his paper, because I was not allowed to help him. In fact, Patrick was told he had to stay in

Michael's Choir until further notice. Patrick giggled, shrugged his shoulders, and said, "I never thought I would be grounded in Heaven."

I did go on my own to where he had hidden the robe, even though I should not have. I did not have permission. But I had to go. The Thrones let me pass, without stopping me. So did the Cherubim, and finally I entered the highest Choir, the Seraphim. They guard the throne of God. They parted and let me pass, too. I thought I would at least be stopped and questioned.

I approached God's throne with my head bowed, and knelt to my knees before him. I did not look at him, and I did not speak until he spoke to me. "I know why you are here, Angilia. You risked reprimand and wrath to come here. Pleading for mercy for him is that important to you." I told him it was. "Very well. Rise and return to your Choir. Perhaps you may teach him restraint." I kept my head bowed and backed away. When I was out of his sight, I ran back down to the Angels Choir.

Uncle Patrick was sitting there, on the edge of the wall, as always, tearing pieces off of clouds and tossing them into space. He smiled and asked what we should do next. I told him that God had said he needed to learn restraint, but he laughed. "God made me this way. He's cool with me as I am. Besides, you are my Spirit Guide. You will keep me out of trouble." He was correct. I had to get him out of trouble many times. I wonder who does that now.

Great-grandfather talked with Patrick and me a lot, and once he said he would have to watch my birth. He had to see you and me reunite, Daddy. Patrick smiled and said he wanted to watch, too, but Great-grandfather just smiled and winked at him. I think that means they were both there, Daddy. They both were watching that day when I was born and when you took me away from that man and held me.

I had waited so long for that to happen. So many times, I wanted to break the rules and laws of Heaven and come to you. I knew if I did, though, it might jeopardize everything, so I refrained. I never stopped seeing you in my mind, never stopped thinking about you, never stopped loving you. When Michael finally came for me, and took me from the Angels Choir, I knew it was time for me to go to you! I would leave the Heavenly Realm and enter the earthly realm.

Eric sat for many moments, absorbing what he had read. It all seemed so real to him. He could see his grandfather's compassion for Angilia, his knowledge that what she would experience that day would alter her irrevocably. He knew his grandfather would want to protect her from that, yet how could he? God had ordained her. God had blessed them. What happened was destined to happen, and now Eric understood why. Everything came together to forge a father-daughter bond and love unlike any other. She really was his angel Angilia.

When Angilia had walked away from him that day thirty-five years ago, she had seemed to walk alone. Eric had not seen Patrick walking alongside her. But he could see it now. He could picture his brother turning to look back, with that Elvis Presley smile of his. Angilia described Patrick perfectly, his essence and spirit. He had always played pranks and jokes, and Eric had often been the target of them. He smiled, even giggled, realizing that Patrick was still Patrick in Heaven, pranks and all. He could hear him say that—"*I never thought I would be grounded in Heaven.*" Patrick had been grounded several times for breaking curfew or doing things he had been instructed not to do. Of course he did the same in Heaven. Patrick may be an angel, but he was still Patrick, fun-loving, rule-breaking Patrick.

Patrick was happy, still full of spunk, and still his brother. Nothing had changed except where Patrick lived now. Eric understood that better than he had before. Patrick had died so he could start his new life in Heaven. Angilia had lived in Heaven waiting to begin her life on earth with Eric. How great a miracle all of this was, he fully realized. He truly was blessed, and he knew that what he read next would add depth and dimension to his existing memories. His little girl would tell, in her words and from her perspective, about her new life as his daughter, beginning with what Eric had felt and believed. She had come to him first, on Christmas Day 1994. Angilia had confirmed that, even though he had never told anyone, not even Marisol, about that sensation and knowledge.

5 February 2001

I do not know what you remember and know, Daddy, although I suspect that you know and remember everything. I do. At the time, I did not know which date it was, but now I do. I crossed the half-light between Heaven and earth and came to you on Christmas Day 1994. My soul entered your heart that day, Daddy, and I remember that you felt me. Almost seventeen and a half years after Uncle Patrick's death I returned to you.

It all began when Michael came to me, while Uncle Patrick and I sat on the ledge talking. I was no longer in the Unborn Children Sphere, but it was (almost) my time. Great-grandfather joined us while Michael explained what God wanted to happen. Michael told me that God wanted me to go to my father, for my soul to stay with him, before it was time for me to enter my mother.

Michael said I would relinquish the physical manifestation of myself until I entered my mother and began growing as a human. I would stay with you, Daddy, in spirit or soul, for a while first. Michael relayed God's plan. I would go to you first so that you would have the knowledge that I was there and real and alive no matter what happened. Uncle Patrick asked Michael what would happen, but Michael would not tell us. I felt sad, and tears fell from my eyes. Great-grandfather held me close. I think he knew what was destined.

Michael said he would escort me soon. Daddy, do you remember when we watched "The Wizard of Oz" last year and I cried when Dorothy had to say goodbye to her friends near the end? That is how I felt when I had to say goodbye to Great-grandfather and Uncle Patrick. I told them I would miss them, and Great-grandfather smiled and reminded me that I would not remember being in the Spheres. I remember thinking how improbable that seemed. How could I forget them? How could I forget any of it? Uncle Patrick hugged me and walked away from Michael and Great-grandfather with me.

He quietly told me something that he said he did not want them to hear. He gave me a message for you. Uncle Patrick told me to tell you this, Daddy: "I'm not always as far away as you might think. You know I live to break the rules, big brother, so I pop around now and then, even if you never see me. It will be a very long time before you join me here, but you will. I love you, Eric." I told him I would tell you.

Great-grandfather said, "She will not remember any of this, you know that." Patrick smiled at me and winked. He said, "You will, Angilia. Someday, tell him everything." I nodded and we hugged again before Michael took my hand and we left the Angels Choir for the last time.

Michael took me to earth, and we stood on the balcony outside the sitting room, Daddy. You were in there, with a huge decorated tree, and so was Mommy, although I only saw her from the back. I never saw her face. I saw you again, and I felt so much love and happiness. Michael told me it was

Christmas Day on earth, the day when people celebrate the birth of Jesus. He said God wanted me to come to you on that date.

Michael did not think I would remember anything, so he let me stand there for a while just watching you. At one moment, you turned toward the balcony and Michael took us out of view. I think you saw us, though, because you stepped out and looked around. I tried to go to you, but Michael held me and told me not like that. I had to leave the manifestation of my physical body and let my soul enter you.

He said that was the perfect moment, actually, and he helped me to prepare. While you stood on the balcony, my soul flew into your heart. You know the moment when, don't you, Daddy? You said it felt like the wind had pushed you, and you took a step backwards. That was me entering you. That was the start of our lives merging as one on earth. That was the moment we both transformed irrevocably.

By now it was early afternoon, and Eric walked into Angilia's bedroom, where she was reading at her desk. She smiled up at him. "How much have you read?"

"You just entered my heart," he replied with a smile. "Let's have some lunch together, Angel." She nodded, and they made lunch together. Eric carried the tray to the back yard, where they sat at the table in the sunshine. He looked up at the clear bright sky. "There aren't any clouds today. What did Patrick do when he could not rip apart the clouds?"

Angilia laughed, and Eric cherished the sound. "He found other ways to make a bit of trouble for himself. He once rearranged the sheaves of sheet music on Gabriel's music stand, and poor Gabriel's masterpiece sounded like a cacophonous mess. There are so many stories I want to tell you, Daddy. If you want to hear them."

"I do, Angel. I thought reading about July 19 would be painful and wretched, but it was actually peaceful and healing. I can just see Patrick running amuck in Heaven causing all kinds of trouble. But why did he stay with you, there? What was his purpose for being in the Angels Choir?"

"I was never told that. Michael only told Patrick that he would have a purpose and that he had much to learn. I don't want to tell you what Patrick said to that."

Eric laughed. "You don't have to. Patrick hated school. He preferred doing things, like sports, to reading, writing, and learning. Good grief, I nearly burst when he was told to write that paper. He would have made you write it for him, too. Michael was right. And that comment about being grounded in Heaven. I could hear him say that. He was always in trouble for something. The problem is, Father and Mother always felt guilty and revoked his punishment. Patrick seemed to get away with anything. I'm not surprised he still does in Heaven."

"He never means anything terrible by any of it. It's all fun and games to him. But when he hid Great-grandfather's robe, that was a bit too risky. He hung it on God's throne! How he ever snuck by all of the upper Choirs I will never know. When I went, I wasn't scared, but I thought they would stop me, question me, even deny me permission," Angilia added, relieved and elated to finally talk about all of this with her father.

"You actually talked to God. To get Patrick out of trouble, no less. Unbelievable. I mean, I believe it, and I love reading it, but of all reasons to approach God. I can't believe they actually let him off, though." Eric smiled, remembering his younger brother's charm and easy-going nature. "I knew you two would get along well."

"We did. Now you know why I hung Great-grandfather's portrait above my desk. And why the Michael figurine is so special to me. I wanted so many times to just tell you, and I started thinking of the perfect day for this. I did not choose to do this today. Patrick actually communicated with me after we returned home, and told me this was the perfect day to tell you everything. He was right."

"He communicated with you? How? Does he come to you?"

Angilia smiled at her father, knowing he would adore the chance to see or to communicate with his brother. "It's like hearing a very soft whisper. He does come a lot, actually. That's what he wanted me to tell you. He is there a lot." She placed her hand over his. "Why do you think Uncle Patrick's room is my Thoughtful Place? I don't need to be in there to feel him or to hear him, but I like being in there. I feel him more strongly in there, because his essence is still imprinted in that room. He often comes at night and stands on his balcony, looking across to your room, watching you through the window. I don't know if you will ever see him, but if you shut out everything else, you can feel him, Daddy."

Eric sat quietly for a few moments, absorbing the truth. "If Patrick had lived, you and I would not have seen one another that day. God planned all of this so that we would meet thirty-five years ago today." He wiped a tear from his cheek. "Does Patrick know his role in our story?"

Angilia nodded, tears filling her eyes. "He was standing behind me the entire time I was there, Daddy. He watched us, even though we never spoke or touched. He knew, and that is one reason he was not sad. He knew that he was the one who allowed us to meet. And he knew, when no one else did, that I would remember everything."

"I always knew the truth about you, even though I had repressed it in many ways. I avoided thinking about or talking about July 19 at all costs, never wanting to relive the pain. But now there is no pain associated with that day. You took my pain away, Angel. What happened is beautiful and blessed, not painful and wretched. You and Patrick have given me such a glorious gift today, baby. Thank you."

"I hoped it would erase the pain, Daddy. Death itself is never scary. When we do die, we will reunite with our family. That is wondrous." Angilia smiled at her father. "Much of what I write after this you already do know. My time with Mommy, beginning with my leaving you and entering her. My birth. Every day since my birth. I do not know why I was created this way, and I do not know if that will ever be revealed to me. I am just eternally grateful to God that he did create me this way and that he made you my father. I love you so very much, Daddy. So very much."

Tears slid from her eyes as Angilia hugged her father, her magnificent father. Whatever God's ultimate purpose for her, for them, she silently thanked him for his blessings and the gift of her father. She was never meant to be anyone except his daughter. She was created Angilia Erica Charity DeBruce Martineau.

CHAPTER 8

On the walk home from church, Matthew and Angilia whispered to one another, much to the others' amusement. Susan smiled, sensing a budding romance, even though Angilia was quite young. When they approached the gate, Angilia nudged him, and Matthew all but ran into the palace ahead of everyone. Angilia craftily fell in step with Katherine and linked her arm through Katherine's. Angilia and Matthew had everything planned so carefully.

"It's such a lovely day. Let's have lunch on the patio today," Angilia said, and before anyone could utter a word, she grabbed her father's hand and led everyone around the side of the palace to the back patio. A buffet was set up, as was a larger table and chairs, and Eric suddenly realized what she and Matthew had planned.

Angilia took Katherine to the head of the table and Matthew entered as if on cue, carrying a huge cake. "Happy birthday, Mom," he said, placed the cake before her on the table, and kissed her cheek. Everyone burst into the Happy Birthday song, while Katherine covered her face with her hands, surprised and touched. She was just one year younger than Marisol would have been, Angilia thought.

The afternoon was blissful, with the family and friends together. Angilia and Eric smiled throughout Katherine's party. In fact, Roger noted, they had smiled constantly for nearly one month, since they had returned from the country house. Whatever happened while they were there in July had done wonders for them.

Roger had known Eric most of his life; they had attended school together before Roger was hired by King Gerard. He had never seen his friend this happy before. He had asked Eric what had happened, and all Eric had said in reply was, "A miracle."

Everyone noticed the almost tangible happiness that filled and surrounded Eric and Angilia, and they were grateful. Matthew seemed even more drawn to Angilia since her return, as if her spell had increased. Mitchell and Katherine had no idea what was happening, but Eric no longer seemed concerned. Indeed, Angilia's gift to Katherine had actually been Eric's idea.

Katherine gasped when she opened the box and saw a colored pencil drawing of her son, sitting cross-legged with a sketch pad in what looked like a Grecian temple. Angilia had drawn a new version of her 2001 sketch for Katherine and had it framed. She had replaced the white tunic Matthew had worn in the Unborn Children Sphere with modern jeans and shirt, but otherwise the sketch was the same.

"Oh, this is amazing. A drawing of my son the artist. I will treasure this always." She stood and hugged Angilia. "Thank you, dear."

Matthew picked up the framed sketch, and Eric noticed his furrowed brow. Had it triggered some latent memories? That did not really matter. Eric realized that Matthew and Angilia were destined to be together, and he was no longer worried about Matthew's intentions. God had sanctioned this relationship by reuniting the two friends. Angilia had known Matthew instantly, even as she fought for her life. She had called Matthew her best friend in Heaven. Eric would not worry about what the future had in store for his daughter. God was in complete control.

§§§§

"Are you ready for your Jubilee week, Eric?" Mitchell asked him as they sat on the patio the evening before the festivities began.

"I don't really have to do anything. It seems like an awful lot of time and money, if you ask me. Have you seen some of what they have planned? How can they afford some of these performers?

How did they get these stars to agree to do this in the first place?" The Jubilee Committee had released the detailed agenda two weeks earlier, and Eric was still flabbergasted by what they had managed to arrange.

"That's easy. They love you, Daddy," Angilia answered as she stepped outside. "You just enjoy the week and let everyone show you love and appreciation."

"You really think this is a good idea, even with people paying for this themselves?"

"I do. They would not have done it if they didn't want to do it, and as far as I understand, no one gave more than he or she could afford to give. You don't worry about the costs. You just enjoy the week." She stood with her arm around his shoulders. "You deserve this and so much more. You would not be King if God had not ordained you as such. You know that. Everything in our lives is part of God's plan for us, Daddy."

§§§§§

Angilia held her father's hand as they, their family, and their friends walked to Christ Church Valmondois for the National Service of Thanksgiving on the morning of August 19, 2012. Reverend Hutchins greeted them cheerfully and reverently and led them down the aisle to their pews. Eric still felt it highly inappropriate to have a church service focused solely on him, but Angilia wanted this, so he smiled and enjoyed her happiness. He picked up the order of service and was thankful that this did not appear terribly long: the bidding, a New Testament reading, the sermon, and the prayer, along with some hymns.

Reverend Hutchins opened with the bidding, declaring the purpose for the day's service. "Welcome to Christ Church Valmondois today to give thanks to Almighty God for the benevolent reign of The King."

Angilia stood, much to Eric's amazement, and walked to the pulpit. Reverend Hutchins bowed and backed away, and Angilia recited from the New Testament. "1 Corinthians 13: 4-13. *'Charity suffereth long, and is kind; charity envieth not; charity vaunteth not itself, is not puffed up, Doth not behave itself unseemly, seeketh not her own, is not easily provoked, thinketh no evil; Rejoiceth not in iniquity, but rejoiceth in the truth; Beareth all things, believeth all things, hopeth all things, endureth all things. Charity never faileth: but whether there be prophecies, they shall fail; whether there be tongues, they shall cease; whether there be knowledge, it shall vanish away. For we know in part, and we prophesy in part. But when that which is perfect is come, then that which is in part shall be done away. When I was a child, I spake as a child, I understood as a child, I thought as a child: but when I became a man, I put away childish things. For now we see through a glass, darkly; but then face to face: now I know in part; but then shall I know even as also I am known. And now abideth faith, hope, charity, these three; but the greatest of these is charity.'"* Angilia bowed her head for a moment and smiled at her father. Charity was her third name for the very reason stated in these verses. Rather than return to her seat between her father and her uncle, Angilia walked to the piano.

She played a hymn she had written just for her father's Jubilee, a piano solo that captured the lilting joy and laughter he brought to her life. The seven minute hymn reverberated from the rafters, from the dome, and filled the church with the most glorious sounds. Eric thought that must be what Matthew had heard when he was in the Unborn Children Sphere with her—amazingly beautiful, soaring sounds unlike any other. The Jubilee was worth it just to hear her play this piece, which she titled "In His Majesty."

When she finished, she returned to her seat, and Eric held her hand as he fought tears of joy. Reverend Hutchins' sermon focused on what Angilia had said the evening before, that God had ordained Eric Richard Constatin DeBruce Martineau as the nineteenth King de Valdavia. The Reverend praised Eric's benevolence and compassion, his devotion to the people of Valdavia, and his complete lack of selfishness. As Eric listened, he strongly suspected that Angilia had at least assisted in writing the sermon, for she had often said those very things to and about him.

At the conclusion of the sermon, the choir sang Eric's favorite hymn, "Christ is Made the Sure Foundation," and then the Reverend told the congregation to rise for a specially-written prayer for His Majesty. "O God Almighty, we thank you for the life and service of our beloved King. We are immensely blessed to have our country and ourselves under his dominion. We fervently pray that you continue your protection over His Majesty, that you continue your loving blessings to His Majesty, and that you continue to shower him with your love and compassion. In your name, Amen." The congregation echoed the Amen, and the Thanksgiving Service concluded with what was becoming the traditional and expected receiving line.

Everyone blessed and thanked Eric for his lifetime of service, and he thanked them for coming. Angilia's eyes shone with love and tears, and she never stopped smiling. Before they left, Reverend Hutchins presented Eric with a tribute book in which the members of the congregation had written messages to him. "There is a similar book in each Valdavian church today, and they will be forwarded to you very soon," Reverend Hutchins informed Eric.

"Thank you. This is too kind, and perhaps the nicest gift." Eric flipped through the book, and noticed that the first message was written by Angilia. His eyes filled with tears. "I can't even see this. I didn't expect this to happen," he said as he pulled his handkerchief from his pocket and wiped his eyes.

Matthew gently took the book and read it aloud. "'*Dearest Daddy, I am blessed by you every moment of my existence, not because you are the King, but because you are the most extraordinary man. God ordained you as my father, just as he ordained you as Valdavia's King. This country could never be more blessed than it is during your reign. I love you. We all love you. xoxo Angilia*'" Matthew cleared his throat and handed the book to Eric, who had turned his back to everyone.

Mitchell patted him on the back. "Nothing wrong with showing how you feel. This is all pretty special, Eric. You two are quite special." Eduardo also hugged his brother-in-law, and Eric felt more than ever that he did not deserve all of these blessings. He looked down at Angilia, that familiar look of love in her eyes, and he thanked God for her.

Eric grabbed her in a hug. "I love you, Angel, more than you know."

"I do know, Daddy. You give me more love than I deserve. I love you."

§§§§§

On Monday morning, Angilia picked up her item for inclusion in the time capsule that was part of the day's activities. In the Central Park, the Committee planned a picnic party, for which the local restaurants and vendors donated food and provisions for everyone. Special food trucks were already in place, tables and chairs were set up, the park was decorated with balloons and streamers, and it would be a fun, informal day. People looked forward to the picnic, knowing they would have a chance to speak with Eric personally. Many people had told her how much they wanted to thank him.

The Committee had asked people to bring things from Eric's twenty-year reign, 1992-2012, for a time capsule that would be sealed at the end of the day and opened one hundred years from now, in August 2112. How thrilling, except Angilia had so many mementoes that selecting just one had proved difficult. Finally, the night before, she had made her decision.

Everyone else had, too, and they all gathered in one of Eric's Rolls Royce convertibles for the drive to the park. Eric drove, with Angilia next to him, while Alejandro, Juanita, Eduardo, Mitchell, Katherine, Matthew, Susan, Roger, and Daniel sat in the spacious back seats. Mike and Tony followed in another car just as a precaution. When Eric pulled into the parking space at 10:00, the park was already crowded with thousands of people, who all burst into joyous cheers when he opened his car door and stepped out. He smiled and waved at everyone, and walked around to open Angilia's door. She smiled up at him and they joined their family and friends.

Eric was surrounded by hundreds of people all clamoring to see him, shake his hand, and wish him well. As soon as he made his way through that crowd, he was seized by a horde of screaming teenaged girls, each yelling louder than the next in order to get his attention. "Just a novelty. Yeah, right," Roger mumbled as he was pushed and bumped. People were desperate to get to Eric.

Angilia was surrounded, too, with people shoving copies of Heart-Glow at her to sign, grabbing at her, and pulling at her. Mike and Tony took charge and barreled through the crowds to rescue Eric. They took hold of his arms and called for extra security officers to rush to the park. "Where is Angilia?" Eric asked, looking panicked. Eric looked over heads and saw Matthew fighting his way through a tight throng of people. "I have to get her," he said, but Mike told him to stay.

Mike and Tony forced the crowd apart, and Mike lifted Angilia to safety. Matthew put his arms around her and helped her to Eric, who held her close. "This is insane. She could get hurt," he said, a hint of paternal anger in his voice.

She smiled up at him. "I'm fine, Daddy. I told you it would be like this for you from now on. This is no passing fancy at all. You are a superstar. They never hurt me. They just get excited, that's all. It looks worse than it is, really."

"Mi nieta, that is frightening. You are all right?" Juanita asked, fear evident on her face. She had never witnessed such frenzy before.

"I am fine, Abuela." Angilia turned to Mike and Tony. "You need to stay close to my father, though. This is going to happen again."

"Again? I don't know if my heart can stand anymore of this," Katherine wearily said. "Juanita is right, this is scary."

Mike, Tony, and several other officers kept people from mauling Eric and Angilia. Roger caught up to Eric and mentioned that there was a podium set up near the time capsule. Eric took Angilia's hand, walked to the microphone, and started a near riot by welcoming people to the picnic. "Thank you all for coming and for planning this event. I am overwhelmed, to say the least. Our family and friends are with us today, my parents-in-law Juanita and Alejandro, my brother-in-law Eduardo, Dr. and Mrs. Taylor, and their son Matthew. Most of you know Daniel, Roger, and Susan, who have been with us for years.

"We look forward to speaking with you throughout the day. All I ask is that you give us some breathing room please." A teenager in the crowd burst into tears and screamed that she loved

Eric. Angilia noticed how uncomfortable he was and she leaned into the microphone.

"Thank you. This is all so new to my father, though. Just ask without overcrowding him, and you'll get your autographs and pictures, I promise. We thank all of you, and we love all of you. Thank you."

Joshua Forte, Mimi Baldwin, and Jessica Campbell approached the podium, and asked if they could make an announcement. Joshua spoke for the Committee. "Ladies and Gentlemen, Mimi, Jessica, and I truly appreciate your support and participation in the week's Jubilee events. Please have fun, enjoy yourselves, and don't forget to add your contributions to the time capsule throughout the day. His Majesty and Her Royal Highness are here to enjoy the day, as well. Thank you."

Mimi, Jessica, and Joshua led Eric, Angilia, and their party to the time capsule, which already contained newspaper clippings, souvenirs from Eric's engagement, wedding, and coronation, copies of his school yearbooks, photographs from public engagements, copies of his speeches, drawings and poems by fans and well-wishers, a copy of his coronation crown, coins with his picture on them, stamps with his image on them, even a set of dolls depicting him and Marisol on their wedding day.

"Oh, I have to find a set of those," Angilia said, looking at the dolls. Katherine smiled and put her arm around Angilia. Now she knew what to find for Angilia's Christmas present.

Eric turned to Roger, who handed him something for the time capsule. Angilia smiled when he placed a copy of her Father's Day/Mother's Day Proclamation inside. The original was indeed framed and hanging in his office. Angilia pulled a small book from her purse and placed it atop the proclamation. On the cover was a drawing of her father and the now-familiar title <u>The Gift of You</u>.

Eric picked it up and looked through it, realizing it was another of her handmade books, this one containing hand-scripted lyrics to her song "The Gift of You." It was illustrated throughout with her drawings. "You can't put this in there. I want this," he said, sounding much like a young child.

Angilia smiled and put her arm around him. "Put it back. There is one waiting for you in your room. I made a duplicate for the time capsule." Roger, Daniel, Susan, Mike, and Tony added their items to the time capsule. Alejandro slipped in a copy of his daughter's first picture with Eric, taken many months before the engagement was announced. Juanita put in a copy of Eric and Marisol's wedding portrait. Eduardo placed a sealed envelope inside, which no one knew contained his own account of his release.

Other people came up and shared with Eric and Angilia their contributions to the time capsule. Thankfully, the titanium box was rather large, since it was filling quickly as the day progressed. "In one hundred years, your great-great grandchildren will open this time capsule and marvel at you all over again, Daddy," Angilia said while they strolled through the park.

Eric smiled down at her, wondering how much of the 21st century he would witness. The thought of Angilia as a grandmother stumped his brain. When he first saw her thirty-five years ago, she looked just as she did today. In fact, she had looked this way since at least the age of eleven. How would she change over the years? Would she change?

Eric's introspective thoughts were interrupted by people asking for his autograph on the CD. The girl who had shouted her love for him stood timidly in the distance, and Angilia motioned her over. When Eric greeted her, she burst into tears again, and Angilia held her while Eric signed her CD and took her hand. He kissed her hand, and she hugged Angilia, overcome with emotion. Finally, Susan walked the girl to a table and got her a glass of water.

"This is too bizarre. How do you put up with this all the time, Angel?"

"It's not the same for me. I'm not you," Angilia said and winked at her father.

"What?"

"She's right. You're a handsome king, Eric. You are every girl's dream man," Katherine added with a smile.

As if to prove the point, a group of young girls restrained themselves and approached Eric with squeals and autograph requests. They jumped in place nervously, screeching with delight when he smiled at them. "So does this make you the new King of Rock and Roll?" Roger asked with a giggle. Matthew laughed, Angilia beamed, and Eric blushed.

The elderly gentleman in the wheelchair caught up to them at that moment, and joined the revelry. "I dare say, you are indeed the newly crowned King of Music. How do you like the festivities, Sir?"

"Hello, Mr. Brennan. How nice to see you here today," Eric greeted him. "It's all a bit much, but it's nice."

"Nonsense. It's not enough, if you want my opinion. Not enough at all. You just wait another twenty years for your 40th Jubilee. Now that will be quite grand, I dare say." He noticed Angilia's broad smile. "You agree with me, do you not?"

"Of course I do. I'm so happy you are here. You are coming to the garden party on Friday," Angilia said and moved to walk beside him.

"I would not miss any of this, my dear. And I don't think we should wait another twenty years to do this. Every five years sounds about right to me," he winked at her.

"All right, you two, that's enough. We don't have to do any more of these, actually," Eric responded with a grin.

"Hello, Princess darling," Billy said as he ran to Angilia.

"Hello, Billy. Are you having fun?"

"Yes, I am. I notice that you have not eaten lunch yet. May I escort you to lunch, Princess darling?"

Angilia glanced at her father, who nodded. "I will be honored, Billy." He took her hand and led her to a table, helped her sit, and motioned for the others to take their seats as well. Billy ran off and returned with a lemonade and salad for Angilia. He disappeared again and returned with the same for Eric, and before he could run off again, Matthew took his hand. Mitchell and Eduardo followed, and they returned with trays of drinks and food for everyone.

Billy sat next to Angilia, and Mr. Brennan sat next to Eric. No one bothered them during lunch, except to wave and greet them, and when they finished and stood, Joshua Forte approached. "Your Majesty, in two hours we will make a formal announcement from the podium, regarding the time capsule. We would be honored if you and Her Royal Highness could join us then."

"Of course," Eric said. "It's 2:00 now, so that will be at 4:00. What do we do in the interim?"

"You sign more autographs," Daniel said, seeing a group of girls approaching quickly. Sure enough, he and Angilia were asked to sign a couple more dozen copies of the CD, which they happily did. Eric and Billy held Angilia's hands as they walked slowly, greeting people and stopping to pose for pictures or to sign autographs. People had come from across Valdavia to attend the week's festivities, and they all seemed to stop Eric to tell him how much they loved and valued him.

After talking with hundreds of people, the two hours were almost over, and Roger directed them toward the podium for the announcement. At 4:00, Joshua got everyone's attention and they all crowded near the time capsule and podium. "Your Majesty, Your Royal Highness, thank you both for coming today. We have all enjoyed this chance to thank you publicly for your years of dedicated service to us and to Valdavia."

Jessica Campbell stepped forward to the microphone. "We have one last item to include in the time capsule, if His Majesty and Her Royal Highness will indulge us. We have a copy of <u>Heart-Glow</u> that we would like them to autograph just for inclusion in the time capsule." She turned to Eric and Angilia. "Would you mind?" Eric took the CD and signed the cover, and passed it to his daughter, who likewise signed the cover. Angilia handed the CD to Jessica, who placed it in the time capsule.

Mimi Baldwin took the microphone and stunned Eric and Angilia with her part of the announcement. "The time capsule will remain open for another hour, and will be sealed permanently at 5:00 by the crew from the steel plant. After that, it will be placed here," she said, while Joshua removed a red velvet covering from a marble foundation stone, large enough to hold the time capsule. "The time capsule shall be placed in this foundation stone, and the stone also permanently sealed this evening."

"Your Majesty, we have a special guest to reveal the purpose for the foundation stone. Mr. Brennan," Joshua Forte called to the gentleman in the wheelchair, much to Eric and Angilia's surprise.

"Your Majesty, this foundation stone has a plaque which I shall read. *'In commemoration of his 20th Jubilee, we, the citizens of Valdavia, dedicate this statue of His Majesty King Eric de Valdavia on this date, 20 August 2012'.* Your Majesty, this is our gift to you and to all future generations."

Angilia could not stop her tears of joy and gratitude. She had no hint of this. Her father looked at her, stunned, and she gently nudged him to step forward. Eric regained enough composure and walked to Mr. Brennan and thanked him. To thunderous applause, Eric stepped up to the podium and thanked everyone. "I don't know what to say. I am completely unprepared for this, you know. How can I thank you for all of this? I truly do not feel that I deserve this, but I do thank you for thinking that I do. You make this the best, most joyous place on earth, and I am honored to live here with all of you. Thank you all so very much."

The thousands of people filling the park cheered for nearly twenty minutes, refusing to stop no matter how much Eric motioned for them to stop cheering. He motioned Angilia to join him as Mimi unveiled the artist's painting of what the statue would look like. Angilia was mesmerized. Her father was depicted in his military uniform, in a semi-casual stance so characteristic of him. Both she and Eric were presented with framed copies of the artist's painting of the statue, with plaques affixed commemorating the date and occasion.

Eric was asked to pose with the painting, and he reluctantly did so, much to Angilia's delight. When the furor finally quieted, Eric thanked everyone again and officially closed the day's festivities.

After another hour of talking with people and signing autographs, they finally got in his car. Angilia smiled at him as he helped her into her seat, and took his framed print.

She held both prints on her lap during the ride home, and looked at them in awe. "How utterly gorgeous and fabulous, Daddy. You are the absolute most perfect father and king."

§§§§

"Today's program sounds very sweet, mi hijo," Juanita said to Eric during lunch. "The children get to perform for you. That is very precious."

"It is, Mamá. I am looking forward to this afternoon."

"So is Miss Yost," Angilia added. "She prepared a special song today with a group of children."

"Miss Yost?" Roger asked, suddenly looking ill. "Miss Yost, the music teacher?"

"Yes, of course. She is so excited to see you today, Daddy. She remembers you, too, Roger. You will adore the song and hand movements she put together," Angilia told them with a smile.

"You mean she still does that stuff? The same song every day, with the same goofy hand movements," Roger shuddered.

"What song?" Angilia asked. Roger shook his head, refusing to utter the title.

"'The More We Get Together,' right Roger?" Eric smiled. "We all did that song, no matter what year we were. So she still works with the school children?"

"She's still the music teacher," Angilia informed them.

"Good grief. She always enjoyed it, that's true," Eric commented.

"And she wore that rainbow apron every day, too," Roger said and rolled his eyes.

"Oh, she still does! The children adore Miss Yost," Angilia smiled. "I do, too. She asked me to visit her classes soon. Susan, I thought we would assist Miss Yost for a week."

Susan dropped her fork onto her plate. "Me? Assist in Miss Yost's music class? Honey, you know I haven't one iota of musical talent. And Miss Yost knows it, too, believe me."

"Oh, it will be fun, Susan. Besides, you will have help. Miss Yost wanted me to tell you to come, too, Roger."

Eric laughed at Roger's horrified expression. "She did not. She couldn't abide me."

"She did. She called you her shy boy, and said this will do you well."

"Shy boy? Roger? He just hated her music class, that's all. He tried to hide behind everyone else so she wouldn't call on him," Eric told everyone. "It was a silly song, but it wasn't all that terrible. You can get through one week."

"No. No, I can't, and you know it. I am not going back there," Roger insisted.

"You don't have to sing, if that's what scares you. You just have to lead the hand movements," Angilia reassured him, which made her father laugh even more.

'No. Susan can handle that on her own. I can't do it," Roger stated.

"I will. It sounds like fun," Matthew piped in.

"Perfect. He's never seen it or heard it. Let him have all of the fun," Roger smiled. "Thank you, by the way."

"It can't be all that bad," Matthew said. "Show me," he said to Roger.

"May I be excused for a moment? I want to get something," Angilia said and went to the sitting room for her iPad. She searched for a certain video online and pulled it up as she walked back to the dining room. She handed it to Matthew, and he pushed the play button.

Roger nearly choked at the sound of Miss Yost welcoming the students to the day's music class, and then singing that song. "It's worse than I remember, and you know it is, Eric. Cruel and inhumane punishment, that's what it was. Every day, over and over. It was like the song that never ends, except I should never say that again. When I did, she sang that one for over an hour."

Matthew and Angilia watched, smiling, while Roger and Susan looked ill. Katherine looked over her son's shoulder and said, "I think she and it are charming. If you don't want to go, Susan, I will be happy to go." Angilia thanked her and Matthew, and said she was excited about this afternoon and about their week with Miss Yost.

"I thought we could have her for dinner that week, too, Daddy. Is that all right? I also want to talk with her about singing harmony on the next album. I used the faculty and students at Oxford in the past, but since Susan has a panic attack at the mere mention of singing, I thought Miss Yost could sing female harmony."

"I think that's a wonderful idea, Angel," Eric told her with a smile.

"So do I, mi nieta. I would like to come with you to the music class, too, if that is all right," Juanita said. Angilia stood and hugged her grandmother, so happy that people were as excited about the music class as she was.

Soon they freshened up and got in Eric's Rolls Royce for the drive to the downtown theatre and the afternoon tribute performances. Eric, Angilia, and the members of their party were escorted to the royal box, where they could see the entire stage. Jessica Campbell came on stage to welcome everyone to the afternoon's Jubilee Tribute Performances, and offered a special welcome to Eric, Angilia, and their party. Eric received a standing ovation, much to his embarrassment, and waved at everyone.

The first performance was by a group of third grade students from Senorine, a city in western Valdavia. Their self-written skit reenacted Eric's coronation, with the tallest brunet boy portraying Eric, clad in black boots, purple robe, and gold crown. Next, a young girl from Plouraide, a northern city, performed a song she had written about Eric and how nice he was to everyone. Angilia smiled and dabbed tears from her eyes. Following her was a high school student who was dressed in his father's military uniform. He recited a speech Eric had given at the United Nations in 1993, early in his reign. Eric was impressed, and when the boy saluted him, he saluted back.

A sixth grade class from Mendelville, from northeastern Valdavia, sang the national anthem, a song dating back to 1431, the country's 100th anniversary. A fifth grade girl from Valmondois read a poem she had written for Eric. A high school girl read Angilia's Father's Day sermon in its entirety, and Eric smiled at his daughter. The Valmondois high school choir sang Eric's favorite hymn.

Angilia smiled with glee when Billy came on stage. He read a story he had written about Eric and Angilia, in which they co-ruled over Valdavia as King and Queen for all eternity. Eric patted his daughter's hand and thought Billy had a pretty fine idea. Eric had thought the same thing in June when she spoke about David and Solomon being co-monarchs. Billy bowed at Eric when he finished and blew Angilia a kiss, much to everyone's delight.

Finally Miss Yost appeared, rainbow apron and all, and announced that a group of students from across Valdavia had formed a chorus just for today's performance of a new song written especially for His Majesty. Eric noticed that Miss Yost winked at Angilia when she had said that. No wonder Angilia had known what Miss Yost was doing for today's program. Had she written the song?

The curtain rose and the students, ranging across all ages and grades, stood on risers, Miss Yost faced them, and a pianist was at stage left. The song was quite an epic, telling of a great king who kept peace and unity in his country against all odds in a world filled with war and upheaval. This king worked tirelessly for his people, who loved him dearly. He was a gracious king, a kind king, a wise king, and a loving king. He was touched by the hand of God, and one day would claim a new throne in Heaven. The so-called hand movements were sign language. While they sang, they also signed the lyrics. Angilia had taught Eric sign language years earlier. This had her stamp all over it, and he could never be prouder of her than he was at that moment.

As the final performance, all of the students who had participated came on stage and joined their voices in a declaration of thanks and love to their King Eric. He received a standing ovation, and at Angilia's urging, he stood and waved in thanks for their wonderful performances. Miss Yost motioned for him to join them on stage, and he obliged, although he disliked all of the public attention. When he walked on stage, Miss Yost hugged him, and the girl who had read Angilia's Father's Day sermon stepped forward and offered him a plaque from the students of Valdavia thanking him for his service and kindness.

Billy came forward and presented Eric with a set of cufflinks commemorating his 20th Jubilee. Eric could not escape without a speech, so he took a microphone from Miss Yost and thanked everyone for coming. "I want to thank the students most of all. Each of you deeply touched me and Angilia, and the rest of our family, truly you did. This afternoon was remarkable, and I am humbled and blessed. Thank you. I know your teachers and parents worked to make this happen, as well, and I thank you all. You make my life richer, more fulfilling, and rewarding."

Eric waved and walked away to another standing ovation. He rejoined his friends and family in the royal box, where Angilia grabbed him in a tearful hug. He held her and whispered in her ear. "Pretty sneaky, Angilia. It's a beautiful song." She looked at him, feigning puzzlement, but her eyes betrayed her. She had written the epic ballad about and for her father, as a way to tell his story for the ages.

§§§§

Wednesday's Jubilee event was a float pageant that began its journey on the border of Spain at sunrise. The floats depicted events from Eric's life and reign, and the designs had been selected by the Committee from submissions by the public. The pageant was expected to enter the capital of Valmondois in mid-afternoon, so Eric and Angilia did not have to leave for several hours. Eric found her in the music room that morning, writing lyrics in a notebook.

He smiled, amazed yet again at how easily and naturally his daughter did so many things. He sat in a chair near hers, the small book from the time capsule in his hands. "Angilia, this book is exquisite. You blow me away with everything you do, baby. I love this little book."

Angilia smiled at him and cocked her head to one side. He wanted to say something. "Thank you. You make creating things so easy. You are my best inspiration. What is it? You want to tell me something."

"I had a thought while I was looking at this again. What if we have limited edition copies of this book for sale? Carol can set up a web site or something where they can be sold. The proceeds can go to our foundations, fifty percent to Open Heart and fifty percent to Learning for Life. What do you think?"

"Do you really think anyone else would want one, though?"

"Of course I do. It's gorgeous, plus it's one of your songs, plus your art. If we have 1000 copies printed and sell them at €100 each, the foundations will make money and people will have a wonderful piece of history," Eric explained.

"If you think it's a good idea, then of course. This is one reason everyone loves you so much, Daddy. You always put others first. You constantly find ways to help people."

He blushed slightly and smiled at her. "It's my duty. Besides, I have been so blessed that I want everyone else to feel as wonderful and loved as I do," he said, and kissed her nose before he walked up to Carol's office.

Eric discussed the book idea with Carol, who said she would work with the print office to make copies of the book. All she had to do was scan the original into her computer and format it in her system's publishing format tool. The print office would print the pages and covers and bind the books. She would handle the copyright and ISBN numbers. She and her staff would set up a web store and send out a press release soon to generate interest and to take reservations.

"Thank you, Carol. It's such a beautiful book, and it should be shared. And if it can raise money for the foundations, even better," Eric told her. "Why don't you all close the office for the afternoon and come with us to watch the pageant?"

The Press Office staff was thrilled to attend, and enjoyed watching the pageant with Eric, Angilia, and everyone else in the royal party. They had arrived to loud cheers and joined everyone else on bleachers set up along the route. They all relished looking at each float, some showing Eric as a boy, others as a serious university student, still more as a husband and father, and many depicting scenes from his reign, such as his coronation, speeches he had made, and official ceremonies. One replicated the cover of the <u>Heart-Glow</u> CD with a giant juke box that played his version of "Sunshine on My Shoulders" repeatedly. Angilia particularly adored that float.

"This is totally awesome, Daddy. I would love to have that," she declared with pure delight.

"Good grief. I hope not," he replied. "A giant juke box that plays nothing but that one song? What a nightmare."

"Oh, stop it. It is not. It would be a dream come true," she smiled.

Matthew could not help overhearing her, and his brain began whirring. What if he could buy it for her? It could not hurt to ask the Committee about the possibility.

After the last float passed out of sight, Angilia put her digital camera in her purse, promising to make a scrapbook of Jubilee souvenirs and pictures. "Aren't you getting a bit carried away, Angel?"

"Of course not. Your 20th Jubilee occurs only once. A scrapbook will make a wonderful addition to the family archives," she beamed at him as they greeted people on their way to their car.

"I think it's a lovely idea, too. I like to scrapbook, dear, and if you ever want any help, you just let me know," Katherine offered.

"Thank you. A scrapbook party sounds yummy," Angilia said, her enthusiasm enchanting to everyone. Eric smiled, always happiest when his daughter was happy.

§§§§§

Eric's car pulled up outside the Embassy Ballroom at 10:30 on Thursday morning for the day's Jubilee event. The Committee had arranged a ticketed luncheon, with one hundred percent of the proceeds donated to Eric's Open Heart Foundation. The event was open to the public, with the ticket price whatever someone could afford. The Committee had taken its lead from Eric and not set high prices beyond everyone's budgets. They had leased the entire third floor ballroom, which could hold up to 25,000 people.

Eric, Angilia, their family, friends, and staff entered the ballroom before most of the guests arrived, and greeted everyone who came, thanking them for supporting Open Heart. Angilia had paid for her ticket with a €25,000 donation. She had also made a donation of €1 million for the rest of their tickets, which was supposed to remain a secret. The Committee members had kept all of her participation tightly withheld, never telling anyone. Angilia was grateful, for she wanted her father to enjoy and have the honor without worrying about who paid for the Jubilee.

Dr. Stanley Garver, the President of Open Heart Foundation, welcomed Eric, Angilia, and their party to the luncheon. "We were not expecting the generous donations, I must say. How very gracious of your family to donate during your Jubilee," he mentioned, not realizing his error.

Eric, although shocked, did not let that show. "You are most welcome, Stanley. You know how much Open Heart means to me." Other people motioned for Dr. Garver, who excused himself. "What was he talking about, Angilia?"

282

"Oh, nothing. I just paid something for my ticket, that's all," she said truthfully.

"I know Stanley. He does not use the word 'generous' lightly. Just how generous were you, my darling daughter?"

"Just €25,000 for my ticket and a little more for the other tickets. That's not important, Daddy. Just look at all of these people, and think of all of the donations to Open Heart," she deflected with a smile.

Eric smiled at her and pulled her to him. "I do love you, my beautiful daughter Angilia. Just when I think you cannot amaze me again, you do."

"She is your daughter, Eric. You could not have named her any more appropriately. Angilia Erica Charity—her name says it all," Katherine claimed with a huge smile.

SSSS

The palace staff was all abuzz and active the next morning setting up tables and chairs on the back lawn in preparation for the Garden Party that began at 10:00. Local restaurants catered the event gratis, and began setting up tents early that morning, along with special equipment to keep the cold and hot foods and drinks safe and fresh. Angilia dressed in a pretty lavender dress and came downstairs rather early to assist. Eric noticed she limped more than usual, and he intercepted her in the middle of carrying chairs.

"Angel, you don't need to do that. If they need help, there are plenty of us here who can lift and carry chairs and things. Besides, we will be on our feet enough today. Let's just relax for a few short hours until we have to stand and walk," he suggested, and led her to the sitting room. Eric moved an ottoman under her legs and propped her right knee up on fluffy pillows.

"I'm fine, Daddy," she insisted, although to him she seemed tired. She saw the concern in his eyes. "Really I am. I just haven't slept much this week, that's all. And before you think or say anything, it's because I am too excited, not sick." She kissed his chin. "I promise."

"Fine, but we still should just relax while we can. It's going to be frantic out there once it starts. Mother and Father held a few garden parties, and everyone is generally polite, but there are always an awful lot of people, and all of them want to talk with you. That means you are the one who never gets a chance to sit and relax. And this one is seven hours. That's a very long time, especially for you."

She smiled at him. "I was a teacher, remember? I was standing most of the day when I was teaching. I am used to it."

"I know, but that was before your knee was injured. I do not want you standing and walking for seven hours. I mean it, Angilia." He did mean it, she could tell.

"I promise."

"I was just going to suggest the same thing," Mitchell said as he entered the room. "I noticed the agenda and how long this is."

"All right. I do promise, really," she smiled at her father and Dr. Taylor.

Eric sat with her on the sofa until 9:45, and then he escorted her to the back lawn to greet the first guests. Mr. Brennan was one of the first to arrive, pushed in by his nurse. Angilia bent to kiss him, and he hugged her. Eric shook his hand, delighted their new friend was there to share the day with them. Mitchell spoke with Mr. Brennan as well, and unbeknownst to Angilia, asked him to get Angilia to sit with him for a while in a couple of hours.

Billy and his parents arrived, and he greeted Eric with his standard salute. He bowed to Angilia and kissed her hand, and then handed her a white rose. "Good morning, Princess darling."

"Good morning, Billy. Is this your first garden party?"

"Yes, it is, but I do hope it isn't my last."

Eric and Billy's parents giggled. "I hope not, either. Our garden parties would be quite dull without you, Billy," Angilia said to him. "Thank you for coming, Mr. and Mrs. Panning."

"Thank you for having us," Mrs. Panning said. "Billy adores you, you know. He has had a wonderful time this week, he really has. You have both made him very happy."

"That's easy. Billy is such a wonderful boy. We both adore him, too," Eric said. "Please, make yourselves at home."

People had come from all cities and towns in Valdavia for a chance to mingle with their King and Princess. The palace grounds were filled with several hundred or more people, all waiting for a chance to talk with Eric. After a little over two hours, Mr. Brennan came to Angilia. "Princess Angilia, I wonder if you would do me the honor of having a cup of tea with me."

Angilia smiled and took his hand as his nurse pushed his chair to a table under an apple tree. His nurse got cups of lemon tea for them, and Mr. Brennan did not have to force himself to enjoy her company for tea and talk. "Your life is so fascinating, Mr. Brennan. You have done and seen so very much. Have you ever considered writing a memoir?"

"Oh, my life is nothing extraordinary except in its length, my dear. I have never done anything important. No one would be interested in reading about me."

"Yes, they would. Why don't we work on your book together? I can record your stories and interview you, and I can put your stories together into a manuscript. We can revise it together. Your life is made for a memoir. I would be honored to help you," she enthused.

"If you think so, I would be the one honored to work with you. For that experience alone, I say yes," he beamed at her. His nurse smiled, knowing that such a project would give him a purpose.

"What has she talked you into?" Eric asked when he walked to their table. Mr. Brennan explained, and Eric smiled at his daughter. "I think it's a marvelous idea, too, absolutely marvelous. She can come to you, and you can come here. Let me know if there is anything I can do to help," Eric offered before he walked to the next table.

Mitchell noticed how engaged Angilia was with the gentleman, and indeed she was already asking him questions. She did not need to write anything, for she would remember their conversation verbatim. She was quite excited to work on Mr. Brennan's memoir. Perhaps her father would write the forward.

In fact, Mr. Brennan and Angilia were so focused on their conversation that they did not notice that the Garden Party was nearly over. She promised to talk with him more soon, very soon, kissed his cheek, and went to join her father at the gate. They thanked everyone for coming, and soon they said good evening to Mr. Brennan, with Angilia's repeated promise to visit him soon so they could continue working on his book.

"Looks like you have a wonderful new friend and a wonderful new project. What a beautiful thing to suggest to Mr. Brennan, Angilia. This will mean more to him than almost anything else," Eric told her with a kiss. "Come on. Let's grab some dinner and relax for a while before the fireworks begin."

A few hours later, Eric, Angilia, and their party arrived at the specially built royal box from where they would watch the Jubilee fireworks display. The Valmondois display would soar above them from the dome of the capital building in downtown. Across the country, nearly every city and town would start their own Jubilee fireworks at the same time, 10:00. Eduardo was particularly excited, since he had not seen fireworks in almost twenty-five years.

Everyone expected the typical, traditional fireworks display, with cascading flames of varying colors filling the night sky. They became pleasantly surprised by the pinwheels in the national colors of red and white, rockets that burst into flaming wheels of brilliant blue and green, and the grand finale, a specially created portrait of Eric that lit the sky when the fuse was lit. Angilia excitedly grabbed his arm and quickly snapped several pictures with her camera. Juanita, Alejandro, the Taylors, and Susan gasped. Roger and Daniel were duly impressed to see their best friend's massive profile illuminating them from far above.

"Oh, Daddy, that was breathtaking," Angilia breathlessly declared. Eduardo agreed, very pleased to have been part of the

Jubilee week. "Listen, Daddy, everyone is cheering for you. Stand up." Eric dutifully did so, pulling her up alongside him, as a spotlight shone on them. They waved, much to everyone's delight.

After 12:30, they finally arrived home and prepared for bed. The day had felt long and had been tiring. Tomorrow concluded the Jubilee Week festivities with a free outdoor concert in the Central Park. Angilia was particularly excited about that, especially since the full lineup had not been released to the public.

§§§§

Angilia rose early on Saturday morning, showered, did her hair, and dressed in one of her favorite long, tiered white dresses. The long skirt hid her knee brace from view. Her knee did hurt, but she expected that after all of the standing and walking she had done all week. Today she needed all of the support she could get, since she had an important part in the day's festivities. Only the Committee members, Sam, and her band knew about her participation, not because she wanted to make a huge splash, but because she wanted to surprise her father.

She read her daily scripture, and then walked down to the chapel to pray before everyone else began stirring. When she returned to the third floor, she was greeted by her father, already attired in a navy suit and burgundy tie. "Are we the first ones up, Angel?"

"I think so. Are you excited about today, Daddy?"

"I am, actually. Today will be fun. Before long, you'll be back on a stage singing, too," Eric wistfully said.

"I know," Angilia smiled. They were joined by her grandparents, and soon Eduardo, and they walked down to the dining room together. Matthew, Roger, Daniel, and Susan entered. Lastly, Mitchell and Katherine joined them. Everyone talked about the lineup for the concert, naming their favorites and debating who would give the best performance. "I wonder how they planned the order of the performers," Daniel speculated. "I mean, why John Colton right in the middle? Why Cliff Richard as the finale?

They're all great, but I wonder if there's any significance to the order."

"You overthink everything too much," Roger grinned. "Just enjoy it."

"Well, I don't care about the order. I'm just thrilled to see all of them, actually," Katherine added. "Cliff Richard is one of our national treasures. He performed at the Queen's Jubilee concert a couple of months ago, too. I have always liked him."

"So have I," Eric said.

"I wish you could have done this, too," Susan smiled at Angilia. "That would have been amazing."

Angilia smiled, hoping her father liked the surprise she had planned for the afternoon. Everyone finished eating and went to freshen before they left for the park at 9:30. Angilia texted Sam and double checked that everything was ready. He assured her it was, and told her to enjoy the concert until it was time for her to excuse herself from her father and join him. Everything was perfectly planned, and everyone was just waiting for their time later that afternoon. She thanked him and said she would see him at 3:30.

As usual that week, Eric's Rolls Royce arrived at the park to cheers and applause. Eric and Angilia were stopped for autographs as they and their party made their way to the royal box. People were excited about the concert, but appeared more excited to meet or see Eric and Angilia than the performers who would grace the stage throughout the day. Angilia was thrilled at the affection shown to her father. He truly deserved this week, despite his protests.

Mimi, Jessica, and Joshua greeted them, escorted them to their royal box above the bleachers, and talked with them for a while. None of them gave any hint of what was scheduled for that afternoon. Angilia had everything planned. At 3:30 she would make her excuses and leave the royal box, presumably for a few moments, and then their surprise for Eric would happen. As they took their seats and got comfortable, Angilia smiled at her father and kissed his cheek.

"What was that for?" he asked her with a huge smile.

"Just because I love you so much," she smiled in reply.

At 10:00 promptly, Dave Rodan, the emcee for the concert, took the stage to welcome everyone and to introduce the first performer, Shaun Lee, who had been one of the most popular teen idols in the 1970s, a favorite of Uncle Patrick's actually. Eric smiled at her, knowing the significance of many of the choices. Local singers and internationally-known singers alternated throughout the day, culminating in what everyone thought was the finale.

At 2:00 that afternoon, Dave introduced Cliff Richard, who wowed the crowd with a lively performance. His songs ranged from the rock-and-roll hits of the 1950s and 1960s, the pop songs and ballads of the 1970s to the present, and even a few renditions of some of Eric's favorite songs. When Cliff sang an old Eric Carmen hit that Eric had listened to in the 1970s, Eric smiled.

When that song concluded, Angilia whispered in his ear. "Daddy, I want to go backstage for a few minutes and talk to some of the people. I'll be back soon." He nodded, and she kissed his cheek again before quietly leaving the royal box. She walked to the backstage area and found Sam waiting for her. He smiled and hugged her, and then led her to the stage right entrance. Cliff finished another rocking song, turned to make sure she was ready, and told the audience he would change pace for the last song. The orchestra and band launched into the operatic "All I Ask of You" from <u>The Phantom of the Opera</u>, and he sang the male verse that opened the song.

Angilia's voice suddenly filled the park, as she sang the verse of the character Christine, and as she slowly walked on stage to join Cliff, the audience erupted in thunderous cheers and a standing ovation. Eric was stunned. Tears filled his eyes and his hands went to his chest. He managed to stand, while Roger and Daniel put their arms around him, thrilled and elated for him. No wonder she had worn that long white dress. It fit the part of Christine.

Matthew's mouth was agape as he watched her and listened to her. Her voice soared to the highest notes flawlessly and easily, and he felt his heart quiver. She was so beautiful, so perfect, and so angelic in her white dress. Katherine noticed her son, and realized that Matthew was truly smitten with Angilia. She could not blame him. Angilia was beautiful, smart, kind, compassionate, and, well, practically perfect. If Matthew and Angilia fell in love, she would be happy for them. Eric and Angilia were already like family to her.

Cliff and Angilia finished their impeccable rendition of the song to a rousing standing ovation. He bowed, she curtseyed, and he kissed her hand gallantly. They exited the stage, and while most people might have thought that was the conclusion of the concert, they were truly stunned to see Angilia's band appear when the stage rotated. She reappeared, her guitar strapped across her shoulder, and launched into a song from early in her career. Eric cried as he watched her on stage for the first time in over five months. The last time had been at the scholarship ceremony in early March.

Eduardo was also crying as he saw his niece perform for the first time. She may be only sixteen years old, but she was so mature and professional. Her set was one hour in length, and ended with the emotional high point of the day, if not the week. The band sat reverently quiet as she played the guitar, looked directly at her father, and sang the heartfelt words of "The Gift of You." The audience was quiet, listening, watching her and turning to watch Eric, feeling the love between father and daughter.

When she finished, she signed "I love you" to Eric, just as she had done in the hospital, and the audience leapt to their feet again. She turned to place her guitar on its stand, and when she looked again at the royal box, she noticed that her father was not there. The audience roared suddenly, and she knew why when he came on stage and pulled her into a hug. Juanita, Alejandro, and Eduardo were crying; indeed, everyone in the royal box was crying.

Eric held her close and spoke in her ear. "I love you, Angilia. I love you. Thank you, baby." She held him for several minutes, while the audience continued their thunderous ovation. Finally, they turned to face the audience, and Eric thanked them. His voice sent them into a more frenzied reaction, and the ovation persisted for over twenty minutes. Neither Eric nor Angilia saw Eduardo leave the royal box.

Finally Eric motioned them to silence. His voice choked with tears, he thanked everyone, the performers, the Committee, and the people of Valdavia for a magical week. He looked at Angilia. "Most of all, I thank my precious daughter for this most beautiful gift. I love her so much."

Over her head, Eric saw Eduardo and nine other people walk on stage, much to his and Angilia's astonishment. Eduardo stood between them and held their hands. Each of the nine former Gulf War hostages spoke for a few minutes, thanking Eric and Angilia for the greatest gift of all, their freedom. Eduardo took the microphone and thanked his brother-in-law and his niece for not just his freedom but for the gift of his family. "I love my family, and I am so honored to be with them." He hugged Eric, and motioned for Bonnie Glaser, a photojournalist, to step forward.

"Your Majesty, in loving gratitude we present you with this plaque of appreciation," Bonnie said as she curtseyed and handed him a black marble plaque thanking him for his compassion and kindness.

Eric was stunned. "Thank you all. I can't tell you how wonderful it is to welcome you to Valdavia. This is far too kind. I did not do anything at all to deserve this, though."

Bill Sturgis, an American reporter, quickly said, "Yes, you did, Sir. By example you taught and guided Her Royal Highness. Without your influence, I dare say she would not be who she is today." Angilia smiled and nodded in agreement, tears shining in her eyes.

Tony Williamson, a French television journalist, spoke next. "Your Royal Highness, your loving compassion engineered our release and our freedom. We can never thank you for that, but we can show our appreciation." Tony nodded at Eduardo, who fastened a gold heart-shaped locket around her neck. Angilia lifted the locket and saw a heart-shaped garnet in the center, and the ten journalists' first names engraved on the back with the year 2012.

"Open it," Eduardo softly told her. She did, and tears slid down her cheeks when she saw pictures of her parents, Eric and Marisol, inside. She hugged her uncle, then each of the journalists, and thanked them for such a beautiful gift. Eric, Angilia, and the ten journalists stood together on the stage, waving at the crowd who cheered them. Eric thought that the week's festivities could not have a more genuine conclusion than this. First, he was surprised by his daughter's performance and then by the former hostages. He silently thanked God, feeling like the most loved and blessed man alive.

§§§§§

25 August 2012

Daddy's 20th Jubilee week was gloriously fabulous! So many thousands of people came to the events and told him how much they love and treasure him. I was not surprised. He is so easy to love, and he truly is the most remarkable man, father, and king who has ever lived or will ever live. It may sound clichéd and sentimental for me to constantly say or write that I am so blessed to be his daughter, but I am.

Today was the free public concert, and I am so happy that so many of Daddy's favorite people agreed to perform for him. When the Committee was arranging the concert, I did make a few calls and send a few emails or text messages. Why not? I know the people, and it was easy enough to ask them if they wanted to come. I was surprised when Mimi, Jessica, and Joshua asked me to perform as a surprise for Daddy, but it was fun. I could see him, and he was surprised.

The duet with Cliff was great fun, but we only had time for one rehearsal, and that was by web cam. I had to go to Jessica's house to do that, just so no one here would hear me and know anything about that. Still, it went well, I think, and it was a nice way to surprise Daddy. I think he liked it. Cliff mentioned we should record the song, which we might just do someday. The proceeds would go to charity, so that is always a reason to do something like this.

I look forward to talking with Mr. Brennan more and helping him with his memoir. His life is so incredible, and he has so many amazing memories. He has lived through and created so much history in his 96 years. I really like him. I'm so glad we met him in January.

Jubilee Week is officially over. In a few days, on 30 August, Abuelo celebrates his 84th birthday. How exciting! Daddy and I have a surprise, and we think Abuelo will like what we have planned for him. I love them all, and I do so hope they decide to live with us. It's so beautiful having Abuela, Abuelo, and Uncle Eduardo here. And the surprise appearance by the former hostages took my breath away. How awesome to see them all together, looking so beautiful and healthy! Thank you, God, for guiding them safely home.

§§§§

On Thursday morning, while everyone chatted happily during breakfast, Eric announced part of his and Angilia's birthday surprise for Alejandro. "After breakfast, everyone needs to change into comfortable travel clothes and shoes. We are taking a day flight to celebrate our Alejandro's birthday."

Now everyone really was buzzing excitedly. "Mi hijo Eric, that is too kind of you. You do not have to go to so much trouble for me," Alejandro said.

"Nonsense. It's no trouble at all."

"Where are we going? What should we wear?" Katherine asked.

"I won't say where yet. Wear jeans or khakis or whatever is comfortable, no dresses or high heels. You might want to bring a light jacket or a sweater, too, just in case you find it a bit chilly there. You can bring a swimsuit if you want, as well, if you wish to swim in the lake," Eric said with a smile.

Everyone quickly went to change after breakfast, although Eric and Angilia were already dressed for the occasion. Eric wore black slacks and shirt with loafers. Angilia was dressed in a pair of khaki slacks, with a white shirt and a pink cardigan. She had a denim jacket and sunglasses with her bag. Ballet flats adorned her feet. She knew her grandfather had wanted to visit their secret destination, and Eric was happy to make it happen for his beloved father-in-law.

Mike drove everyone to the airport, and he, Tony and the royal party boarded one of Eric's planes. Soon they were soaring amidst the clouds, and Angilia smiled at her father. They both pictured Patrick shredding clouds and wondered if he were nearby. Matthew sat across from her and watched her as she smiled. She

293

smiled a lot now, he thought, and he felt happy for her. She deserved happiness.

Two hours later, they were at Lake Como, Italy, and Alejandro stared at Eric in wonderment. Angilia held her grandfather's hand, smiling up at him, knowing he was happy. "I don't know what to say. I have wanted to come here, but I never have. How much I love being here with all of you on my birthday," he told them.

Angilia stood on her toes and kissed his cheek. "Happy birthday, Abuelo. I love you."

He hugged her, tears in his eyes, and kissed the top of her head. "I love you, mi nieta. I am so very happy that you are here today."

A cabana had been set up for them on the beach, and they all settled in its shade. Most everyone took their shoes off and enjoyed the warm sand on their feet as they strolled along the beach. Matthew wore swim trunks under his white slacks and pulled off his pants and shirt. He walked out into the water and dove in, resurfacing in the distance. Katherine, Mitchell, Roger, Daniel, Susan, and Alejandro changed in the nearby dressing huts and joined Matthew in the famous lake.

Angilia preferred the beach to the water and sat with her father under the shade of the cabana. Juanita sat with them, saying she never much liked deep water. "It is gorgeous here, though. I can see why that poet of yours liked it here so much," she commented to Angilia.

Angilia smiled. 'He did write that *'This lake exceeds anything I ever beheld in beauty.'* It is beautiful and peaceful. Daddy, is it all right if I walk along the beach for a while? I want to look at the villas. I'm sure most of them were here in 1818 when Shelley lived here." Eric nodded, and she picked up her notebooks and pencils. What would she draw or write? Eric wondered what inspiration she would find in Italy.

Ninety minutes later, Matthew found her sitting on a pile of rocks sketching a row of villas. "Do you mind if I join you?" he asked. She shook her head and smiled at him. He sat beside her, his own sketch pad and pencil in his hands. They remained there for a while, until Mitchell called them back.

"I thought we would have dinner in a real Italian restaurant," Eric told everyone. "As soon as everyone is ready, we will go to L'Ora della Pasta. We have reservations, actually, and they do have a vegetarian menu," he smiled at his daughter. Like her poet Shelley, Angilia was a vegetarian, and Eric always considered that when making reservations.

Those who had gone swimming showered in the nearby huts, changed into their clothes, and soon they were on their way to the restaurant for a luscious dinner. Eric was surprised when he was surrounded by a group of Italian teenagers and asked for his autograph. Angilia smiled, honestly pleased that people adored her father. Paparazzi spotted them and snapped pictures as they walked to the restaurant. In his dark sunglasses and black clothes, Eric looked very much like a rock star. His handsome looks certainly did not hurt newspaper and magazine sales or discourage his admirers.

During dinner, everyone talked and enjoyed themselves immensely, especially Alejandro. After they ordered desert, Angilia excused herself and sought out their waiter to order a small birthday cake for her grandfather. Fifteen minutes later, Alejandro was serenaded in Italian and the cake presented to him. "How did they know? You told them when you made the reservation, did you not?" he asked Eric.

"I can't take credit for this, Papa," Eric admitted and smiled at his daughter.

"Mi nieta that is where you went? You are very sneaky in a nice way. Thank you." He kissed her cheek and looked at her with such love in his eyes. "This is a wonderful birthday today. Thank you, mi hijo."

"It's not over yet, Papa," Eric winked.

He was right. Once they were back on the plane, the gifts emerged from hiding, and Alejandro opened his birthday presents as they flew above the nighttime clouds. He marveled at them all, but when he opened Angilia's gift, he cried. "This is too wonderful for me, mi nieta." He held his arms open and she went to him in a loving embrace. "You are my beautiful gift from God, Angilia. Thank you for this."

Juanita picked up the box and smiled. Angilia had done a watercolor portrait of Alejandro from long ago, with his two young children. Marisol sat on his lap, and Eduardo stood beside him. The portrait was not copied from a picture but painted from her imagination and love. The painting depicted how she saw her grandfather, mother, and uncle: loving, united, and beautiful.

Eric smiled at Angilia, yet again astounded by her ability to create beauty. Eduardo pulled his niece onto his lap and held her close to him. His family meant everything to him, and because of her he was with them. His parents were alive and healthy. He had Eric, his brother, and Angilia, his niece. He loved them dearly. They were extensions of his sister Marisol, the older sister who had protected him when they were children. Angilia was her daughter and his savior. He praised God silently and thanked him for this young lady who amazed him constantly and who really was his guardian angel.

CHAPTER 9

"You're sure everything is arranged for tomorrow?" Eric asked Roger on Sunday afternoon behind his locked office door.

"Yes. Everything is planned, prepared, and ready. Franklin and one cameraperson will arrive at 11:30 tomorrow morning and get the lights and camera set up. It will be just the three of you in here. I'll ask Angilia to join us in the sitting room, and we'll all watch it live from there. No one else knows anything, just you and I. Her desk is getting delivered at 9:00 tomorrow morning, so the only thing we need to do is keep her from seeing any of that," Roger explained.

"I'll take care of that. I've got some things ordered from the stationer's, actually, which are part of the surprise, so I plan to ask Mike to drive her there to pick them up. I've also got a list of other things for her to buy there, just to kill some time during that hour. I just want this to be a surprise for her," Eric said with a smile.

"It will be, I'll make sure of that," Roger assured his friend.

§§§§

Everything went as planned after breakfast the next morning. Angilia happily went to the store to pick up her father's order and buy the other things on his list. She had rarely known him to make such a large purchase at the stationery store, but she was pleased to help him. By the time she finished and paid for everything, an hour had passed, just as Eric had planned. Mike drove her back to the palace, and helped her carry the bags inside.

Eric was strategically waiting on the patio, and he took the bags from Mike and Angilia. "Angel, I have something very important to attend to, so I will be in my office for a while. Thank you for getting all of this," he said and kissed her nose.

"Okay. I'm going to walk to the sable and visit Starlight for a while, Daddy."

"That's perfect. Have fun," he called as he rushed up the stairs.

Angilia spent over an hour walking Starlight, longing to ride him. Roger called her cell phone and asked her to come to the sitting room for something important. Joseph finished Starlight's cool down, and she walked back to the palace and up to the second floor. "What is it? What's wrong?" she asked Roger, looking panicked seeing everyone there except for her father.

"Nothing's wrong. I want you to see this," he said and turned on the television to the midday news.

"Roger, what happened?" she asked, fear rising in her.

"Just watch and listen," he insisted.

No one knew what had happened that was so urgent that they had to gather for the noon news. Laurie Dougray came on first. "Welcome to the midday news for this Monday, September 3, 2012. We have breaking news from the Palais Royale de Valdavia. Franklin is at the Palais. Franklin?"

Angilia's heart pounded, and she turned to rush to her father's office. Roger grabbed her, and whispered that everything was all right. "Thank you, Laurie. We are honored to bring you this official announcement from His Majesty, live from his office."

The camera showed Eric seated at his desk, and Angilia took a deep breath and calmed. "I am deeply honored and privileged to make this proclamation official on this date, September 3, 2012. I mentioned on my daughter's birthday, when I bestowed the title of

Duchesse de Valmondois upon her, that Angilia is a valuable unofficial consort to me. She indeed is. Today, that becomes official. As of this moment, my daughter's official title is Her Royal Highness The Princess Consort Angilia, Duchesse de Valmondois. Angilia has long assisted and accompanied me, but now she does so as my Consort."

"Thank you for giving us the honor of sharing that amazing news with everyone, Your Majesty," Franklin said with a huge smile.

Eric stood and shook Franklin's hand. "Thank you for allowing me to make the announcement to the country," Eric smiled into the camera, straight into his daughter's heart.

Angilia's hands covered her face as she stood watching her father on the television. Juanita walked to her and hugged her granddaughter. Eduardo congratulated her with a kiss, as did Alejandro and Susan. Daniel was stunned. Eric had kept this secret tightly sealed. Katherine and Mitchell hugged her, too, and Matthew smiled at her. He was afraid to hug her in front of everyone. He could barely look at her without turning into a lunatic who thought only of clouds, angels, and piano music.

Carol, her staff, and everyone else stood and applauded when Eric entered the room a moment later and walked to Angilia. She was already crying, but her tears became torrential when she hugged him. It was not the title that mattered to her; it was him and his love for her. He told her he loved her several times each day, but more importantly he showed his love constantly. Every action demonstrated his love for her, and she was so grateful to him and to God.

"You know what this means, don't you, Angel?" His eyes twinkled. "You have to spend more time with me now. Do you think you can handle that?"

She looked up him, tears spilling from her eyes, and nodded her head. She held him close to her and cried against his chest. "I mean a lot more time. Come with me," he said and took her hand. He motioned for everyone to follow him to his fourth floor office. The large group dutifully followed, and when everyone was in the hallway outside the office, Eric opened the office door.

Angilia saw a desk identical to her father's, next to his, and then she noticed the brass nameplate on the desk: ANGILIA. Her desk was stocked with new accessories, such as a pink marble pencil cup and a pink desk lamp. Many of the things on and in her desk were the things she had picked up at the store that morning. "Since we'll be working together a lot more now, you need to be close to me. What better solution than we share the office?" he asked with a smile.

She turned and tearfully hugged him again. "Oh, Daddy, I can't think of anything better. Thank you."

As he held her and laid his cheek on her head, Eric, too, cried tears of joy. He could not think of anything better, either, than to share his duties with his daughter, his miracle angel. He had planned this since their return home, although he was already thinking ahead to his next announcement proclaiming her his co-monarch. At some point in the future, he would make that proclamation official, and she would then become Queen Angilia.

§§§§

Angilia was working at her desk in the office she shared with her father when Susan knocked on the open door. Since becoming Angilia's Lady-in-Waiting and Personal Assistant five years earlier, she handled most of Angilia's public schedule. "Angilia, a group of high school students would like to meet with you to discuss Christ on Campus with you," she informed Angilia. "You have some time next Wednesday afternoon, which is the 12th. Would you like to meet with them then?"

"Of course. Did they say why they want to talk to me?" Angilia asked.

"No, but they did say it was important," Susan added. "I will add it to your schedule, and call them with the date and time of the appointment."

"Thank you, Susan. Are you sure you don't want to come with us to Miss Yost's music class next week?" Angilia asked.

Susan smiled. "I'm quite sure. I love to listen to music, but that's as much as I can handle. You four will have fun. If you do need me to go to help you, I will."

"No, we'll be fine. Matthew will be there anyway," Angilia smiled.

Susan returned to her office, which was across the hall near Roger's. Eric smiled, realizing that Angilia was taking on more duties and making more appointments. She had already helped him draft an important speech he had to make in two days. She had always helped him voluntarily, and he relished the chance to see her thrive and blossom in her growing royal duties. She caught him staring at her with his charming smile.

"What are you smiling about?"

"You, Angel. You are really coming into your own, and I love watching you work."

"You love watching me annotate articles for research? Seriously Daddy," she said, unable to hide her smile.

"Seriously. You are so diligent and focused. What are you researching anyway?"

"History curricula in other European countries." She noticed his furrowed brow. "The high school board asked me to revise the history curriculum for next academic year before their winter break so they can train teachers over the months leading up to August 2013," she explained.

"They asked you to write the new curriculum? Isn't there a program director who is supposed to do that?"

"Yes, but he can't right now. Mr. Bastille is ill. I didn't press for details, but they told me he is very sick and is on extended leave. I don't mind doing it. I've done this sort of thing before, but not at this grade level. I just need to understand the guidelines and what is expected for the students to learn. After that, it's easy," Angilia added.

"Maybe to you. I'm glad they didn't ask me to do that. See, that's what I mean. You are able to do so many things, and do them well. You don't have to do this, but you are. You really are my best asset and ally. I could never ask for a better Consort, Angel." Eric stood and leaned over her chair to hug her. She smiled up at him, and he kissed her nose.

§§§§

Angilia, Matthew, Katherine, and Juanita arrived at the King Stefan Middle School at 12:30 on the afternoon of Monday, September 10 to assist in Miss Yost's afternoon classes. Miss Yost gleefully greeted them, and explained the agenda for each of the two afternoon classes, even though they seemed essentially the same to her four guests. Miss Yost asked if any of them could play the piano, the recorder, or the cymbals. No one could, except Angilia, who they all knew was a piano prodigy.

"Oh, but I don't want you behind the piano, dear, no I don't. I want you out here with the wee ones, yes I do. I will play the tape of the music, which is what I usually do, so that I can be out here with all of you, oh yes. Oh my, I am so excited. I told the children we will have special guests this week, but I didn't tell them who, no I didn't," Miss Yost enthused with a huge toothy smile.

"What do you want us to do?" Katherine asked, knowing she could not sing worth a nickel.

"Oh, you will lead groups of children in the singing, yes you will," Miss Yost smiled. "Some of them, well, most of them, are very shy little things, yes they are. They need encouragement, yes they do."

"What song is it they're doing today?" Matthew asked, now nervous.

"Oh, you must know the song, surely you must. It is quite a lovely song, and my favorite to do with the children, yet it is. It's called "The More We Get Together," and the children do adore the song, yes they do. They are just shy about singing it, is all," Miss Yost continued to smile.

Matthew snickered, forcing himself not to laugh. Katherine slapped his arm and gave him a stern look. "Yes, it is a charming song," Juanita agreed. "We are happy to help, even though only one of us has any talent for singing at our own admission."

"It is all about the joy of singing in my classes, yes it is" Miss Yost still smiled. "You will make the children open up and have fun, yes you will. Oh my, yes you will."

"Well, if you don't care how we sound, then we won't either," Katherine promised. "Right, Matthew?"

"Oh, yes, of course," he mumbled. What had possessed him to volunteer for this? He knew cardiology and art, not music. He suddenly felt inept and out of place, until Angilia took hold of his arm and smiled at him. He smiled back, willing to do whatever he could to make her happy—and make her like him as much as he liked her. He would even make a fool of himself for her.

Suddenly, a bell rang and the room filled with seventh grade students. They unenthusiastically took their seats, knowing what they had to do again today. The students talked with one another, not paying attention to Miss Yost. Most of them saw Katherine and Juanita standing in the front of the room with Miss Yost, and they saw most of Matthew's head over his mother. They did not see Angilia, though, who did not tower over her grandmother enough.

Miss Yost pounded a tambourine, getting her students' attention when the bell rang the start of class. "Children, I told you last week about our special guests, and they are here for our class today, yes they are. I want you to welcome them with your typical kindness. Mrs. Katherine Taylor, who hails from England, her son Matthew, also from England, is a cardiologist, Mrs. Juanita Martínez is from Spain, and of course you all know our beloved Princess Angilia, yes you do."

Angilia stepped from behind her grandmother, and the seventh graders burst into screams of delight. Most of them ran to Angilia, hugging her, crying, and begging her to sing for them. She finally got them quiet enough to tell them why she was there. "We are going to sing with you today. Will you like that?" Thirty voices screamed they would like that very much. Angilia smiled and asked them to take their seats so they could get stated. Thirty students hurried to their chairs.

"All righty children, here is what we are going to do today, yes we are. There are thirteen rows of chairs, and I will split you into groups, three groups of three rows and one group of four rows, yes I will. Each of our guests will lead one group, yes they will. Let's see, these first three rows will be led by Mrs. Martínez, oh yes. The next group of three rows by Mrs. Taylor, yes indeedy. The third group of three rows by Matthew, oh my. The last group of four rows by Angilia, oh goodness yes," Miss Yost explained. The last four rows erupted in loud cheers.

"Quiet now, children. Please show our special guests how nicely you can sing our favorite song, yes. I will start the music and you will sing with your group leaders, yes you will. I will conduct everyone and lead the singing, yes I will," Miss Yost continued and walked to the tape player to turn on the music. "Oh, children, do not forget our famous hand movements, please, oh no. You will teach the hand movements to our guests, yes you will."

The music began and even though the students did not consider this their favorite song by any definition, they wanted to impress the Princess. They sang boisterously that day, all of them seeming to watch only Angilia. Her voice was clear, strong, and in perfect pitch as always, while the other three group leaders struggled to find their comfort zones. It did not really matter, though, for Juanita, Katherine, and Matthew were barely heard over the seventh graders' loud singing.

Matthew could not master the hand movements, and he began to empathize with Roger. If it were not for Angilia, he would have run from the room long ago. What had possessed him to say that this was charming? Angilia smiled at him as they sang with the students, and he remembered that she had possessed him. He had to do something about this before he went insane.

After the longest thirty minutes, the song finally ended. The students clapped, mostly for Angilia, although Miss Yost misunderstood. "See, children, I always tell you that if you give it your all you can sing wonderfully, yes I do. I am always right, yes I am. Why don't we sing "The Song That Never Ends" next?"

The students all said an emphatic "No" in unison. One girl raised her hand and when asked what she wanted, she said, "We want Angilia to sing for us. Please, Miss Yost?"

"Well, now, we cannot impose on Her Royal Highness, no we cannot. She and her grandmother and the Taylors came to help us today, yes they did. Isn't that right, Matthew?"

"Oh, yes, Ma'am, we did. But if you don't mind if Angilia sings, then we certainly won't. Will we, Mom?"

"Oh, well, no, we would not mind at all," Mrs. Taylor said.

"Your Royal Highness, would you mind at all indulging the students? Other than me, myself, and I, the children rarely hear professional singers, no they don't," Miss Yost said with a curtsey to herself. Katherine pinched Matthew's arm as she noticed he was on the verge of laughter again.

"I don't mind at all. I didn't bring my guitar, though. I suppose I can sing a cappella," Angilia reluctantly agreed. The students cheered loudly, drawing the attention of other classes who suddenly wondered why Miss Yost's class was so exuberant that day. She sang one of her earliest songs, one she had written when she was four, and they all sat staring at her in rapture. When she finished, they burst into more cheers. The bell rang signaling the end of class, and they all hugged and thanked Angilia, reluctant to leave her.

The next class filed in, anxious to learn what all of the screaming had been about, when they saw Angilia standing with Miss Yost. They, too, ran to Angilia in fits of screaming, hugging, and begging her to sing for them. The students who had just left were excitedly telling everyone that the Princess was in the music room, and soon hundreds of middle school students overflowed the room. The other teachers could not control their own students nor get their attention. The principal came, realizing there was a near riot in progress, and ordered everyone to their classrooms immediately.

"I apologize, Your Royal Highness. I doubt they are going to pay attention to their teachers now, though. This is the last class of the day. Would you be agreeable to singing a few songs to all of the students in the auditorium instead of just in Miss Yost's room?" Mr. Gruder asked in desperation.

Angilia was stunned. "I never thought this would happen. We—my grandmother and our friends—were here to assist Miss Yost for the week, that's all. I am very sorry," she replied. She looked at her Abuela, who nodded her head.

"I think it is a nice idea for you to sing a few songs to the students, mi nieta."

"All right, then, I suppose it couldn't do any harm except to take them out of classes," Angilia agreed.

"Wonderful," the principal said and led them to the auditorium. Angilia was settled on the stage with a piano, and the principal went to his office. His voice boomed over the loud speakers. "Teachers, please bring all of your last period students to the auditorium immediately."

Many of them presumed they were in trouble for the so-called riot moments earlier. When they entered the auditorium and saw Angilia on the stage, they burst into cheers again. They quickly took the closest seats to the stage they could find. When everyone was seated, the principal told them that Angilia would sing a few songs for them, but if their behavior got out of control he would stop the performance and keep them after school.

They promised to behave, and Angilia told them she was happy to be at their school. She sat at the piano and played and sang six of her songs for them, and when she finished, they gave her a standing ovation. "Thank you all for welcoming me, my grandmother, and our friends, Mrs. Taylor and Matthew Taylor. We have enjoyed being here this afternoon," Angilia told them. The students thanked her, and were led back to their classrooms to prepare for dismissal.

Mr. Gruder called Miss Yost to the stage and talked with her and Angilia. "Given today's response, I have to say that, as much as

I thank Her Royal Highness for volunteering to help, we just cannot allow it anymore. The risks are too great, I am afraid. I am truly sorry, Your Highness. Miss Yost."

"Oh, that is such sad news, yes it is. But I do understand, Mr. Gruder, yes I do. Thank you all for coming this afternoon. The students really sang well today, yes they did," Miss Yost said.

"I am very sorry, too. I wanted to help you this week, Miss Yost. I would like to invite you to dinner with us, though."

"Oh my, that is very exciting, yes it is. I most gladly accept, yes I do. You say when, and I will be there, yes I will," Miss Yost said with her toothy smile.

"How does Thursday evening sound?" Angilia asked.

"Oh, that sounds perfect, yes it does. I will be there, oh, yes I will. Thank you, my dear. You tell your father and Roger I will see them, yes I will," Miss Yost remarked, and patted Angilia's cheek.

Angilia, Juanita, Katherine, and Matthew left the school building and got in the Rolls Royce that Mike had driven them in that day. Matthew burst into nervous giggles when they pulled out of the parking lot. "Oh, my gosh, I couldn't believe that." He noticed Angilia's disappointment. "Miss Yost is very charming, isn't she, Mom? I really had a lot of fun, but boy did those students raise the roof."

"Yes, Miss Yost is sweet, Matthew. I'm sorry we can't go anymore," Katherine commented. "Except, there is no reason you and I can't go, Matthew. It's Angilia who caused the students to get excited. We can still go the rest of the week," she beamed at her son. Matthew saw Angilia's smile and happiness.

"Sure we can, Mom. I'll call Miss Yost when we get home," Matthew promised.

"Thank you, Mrs. Taylor, Matthew. This means so much to me. I never meant to ruin this for Miss Yost," Angilia said sadly.

"You didn't ruin anything. None of us expected that to happen, dear. Matthew and I are very happy to visit Miss Yost's classes," Katherine assured Angilia.

"Of course we are. It really was fun, even if I sound like a piece of road kill when I sing. Once I got over it all, it was fun. I wish you could come with us, but it is too risky," Matthew said. Honestly, he was happy to help her. Going to a few music classes would not kill him, he told himself.

That evening at dinner, Roger asked how their first day with Miss Yost went, and Angilia looked like she would cry. Eric asked what was wrong, and Katherine explained what had happened.

"I'm sorry, Angel. I know how much you want to do this. You can find other ways to help, though. Thank you, Katherine and Matthew, for going anyway. That's very kind of you," Eric said.

"We really want to," Matthew said with a huge smile. "It really is fun, actually." Roger looked at Matthew as if he were totally crazy. How could anyone enjoy that sugary song and those goofy hand movements?

"Daddy, I did ask Miss Yost to dinner for Thursday evening. She said she looks forward to seeing you and Roger again," Angilia smiled at her father and then at Roger.

"Wonderful. You are very sweet, darling," Eric smiled.

"Yes, you are. I can barely wait," Roger said with a forced smile that almost made Eric choke on his food.

§§§§

Matthew rushed up to the fourth floor office at 10:45 on Wednesday morning, a huge smile lighting up his face. "Angilia, Mom and I just got back from the school. It was a lot of fun today. I think I'm getting the hang of the whole thing finally. I asked Mr. Gruder if I could volunteer to help in the science classes, and he said I could. So it looks like I found something useful to do with my time."

Angilia smiled at him, her eyes flashing with happiness. "That's wonderful! Thank you, Matthew. I'm glad you and your parents are here."

"So am I," he said with a smile and a wink, and Eric watched the two of them. They did like each other, he could see that. Where it would lead them, he could not know, but he suspected that they would eventually discover their love and marry. If they did not, that would actually stun Eric, especially after what he had learned in July.

A short time later, they went downstairs to eat lunch. Eric had an afternoon meeting to attend, and Angilia had her appointment with the high school students. He walked her back to the office, picked up his briefcase, and kissed her nose. "I should be home no later than 4:00," he told her. "What time is your appointment?"

"The group of students is coming straight after school, so they will be here at 3:30. We can meet in another room so we don't disturb you."

He shook his head. "No. I think I'll go to my room after I get home, change clothes, and go give your Starlight some exercise. I want some fresh air and sunshine, too."

"Thank you, Daddy," she smiled and hugged him before he left for his meeting. Still smiling, she sat at her desk and wrote the history curriculum. She knew how it should flow, she knew what it should require, and she knew how much work would help the students meet the standards. Angilia worked throughout the afternoon, and by 3:00 the curriculum was finished. She saved the document as a PDF file and forwarded it to the members of the school board. She answered a few e-mails, and just after 3:30 Susan tapped on the office door.

"Angilia, the high school students are here for their appointment with you," Susan announced. Angilia asked her to show them in, and she stood to greet them.

Angilia motioned them to the sofa, where the five girls and one boy sat. Angilia sat in the matching chair. "I understand that you want to discuss Christ on Campus with me."

"Yes, Your Royal Highness," one of the girls confirmed.

"Please call me Angilia. Please tell me your names, too, so we can get to know one another."

The girl who had spoken said her name was Shannon. The others introduced themselves as Amanda, Amy, Nicole, Darlene, and Scott. Angilia smiled at them. "How can I help you?"

"We are starting a chapter of Christ on Campus at the King Philippe High School, and we need a sponsor slash advisor. We want someone who is intelligent, powerful, and wise, a strong Christian, and closer to our ages than the teachers are," Shannon explained.

"You want me to help you select your sponsor-advisor," Angilia said, presuming that was their request.

The high school students looked at one another nervously. Darlene cleared her throat. "Actually, we want to ask you to become our sponsor slash advisor."

Angilia had not expected that. "You want me to do that?"

"Yes, we do," Scott said. "When we got together to start the chapter, we went through a very long list of potential sponsors. We kept narrowing down the list for various reasons, and yours was the only name remaining."

Amy added, "Please consider this, at least. We need someone we can trust, someone who will understand us and what we are going through, someone who will maintain confidentiality, someone who lives a Christian life. We need you, Your—Angilia."

"Our group will meet at least once each month, either at the school auditorium if it's available, or a church meeting room, or somewhere else private. Our sponsor will attend the monthly meetings, and also be someone any of us can contact when something comes up and we need her advice or help. We also want to have a Bible study group. You wouldn't be required to attend those sessions, but if you could we know you can really help us learn more about the Bible," Shannon explained more fully.

"You don't have to answer now. We want you to think about it. We got these leaflets from the main chapter of COC, and you can read these, too," Nicole added.

Angilia's brain felt panicked. She was closer to their age, and she was a strong Christian, but her experiences had not been anything like theirs. She had not attended public schools and dealt with peer pressure, dating, bullying, eating disorders, or any of the more typical high school experiences. She had never had friends her own age. Her classmates and friends were always much older. How could she advise high school students about their problems, fears, and concerns? "I am truly flattered you think I am the person for this," she told them. "I promise to read the leaflets, seriously consider this, and I will pray about this. I want the best person for your COC chapter, and if I determine that I am not the best person, then I promise to help you search for that person."

The six students knew Angilia would do what was right and best, and as much as they preferred her, they could not force the issue. "Thank you, Angilia. Really, we so appreciate this. That's all we ask of you right now, to just seriously think about this. We know you are the best person, but we will trust your judgment," Shannon stated.

They all stood, and Angilia walked them downstairs to the main entrance and to the gate. She promised them she would call them as soon as she came to a decision. She felt so out of her league with this request. Sighing heavily, she entered the foyer and immediately turned down the hallway to the chapel. She needed to pray about this and attempt to clear her head.

Thirty minutes later, Eric came in from his ride with Starlight, and asked Susan where Angilia was. "I don't know, Eric. She met with the students and when they finished, she walked them to the front door. I haven't seen her since."

Eric knew where she was instinctively. He walked to the first floor and went to the chapel. He quietly opened the door and saw her sitting on the first pew, her head bowed in prayer. What on earth had they mentioned? He knew it was about Christ on Campus, but not much else. Eric quietly closed the chapel door and sat in a chair in the foyer waiting for her to finish. Twenty-five minutes later, Angilia reentered the foyer, and smiled when she saw her father sitting there.

Eric stood and walked upstairs with her. "How was your meeting? What did the high school students want to talk to you about? I know it was something to do with Christ on Campus."

"I need to talk with you about that, Daddy," Angilia replied.

They entered their office and sat together on the sofa. She picked up the leaflets they had given her and handed them to Eric. He looked at their titles, *Your Role as a COC Sponsor/Advisor* and *Working with Your Local COC Chapter.* "I take it they asked you to be their local sponsor. That's perfect for you."

"I'm not so sure. The sponsor is also the advisor, and is supposed to council the students when they have problems, issues, or concerns. I can't do that, Daddy."

"Sure you can. You know the Bible thoroughly."

"It's not just about the Bible, although they do want to have a Bible study group started, as well. I don't have any concerns about that sort of thing. It's everything else. I'm not knowledgeable enough or experienced enough to help them, Daddy, not with what concerns them most. I've never had life experiences similar to theirs, like attending high school, peer pressure, dating, family problems, eating disorders, bullying, just pretty much everything most high school students deal with either first-hand or through their friends. I don't know what any of that is like. How can I advise them? I've never experienced any of that."

Eric sat quietly for a few moments, gathering his thoughts. "I understand your concerns, Angilia. You don't always have to experience something yourself to understand what it's like for other people, though. What about all of those novels and stories you read in which the characters do things you know you will never do? Does that stop you from understanding what it's like for them? When someone has a problem, we don't always have the personal experience to draw upon to help that person solve the problem. We do have a clear head and other knowledge that do help, though.

The most important thing when helping others is compassion. You have that in droves, Angel."

"What if I give the wrong advice? What if something terrible happens because of my advice?" She looked at him with dread in her eyes.

"Even when we give the right advice, wise advice, some people will still do what they want to do. There are always people who disregard our advice. I doubt you would offer ill advice, but if you do, it becomes a learning experience for you. You have always been wise and your instincts are strong. Why did these students ask you anyway? Did they say?"

She nodded and explained what they had told her about their criteria and how they created and then narrowed their list of potential sponsors/advisors. "I just feel overwhelmed. This is so far out of my range, Daddy. Their lives could be at stake with some of these problems they deal with. I want to help them, but I don't think I can help them. I don't have what they most need."

"I think you do, and I would never say that in such a serious situation as this if I did not believe that. I really don't think first-hand experience is the key here, Angilia. Empathy and compassion are the keys. Their sponsor and advisor must have those to be able to treat the students with respect and kindness, which I think is crucial. If they trust you and believe in you, that is half of the battle when they come to you for advice. They know you will listen to them, care about them, and guide them with wisdom and truth."

"I trust you, Daddy. If you think I can do this, I will do my best. I'll call Shannon tomorrow and tell her I accept," Angilia said with a deep sigh.

"Wonderful. You will be fine, Angel. Trust your instincts. I know you pray about decisions, so that is your biggest strength going into this. I am so proud of you," Eric said and pulled her into a loving embrace.

§§§§§

The next afternoon, after school, Angilia called Shannon from her office telephone and told her that she was pleased to be their COC sponsor and advisor. Shannon thanked her, said she would call the others, and that they were ever so grateful to Angilia. Angilia asked when their first meeting would be, and Shannon explained it would be sometime in mid-October. She would forward all of their notes and ideas to Angilia soon.

Angilia hung up the phone and sighed, both relieved and anxious. Eric smiled as he typed an answer to a message, knowing she would do more for those students than anyone else would. She resumed her work, writing a grant proposal for the high school music program. She constantly worked on projects or tasks at others' requests. She truly awed Eric, and he often had to force her to stop working in the evenings.

An hour later, he did so again. "Angilia, let's stop work for today. Miss Yost is coming this evening, and I thought we could spend some time together before she arrives. Let's change into jeans for a while and go outside."

He was smiling at her, and she wondered what he was planning. She didn't care, though, and she saved her work on the computer and walked to the third floor with him. She quickly changed in her dressing room, and joined him on the landing moments later. Outside, he took her hand and walked toward the stable. She smiled. "You want to ride Starlight again. I get to see my boy run again," she enthused.

Eric grinned at her. "Yes, I do, Angel." He could barely keep her from running to the stable. When they neared, she saw Starlight in the paddock with Joseph, ready for his ride. When Starlight saw her, he stood on his hind legs and whinnied with delight. She entered the paddock and hugged Starlight. He kissed her cheek, as he always did when she visited him.

Eric mounted the horse and surprised Angilia. "Come here, Angel." He held his arm out to her, and she looked confused. "Ride with me for a while." Joseph and Eric lifted her onto the saddle in front of her father, and he held both her and the reigns. Joseph opened the paddock gate, and Eric walked Starlight out and onto the lush green land. He kept the horse at a steady walking pace for a while, not wanting to jar and jolt Angilia.

It had been just over six months, and he knew how much she wanted to ride her horse. Eric had talked to Matthew and Mitchell the previous evening, and they assured him that as long as her heart did not receive too much exertion she would be all right. She turned her head and smiled up at her father, happy beyond words just to be riding her horse again. She had not been able to do so since the morning they had departed for Oxford. Starlight somehow understood to keep his pace slow and steady, and Eric was pleased. They rode for an hour at their more leisurely pace.

Finally, Eric walked Starlight into the paddock and dismounted. He lifted Angilia off of the saddle, and she hugged him. "Thank you, Daddy! This was the most wonderful surprise. Wasn't it Starlight?" She turned and hugged her beloved horse, and he whinnied. She kissed him, and Joseph said he would walk Starlight for the cool down so that they could get ready for dinner with Miss Yost.

"Nothing makes me happier than seeing you happy, Angel. I love you." Eric had his arm around her shoulders and he pulled her closer to him and bent to kiss the top of her head. Angilia was happy, and the smile she gave him proved that.

§§§§

Angilia and Eric greeted Miss Yost at the main entrance when her yellow car pulled into the courtyard that evening. She was, as always, the same as Eric remembered her from middle school: a yellow peasant-style blouse, a black dirndl skirt, her famous rainbow-striped apron, and her white blonde hair braided and twisted atop her head. She emerged from her car with her seemingly permanent smile and grabbed Angilia into a hug. She then turned to Eric and squeezed his cheeks, something she did every time she saw him.

"Welcome, Miss Yost," Eric said with a smile. "We are so happy to have you join us this evening."

"I am most delighted to join you my dear boy, yes I am." She walked past him into the foyer. "I feel so at home here, yes I do. You have a very lovely home, yes you do."

Eric smiled, feeling like a twelve year old all over again at the sound of her voice. She still talked the same way, with her unique phrasing. "Miss Yost, please join us all in the sitting room before dinner is served," Eric motioned toward the staircase. He and Angilia escorted her to the second floor, and when she entered, those who had not yet met her were quite amazed.

Miss Yost went straight to Matthew and grabbed his cheeks. "There is my little helper, yes he is. I have so much fun with him, yes I do."

"Thank you, Miss Yost. It's my pleasure. I really do enjoy it. I can't believe tomorrow is our last day," Matthew said to her. "Miss Yost, you know my mother. This is my father, Mitchell Taylor," he added.

Mitchell stepped forward and shook Miss Yost's hand. She reached up and squeezed his cheeks, too. "It is so nice to meet you, yes it is. Little Matthew's daddy, yes you are."

"Is she for real?" Eduardo whispered behind Eric. "If she does that to me, I am leaving, Eric, I promise."

"She will. She always does. I am sixty years old, and she still calls me a wee boy. Did she have to wear that costume tonight?" Roger whispered between his clenched teeth. Eric shushed them as Miss Yost made her way around the room.

Angilia went to Miss Yost while she greeted her dear sweet Juanita, and introduced Miss Yost to her grandfather. She miraculously did not attempt to squeeze Alejandro's cheeks. Instead, she grabbed him in an exuberant hug. He was stunned and gently pulled out of her grasp. "It is very nice to meet you, Miss Yost. I have heard quite a lot about you and your music class," he told her.

"Oh, I am quite sure you have, yes I am. If I do say so, everyone loves my music class, yes they do" Miss Yost said, still smiling. Roger coughed, much to his dismay, for she was on her way to him.

Soon Miss Yost had Roger in a tight hug. "Here is my shy boy, yes he is. He is still shy, hiding behind his friends, yes he is. There is no need to be shy, no there is not." Roger's face turned red, in frustration and anger, although Miss Yost characteristically misread the cause. "See, he is blushing now, yes he is. We must break you out of your shell, yes we must."

"Good evening, Miss Yost," Roger managed to say with the worst forced smile any of them had seen. Eduardo moved away from Roger, trying to escape her, but she playfully chased him and grabbed him.

He looked at Eric, his eyes seething. "Who is this little fellow?" Miss Yost asked. How ridiculous. Eduardo stood over six feet tall and was muscular.

Angilia rushed to her uncle and took his arm. "Miss Yost, this is my uncle, Eduardo Martínez."

"Oh my, then you are my dear Juanita's little boy, yes you are. Oh my, you should have come with your mother the other day, yes you should have. How sad that she had to stop coming, yes it is." She let him go and grabbed Angilia again. "But our dear little girl caused a riot, yes she did, and she is not permitted to return, no she is not."

Miss Yost turned, looking for Susan, and spotted her in the far corner with Daniel. Miss Yost bounced to them and grabbed Susan's cheeks. "My favorite little girl student, yes she is. She is precious, yes she is. She is shy, too, just like Roger, yes she is." Susan hugged her and said how nice it was to see her.

"Miss Yost, have you met Daniel?" Susan asked, her only defense at the moment.

"I have met him before, yes I have. You are from somewhere else, yes you are. You were not lucky enough to be my music student, no you were not." She squeezed his cheeks and then pounced back into the center of the room, terrifying most everyone. What would she do next?

Thankfully for them, the chef appeared to announce that dinner was served. Miss Yost grabbed him before he could escape and squeezed his cheeks. "You are such a sweet young thing, yes you are. I could eat you, yes I could." Chef Antoine looked absolutely horrified and excused himself. "He is very shy, too, yes he is. You have quite a lot of shy people here, little Eric, yes you do."

"Apparently I do," he wryly agreed, and took Miss Yost's arm to escort her to the dining room. He knew better than to ask Roger, Daniel, or Eduardo. Eduardo linked arms with Angilia and gave her a look that let her know how much he disliked this. At the table, Miss Yost was seated across from Angilia, to Eric's left side. Eduardo grabbed the chair next to his niece. Roger, Daniel, and Mitchell sat as close to the other end of the table as they could. Matthew gleefully sat beside Miss Yost, his smile, like hers, plastered across his face. Roger looked at Matthew, certain the boy had lost his mind.

Miss Yost talked constantly during dinner, leaving many of them with headaches. After dinner, Angilia asked if she and Miss Yost could go to the basement recording studio. Eric said they could, knowing Angilia wanted to ask Miss Yost about singing with her. When they were out of earshot, everyone voiced their thoughts. "She is quite a character," Daniel said. "I thought surely you had exaggerated, but no, you were right," he told Roger and Susan.

"You could never exaggerate that," Eduardo said.

"Come on. Miss Yost is a sweet lady," Matthew protested. "She really is. I've never met anyone else like her."

"You won't either, thank goodness," Mitchell said. "She is certainly one of a kind, isn't she?"

"Did you say she teaches middle school, mi hijo?" Alejandro asked Eric. Eric nodded. "Her students are too old for her to talk to them like they are babies, if you ask me."

"See? Didn't I tell you all how horrible it is?" Roger replied. "Right, Susan?" She nodded, too stunned to say anything.

"Dr. Matthew is right. Hilda is a very sweet woman," Juanita stated. Katherine voiced her agreement.

"Hilda? Her first name is Hilda?" Roger asked, stopping when Eric shot him a look of disapproval. "I'm sorry, but you know how much torture that was for me. I am not exaggerating when I say it traumatized me for life."

"Let's return to the sitting room so we can relax while Angilia and Miss Yost are in the recording studio. The least we can do is say good night to her before she leaves," Eric told them. They all dutifully did as he requested. One hour later, Angilia and Miss Yost entered the sitting room, and Eric stood. The other men followed suit.

Angilia was smiling. "Miss Yost listened to the new song I wrote, and she agreed to sing backing vocals on the track. Isn't that wonderful?"

Everyone said it was, and Juanita and Katherine went so far as to hug her and Miss Yost. Katherine stunned Mitchell by asking Miss Yost to join them for tea on Saturday afternoon at the house. Miss Yost agreed with a bouncy hug for Katherine and a cheek squeeze for Matthew's daddy.

"I have to prepare tomorrow's lessons, yes I do. I am afraid I must say good night to all of you, yes I do. Good night," Miss Yost sang. They all said an enthusiastic "Good night" in reply, relieved that she was leaving. Eric, Angilia, and Matthew walked her to her car and waved to her as she drove away.

"I really do like Miss Yost," Matthew said. "She should visit more often."

"I'm afraid I would have a revolt on my hands if that happened. Her class really is a bit much, if I do say so. I wonder what she's preparing. She always did the same things every day," Eric speculated.

"She does, but she writes a formal lesson plan for each day anyway. She's done that as long as she's been teaching," Matthew shared.

"Really? Well, at least she is organized," Eric replied. "I am happy for you that she agreed to sing on your song, Angel. I know you wanted her to."

"I am, too, and she will enjoy it, I think. I don't think most people take her seriously, Daddy. Miss Yost doesn't have any family here, and her teaching is all she has. I think she's lonely, so she fills her time doing things like the formal lesson plans. We do need to ask her over more."

"Perhaps, Angel, but maybe not to a formal dinner with everyone. If it's just those of us who enjoy her company, that would be kinder. Maybe she could come to lunch sometimes."

"Thank you, Daddy. I love you."

And I love you, Angilia, Matthew thought, but dared not say. Miss Yost can pinch my cheeks all day if it makes you happy.

§§§§

Eric, Angilia, and their group walked to church as usual the following Sunday, September 16, 2012, although that day was not quite usual. Angilia's red and white suit and Eric's red and white tie were the national colors of Valdavia. The flags that proudly flew throughout the country were red and white with the spread-winged eagle emblem in the center. Reverend Hutchins' prayer that morning was for the continued protection and peace of Valdavia.

The sermon told of Valdavia's 681 years of existence as an independent country who had never waged war, as the citizens celebrated Valdavia's Independence Day that day. Valdavia had existed in peace for nearly seven hundred years, and Reverend Hutchins read scripture which supported their shared belief that Valdavia was ordained and protected by God as a country of peace and love. Certainly the nineteen kings who had thus far ruled over the country were men of God whose own lives were examples of love, charity, and peace. The day's service concluded with Angilia's version of Ecclesiastes 3 that had debuted on Father's Day.

At noon, Roger called everyone to the television for the news. The weekend anchor, Melissa Gibbons, showed the 2012 Independence Day photographs that had been released by the Palais Royale de Valdavia to mark the country's 681st anniversary. "These are quite special, are they not? King Eric is wearing his formal military uniform, looking very handsome and dashing." Roger poked Eric's arm, grinning. "Princess Angilia is shown wearing two different outfits. The first is her fourth great-grandmother Queen Consort Sarah's Regency-style floral print day dress from 1816. Is that not adorable? The second outfit worn by the Princess is her great-grandmother Queen Consort Sabrina's 1901 going-away ensemble. That outfit is just stunning. For comparison, we have a photograph of Sabrina on her wedding day wearing that very ensemble. What a fun, beautiful way to honor the country's heritage. One other historic note is the photographer. Bonnie Glaser was given the honor of photographing the King and the Princess for Independence Day. As you recall, Bonnie Glaser is a photojournalist and one of the former Gulf War hostages whom the Princess helped to free. How fitting that she take these historic photographs."

Eduardo was smiling broadly, even though tears shone in his eyes. He hugged Bonnie, who had stayed with them for several days to take the photographs and enjoy Independence Day with them. She had sat with Eduardo at church that morning. She was smiling, too, so happy to share their joy. "Thank you all so much," she said. "I am still trying to wrap my head around all of this. I can never thank you enough for this honor, Your Majesty."

"Remember, call me Eric please. Bonnie, Angilia and I would like to ask you something. You do not have to answer immediately, of course. We know you need time to think and to come to a decision. Would you consider becoming our official photographer? We cannot think of a more talented and wonderful person to whom we would like to offer this position. Right, Angilia?" Angilia nodded, hoping Bonnie would accept. They both liked Bonnie and her work was consistently beautiful.

Bonnie's hands covered her face and tears spilled from her eyes. Eduardo was thrilled for his friend. Through her hands and her tears, she asked Eric, "Are you serious?"

"Absolutely, we are," he replied with a smile, while Angilia leaned on his arm, tears in her eyes, as well.

Bonnie took a few minutes to catch her breath and to regain her composure. She dried her eyes and held her hand out to Eric. "I accept. You have a new photographer."

Angilia hugged her, so happy for Bonnie. In fact, everyone hugged her and welcomed her to the extended family. "Why don't we all head to the park for the Independence Day picnic?" Eric suggested. Mike drove them all in Eric's largest Rolls Royce, and the happy family and friends enjoyed the day mingling with people, signing autographs, posing for pictures, and even eating lunch.

As they sat at the table, they joined hands and Angilia said the prayer. "Dear God, Thank you for your loving grace and protection over us. We ask that your loving embrace remains around us for all eternity, even after we depart this earth for the splendors of your Kingdom of Heaven. Thank you for your many blessings. Amen."

Everyone repeated her "Amen," and Bonnie added her gratitude once more for Eric's and Angilia's love and compassion in helping them to freedom. Eduardo embraced her, and they all felt more than ever that they were indeed under God's protection and care.

§§§§

The following Wednesday, September 19, was also a special occasion, for Mitchell turned 62 years old that day. After lunch, Eric asked everyone to join him in the sitting room, and soon everyone was gathered. Matthew and Angilia had strategically kept Mitchell near the back of the line, so that when he entered the others could surprise him with a shout of "Happy birthday!"

"I don't know why I'm surprised, actually, since birthday parties seem to happen regularly here," Mitchell proclaimed. "But I am surprised. Thank you all, especially Matthew, who is the likely culprit who disclosed my birthdate."

Matthew could not help but smile. Like they had done with Katherine's party the month before, Matthew and Angilia had engineered his party, with help from the others. A sheet cake waited on the table, as did stacks of gifts. Angilia stood on her toes and kissed his cheek. "Happy birthday, Dr. Taylor."

He hugged her, literally amazed at her progress in just six months. She was so much stronger and healthier than he had expected her to be at this point. He had gotten drawn into their lives on the worst day of their lives, and he was grateful for that. Eric and Angilia felt like family to him, to Katherine, and of course to Matthew. "Thank you, sweetheart."

"Cake! Cake!" Katherine demanded, and her plea was soon joined by several other voices. Mitchell obliged, and joked that he was glad they had not lit 62 candles on his cake. Instead, there was one, a star-shaped candle in the center. He dutifully blew out the wick and then Katherine cut the cake, giving the first piece to her husband. Everyone stood while they ate cake and chatted, except for Angilia, who strolled onto the balcony. That was where she had come to her father on Christmas Day 1994.

Eric saw her standing there, looking up at the sky, and he knew what she was thinking. He went to her and put his hands on her shoulders, and she smiled up at him. They did not have to say anything. They stood together, wrapped in their love and their memories for several minutes. They rejoined everyone when they heard Matthew urge his father to open his presents.

Mitchell received several books he had mentioned wanting to read, a year's pass to the nearest golf course from his wife, a new watch from Eric to replace the one he had recently broken, a portrait of Katherine and Matthew from Bonnie, and a joint gift from Matthew and Angilia. How prophetic it felt to see their names together on the gift tag, he thought. What could they have bought together?

He looked at them quizzically, and tore off the wrapping paper. Inside the box was a book. On the cover it said <u>Demon Slayer</u>, "Written by Angilia" and "Illustrated by Matthew." He was speechless. Angilia had written a modern fairy tale about a kind doctor who saved a princess from an evil demon. It was her way of thanking him for all that he had done for her and for her father. She could have illustrated it, but she felt it would be far more special if his son did. She had taken the book to Matthew and asked him if he wanted to illustrate it as his father's birthday gift. He read the story and was dumbstruck, too, by the plot.

He had happily agreed, and now Mitchell was showing their beautiful book to Katherine and Eric. Everyone was amazed, especially Eric. Once again, Angilia had turned something ugly and horrifying into something beautiful and soothing. How she had the wherewithal to constantly do that Eric never determined except to credit it to her background as an angel. He was pleased that the two former Heavenly Realm friends were friends on earth. Eric knew in his heart that Angilia and Matthew were destined to be together forever. In earthly terms, Angilia was much too young to consider a serious relationship or marriage, but in time it would happen—with Matthew.

§§§§

24 September 2012

I have never felt as unsure about anything as I did today. After school was dismissed, Shannon called me and said a friend of hers was very distressed and needed help. Could I talk with the girl? Shannon didn't want to say much over the phone, so I told them to come here. I took them to the sitting room, closed the door for privacy, and Shannon finally got her friend to talk to me. I asked her name, and she told me it is Molly. I asked how I could help her and what was wrong. She looked at Shannon, and Shannon told her to just tell me.

Finally she did. She said she is pregnant. She is 17 and pregnant. She kept talking, saying she just wanted to go somewhere alone and get an abortion. I was stunned, of course. I asked her if she had talked to her parents, and she laughed while she cried. She said her father was away for work, but he would kill her if he knew. She said her mother would kick her out of the house and disown her. She could never talk to them about this.

After about an hour of convincing her that she could not do something she would likely regret, like abortion, she listened when I said she was safer confiding in her parents. They loved her, or they would not have taken care of her and provided for her, I said. Molly said they had to or they would go to jail.

I reminded her that they could have given her away for adoption if they really did not want her. She finally agreed that they loved her, though she was still terrified to tell them she is pregnant.

I asked her if she wanted me to call her mother and ask her to come here, too. We would tell her mother together. She alternated between wanting to do that and being terrified of doing that. After a long time, she dialed her telephone number and I talked with her mother and asked her to please come here. She wanted to know why, and I assured her we would tell her after she was here. I called Daddy and told him the girl's mother was coming and asked if he would let her in and escort her to the sitting room. He did, and he never said or asked anything.

We finally told Molly's mother, who was very angry at first, telling Molly how awful she was and calling her names. I was horrified. See, I never thought parents would talk like that to their children. Never. I am still in shock over that. Molly cried and apologized, which seemed to make her mother angrier. Finally, I told her mother that Molly was frightened and alone except for her parents. She needed them more than ever. She needed their love and support, even if they didn't agree with or condone what Molly had done.

Her mother paced the room for a long time, and Molly kept weeping. Her mother finally sat next to me and asked me if I had ever done anything like Molly had done. I told her I had not, and she looked at me for several minutes. "Then how are you so wise about all of this?" she asked me. I was really stunned then! She went and sat beside Molly and hugged her. She told Molly everything would be all right. They would talk to Molly's father when he got home tonight. They would take it one day at a time and get through this together.

Molly was stunned, I was stunned, and I know Molly's father was, too. Molly and her parents called me tonight and told me that while none of them were pleased with what had happened, they would make sure that Molly and her baby were cared for and loved. Molly told me she could have never faced her parents without my urging and advice. I don't think I did much. Daddy was right, because everything I told Molly and her mother was what most people call common sense. I just spoke from my heart and told them what I knew was right. It worked. I am amazed and very grateful to God for guiding me through this crisis. After this, I think I can handle anything that the teens in COC bring to me. Thank you God!

CHAPTER 10

Before they left for church on Sunday, September 30, Angilia finished her birthday card for Matthew. She left it on her desk so the ink would dry. Her gift for him had been wrapped for quite a while, since she had bought it at the gift shop with her father. She felt it the perfect gift for her best friend—she always thought of him as such, for he was still the Matthew she had known so long ago in the Unborn Children Realm. She was so happy God had brought them together on earth, because she had never forgotten him and had hoped she would someday, somehow meet him again. It took a tragedy to reunite them, but that was God's doing to counter-balance what one of Satan's fiends had done.

During Reverend Hutchins' sermon on the eternal battle between God and Satan, he mentioned how those people who open their hearts to Satan actually become his workers on earth. They did Satan's bidding, bringing pain and misery to those who had opened their hearts to God. Angilia could not help but to pity Gregor Jamieson, for he had been under Satan's control. Yes, he knew what he was doing, and he was ultimately responsible for his actions. Still, he had allowed his anger over long-ago events to let his soul and heart be overtaken by Satan. How very sad, Angilia thought. She prayed that those who had not opened their hearts to God would do so.

As they walked back home, Angilia hugged her father, ever more grateful that he was her father and that he was free from Jamieson's threats. Eric put his arm around her and felt such a surge of joy when he looked down and saw her beautiful smile. Matthew watched them, realizing how close father and daughter were, almost envying their closeness. Angilia loved and adored her father, Matthew knew that. Heck, she had said her father was her very best friend. How could he ever compete with that? Did he stand a chance of earning her love? His heart ached every time she was near him, every time he thought of her—in other words, constantly.

Angilia whispered to her father, he nodded, and she went ahead of everyone into the courtyard and palace. She walked as quickly as she could to the second floor music room, wanting to make sure everything was in place and ready. It was. The chef was putting the finishing touches on the buffet lunch. Matthew's cake was centered on the table and surrounded by the gifts. She quickly went to her suite, sealed his card, and picked up his gift. She slid the card underneath the ribbon on the gift, and returned to the music room. She placed her gift on the table with the rest.

"Thank you, Antoine. You are a miracle worker. Everything looks perfect, his favorite foods and drinks, the lovely cake, the decorations. Thank you so much," Angilia said to their chef and hugged him in gratitude. They heard the others' voices, and Antoine quickly exited and went down the back staircase.

Angilia took her place at the piano and took a deep breath. Matthew knew by now that birthdays were celebrated here, and he honestly expected a not-so-surprise party. He actually turned toward the sitting room, which was opposite the music room, when he heard the most glorious sound coming from the music room. He walked to the open door and saw Angilia sitting at the piano, playing a piece he had never heard before. Or had he?

Matthew walked slowly toward the piano, entranced, his head slightly cocked to one side. He had heard that before, he swore he had. But how? Angilia had not played it while he had been here, and she had not recorded that piece. How and when could he have heard it? Matthew's brain was spinning out of control as he watched her and listened to her music. She smiled at him, and his knees went weak. He held onto the edge of the piano to maintain his balance. He no longer felt like he were standing, but rather floating above and looking down on the scene. How very odd.

Eric, Mitchell, Katherine, and everyone else watched, too, and they all now knew beyond any doubt that Matthew did love Angilia. That was more than evident. And that music, that breathtaking music. Katherine wondered whether Angilia had written that just for Matthew's birthday. It was lilting, joyous, and bright. When it ended, everyone applauded and gathered around Matthew near the piano.

Angilia stood and came around the piano, and Katherine hugged her. "That was stunning, dear. When did you write that?"

"Oh, a very long time ago," Angilia mysteriously said, and winked at her father. It was a piece she had played for Matthew a very long time ago indeed, when they sat alone in the tower of the Unborn Children Realm. She had seen Matthew's reaction, and she knew it had triggered an underlying memory. She had told her father about the piece, and he had encouraged her to play it for Matthew on his birthday, whether he remembered it or not. It had been written for him originally, and it would be a nice surprise and gift for him, Eric had commented.

Matthew regained some of his senses and turned to face Angilia. "That was jubilant and heavenly, Angilia. Thank you." She looked up at him with those eyes and that smile, and he wanted to pull her into his arms and kiss her. It took every ounce of his willpower not to do that. He cleared his throat and thanked her again, not knowing what else to do or to say at that moment.

Eric saw Matthew's distress, and he sensed that the young man was confused. Had he remembered something? "Well, lunch is set up, everyone. Help yourselves. Birthday boy goes first in line," Eric said with a smile. Matthew somehow managed to walk to the buffet, his parents behind him, followed by Juanita, Alejandro, Eduardo, Bonnie, Susan, Daniel, and Roger. Eric motioned for Angilia to go before he did, and Eric was the last to fill his plate.

Both seats next to Matthew were taken, and he looked utterly crestfallen when Angilia, holding her plate, looked for an empty chair. Mitchell noticed and stood. "I think I'll sit with the men," he said and motioned toward Eduardo and Eric. He offered his chair between Katherine and Matthew to Angilia. "Why don't you keep Katherine company?" he asked her, never revealing his true intentions.

Angilia smiled at Katherine and then at Matthew. Matthew felt his throat tighten when she asked him if he liked the menu. "Your mother and I planned the menu with a lot of your favorite foods. Antoine did an amazing job preparing everything, didn't he?" she said to Matthew.

Matthew forced himself to swallow. "Yes, he really did. Thank you Mom, Angilia. This is very sweet of you."

Angilia smiled. She had wanted Matthew's first birthday party with them to be extra special. When everyone finished eating, Angilia began collecting the plates. Katherine, Bonnie, and Susan stood and helped her carry them to the cart Antoine had placed at the end of the buffet table. Eric stood and lit the twenty-six candles and announced that it was time for Matthew to make his wish and to blow out the candles on his cake. Matthew blushed, but stood, made a secret wish that Angilia love him in return, and blew out the candles with one giant breath. Everyone applauded, and Katherine took the cake knife and cut pieces of cake. She handed the first piece to Matthew.

After half an hour, Susan and Bonnie collected the cake plates and added them to the cart. "Son, now you get to open your presents," Katherine said. Matthew hesitated for a few seconds, embarrassed that so many people were watching him, but he finally reached for a gift. It happened to be his mother's, another cardigan sweater. She seemed to always buy him sweaters. His father's gift was an artist's box with colored pencils and various paints and brushes. Matthew was pleased that his father accepted his art. Other gifts were more art supplies, such as canvases, pencils, and a new large easel, since few people knew what else to get a cardiologist-turned-artist.

Eric gave him a pseudo plane ticket to take one of Eric's planes to France for the following week—Matthew's first foray into France since his arrival. Matthew was stunned and looked at Eric in gratitude. "Thank you, I mean really thank you. I don't know what to say."

"Open the ticket," Eric said. Matthew gasped. Tucked inside the ticket were unlimited passes to a dozen museums in Paris, France. Matthew looked like he would cry, he was so happy. "Now you can put all of these art supplies to good use," Eric added. "If one week is not long enough, stay longer. Your hotel reservations are included in that stack somewhere."

"This is remarkable," Matthew gushed. No one had ever given him such a marvelous gift.

"There is one more gift, son," Katherine reminded him.

Matthew picked it up and recognized Angilia's handwriting on the envelope of the card. He untied the ribbon and opened the card first. She had made it, with a drawing of him sitting in his sitting room window sketching. Inside she had written him a prayer that his birthday and every day be glorious and full of his dreams come true. "It's beautiful, it really is. Thank you," he said softly.

Daniel, who sat next to Matthew, gently nudged him to open the present. The boy seemed too enamored over just the card. Matthew cleared his throat and unfolded the handmade wrapping paper, wanting to keep it for an art project. He stared at the book she had bought him, <u>Celestial Art Through the Ages</u>. He flipped through it, seeing paintings of angels, God, and Heaven. Inside the front cover, Angilia had written a brief note to him: *Dearest Matthew, Follow your heart and your dreams wherever they lead you. Thank you for your beautiful friendship. xoxo Angilia.* He stared at her note until the tears in his eyes blurred his vision. He knew where his heart and his dreams led him—to her.

Angilia put her hand on his arm. "I didn't mean to upset you. I'm sorry."

Matthew shook his head. "You didn't. It's the most beautiful book I have ever seen," he croaked through the tears that choked him.

Eric, Mitchell, and Katherine looked at one another, dazed by Matthew's reaction. Eric knew more than ever that in a few years their children would marry. That was inevitable. The art book of Heavenly paintings was an innocent enough gift from Angilia, one she had bought a few months earlier. It was a gift of friendship. It touched something deep inside Matthew, though, that perhaps he did not yet or may never fully comprehend. Eric knew, though, that Matthew and Angilia were bound together for eternity.

§§§§

"What did you do in Paris?" Angilia asked Matthew as they walked for a couple of hours the Wednesday after his return. Although it was fall, the temperatures remained in the high 60s up to the mid 70s. The weather in Valdavia was generally pleasant throughout the year, with its Mediterranean locale. The days were quite mild, with winter nights averaging in the mid 50s. Matthew and Angilia wore jeans and t-shirts as they enjoyed the sun's warmth.

Matthew smiled broadly, genuinely happy. "What did I do? I all but lived in the museums. The first day I went to The Louvre, and I wanted to cry, I was so happy. Everything there just blew me away, Angilia. I spent the entire first day there, walking around and staring at painting after painting, just absorbing it all. I can never describe what it felt like to see these great works up close. They came to life for me. I left there when they closed and walked the Paris streets for the longest time, and finally just sat and drew whatever and whoever I saw. Oh my gosh, it was like Heaven."

Angilia smiled. "I'm sure it was, Matthew. Your first passion is art. It always has been." Had she just said that? She had to be aware of what she said to him.

"What? What do you mean? I never thought of art until a few months ago when we were still in Oxford at the hospital. I still don't know why art pulled me so strongly," he said, mystified by her comments. Sometimes it was as though she knew him better than anyone had ever known him.

"That must mean that art is your first love, then. Somewhere inside of you it was there. Regardless of what brought it out, this was meant to be your path, your destiny. You would never have pursued art if it were not your destiny."

"All I know is that it came to me while we were still at the hospital. It consumed my thoughts. I did write a resignation letter, and I was going to submit it when you were released. I was going to leave medicine and go to France. And then you asked me to come here, and so it is. Maybe you're right and it was meant to be. Otherwise, it sure doesn't make much sense to me. It's like you pushed me toward art, but that isn't right, either. My mind is all mixed up with so many feelings after last week. One thing I do know is that I made the right decision to come here," Matthew confessed to her.

Angilia smiled. "Other than art, what is most important to you, Matthew?"

Dear God, he prayed. He could never answer that question truthfully, not yet. She was. "Family," he said instead. "I know your family is very important to you, too. Do you ever regret being an only child?"

Angilia shook her head. "No. I don't regret anything about my life. I never have and I never will. I am far too blessed for regrets. God is first in my life always and forever, and then my father. I love him so much. I can never express that love with mere words."

"You don't have to. Your love for him shows in your eyes. He loves you more than I have ever known a father to love a child. You two share a love and a bond I don't quite understand, probably because I had never seen anything like it until I met you both. It's always been that way for you and your father. I mean, when we watched those home movies, it was so clear. It's almost spooky how tight you two are."

Angilia looked somewhat puzzled. "Spooky? What do you mean?"

Matthew sighed. "That's not the right word. I'm not a wordsmith at all, so forgive me if I seem to say something wrong. I guess what I mean is otherworldly or something."

"Like Heavenly, perhaps?" Angilia suggested. Matthew nodded. "It is. God ordained that we be father and daughter, and he blessed our relationship. I suppose that is the simplest explanation I can offer."

"Hmmm. I believe you. It's ironic how I have always believed in God and all, but until I met you and your father, that was really not a huge part of my life. I'm sorry if any of this offends you." Angilia shook her head as he talked. "It's just that as a cardiologist, I was trained to think scientifically and kind of ignore the spiritual stuff. Then the two of you whizzed into my life with your prayers and talk of destiny, and something in my head and in my heart changed. I changed."

"That is a beautiful thing to say. I never try to force my beliefs on others, but they are a major part of who I am, and I will never deny or forsake them for anyone. If how I live can or does influence anyone, then that is part of God's plan, too. I never want to do anything that would dishonor God or my family," Angilia confided. It was still so easy to talk with Matthew and share her feelings with him. That had not changed at all, even if he did not remember their shared past.

"You have to think about that more than most people do, though. You're a public person, a princess and a singer. How do you deal with all of that, with people demanding to know everything about you constantly?"

"Most people don't actually demand to know everything about me. The press does, of course, but I largely ignore them. Sure, people ask for autographs and pictures, but that's the least I can do in return for their support. Without them and their interest in my work, there wouldn't be much purpose in making music for the public. I'd probably still write music, but no one outside these walls would hear it. That would be all right, too. This all started so quickly and even then I felt it was meant to be. Why else was Tom outside the palace gates that day to hear me? That day started the whole music career. That was part of God's plan for me, too," Angilia said as she looked up at the clear sky and smiled.

"God sure has some grand plans for you, girl. You were born heir to a kingdom, you are a composer and singer, you were a university professor, you are a writer, you are an artist, and you are a humanitarian. That's quite a life to be just sixteen years old," Matthew told her as he glanced at her with a smile.

"I suppose. But your life is just as amazing. You were a teenage surgeon, after all."

"Yeah, I was. It had its ups and downs, but the best thing that came of it was you. If I hadn't been the cardiologist on duty that day, we would never have met. Is that God's plan, too, Angilia?" Angilia studied his face. Matthew was not smiling. His brow was furrowed. His question was not in jest. He was serious. Her heart pounded heavily.

"Yes, it was. That day brought our families together, Matthew. That was meant to happen for whatever reason," Angilia truthfully answered.

I know the reason, Matthew thought. I love you. I want to marry you.

After their walk, when she went to her suite to shower, Matthew ran to Eric's office and tapped on the door. "Matthew, come in. Is Angilia all right?"

"She's fine. She's taking a shower right now. We had a long walk, and she didn't run out of breath or get tired. Her knee is sore, but she's doing much better."

"Wonderful! Thank you. What can I do for you then?" Eric asked.

"Actually, I need to make an appointment to talk with you privately," Matthew forced himself to say. He felt so nervous that his body trembled.

"An appointment? Just to talk to me?"

"Yes. It's quite important, and it is private," Matthew insisted.

"That means it should be when Angilia isn't here." Eric opened her calendar on his computer. "She has her COC meeting at the high school one week from today, on October 17, from 4:00-6:00 that afternoon. How does that sound?"

"That's perfect. Thank you."

"May I ask what this is about?" Eric looked concerned. "You aren't thinking of leaving, are you? That would break Angilia's heart."

Dear God, Matthew prayed. He knew Eric and Angilia did not intend to torture him, but they sure did. "No, not at all. It's personal. I'll tell you everything next week."

"All right. If there's ever a problem, please let me know," Eric said.

"I will. Thank you," Matthew said, and took a deep breath as he walked to the third floor. One week was not long, but it would feel long to Matthew.

§§§§§

Finally, the time had arrived. Matthew watched Angilia leave for her COC meeting, driven by Mike, and he took a deep breath. Why was he so darn nervous? He walked upstairs to the office and tapped on the door at 4:00 promptly. Eric smiled and told him to close the door. Matthew sat in the chair across from Eric's desk, his hands clasped tightly in his lap. This was it, Matthew thought. His future, and possibly his life, was on the line and in Eric's hands.

"Thank you for meeting with me," Matthew said, his voice seeming to crack.

"What can I help you with? You said it was personal and private. Have you talked with your parents?"

"No, I haven't. I need to talk with you, Sir." Eric's brow furrowed. Something was wrong, he thought. Matthew was quite nervous and very formal.

"All right. Whenever you're ready, I'm here to listen," Eric assured him.

Matthew cleared his throat. Eric stood and opened a small refrigerator hidden in the bookcase. He handed Matthew a bottle of water, and Eric watched in bewilderment as the young man drank the whole bottle in one huge gulp. Matthew cleared his throat again and steeled himself. Why could he not just say it? He did.

"I love her. I want to marry her. After the past seven months with her, I know my love is real and deep and true. I feel it. I know it."

Good grief, Eric thought. Matthew was a complete nervous wreck. Eric, though, smiled and relaxed. For a moment he thought Matthew would tell him he had a terminal disease, he looked so forlorn and serious. "I know, Matthew."

Matthew looked like Eric had punched him. "You—you know?" His voice cracked like a thirteen year old boy's voice, and Eric controlled his laughter.

"Yes. I saw it in the hospital, at the stable, at your birthday party, and every other time you look at her or are near her."

Matthew suddenly looked utterly panicked, his eyes huge. "Does—does—does she know?" Now he was stuttering.

"No. Angilia does not know. She has no experience with this, so she does not recognize the signs. She considers you a great friend, I know that. But she doesn't suspect anything other than friendship, no," Eric told him.

Matthew seemed to relax, but then nearly jumped from the chair again. "Are you—are you mad?"

"Mad? No. I'm neither surprised nor mad, Matthew. What do you propose to do about this?" Eric asked, resting his chin on his hand.

"Propose? Not yet." Eric bit his finger to keep from laughing. Did Matthew think Eric would behead him for admitting the truth? "I do love her, I really love her. I tried to deny it. I tried to fight it. It was futile. Sometimes I feel so odd, like I've known her forever. I think I've gone mad since I met her."

There it was, Eric thought. Matthew did intuit at least tiny pieces and memories from his past. "Matthew, no one can deny his feelings. Do not even try. Mad? Love does that to a lot of people."

"What do I do? She is so young still. I love her so much. I will wait for her for as long as it takes, whatever her feelings are, I will wait. I want her to love me, of course I do, and I will die of heartbreak if she does not, I swear I will. But if she ends up loving another, I will have no choice but to accept it and wish her happiness. I will wait for her. I have to wait for her. I cannot live without her." Matthew sounded like a love-struck Shakespearean character—like Romeo. Eric felt for him, but he did find Matthew's angst rather amusing. If only he knew what Angilia had shared with him in July.

"Relax. Love has its foundation in friendship, even love at first sight. Believe me. I know. You have to like the person you love, and Angilia really likes you a lot. Give her time and space and understanding. Ultimately, it is Angilia's decision, whatever it is. If she loves you, that is fine. But you have to give her time to adapt to and grow into her feelings," Eric lectured.

"I will. I promise I will. I mean it. I am willing to wait as long as it takes. Before I met her, I would have never said or done that. She changed me. I can't explain it, but she has changed me. I won't do anything to upset her or hurt her or alienate her. I couldn't do that." Matthew took a deep breath and seemed to regain some of his senses.

"That's all I ask," Eric reiterated.

"But what about her social status?" Matthew asked, looking worried.

"What about it?"

"Well, I'm a British commoner and she's a princess," Matthew said.

"Do you think that really matters, Matthew?"

"No, not to you or to her, but what about the people? They might not approve," Matthew clarified.

"It's Angilia's life. It's her decision alone. No one cares about that sort of thing anymore anyway, and if they do, don't pay it any attention," Eric sternly said.

Matthew sat up straight, looked more serious, and cleared his throat again. "I want to ask you something." Eric looked at him, waiting for him to ask. Finally he did. "I want your permission to give Angilia a promise ring on her seventeenth birthday." There, he said it. "First, though, I would like to get a sense of how she feels. May I talk with her on Christmas Day and tell her how I feel for her? Would you mind if I tell her that I love her so that on her birthday the promise ring is not a complete shock to her?" Matthew felt and heard his heart pounding as he looked at his potential future father-in-law. What did Eric think? What would he answer? Matthew anxiously wanted to know.

Eric smiled. He knew their union was destined. "That's fine, Matthew. If she accepts, or does not accept, that is her decision."

"Thank you. I will wait as long as I have to, as long as it takes," Matthew said yet again. "I love her far too much not to wait."

"You do understand that if she eventually agrees to marry you, then you will have to sacrifice a lot of your privacy. Such a marriage comes with scrutiny, public demands, and press interest. That is often very trying on a person."

"I understand. I have seen that, and I understand that. I know none of that will be easy, but my love for her is so much stronger than any fear or concern I might have about any of that. Besides, she is the one everyone loves and is interested in, and I can help her and support her," Matthew asserted.

"I hope so, Matthew, for both of you." Eric stood, and Matthew did as well. The men walked down the hallway and the stairs, Eric's arm around Matthew's shoulders. "I warn you, though, if you do anything to hurt or to offend my little girl, if you break her heart, I will. . . ."

Matthew turned pale, looked horrified, and stopped walking. "I would never do that."

Eric smiled and winked at him, and Matthew sighed in relief. Eric skipped down the stairs, but turned around on the landing and looked up at Matthew. "I am very serious." Matthew loosened his tie. He knew Eric was serious, but Matthew felt more elated than afraid. Eric approved of the relationship, and that was all that mattered. Except for Angilia's feelings. January 3, 2013 was still over two months in the future. Matthew had to do as he promised and wait until Christmas to even broach the subject with Angilia. He smiled and told himself he could do that. For her, he could do anything.

§§§§§

When Angilia returned from her COC meeting, she took her briefcase to the office and was surprised that Eric was still working at his desk. "Good evening, Daddy." She walked over and kissed his cheek. "What are you still doing in here working?"

"I'm just catching up on a few e-mails and waiting for you," he smiled. "I saw an interesting advertisement in today's newspaper, Angilia."

"Oh? What for?"

"A benefit performance of Shakespeare's <u>Romeo and Juliet</u> to be done on the evening of my birthday. Apparently, it is your acting debut."

"Oh, that," Angilia wrinkled her nose.

"Yes, that. How come you never said anything about this?" he asked her.

"I guess I forgot. Really. They asked me to do it, figuring I know the play already and said since it's your birthday it would be nice. It's for charity anyway, so I suppose I can stumble my way through it once."

"Who is Romeo?" Eric asked, fighting a laugh at the memory of Matthew's angst-ridden protestations that afternoon.

"Scott Ransdale. He is with COC and actually came to talk to me about that with the girls that day. The other performers are from the high school drama departments, including the adults. They want to raise funds for the fine arts programs at the high schools. That's the only reason I agreed to do this."

"Well, you will outshine them all, Angel. I can't say I look forward to the end of that play, but it's all make believe. I suppose I can deal with it," he grinned. "Do you realize this is your first school performance?" he smiled. "I've seen you on stage hundreds of times, but never at a school recital or play. I guess we are catching up, aren't we?"

She kissed his forehead and hugged him. "I guess we are, Daddy."

§§§§§

31 October 2012

Tonight, believe it or not, I am having a slumber party! My first slumber party. At first, when I thought of it, I felt oddly too old for such a thing, but then I remembered that I am 16 and have never been to or hosted a slumber party. A slumber party is practically a must-do for every teenage girl. Two weeks ago, after the first COC meeting, I asked Daddy if I could host a slumber party here, and he smiled and said yes! I am so happy.

Shannon, Amanda, Amy, Nicole, and Darlene are coming. I know I am their COC sponsor/advisor, but I feel it's appropriate to do things with them socially. I like them, and they like me. I see no harm in our being friends. In fact, I feel that will only strengthen our trust. They will arrive this evening a couple of hours after high school dismisses. They do not have school tomorrow due to teacher meetings, so this is the perfect night. Instead of celebrating Halloween, we will have a COC friends slumber party! Now I do feel more like a typical teenager.

§§§§

Just after 5:00, Eric and Angilia greeted her five friends and welcomed them for the night. Each girl had a sleeping bag and a suitcase. Darlene kept her head down and did not speak. Eric thought she was extremely shy. Angilia escorted them to her suite, where they would all sleep that night, and Eric smiled as he watched them. Angilia had never had friends her age before, and suddenly she had five. Their chatter and giggles wafted down the staircase and filled his heart with joy.

"Oh my gosh, your room is to die for gorgeous," Amy gushed. "This really is like a fairy tale princess' room."

Angilia smiled. "Thank you. Put your things anywhere. I thought we would sleep in the sitting room since it's larger." The five girls stood quietly. "You don't want to stay in here? It's just that the bedroom has less space, because the bed is large. It's not large enough for six people though. It can hold two or three of you if you would rather we sleep in my bedroom."

Nicole nudged Shannon. "It's not that," Shannon said. "Should you sleep on the hard floor? I mean, you know."

Angilia did know. "Oh, that. Well, actually, Matthew told me I should sleep on the sofa here, if you all don't mind. Is that okay?"

The five girls sighed in relief and smiled. "That's fine." They finally put their sleeping bags and overnight cases on the floor and asked Angilia to show them around her suite. "Holy smokes. This bed is just the most." "A spa tub. How luscious." "This bathroom is humungous. My bedroom is the size of this bathroom." "Oh my! Oh my! Oh my! This closet is the absolute dreamiest closet I have ever in my life seen! Oh my!" "I always wondered where you kept all of your clothes. I mean, I knew it had to be large, but this is like a department store!"

Back in the sitting room, they walked out on the Juliet balcony and giggled. "This totally rocks, really it does." Next the girls wandered through the room, taking it all in and talking non-stop. "This desk is gorgeous. Heck, I'd do my homework if I had a desk like this." "Oh, your parents. That is so cool," Darlene sighed and pointed to the 1991 wedding plate. "Your dad is the coolest dad ever, Angilia," Amanda said. "He is. Really he is," Shannon agreed. "I think I'm in love with him," Darlene sighed. "You are so lucky, Angilia," Nicole smiled.

Angilia smiled. "Thank you. I'm not lucky. I'm very blessed that God gave me to my father. He is quite amazing." The girls whimpered and said she really was blessed.

"I have never known anyone with a father like yours, Angilia, I mean it. He loves you so much, and he is just so protective and supportive of you," Amanda said. "A lot of us envy you, you know, even though we know it's wrong. You have such a special relationship with your dad."

"I do, and I am so grateful for him. I have never met anyone like him. I love him more than I will ever love anyone," Angilia smiled. The girls whimpered again and hugged her.

They sat in her room talking for a while, listening to CDs. Darlene pulled a CD from her bag and asked if she could play it. Angilia nodded, and soon Eric's "Sunshine on My Shoulders" was blaring at full volume, filling the third floor and wafting to the fourth and second floors.

Eric, Matthew, and Roger heard it from their seats in the sitting room. "Good grief. They can't find something else to play?" Eric groaned. Roger snickered.

"Get used to it. I understand they're smitten with you, as Angilia put it, especially one of them," Matthew said. "Apparently that's her ringtone, her alarm, it's on constant rotation on her iPhone, and she falls asleep with it playing through her ear buds."

"Super," Eric frowned and snapped the newspaper he was reading.

At dinner time, the six girls announced their arrival long before they entered the dining room. Their voices carried down the stairs ahead of them. When they entered, Angilia turned to introduce the girls to everyone. Eric stood, smiled at them, and

Darlene gasped. She fainted and fell to the floor. "Oh, good night," Shannon said. "She did it again."

"She did what?" Mitchell asked and went to Darlene. "Is she ill?"

"No, I mean not physically ill." Nicole whispered, or attempted to whisper, to Dr. Taylor. "She has a major crush on King Eric." Roger started to laugh, but Eric gave him a stern look and he forced himself not to laugh. Eduardo rolled his eyes.

Mitchell revived Darlene and helped her to her feet. He walked her to the table, and mistakenly pulled out the chair opposite Angilia's on Eric's left side. When Darlene saw where she was supposed to sit, she fainted into Mitchell's arms. "Are you certain she's not ill?"

"We're certain. We're very sorry. We should have known this would happen, though," Shannon said. "She'll be all right. Just put her way down here." Shannon pointed to the empty seat next to Eduardo, and he rolled his eyes again.

Mitchell revived Darlene again and helped her into the chair between Eduardo and Matthew. She smiled, keeping her eyes on her plate lest she faint at the sight of King Eric again. Roger filled his mouth with water to keep from laughing. Everyone took their seats, and Antoine served dinner. Level-headed Shannon sat across from Angilia, for which Eric was grateful. Truly grateful.

"What do you young ladies have planned for tonight?" Eric asked them with a smile and looked at each of them in turn. He should not have smiled and looked at Darlene. Her dinner roll caught in her throat and she began choking. Matthew quickly grabbed her and performed the Heimlich maneuver to dislodge the food.

"I'm so sorry, really I am. I just can't help it," Darlene said as she stared at her plate and caught her breath.

Eric started to respond, but Shannon motioned him not to speak. "It's all right, Darlene. Just relax and eat slowly," Shannon said. Slowly? Most everyone seemed distraught at the thought. The poor girl would not survive the meal.

Eric whispered in Angilia's ear. She nodded. "Come with me, girls. We are having pizza for dinner. It will be here soon, and Antoine will bring it to us. We're going to the media room to watch movies."

Shannon, Amanda, Amy, and Nicole squealed with delight, and went to help Darlene to the basement. When they were gone, Eric put his head in his hands and said a silent prayer that they all survive the slumber party. "Good grief, that girl has it bad," Mitchell said. "I've never seen anyone react that way to someone."

Roger finally giggled. "Angilia was right, you know. You really are bigger than Bieber." Susan kicked his leg under the table to stop him. "Sorry. You know it's true. You just have to get used to it, Eric. You are a huge star now."

"Let's all just eat, please. Hopefully, they will spend most of the night in Angilia's room and we can avoid one another," Eric hoped.

"Yeah, and your room is right across the hall," Roger said, earning another stern look from Eric.

Thirty minutes later, Antoine carried a tray with the pizza, paper plates, napkins, and chilled drinks to the media room. He reported that the girls were watching The Ghost and Mrs. Muir at the moment, a sappy romantic tale of a widow and a ghost who fall in love. They were giggling and sobbing simultaneously. Roger snickered again, as did Daniel. Eric stood, looking exhausted before the night had begun. "I'll be in my office," he told them. "With the door closed."

"Oh dear, how uncomfortable," Katherine said when Eric was out of earshot. "Maybe I should chaperone the girls and let him and Darlene get some peace." Mitchell said that was a wonderful idea, and Matthew silently agreed. He did not want to save Darlene's life again that night. Katherine went to their house and fetched a small overnight bag and decided to spend the night in the empty suite next to Eric's. She had brought a book to read and was seated comfortably in the chair when Eric came upstairs to seclude himself in his room.

"Katherine? Is anything wrong?"

"No. I just thought it might be best if I chaperone the girls. Call me old fashioned, but it would make me feel better," she smiled. She told the truth, but she just did not mention the part about keeping him as far from Darlene as possible. "You best get in there. Their movie should be over soon," she suggested.

Eric thanked her and closed his door just as they heard female voices getting closer. Moments later Eric heard a knock on his door and Angilia's "Daddy." He opened the door, and Angilia entered and smiled at him. She also looked a bit sad. "I'm so sorry, Daddy. I had no idea. Darlene feels terrible about it, too. We'll stay in my room, with the door closed. You don't have to be a prisoner in your home." She hugged him.

"It's not your fault, Angel. You and your friends have fun, lots of fun. I'm all right, really. Katherine is next door tonight, by the way. She feels girls need a woman chaperone, so she is spending the night. But you come to me if you need anything at all. Promise?" She nodded and smiled up at him. He kissed her forehead. "I love you, Angilia."

"I love you, Daddy. We won't stay up all night, I promise. We're going to talk some more and do a scripture study, and then we'll turn off the lights. I'm going to tell Mrs. Taylor our plans, too." She kissed his cheek and went next door to inform Katherine of her plan to keep her door closed so no one could see her father. Katherine smiled and said she would check on them later.

Angilia rejoined her friends, who were now in their pajamas with their sleeping bags spread on the floor. She excused herself and went to her dressing room to change. She brushed her teeth, and then returned to the sitting room and her friends. "Angilia, we don't want any ghost stories tonight. Instead, will you tell us some true stories about your family? You know, from long ago?" Amanda asked.

Angilia sat on the sofa and took a deep breath. First she repeated the story Abuela had told her about the night her parents had met. The five girls sighed, oohed, and moaned throughout the story. "That is so romantic," Amy remarked. "It sure is," Shannon agreed. "Your father was the most handsome groom ever," Darlene said dreamily. The girls rolled their eyes at her. "He still wears his wedding ring. Now that is romantic," Amanda said. They all agreed.

Angilia smiled and said, "True love never dies." The girls nearly swooned over that.

"Now I want to go far back in time to a trio of men," Angilia teased. "Have you seen the film <u>Braveheart</u>?" The girls said they had, though some of them several years earlier. "The truth about the three main figures and what really happened is far better than the Hollywood version. Do you want to hear the real story?" They nodded their heads and said they did. Angilia elaborated on the facts she had told the police and her father at the Oxford police station in April, providing all of the details that myth and Hollywood ignored. Her story was long, but engaging, exciting, even blood chilling in its accuracy and detail. William Wallace's execution was gruesome, Robert the Bruce's death was sad and tragic, and Edward I's contradictory nature and cruelty were frightening.

When Angilia finished, the girls shivered. "How does that relate to your family, Angilia?" Amy asked.

"Each of the three main participants is an ancestor of mine. William Wallace is my 18th great grand uncle. King Edward I of England is my 20th great-grandfather. Robert the Bruce is my 18th great-grandfather," Angilia explained.

"Really? That is so cool!" Shannon enthused.

"How do you deal with that? I mean, they all fought for what they believed in and thought was right, but all three were not right. Edward I seemed so cold and heartless at times. How can you accept them all three? I mean, how can you love all three men, or do you?" Amanda asked.

Angilia smiled at Amanda. "I do love each of them. Do I love them each the same? No. Do I condone everything each of them did? No. Each of them is part of my lineage and my history. Each of them is part of me. Each of them contributes to who I am. How can I hate them or disown them? I cannot do that. We each make mistakes and do things we know are wrong at times. That does not define who we are for all time. The key is to accept and to love people for who they are, not for who we want them to be. That is the danger of mythologizing our heroes. I accept Robert, Edward, and William for who they were. I learn from their good deeds and their wrong doings. Each of them has taught me many important life lessons about family, honor, respect, duty, love, faith, and obedience. For that, I do love them each."

"Wow. That is totally awesome. You should write a book about that, what you just told us. How many people share a lineage with all three of those men?" Amanda suggested to Angilia.

"Who knows? Maybe someday I will write that down. I find it fascinating, but whether anyone else would, I don't know," Angilia smiled. They all told her how much they would love such a book, to read and to look at.

"Besides, knowing you, the one who is related to Robert, Edward, and William would make the book all the more special," Shannon stated.

"I will certainly think about it," Angilia promised. "Let's do our scripture study now, okay?" They spent an hour discussing what John 8:31-32 meant to each of them and how they could apply its message to their lives.

By then it was well after midnight, and a few of the girls were starting to yawn. Angilia excused herself and said she wanted to say goodnight to Mrs. Taylor. She did go to Katherine's room first. "Mrs. Taylor, we are going to turn off the lights and go to sleep in a few moments. I'm going to leave the door closed, though. You get some sleep soon."

"I will, dear. You girls know where I am if you need anything," Katherine told her with a hug.

Angilia tapped on her father's door and heard his "Come in" from his bedroom. She went to his bedroom door and peeked in. The light was on, and Eric was sitting in bed reading. "I just want to say goodnight, Daddy. We're going to bed in a moment." He held out his hand, and she went to him and kissed his cheek. He hugged her and kissed her nose. "I love you, Daddy."

"I love you, Angel. Is everyone having a good time?"

"They are. We talked and they asked me to tell true stories about my family and ancestors in lieu of ghost stories. It was great fun. They seemed to enjoy the stories. They even said I should write a book about one of the stories," she giggled.

"That's wonderful. Get some sleep. I know they don't have school tomorrow, but they also don't need to stay up all night."

"We aren't. I just wanted to say goodnight to you and to Mrs. Taylor." She kissed him again and closed his door after she left.

Angilia turned off her sitting room light and settled on the sofa, while the girls snuggled in their sleeping bags. Everything was soon quiet, and Angilia smiled at the moonbeams that shone on her ceiling. Maybe someday she would write that book, she thought. She enjoyed writing. Maybe Matthew could illustrate the book. She thanked God again for bringing her best friend back into her life. Soon she was asleep, deep asleep, for the duration of the night.

The next morning, Angilia awoke rather early and looked at her five friends asleep on her floor. She smiled. She was glad she had invited them over despite Darlene's constant fainting spells. Breakfast should prove interesting, she thought. How could they all eat together and yet prevent Darlene from seeing her father and fainting again? They would have to figure a solution.

She stood and grimaced in pain. Her right knee hurt horribly. She tried to take a step but winced and moaned. "Angilia? What's wrong?" Shannon asked.

Angilia shook her head and took another step. Her right leg caved under her and she crumpled to the floor. Shannon stumbled over other girls getting to Angilia, and soon they were all frantic. Darlene was crying. Shannon held Angilia to her, the princess' head on her shoulder. Amanda raised the leg of Angilia's pajama pants to look at her right knee, which was red and hot. Darlene cried hysterically and looked sick. "I'm all right, Darlene, really. I must have slept wrong or something. Help me up please?"

Shannon shook her head. "No. You stay there. Which room is your doctor in?" Angilia protested. "Fine. Amanda, go get her father then."

"No, please don't. I'm okay." Angilia's words were futile, for Amanda ran across the hall and banged on Eric's door. He said to come in, but Amanda did not.

"Sir, it's Amanda. Please come quick." Eric bolted to the door, panic on his face, and ran to Angilia, who was surrounded by scared-looking girls. He looked at her knee and ran down the hall and awakened Matthew. Matthew grabbed his medical bag and he and Eric ran to her room. Matthew told the other girls to please leave for a while, and they did. Shannon closed the door, while the worried girls formed a prayer circle in the hall.

"We need an MRI," Matthew insisted. "Now. I can't tell what's wrong just by looking. It could just be overexertion, it could be a sprain, or it may be an infection. I don't know until we get an MRI and I call in the orthopedic specialist for a consult."

Eric nodded and rushed to his room to get dressed. Matthew called his father, who quickly dressed and soon came to the third floor. He also sped to the room where his mother slept and told her to stay with Angilia while he dressed. Katherine followed her son's orders and refused to let Angilia move. Angilia called her friends into her room and apologized to them.

"No, please, don't. We'll grab our things and dress in the room Mrs. Taylor was using. I'll call my parents and one of them will pick us up. We'll be fine. We'll just get out of the way as soon as possible. We are praying for you, Angilia," Shannon said. The girls quickly scooped up their things and rushed to Mrs. Taylor's room out of the way.

Eric was dressed and beside his daughter again in minutes. So was Matthew. Mitchell arrived a moment later. Mitchell and Matthew supported Angilia while Eric and Katherine slipped her robe on her. Eric also wrapped her in a blanket and carried her to the car. Katherine told her not to worry about her friends. She would stay with them until one of their parents came to get them. Angilia thanked her.

Two hours later, Eric, Matthew, Mitchell and Dr. Stephen Setterfield looked at the MRI results. "Everything looks fairly normal," Dr. Setterfield stated. "Of course, there is scar tissue. There is a bit of inflammation, but no signs of any tears or ruptures. She probably strained it. She needs to wear a brace to give added support and strength to the knee. If she can take them, I can prescribe some anti-inflammatory pills to reduce the swelling."

"Which pills?" Matthew asked. He pulled them up on the computer and read the effects, active and inactive agents, and side effects. "She can't, not those. Anything that could potentially affect her heart is out of the question," Matthew insisted.

Dr. Setterfield looked at the options and showed one to Matthew. "This one is much milder and won't have the same impact in reducing the swelling and pain, but it's better than nothing," he said. Matthew agreed that the milder prescription would be all right for Angilia.

Dr. Setterfield turned to Eric. "She needs to stay off her feet and keep her knee elevated for three days, though. If it's all right with you, I will come to your home and check on her tomorrow and the following day. If she takes the medicine and keeps the knee elevated, with an ice pack, the swelling will reduce."

"Of course. Will she be all right?" Eric asked.

"She will. This is fairly common in the first year after a traumatic knee injury. The Princess has done a lot of walking, which has just taken a toll. Walking is wonderful exercise, and she does need to move her knee. But too much walking can cause strain."

"It's all of those stairs," Eric sadly said. "Angilia is up and down several flights of stairs several times each day. We need an elevator. I'm going to have someone install one immediately."

"That will certainly reduce undue strain on her knee, but until the elevator is installed and working, she needs to restrict the climbing," Dr. Setterfield advised.

"I'll carry her," Eric said firmly.

And he did. He carried her to the car, into the palace, and up to her suite. He placed her in her bed and propped her knee on pillows. He covered her with a soft blanket and smiled at her. "No more stairs for you, Angel. I was thinking about getting an elevator anyway, for Abuelo and Abuela mainly. Now I will." He called Roger to Angilia's room and told him to call a residential elevator company about installing an elevator immediately. Cost did not matter. Roger rushed to his office and soon had an appointment with someone that morning. He texted the information to Eric, who told Angilia.

"I'm sorry, Daddy. I keep causing you problems," she said.

"No, you do not. I was going to do this anyway. I just hadn't gotten around to calling anyone yet. Besides, someday I will need that elevator, too, you know," he winked at her and she smiled. "This place has five tall floors and hundreds of stairs. An elevator will make things easier on everyone, such as Antoine and the maids who have to carry heavy loads. I should have done this years ago."

"Speaking of Antoine carrying things," Angilia said when he entered with her breakfast tray. He smiled and sat it on her bedside table. "Thank you."

After she ate, Eric brought her iPad, her diary, her Bible, and her sketch pad, along with sundry pens and pencils. He moved a table next to her bed, and she worked in bed over the three days she was restricted to rest. Eric ate lunch with her a few hours later. Her uncle popped in for an early afternoon visit, as well, and sat with her while Eric reluctantly went to a meeting.

When he returned, he leaned down and kissed her and told her he had a surprise for her. She smiled and reached inside his suit jacket. She pulled out a brown paper bag with a yellow label on the front. "Lemon sours," she smiled. "Thank you, Daddy." She kissed his cheek and popped one in his mouth. She held the bag to Eduardo, who took one. She finally put one in her mouth and smiled again. Eric had brought her a bag of lemon sours as a treat whenever he could while she was growing up.

She slept peacefully that night, with Eric sitting in the chair near her bed. She did not wake up or seem distressed. Eric was relieved, and when Dr. Setterfield came the next morning, he was pleased with her improved condition. The next day was just as non-eventful for Angilia, with her father working next to her bed on his laptop so he could keep her company. They ate breakfast and lunch together, and were drafting a speech when Dr. Setterfield arrived that afternoon.

He examined Angilia's knee, noticing that the redness and swelling were gone. "Do you feel any pain at all?" he asked her.

"Just that ache I feel every day," she told him. "I've gotten used to that."

"Well, let's try some walking and see how your leg looks and operates." He and Eric helped her out of bed and gently held her arms while she took a few steps. At the doctor's urging they let go and spotted her as she walked on her own. "Everything looks fine. Walk down the hall and back for me." He watched her closely while she walked effortlessly. "All right. Just keep from overdoing anything, and remember, no stairs. There are plenty of strong men here who can carry you until that elevator is installed, which I can hear is in progress already. Got it?"

"Yes, Dr. Setterfield. Thank you," she said.

"Thank you," Eric repeated, heaving a sigh of relief. Matthew walked Dr. Setterfield to his car while Eric carried Angilia to the first floor. She walked to the patio with her father and they sat at the table enjoying the comfortable fall weather. Maybe this did happen so that her grandparents would have an elevator. She had watched them and noticed that Abuelo in particular struggled more in climbing all of those stairs.

Angilia told her father her thoughts, and he smiled at her. "I hate to think you had to suffer to nudge me into getting that elevator, Angel. Whatever the reason, the elevator will serve everyone well," Eric said. "I do think Abuelo and Abuela are staying here with us, baby."

She smiled and hugged him. "Really? Oh, Daddy, that is wonderful!"

§§§§

After her knee ordeal, Angilia was determined to keep her appointment with Mr. Brennan to work on his memoir. "Mr. Brennan is coming here today, Daddy. Since neither of us can climb the stairs, we were going to have lunch and work on the patio, but it's a bit too chilly for him to be out there. Where else can we work?"

"Use the dining room table, Angel. After lunch, you two can just stay there. You could use the waiting room, although that is rather small I think." Eric smiled at her. "The contractors are working all day every day on the elevator. They should have it finished in five weeks, sometime in early December. So, it will be somewhat noisy for a while, but it's worth it. When Mr. Brennan comes at Christmas, he can take the elevator anywhere he needs to go. So can you, Angel." Eric smiled and kissed her.

"That will be nice for him, Daddy." She thought about her father's birthday soon and how Mr. Brennan would get to the fifth floor. Some of the men could carry him, she supposed, since that would be before the elevator was completed. She planned to invite him of course. He would adore coming for her father's birthday.

Mr. Brennan and his nurse arrived at 11:45, and Angilia had the front door open for them. Eric and Angilia greeted him with huge smiles and hugs. Angilia took their coats and hung them in the coat closet discreetly hidden behind the staircase. "Lunch will be served shortly. Why don't we sit here while we wait?" Eric asked and motioned toward the sofas and chairs in the corner of the foyer.

They chatted until it was time to enter the dining room. Angilia had removed the chair across from her so that Mr. Brennan could sit next to her father. Nurse Ginny pushed his wheelchair to the table and made sure he was comfortable, and then sat next to him. Everyone started filing into the dining room and they all joyfully greeted Mr. Brennan and his Nurse Ginny. Antoine served the lunch of salad, Juanita's famous stuffed green peppers, and cheesecake for desert. Most of the talk centered on Mr. Brennan's memoir and what surprises it would hold.

Angilia smiled, pleased he was the focus of attention. He smiled at her and told everyone, "Well, I can't tell you now, can I? If I did, they would not be surprises when the book is published." Everyone giggled and relented.

"What can you tell us, Mr. Brennan?" Matthew asked.

"I was born in 1916 during King Gerard III's reign. I was four years old when your father was born," he said to Eric. "I have seen the reigns of four Kings de Valdavia and the births of two Kings and one future Queen. In my 96 years I have seen a lot of advancements and changes, but through it some things remain constant. One of them is the peace and harmony in Valdavia. Another is the strength of character and compassion of the Kings and this Princess. I know I will not live to see her coronated Queen, which is as it should be. I have seen three coronations, beginning with King Stefan's in 1926. The second was your father's in 1963, and the third was yours in 1992," he said again to Eric. "I was in the crowd at each event, including your wedding and when you carried this Angel out of the hospital four years later."

Susan dabbed tears from her eyes and everyone else smiled. "That is beautiful, Mr. Brennan," Eric said, placing his hand over the elderly man's.

"My great-grandfather and you would have been wonderful friends," Angilia added. "He was passionate about history, as well, and I know he will love to hear your stories someday, too."

"You know who should write a book? Princess Angilia. If she wrote down everything she felt and believed about God, Heaven, death, and eternal life no one would ever be afraid to die or would ever doubt God's existence again," Mr. Brennan stated, much to Eric's surprise. Angilia was just as surprised. She had not told him anything about her past. They had, of course, talked about their faith and their beliefs.

"I think so, too, actually," Matthew replied, his voice soft and introspective.

Roger asked Mr. Brennan about his work. "I delivered the mail for fifty years. Among the addresses on my route was the Palais. Every day I drove the mail truck to the gate at the courtyard and handed the guards there at least one large burlap bag filled with mail, sometimes more. I began working for the postal service when I graduated high school, and I retired on my 70th birthday. I enjoyed my work. I got to meet many people because of my work. I even met the Emperor of Japan one day while I was delivering the mail at the gate and his car drove up. He rolled down his car window and talked to me for a good fifteen minutes," Mr. Brennan told them all with a wistful smile.

The conversation continued for another hour, and Angilia listened attentively to every word. She would remember every word, too, and type it all up later that afternoon. Finally, Ginny spoke up. "I am so sorry, but we must go home now. Thank you for inviting me." Mr. Brennan smiled at Ginny and patted her hand.

"We did not discuss the book, Princess. I am sorry," Mr. Brennan apologized to Angilia.

She smiled at him and shook her head. "Oh, but we did. All of the stories and memories you shared with us today are exactly what your memoir needs. I will just type them all up later today and add them to the working draft of your manuscript."

Angilia stood and walked to him. Eric and the other men stood, and Eric shook his hand. "Thank you for joining us for lunch, Mr. Brennan. I know I speak for all of us that we truly enjoyed your company. Come anytime you want to."

Mr. Brennan beamed and thanked Eric. Ginny pushed him into the foyer, and Eric assisted him into the car. Nurse Ginny covered his lap with a blanket, and Angilia leaned in and kissed his cheek. "Remember, I am coming to visit you next Saturday, Mr. Brennan."

"I look forward to that, Princess." He waved at them as the car turned and left the courtyard. Angilia hugged her father and said a silent prayer for Mr. Brennan's continued health and happiness. He, like Miss Yost, was alone. His wife had died nearly twenty years earlier, and his son was dead, too. His daughter was married and lived in Australia with her family. She had not returned to Valdavia since her wedding nearly forty years ago. Angilia knew how lonesome Mr. Brennan often felt, and she was grateful God had aligned circumstances so that they had met him in January and were now his friends. She enjoyed his company immensely, and she knew he, too, enjoyed the idea of his memoir.

Eric kissed her head, sensing her thoughts and feelings, as they returned to the foyer. "I take it you want to start typing up those stories of his?" Eric asked her. She smiled up at him and nodded, so he carried her to their office where she could use the computer. He sat at his own desk and answered important e-mails and worked on a speech. After three hours, Angilia finished and helped him complete the speech.

The following Saturday, as promised, Angilia arrived at Mr. Brennan's charming house. Ginny answered the door and smiled at her. Soon Angilia was sitting in his living room next to him on the comfortable sofa. They talked for nearly four hours, during which time Ginny brought them tea and sandwiches. Angilia adored listening to Mr. Brennan's stories, and she adored him. He saw her smiling at him as they talked and sipped tea.

"What are you so happy about, Princess?"

"You," she replied. "I am so happy that God planned it for us to meet and to become friends."

He patted her hand. "I am too, Princess. I have watched you from afar your whole life, and your father, too. I can never tell you how thrilled I am to know you both."

"Mr. Brennan, next Saturday is my father's birthday," Angilia said, as he smiled and nodded. "I have planned a party for him, and I want to invite you and Nurse Ginny to come. Please say you will."

Mr. Brennan's smile seemed a mile wide. He clasped her shoulders and said, "Of course I will come, Princess. I am honored to come to the King's birthday party. Nurse Ginny and I will wear our best clothes and have a wonderful time helping King Eric celebrate."

"Oh, thank you! My father probably won't really be surprised that I invited you, but he will be so thrilled. I will send Mike to pick you both up, all right?"

"In one of your father's cars? Oh, now that will be splendid, Princess."

§§§§§

Angilia was in the fifth floor ballroom most of the day on Friday decorating it for her father's birthday party. He knew she would give him a party, but he most likely expected it in the sitting room or the music room. He would never suspect the ballroom. She had to recruit some of the staff to help her, since she first of all needed help getting to the fifth floor and second of all reaching the high ceiling. Men gladly hauled ladders up the back staircase and stood on them to hang streamers, balloons, a huge Happy Birthday sign, and even a glitter ball for fun.

They all spent several hours getting it all decorated and ready for the food, drinks, cake, and gifts. Tables and chairs were brought up and decorated, as well, so that people could sit, eat, and relax between socializing and dancing. Angilia had no choice but to ask Mike to sneak her present for her father out of her room and up to the ballroom. "It's draped in a huge red velvet cloth in my dressing room," she told him. "It's along the back wall, out of sight." Several minutes later he returned carrying her large present.

She had the perfect place for it. She had him lean it along the center north wall, against what her grandmother had called the sculpture display, and then she closed the gold drapes that were held back on either side of the sculpture kept there. Her present would remain out of view until she gave it to him the next day at his party. No one knew what it was, although to Mike it had felt like a huge picture or painting. Whatever it was, she seemed both nervous and excited. Finally, Angilia looked around and declared the ballroom perfect.

"Thank you all so much for your help. I have to leave now for the final dress rehearsal of the play for tomorrow night. Please remember, Daddy's party starts at 11:00 tomorrow morning and lasts most of the day. I will have to leave at 6:00 tomorrow evening to be at the high school." Mike said he would drive her to the dress rehearsal and tomorrow's performance. She thanked him and they headed toward the stairs. He picked her up and carried her down them.

At dinner, everyone wanted to know about the dress rehearsal, and Angilia said it went well. "We bought our tickets immediately," Katherine said. They had all bought tickets even though everyone would sit in the royal box with Eric. "It's such a great cause, too," Katherine added. Matthew did not divulge that he had paid four times the ticket price for his one ticket. He felt it only right that he follow her example in donating to worthy causes generously. He was, after all, financially comfortable and could afford to share his good fortune—or blessings, as Angilia would say.

Angilia awoke typically early the next morning and tiptoed across the hall to hear if her father was up and about yet. She heard him moving, so she softly knocked on his door. He leaned out of his bedroom and smiled at her. "Good morning my beautiful daughter Angilia."

She smiled and went to him, her arms open for a hug. "Good morning, Daddy," she said against his chest. "I love you more today than I did yesterday." She looked up at him and took a small present from her dress pocket and slipped it in his hand. "Happy birthday, Daddy."

Eric kissed her nose, so happy and grateful they were together. The memories of March never went too far away, always reminding him how blessed he was to have his little girl still with him in this life. He opened her gift, their so-called private gift exchange early on their respective birthdays. The gifts were often sentimental and personal. He stared at the small box and felt tears fill his eyes.

"Wherever did you get this?" he asked her.

"It was in an auction catalogue online, in a sale of someone's private royal collection. Something told me to look, and when I saw this I knew why." She pulled an envelope from her pocket and handed it to him. "This is the certificate it came with. Apparently it's one-of-a-kind and made of onyx and gold. It is meant to be yours, Daddy."

"Someone had a tie tack made with your mother's profile engraved on it? How incredible. And how unbelievable that you found it," Eric said, incredulous to say the least. "How did you find it?"

"I read about the auction. Most of the items dealt with the British royal family, but he collected other people, too. He had a lot of Romanov pieces and some Princess Grace things. I just went to the online catalogue and looked through everything. It's all very interesting, of course. Then I saw her, and that sealed it. I registered to bid, they approved my application, and I placed my bid. Now she's here with you where she belongs."

"Did they know who you are?"

"I don't know. I had to use my real name and everything, because they needed a reference from the bank that I could cover the bid. But none of that matters, because she's yours now and always." Angilia smiled at him.

Eric hugged her close to him. "Yes, she is, darling. She most certainly is."

He removed his tie tack and replaced it with his wife's profile. He smiled as he carried his daughter to the first floor for breakfast. Roger and Daniel had just entered and noticed Eric's happy smile. They knew that Angilia was planning a surprise party for him later that morning, but she had kept the details quiet. Soon the table was full and Antoine served their breakfast. He smiled at

Angilia, silently letting her know that most of the food for the party was done and waiting to be transported to the ballroom later. She smiled in return.

Roger had scheduled a brief meeting at an office in downtown Valmondois for 9:30 that morning so that he could get Eric away during the final preparations. After Eric kissed her goodbye and grabbed his briefcase, he and Roger left together. Angilia went to the kitchen and made sure everything was in order. Antoine had men carrying hot plates and cold plates up to the ballroom buffet table so they would be ready. He and his assistant would carry the food up at 10:30 and he would bring the cake up right after that. Plates, cups, flatware, and napkins were already in place.

Angilia texted everyone at 10:50 and told them to come to the ballroom. Katherine, Mitchell, and Matthew were really surprised. They had not yet seen the ballroom. Mike and Tony carried Mr. Brennan and his wheelchair to the ballroom as everyone began arriving. Mike and Nurse Ginny helped him settle into his wheelchair, and Angilia leaned down and hugged him. "Thank you so much for coming, Mr. Brennan."

"I am delighted to be here today, I really am," he smiled at her.

Angilia's phone beeped. "Roger just texted me. He and Daddy are here. I'm telling Roger to get up here now. I will get Daddy up here. You just be ready to shout when he comes in." Roger raced in, she thanked him with a smile, and closed the double doors.

Angilia stood at the top of the landing and shouted for her father. "Daddy, I need your help please. Can you come to the ballroom now?"

"Angilia?!" He bolted up the two flights of stairs from outside his suite, panicked. He was breathless when he reached her. "How did you get up here? What's wrong?"

"I need your help with something in the ballroom," she said, and pointed to the closed doors. He looked concerned. "I'm okay, but I need your help," she repeated. She took his hand and opened the doors.

"Happy Birthday!" everyone screamed in unison as soon as the door opened.

"Good grief. You scared me, Angilia. This is one way to surprise me," Eric smiled and took a deep breath. They walked in to a huge crowd. Eric talked to everyone, especially to Mr. Brennan, and thanked everyone for remembering him. "I suppose you didn't have much choice, though, with Angilia planting not-so-subtle hints in your ears."

"Nonsense. The whole world knows when it's your birthday," Katherine smiled. "I know you saw all of those people out front." They saw Angilia talking with some of her friends from COC. "Don't worry. Darlene isn't here. She sent a gift and a huge card, though."

Eric rolled his eyes at her and made his way to the girls. "Welcome, ladies," he said. They all curtseyed, as they had been taught, and thanked him and Angilia for inviting them. At noon everyone got some food from the buffet and relaxed at the tables. Juanita hugged Eric as she took her seat next to him, and she noticed the tie tack. "Isn't this gorgeous?" he asked her. "It's the only one like it in the world, and my daughter found it."

"Yes, it is very beautiful, mi hijo. It is meant to be yours," she said with a smile and a kiss. "You give the most thoughtful and wonderful gifts, mi nieta."

Mr. Brennan smiled and patted Angilia's hand. "She is a very thoughtful young lady. Someone taught her well and wisely," he bowed his head to Eric.

"Thank you, Mr. Brennan. I'm happy with her. I think she's a keeper," Eric teased. Angilia smiled at her father.

As people finished eating, music began playing and a glitter ball that no one had seemed to notice suddenly filled the room with sparkles. Music from Eric's teen years of the late 1960s and early 1970s filled the room. Angilia nudged her father to dance, but he refused.   Matthew whispered to his mother, and Katherine approached and grabbed Eric's hand and led him into the center of the room for a dance.   Eric was a good sport, and he did enjoy himself.   He and Patrick had done their share of disco dancing nearly forty years earlier.

People paired up and joined the dancing, having fun and laughing.   Eric next danced with his mother-in-law, much to Eduardo's amusement.   Angilia smiled as she watched her father. She wanted him to have fun and to relax with his friends.   She led the applause when the dance ended.   A few songs later a waltz began and Eric walked to Angilia and held out his hand.   She took it and walked onto the dance floor with him.   They had danced dozens of times over the years, at formal balls and for fun.   Even with her knee brace, they danced flawlessly and perfectly, seemingly gliding across the floor.

Everyone else stood watching them, entranced and awed. Juanita, Susan, Katherine, and Angilia's four friends all sobbed. "Aren't they so beautiful?" Amanda wistfully said.   "It's like watching Cinderella, only better," Nicole sighed.   Even Mr. Brennan wiped tears from his eyes at the sight of them waltzing.   Eduardo held his mother, both of them smiling through their tears.   If only Marisol could see her husband and her daughter and how much they loved each other, Eduardo thought.

When the waltz ended everyone quietly applauded and sighed.   The dancing continued for another couple of hours, and during the next slow song, Mr. Brennan asked Angilia to dance with him.   "Will you sit on my lap while I move the wheelchair, Princess? You will not hurt me, will she Ginny?   She's such a tiny thing." Ginny said it would be all right, so Angilia obliged Mr. Brennan. Eric smiled.   Angilia made Mr. Brennan's life happy and meaningful. She gave him light, love, and purpose.   Angilia laid her head on his shoulder, and he smiled throughout their special dance.

Finally, it was time for Eric to open his presents.   The COC girls had pooled their money to get him a gift, except for Darlene who sent her own gift with them.   Her huge card had a castle on the front and a handwritten "Happy Birthday" and a heart inside.   She had made Eric a crocheted winter scarf, which was an odd gift considering the rather mild temperatures. The other girls had bought him a five-volume set of history books that included several chapters about Valdavia and his ancestors. "Thank you, ladies. These are lovely books. Please give Darlene my thanks, too," he almost regretted saying, picturing her fainting again.

When he opened Mr. Brennan's present, Eric smiled. Mr. Brennan had put together a photograph album spanning most of his life. The pictures were copies of those Mr. Brennan had taken of Eric's family from 1926 to the present. "Mr. Brennan, this is remarkable," Eric said while he flipped through the album. "I can never thank you enough."

"I am honored to share your birthday, Sir. I would like to add one picture from today to my collection, if you will give me the honor. Would you allow Ginny to take our picture, Sir?"

"Absolutely," Eric smiled and stood next to Mr. Brennan, his hand on the gentleman's shoulder. Mr. Brennan motioned for Angilia to join them, and she stood on his other side. Everyone applauded, knowing what the simple picture meant to Mr. Brennan. He was an ardent royalist and a loyal subject, and he was obviously proud to count Valdavia's King and Princess Consort among his friends. Angilia kissed his cheek after Ginny snapped the picture.

Eric opened his remaining gifts and looked at his friends and family. "Thank you all for sharing the day with me. This has been. . . ." Angilia gently tugged his sleeve. She pulled him closer and whispered that there was one more present he had to open. "You already gave me your present, Angel."

"I have another one for you, Daddy." She led him to the gold drapes and pulled them back. "I hope you like it, Daddy," she said, nervous again. What if he hated it? She touched the red velvet cloth and he removed it to a room full of gasps. The four feet by six feet canvas looked regal in an antique frame. Eric had one arm around Angilia and one hand over his mouth. Juanita, Alejandro, and Eduardo walked to them and stared with tears in their eyes.

Everyone waited for Eric to speak first, but he could not. He pulled Angilia to him and cried as he held her. Juanita cried, too, and Eric reached one arm for her. She put her arms around Eric and Angilia, and soon so too did Alejandro and Eduardo. Susan burst into tears and as usual leaned on Daniel. Katherine turned to Mitchell, who held his wife while she cried. The four teenage girls huddled together crying. Matthew looked at Angilia's portrait of her mother and felt such warmth and peace. Roger watched his best friend and tried valiantly to fight his tears but lost. Mr. Brennan did not even try to fight his tears. He had never witnessed anything more beautiful or emotional.

"I love you, Angilia," Eric finally said, his voice choked with tears. "I love you." She held onto him, although her own love for him was too much for her to hold. "I have received wonderful gifts before, but this portrait of my wife is the most beautiful gift anyone has given me," he told her.

Eduardo stared at the portrait while his hands held onto Angilia. "Marisol looks so alive. That is my sister." He bowed his head and kissed his niece's cheek. Juanita stroked her son's back, and Alejandro held Juanita. "You brought her to life again, Angilia."

Eric turned her face to him and smiled at her. "I keep saying that you amaze me constantly, and you do, Angel. When and where did you do this to keep it a secret?"

"I had to do it in my wardrobe/dressing room, where I could prop it against the back wall out of view. I had the canvas snuck to my room in May after we returned home," she admitted.

"When did you find the time, though? That's only five months."

"Early mornings, evenings, whenever I had time. I got the idea on my birthday when Abuela noticed the gown I wore for my portrait was Mommy's. Hers is the only portrait that is not in the museum, Daddy."

Eric sighed. "I know, baby. But her portrait is here, where she belongs."

Angilia smiled and walked to the portrait. She reached behind it and removed a stack of envelopes. She handed one to her father and told him to open it. Eric burst into tears again and grabbed Angilia into another hug. Angilia handed Eduardo the envelopes and asked him to give one to everyone in the room. As he did, they opened them and were surprised by what they read. Juanita and Alejandro read theirs and hugged one another. The four girls sighed and sobbed again. Susan erupted in tears, too.

Muriel Laperen invited each of them to a private unveiling at the Musée National de Valdavia on Monday evening. A portrait of HM Queen Consort Marisol de Valdavia, painted by her daughter HRH The Princess Consort Angilia, Duchesse de Valmondois, would be installed alongside the most recent portrait of her husband HM King Eric de Valdavia. "I painted another one for the museum, Daddy. Is that all right?" Angilia asked softly.

"All right? Angel, that is perfect. Your mother belongs there, and I cannot imagine a more beautiful portrait and tribute to her than your portrait." Eric wiped at his tears and then giggled. "Did you just tell me that you painted two of these portraits in five months? You just broke your record for amazing me, Angel."

Everyone smiled and applauded, while Eric hugged his daughter. Nothing could have filled and warmed his heart as much as her loving tribute to his wife. He glanced at his wedding band and then at the portrait of Marisol. Eric had now celebrated 58 birthdays, and none had touched him as this one had. His little girl never ceased to fill him and his world with love, beauty, and hope. She was the best gift he had ever received, and for that he once again closed his eyes and thanked God.

§§§§

Angilia kissed her father before she had to leave for the theatre. Eric smiled at her and lifted her in his arms to carry her downstairs. He walked her to the car and helped her in while Mike turned the key. She waved at him as they pulled away, and their car was greeted by screams when it left the gate. Eric was still astonished by the breathtakingly lifelike portrait of Marisol and the reality that Angilia had painted a duplicate for the museum. In a couple of hours he would watch her acting debut.

Eric changed into an evening suit and affixed the Marisol tie clip to his black tie. He could not stop smiling, knowing how much he was loved by his staggeringly awesome daughter. Daniel smiled as he gave a final brushing to Eric's suit, grateful that his best friend's birthday was such a joyous day. More happiness would follow as they watched Angilia from the royal box that evening. Eric turned and clapped Daniel on the arm, and they went to gather everyone. Daniel assisted Alejandro, Eduardo held his mother's arm, and the four of them went down to the foyer.

Matthew called his parents to rush them, and Eric called Susan to rush her. The two men walked to the foyer together, Matthew more excited than he would admit aloud. Angilia as Juliet—how fabulously romantic and sad. Dear God, please do not let me cry tonight, Matthew prayed as he stood next to Eric. He knew the suicide scene alone could wreak havoc on his emotions. He took a deep breath as his parents entered and finally Susan appeared. They all headed to the garage and climbed into one of the larger Rolls Royce cars. Eric drove and Roger sat in front with him. Mike had driven Angilia and was there with her.

Eric parked his car and helped Juanita and Susan from the car. Everyone smiled as other attendees greeted them and said how excited they were to watch the Princess' performance. They also wished Eric a very happy birthday. He thanked everyone as they entered and were greeted by the theatre manager, who escorted them to the royal box. Eric spotted Sam and the four band members in the audience, quite unexpectedly, and texted Sam quickly. Sam looked up and waved, and Eric motioned for them to come to the royal box. In a few minutes, they were seated with Eric's family and friends. What no one knew yet was why they were in Valmondois. That would be the ultimate surprise of the evening.

The lights dimmed moments before the curtain rose and the play began. Everyone knew, or thought they remembered correctly, that Juliet's first scene was at the party at the Capulet house. That was where Romeo first saw her and fell in love with her. Matthew had looked it up. It was Act I Scene V. Soon. He would see her soon. He prayed again that he not cry, at least not in the theatre. His heart pounded as Scene IV ended. He gripped the arms of his chair.

There she was, on the arm of the man portraying Capulet, Juliet's father. Matthew could not breathe. Angilia was stunningly beautiful in her blue dress and cap. No wonder Romeo had fallen in love with her at first sight. So had Matthew. When Romeo asked the servant who she was and waxed poetic about her beauty, Matthew understood how he felt. *'Did my heart love till now?'* Romeo asked. That is what I asked myself when I first saw her, Matthew thought. I never knew love until I knew my Juliet. I love her.

Romeo approached Juliet and in his poetic way said he wanted to kiss her. Matthew gasped audibly, and Eric glanced at him. He took a deep breath and watched his daughter. God, help that boy. The play had barely begun, and he was in the throes of a real-life Romeo syndrome. What would Matthew do when Romeo did kiss Juliet? Eric smiled as Angilia embodied Juliet and spoke the lines with emotion and credibility. Angilia may never have experienced what Juliet does, but she could interpret it and understand it. She was brilliant, Eric admitted.

Juliet loved Romeo at first sight, too, bemoaning her fate when she learned his true identity. Their families were sworn enemies and a union betwixt them forbidden. Juliet picked up a dagger, and Matthew gasped in horror. She of course did not kill herself, yet, but Matthew's heart nonetheless jumped in his chest. When Juliet appeared on her balcony, while Romeo stood below, Matthew fervently wished he was the one standing there looking up at her and proclaiming his undying love unheard by her, while she so angelically uttered her love for him. Matthew prayed for that to happen. He prayed for Angilia to love him, as Juliet loved Romeo.

Their secret marriage. Romeo had his fair Juliet, Matthew sighed again. How long would he, Matthew, have to wait for his fair Angilia? He promised he would wait, and he would, but he was so tortured. No wonder Romeo died for Juliet, when he thought she dead and he would have to live without her. And Juliet seeing Romeo dead, not wanting to live without her true love. Matthew watched as Angilia grabbed the dagger from Romeo's sheath and stabbed herself in the chest.

Eric watched, too, knowing it was stage blood, but still shocked by the sight of blood once more oozing from his daughter's chest. He took a deep breath and relaxed, but Matthew grabbed Eric's arm. Eric looked at Matthew's pale, sick face. Eric motioned for Mitchell, who roused his son and wondered what on earth had happened. Matthew did not watch the funeral procession of the two dead lovers. He could not watch Angilia carried on a slab and wearing a burial robe. That was too much for his heart to bear. Soon he heard the audience applaud and dared to look up. The curtain was down and it was over. He had survived her death. He took a deep breath and when she and Scott reappeared for their curtain call he was the first to stand. She was so beautiful with her braided hair and huge turquoise eyes. Scott bowed and Angilia curtseyed to Eric, and she blew her father a kiss when she rose. If only that kiss had been for him, Matthew thought.

While the other actors made their curtain calls, Angilia rushed to change back into her custom made blue gown and cap from earlier in the play. The orchestra was ready in their pit, and she held a cordless microphone, ready when the director gave her the signal. After the curtain calls, the orchestra began playing the love theme from <u>Romeo and Juliet</u>, "A Time for Us." The curtain slowly rose as Angilia began singing the words and walked to the center of the stage. Everyone was pleasantly shocked, no one more so than Eric.

Angilia's voice was more beautiful than ever as she hit the operatic high notes effortlessly. The emotions in her voice brought tears to many peoples' eyes, including most in the royal box. Matthew watched her, so young, so beautiful, so angelic, so perfect. He leaned forward in his chair to the point that Eduardo thought he would fall over the rail and tumble to his death. He pulled Matthew back into his seat and watched his niece.

Angilia curtseyed to her father when she finished and smiled at him. She waved at the audience and walked off stage to a standing ovation. She returned on the director's arm. "Your Majesty, ladies and gentlemen, thank you all for attending. I am honored to announce that Her Royal Highness has recorded "A Time for Us." The song will be available beginning this coming Tuesday, and one hundred percent of the proceeds will go into our arts fund. We are most grateful to Her Royal Highness for her kindness and support." He handed her a dozen long-stemmed red roses and bowed to her. The audience remained standing as she waved and thanked them.

She was forced to make three more curtain calls before she finally told the director she wanted to join her father and her family. She grabbed her small duffle bag, which held her street clothes, and walked to the royal box wearing the blue gown. It was hers—she had designed it—and she wanted to enjoy wearing it a little while longer.

Everyone in the royal box was either crying or talking excitedly about how wonderful Angilia's performance was. When they saw her enter, they applauded her, which drew the audience's attention. They turned to applaud her, as well, and to wave at Eric and Angilia. Many even shouted happy birthday to Eric, before the high school actors rushed on stage to serenade him with the birthday song. Angilia smiled while she held her father's arm, elated yet again at the love people felt for him.

After the furor, Eric hugged her, and with tears in his eyes looked at her. "You were absolutely brilliant, Angel. No one has ever portrayed Juliet so perfectly."

Everyone added their praises, except Matthew, who stood looking like a fish gasping for air. His mouth was open as he stared at her. Mitchell nudged his son, realizing the boy was love-struck. He took Matthew's arm and shepherded him to the car, where Angilia was helped into the front passenger seat next to her father. Angilia turned her head and smiled at everyone, and she thanked them for coming.

"I don't think I would want to do that every night, but it was fun. It was for a good cause, too, so that is always wonderful. I wonder how much money they raised," she wondered aloud. "Thank you all for donating."

She did wonder, too, why everyone talked to her except for Matthew. He looked ill. Angilia had to ask. "Are you all right, Matthew? You don't look well." Dear God, Eric thought. If she only knew what was wrong with him, what would she think? He was sick all right—lovesick.

"Oh, he's fine, dear," Mitchell assured her while he poked Matthew's arm.

"Huh? Oh, sure, I'm fine. I just got a bit dizzy up there," Matthew muttered.

Eric bit his lip and fought his smile. Poor Matthew. Angilia's birthday was still six weeks away, and she still failed to recognize his feelings for her. Her heart would feel that love, too, and when it did she would know. Maybe it would take Matthew's confession of love for that door to open in her heart. Eric hoped so, for Matthew's sake. Otherwise, the boy would wither away before their eyes. Eric glanced at his daughter, so young, wise, yet innocent. Her heart would mature soon, he knew that, and in a few short years Valdavia would celebrate another royal wedding, the first since his own to Marisol. He touched the tie clip and smiled. He wished that kind of deep, true, eternal love for their daughter.

§§§§

Nearly two weeks later, on November 30, huge crowds yet again filled the Central Park. Eric and Angilia would light the city's official Christmas tree in the heart of the park near the sight of his future statue. Angilia wore a pretty cream coat-dress with the cameo of her mother pinned above her heart. Eric wore a black suit and red tie, which was held in place by his Marisol tie tack. Marisol was truly with them, visibly and spiritually.

"Ladies, gentlemen, and children, welcome to Valmondois' annual Christmas tree lighting ceremony," Eric said from the podium. "Angilia and I are delighted to welcome a very special guest who will assist us this evening," he smiled and Angilia stepped to the microphone.

"As you probably know, we held a contest for children between the ages of three and fourteen. They each submitted a drawing depicting what Christmas means to them. Their drawings are wonderful, and all of them are on display at the museum through January 16, 2013.

"There was no way my father or I could choose one favorite drawing. Instead, we placed all of the drawings in a huge box and

371

together we pulled one from the box. That person will help us flip the switch and light the city Christmas tree. Veronica Mills is a fourth grader at Saint Michael Elementary School. Veronica, please join us." Angilia led the applause to congratulate and welcome Veronica to the stage. She sweetly curtseyed to Angilia and to Eric. Her proud parents snapped dozens of pictures while she stood with the Princess and the King and waved to everyone.

Angilia took her hand and the three of them walked to the massive evergreen tree. The audience counted down, 5-4-3-2-1, and the three of them joined hands and pulled the switch together. The giant tree was suddenly aglow in twinkling purple lights and a large Star of Bethlehem atop its tip. People cheered and took pictures, including Mr. Brennan, who smiled and waved at them from the front of the crowd.

Eric and Angilia thanked Veronica and her parents, and then mingled with everyone for a long while. Billy ran to Angilia and handed her an ornament he had made of baby Jesus. "Billy, this is beautiful. Do you mind if we hang it on the public tree?" Billy smiled and shook his head. Angilia and he walked to the tree, and he pointed to a branch above her reach. Matthew noticed her trying to stretch and ran to them. He lifted Billy, who hung his ornament on the branch. Billy thanked Matthew and kissed Angilia's hand.

The three of them joined hands, Billy between them, and made their way through the people. Eric watched them, thinking how much like a young, happy family they looked as they smiled and chatted. He knew one day they would have a child together and share their love and happiness. What a beautiful feeling, Eric sighed, and touched his wedding band.

§§§§

Angilia surprised everyone yet again during breakfast the following Tuesday. The radio was on, rather softly, and Dave Rodan announced the next song. Eric's attention peaked when he heard Angilia's name. He quickly turned up the radio. "Listeners, we have a very special Christmas song to debut this morning. Princess Consort Angilia wrote and recorded this song, with harmony vocals by none other than our own Miss Yost. This song is Angilia's Christmas gift to everyone, available for free download everywhere, including her web site. Here is the world debut of "Love Was Born on Christmas Day." Listen to the words everyone."

Everyone listened quietly, never knowing until now that she had recorded this song when she recorded "A Time for Us" in early November. Her lyrics filled them with warmth, as she made the analogy that Jesus is Love. Eric smiled and took her hand, recognizing the reference to their union on Christmas Day 1994, when their love was solidified: *Love was born on Christmas day, to enter your heart to stay. Like a falling star it flies, far from Heaven through night skies.*

Matthew too smiled, feeling unexpectedly calm, sure, and hopeful. He somehow now knew that he and Angilia were meant for one another only. It was almost as if Matthew heard God's voice telling him that, reassuring him that Angilia would become his wife. Matthew's angst disappeared miraculously, replaced by peace.

"That is amazing," Roger said when the song ended. "Miss Yost sounds so different there, not bad at all. You know what I mean," he smiled.

"Thank you, Roger," Angilia replied. "Miss Yost really is a wonderful singer."

Everyone else commented on how lovely the song was. Eric never said anything, though. Instead, he typed a text message to his daughter while she talked with the others. Her cell phone vibrated while she leaned to talk with Eduardo, and she pulled it from her pocket and opened the message: 'My beautiful daughter Angilia, I love you eternally. You are the absolute most precious Christmas gift I will ever receive. Daddy.' A lone tear slid from her eye as she looked at him and signed "I love you" in reply.

CHAPTER 11

At 11:30 on Christmas Eve night, Mike drove Eric, Angilia, Juanita, Alejandro, Eduardo, Katherine, Mitchell, Matthew, Daniel, Roger, Susan, and Bonnie to the Christ Church Valmondois. The midnight Christmas service began soon, and Eric and Angilia welcomed everyone alongside Reverend Hutchins. Mr. Brennan and Ginny were among the first to arrive, and Angilia kissed his cheek. He kissed her hand. When the Pannings arrived, Angilia beamed. Billy looked so grown up in his suit and tie. He bowed to Eric, as he always did, and greeted Angilia in his typical fashion.

"Merry Christmas, Princess darling. You look especially beautiful tonight," Billy said.

"Merry Christmas, Billy. Thank you, dear."

Finally the church bell chimed, announcing midnight and the arrival of Christmas. Reverend Hutchins, Eric, and Angilia made their way to the front of the church. Eric and Angilia stood at their seats in the pew, while the other parishioners stood and Reverend Hutchins went to the pulpit. He said the opening prayer. Angilia held her father's hand while they bowed their heads to pray. After the "Amen," Eric squeezed her hand, she smiled at him, and he walked to the pulpit. As he had done every year since 1979, when he was 25, Eric read the nativity story, Luke Chapter 2.

Angilia felt warmth surround her as her father read, a familiar warmth. She often felt that warmth when she sat in Uncle

Patrick's room. She smiled, knowing that her Uncle Patrick was there with them, in the church, watching and listening to his brother. Would he? Dare he? For Eric?

He did! Patrick manifested. Angilia saw him sitting next to her in Eric's seat. They smiled at one another. Angilia looked at her father, such love on her face. Eric looked at her, and she knew he, too, saw Patrick. Her father's face told her so. His eyes filled with tears. His smile was joyous. His color heightened with his emotions. Eric looked only at his little brother as he recited the remainder of the nativity story, though most people presumed he looked at his daughter.

Eric finished and somehow maintained his composure to walk to his seat. Patrick stood against the wall next to Eric, his hand on Eric's shoulder. Angilia looked into her father's eyes, and he nodded. He saw and felt Patrick. She leaned over and kissed his cheek, knowing what an unconditional miracle and blessing her father received that Christmas Day.

Angilia squeezed his hand and stood. So did Miss Yost. They walked to the piano, where Angilia sat on the bench and Miss Yost stood behind her. Angilia played and sang "Love Was Born on Christmas Day," Miss Yost singing her harmony part. Love was indeed the heart, soul, and purpose of Christmas. Eric knew that well. Not only had his baby first come to him on Christmas, but his brother was there with him. Eric glanced at Patrick, who was watching Angilia, that Elvis smile achingly familiar. Had it been over thirty-five years since Eric had seen Patrick? He still looked the same, his handsome, playful, charming 19 year old little brother.

Angilia approached her seat, and looked at Patrick with a smile as she turned to sit. She looked again at her father, her smile huge and happy. Eric leaned his head close to hers and whispered a question. "You see him?" She nodded and looked at him with love, happiness, and joy that outshone the stars. Eric held Angilia's hand and felt Patrick's hand. His daughter and his brother were on either side of him on this most blessed and holy of days.

Patrick remained beside Eric throughout the service. He stood behind Eric in the receiving line. Eric felt his brother's hands on his shoulders. Everyone who greeted him that night noticed how radiant, peaceful, and joyous Eric looked. They attributed it to the Christmas Spirit. Eric knew it was a miracle, a Christmas miracle. After the parishioners left, Reverend Hutchins bid them good cheer and left.

"You all take the car and go home. Daddy and I want to stay here a little while longer," Angilia told their family and friends. They protested, but Angilia assured them that she and Eric would be fine. They reluctantly departed. When Angilia, Eric, and Patrick were finally alone, Angilia turned to her father, her smile broader and happier than ever. "Merry Christmas, Daddy."

"Merry Christmas, Eric." Angilia's eyes widened at the sound of his voice, and she looked at Patrick. He giggled. "Don't worry. I've already broken enough rules tonight. What's one more?"

Eric stood staring at his brother, more astonished than he had ever felt. Angilia knew how intense and overwhelming this was for her father. "Daddy, this is your present from Patrick."

"Actually, she did this. Angilia went to my room today and evoked me. She asked if I could do this for you tonight. She even reminded me to get permission. I didn't. I just came." He smiled at Eric and threw his arms around his brother.

Eric actually saw, heard, and felt Patrick. He did not know what to think, do, or say. All he could do was embrace his brother and cry. "I love you, Eric," Patrick softly said, which made Eric's heart soar and pound and made Angilia cry.

"I love you, Patrick," Eric managed to tell his brother though his tears and shock. The two men held one another for several minutes, both overwhelmed by the experience. "So you broke the rules again? Not much has changed, has it?" Eric smiled as he held Patrick at arm's length to look at him.

"Not really, except I am officially an angel," Patrick laughed. "How long has it been, Eric?"

Eric took a deep breath. Did Patrick just ask him how many years ago he had died? Eric's brain was on overdrive, fighting to comprehend and take in everything. The real miracle was that it really no longer caused him pain to think or to talk about Patrick's death. Eric knew that for certain now. "Almost thirty-five and a half years," Eric replied with a smile.

"That long? Really? Good grief, if I were still here, I'd be 54," Patrick giggled. "But look at you. You do not look 58 at all. And she is exactly the same as the day we first saw her. It was so odd seeing her as a tiny baby, though, with all of that curly hair," Patrick said, one arm around Angilia.

"So you and Great-grandfather were there?" Angilia asked her uncle.

Patrick nodded. "I've been around a lot, you know that," he told her. "I'll always be around," he said and looked at Eric. "You might not always see me, but I'll be here. And here," he softly said as he placed a hand over Eric's heart.

Patrick and Angilia suddenly looked up and then at each other. "They know what I did. It took them long enough," he giggled. Angilia lightly slapped his arm. "What can they do? They know this is for you."

"You're in trouble again?" Eric smiled.

"Michael's yelling for me to return immediately," Patrick said, his voice deep in imitation of the Archangel. "They won't do anything. It's Christmas and at her request. She is still talked about there." Patrick smiled at her. "The new angels are taught how to be angels by hearing about you, you know. You are the gold standard for all angels. Except for me, apparently," he giggled again.

Eric smiled. This conversation between the three of them was so natural and so real. It was real. Angilia was not smiling, though. "What is it?" Eric asked her.

"Michael is screaming now." She looked at Patrick. "You have to return. Otherwise, you will spend Christmas in isolation again."

"Again? Good grief, Patrick, you really are the rebel angel. I wish you could stay, but you belong with the angels," Eric said, smiling as tears filled his eyes.

"Yeah. I'll manifest again someday," Patrick promised him. He pulled Eric to him in a hug that felt so real and human that it sent a shockwave through Eric's body. "I love you, Eric." He hugged Angilia with one arm while he still held his brother. "I love you, Little One."

"I love you, Uncle Patrick," she whispered.

Eric hugged him one more time. "I love you, Patrick. Thank you for this." Patrick nodded, still smiling, and flashed a peace sign as he disappeared. Eric stood staring at where his brother had been, struggling to assimilate the experience.

Angilia held his arm, understanding that he needed to process what had happened. After several minutes, she softly asked, "Daddy? Are you all right?"

Eric turned, smiled, and pulled his daughter into an embrace. "I am fine, Angel. I don't know what to say. Thank you seems rather insipid and inadequate. He was really here. Patrick was here. I saw him. I heard him. I felt him. How can I thank you for such a miracle?"

Angilia smiled and shook her head. "You don't have to, Daddy. There was nothing else I wanted to do for you this Christmas, especially after what we shared in July. I just didn't expect him to show up in church while you read the nativity story," she giggled. "I shouldn't be surprised by that, though."

"He looks just the same. Is that how he looked when you were there?"

Angilia nodded as they slowly walked down the aisle to leave. "He will look like that for all eternity. I just hope they do not send him to isolation. He hates that."

Eric laughed. "I'm sure he does. Patrick never really liked being alone." They walked in silence for a few minutes, their arms around one another. "Patrick said you evoked him today. How do you evoke him?"

"Oh, that's easy. I just call him and tell him I need to talk to him. He always comes, but he rarely manifests. Usually it's a sensation, which is how I knew he was beside me in the church. I feel warmth all around me and I know he is here. Remember the warm air around us on Mommy's birthday? That was her. It's a lot like that, Daddy."

They neared the palace gate and the guard unlocked it for them. Angilia watched her father and sensed his thoughts. She put her hand on his arm and stopped him outside the main entrance. "Now that Uncle Patrick has manifested and connected to you in his physical form, you can evoke him, too, Daddy. When you are alone and it is quiet, just call to him. Say his name and ask him to come to you. Uncle Patrick will, most often in spirit form, which is the warmth I mentioned. I know people talk about spirits feeling cold, but angels feel warm. You will know when he is with you." She smiled at him. Eric kissed her forehead and they entered the foyer.

He walked with her to the elevator and they both entered. Almost simultaneously they reached for the second floor button and giggled. "The sitting room?" Eric softly asked. Angilia nodded, and they entered the sitting room at 3:00 on Christmas morning, the room and the date they had first come together. Eric turned on the lights, and they sat on the floor in front of the fireplace. Its soft golden glow bathed them in warmth and light.

"I spent two Christmases with you before I was born, Daddy. The first was here in this room when I came to you. The second was in 1995, nine days before I was born. You spent the entire day with me. You talked to me and told me stories. You gave me my first Christmas present, the stuffed toy lamb I keep on the shelf in my room. Lambchops, I named him. You sang Christmas songs to me, like "Silent Night" and "Little Town of Bethlehem." You read the nativity story from Luke 2 to me, just like you read it in church every year. I remember feeling such love. I knew somehow that it was almost time to be born and see you."

Eric smiled at her. "Speaking of Christmas gifts, I have one for you. It's not from me, though," he said as he went to a cabinet and removed it. He sat next to Angilia again and handed it to her. The wrapping paper was sweet, depicting Mary holding baby Jesus. Angilia removed it very carefully, saying she wanted to keep it.

"It's from Mommy," she said as soon as she saw the Spanish book. She ran her finger over the cover, and Eric smiled while he watched her. She opened the book, seeing an inscription written in flowing cursive handwriting. It was in Spanish, which of course Angilia spoke, read, and wrote fluently: *To our precious daughter Angilia—I love you so very much. I am forever in your heart. Love, Mommy.* Tears filled and began to overflow her eyes as she traced her mother's writing.

Angilia noticed an envelope protruding from the book, and she removed it. She carefully opened the flap and pulled out a handwritten letter. "Daddy, I can't see it," she said, her tears too thick and blinding. "Will you?"

"Of course, baby," he replied. He put his right arm around her as she leaned against him. He held the letter in front of them and he choked back his own tears, seeing his wife's last letter, written six days before she died. He remembered her writing it, both of them knowing she was dying. Now Eric read it aloud to their daughter:

17 October 1995

My Dearest Angilia,

You are so very precious and so very loved. I have treasured every second of these six months with you, feeling you, enjoying how you respond to your father. I know in my heart how very special you are, my darling daughter.

I can write this to you today, knowing I shall never see you, but full of peace, joy, and love. My heart overflows, immensely touched by watching and sharing your daddy's love for and joy in you. His love for you is unlike any love I have experienced, witnessed, or even read about before! A truer love has never existed! A glow emanates from within him since you have been with us! To see this, I know it must be a miracle. By now, Angilia, you have seen this many times, and you know how much a miracle his love is.

I know that you will always be surrounded by that glow, and that you will know such wondrous love. Your father has loved you from the very first second! He knew you were here before I felt or sensed you, before you were confirmed by the doctor. He just knew! And he knew you were his beautiful daughter, long before there could even be a thought of a test to confirm this—though he was quite adamant that such a test was unnecessary. He told me that he knew you so very well! Many times.

He talked about knowing you, feeling you, seeing you. I was never quite sure just what he meant, though the look in his eyes made me believe him. He was so intense, so serious, so full of love. I had to believe him. All I know is that I felt you inside of me, and when you heard his footsteps or his voice, you became quite excited! How you knew his footsteps, I never understood. But the two of you have had a special connection from the very beginning.

Another unusual thing. Everyone—my mama, friends, the doctors—told me I would have morning sickness, which I must tell you did not thrill me! I dreaded that so. But I was never once sick while you were with me—not from anything. It is as if you protected me, my Angel, and made my last months the very happiest. You are such a blessing!

I know your daddy loves you and protects you. You must take care of your daddy, too, Angel, for it is just the two of you now. Promise me, precious daughter, that you will stay healthy, strong, and faithful for both of you. It might seem silly to write this today, while you are still with me, but I know you are very strong, wise, and protective of your daddy. You are already a comfort and a blessing to him, and that will only increase with each passing year. I know I do not have to worry about either of you, my dear—you have one another. I can accept the future with a calm heart and soul.

You may never see me as you journey through this life, but you will feel me with you, Angilia. I want to close this letter to you with a line from the Winnie the Pooh movie. Your daddy reads the book to you every day—it must be a favorite, for you seem to reach for him when he is reading—'If there ever comes a day when we can't be together keep me in your heart; I'll stay there forever.'

All my love forever,

Mommy

Angilia's head rested on Eric's shoulder, and tears fell from her eyes. Eric folded the letter and returned it to the envelope. He held Angilia, kissed the top of her head, and smiled. He had not read Marisol's letter at the time she wrote it and sealed it. Her words sent a surge of love and peace through him.

Angilia smiled up at him, dried her eyes, and picked up the book, <u>The Selected Poems of San Juan de la Cruz</u>. Angilia was familiar with a few of his poems from the 16th century. She opened it to the page where the ribbon bookmark was placed and read the poem aloud in its original Spanish:

Canciones Del

Alma en la intima communication

De union de amor De Dios

del mismo auctor.

O llama de amor uiua

que tiernamente hieres

De mi alma en el mas profundo centro

pues ya no eres esquiua

acaba ya si quieres

Rompe la tela deste dulce enquentro.

O cauterio suaue,

o regalada llaga,

O mano blando, o toque delicado

que a uida eternal sabe

y toda deuda paga,

matando muerte, en vida la as trocado.

O lamparas de fuego

en cuyos resplandores

las profunda cauernas de el sentido

que estaua oscuro, y ciego

con estraños primores

Calor, y luz dan junto a su querido.

Quan manso, y amoroso

recuerdas en mi seno

Donde secretamente solo moras

y en tu aspirer sabroso

de bien y Gloria lleno

quan delicadamente me enamoras.

As she began reading, Matthew came down the stairs quietly. He had awakened early and wanted a snack, so he was headed to the kitchen. Instead, he stopped outside the sitting room and listened to Angilia read the poem. He did not understand much Spanish, but he smiled at the sheer beauty of the words. When she finished reading, he quietly said, "That's beautiful."

Eric smiled at him and motioned Matthew to join them. He did, and sat on the floor facing them. He smiled and asked Angilia, "What does it mean?"

Angilia smiled and translated the poem into English, looking into the flames dancing in the fireplace as she spoke. Matthew and Eric both watched her, both loved her, and both felt the power and beauty of the words. Matthew smiled at her. "That really is beautiful."

"It's from my Mommy," Angilia told him as she showed him the book.

"She told me to give it to you on your 18th birthday. Considering everything that happened this year, I don't think she'll mind that I gave it to you now," Eric said, his voice soft and gentle.

"Mommy kept me alive, Daddy. I died, I know that, but Mommy came to me and brought me back to you. I felt her," Angilia confessed to her father, taking him by surprise.

Eric cried, remembering looking down at Angilia lying on the ground, bleeding to death, knowing he was losing her. He remembered her dead in his arms. He remembered her coming back to life and whispering 'Mommy.' He remembered Matthew telling him the bullet to her aorta should have been fatal. He remembered Matthew saying that Angilia's guardian angel had kept her alive. Marisol.

Eric looked at his daughter, tears sliding down his cheeks. He smiled at her and took her hands in his, words failing his brain—until his daughter's next question stabbed his heart. "Daddy, there was only one question I needed to ask you for total peace and closure. I never have, because I knew it would hurt you. But Mommy answered it in her letter, actually. Did I, did her pregnancy, cause her to get sicker, weaker? Did I cause her to die?"

Eric's heart lurched. He gently cupped her face with his hands, his eyes betraying his pain. "Oh, baby, is that what you thought? No. No, Angel. In fact, Mommy was right. She hadn't felt so healthy in at least two years. It's as if your energy filled her and kept her well and alive. I've never yet told you this, but now is the time. In May 1994 the oncologists told us that Marisol would live another year and a half at the most, probably less.

"She wanted to have our baby. That's all she wanted. You know that I first felt you on Christmas Day 1994. I felt you in my heart. You were so alive, so real, and I knew you. I knew you. That's what Mommy meant in her letter, baby. You came to me. You were alive, and you came to me.

"Mommy wrote that I knew when you were inside of her. I did. You went from me into her. Just about eleven months after the doctors told us Marisol had a year and a half, you entered her, on April 16, 1995, Easter Sunday. Yes, the doctors feared pregnancy might cause her some serious problems, even kill her, and they wanted to perform an abortion. We were horrified. We would and could never do that to you, not ever. She stood there and told them that you were her sole life's purpose, and that no matter what, you came first. That's when we began meeting with the doctors and making all the arrangements, if needed, to keep Marisol alive until you were born. It's what she wanted, and that's what happened, you know that.

"But the first six months of the pregnancy were filled with love and happiness. She was never sick, not even from the leukemia. Never. It wasn't until the third trimester began that she got sick. But that had nothing to do with you, Angel. Her leukemia was very aggressive, and we all knew it would take her from us. It was the disease, baby, not you. You brought her such joy, peace, and love. She was never more beautiful and alive than she was during those six months with you.

"She loved me. She loved you. She wanted you even though she knew she would never be here, physically here, with you. You were meant to be, Angilia—you are my gift from God. You came to me first, because God knew it would be the two of us, and He gave you to me. He solidified our bond. I loved you, I knew you, and I saw you before you were born, Angilia. I can never explain it any other way." Eric's turquoise eyes stared into her soul, emitting love and truth.

"Daddy, you are the greatest love of my life. You made me. From your love, you created me. I love you, Daddy," Angilia told him, putting her arms around him and holding him close to her. Matthew smiled through his own tears, feeling blessed to share their intimate, heartfelt moment.

§§§§§

A short time later, others began waking up and joining them, and everyone noticed that Eric and Angilia still wore the same clothes from church. They had not gone to bed, but they did go to their rooms to change clothes before breakfast. After breakfast, everyone gathered in the sitting room, mostly to share company, friendship, and love. Angilia could not remember a Christmas when this many people filled their home with laughter and love.

Throughout the morning, they watched old Christmas movies, listened to Christmas music, and told stories. Katherine and Mitchell told about Matthew's first Christmas, much to his embarrassment. "He threw up all over himself and me right in the middle of the Christmas morning church service. We were smelly, sticky messes, and as much as we hated to leave, we had to. Mitchell had to clean Matthew while I cleaned myself," Katherine said with a laugh.

"Do you remember any of that?" Eric asked Matthew with a smile.

"No. I don't remember anything much at all before the age of three," Matthew admitted. "I'm not like she is," he grinned.

"Tell everyone about your first Christmas, Angilia," Katherine requested.

Angilia smiled and looked at her father. "Which one?"

"I don't understand, dear. What do you mean?" Katherine looked as befuddled as she felt.

"I suppose it depends on what you mean by first. My first one after I was born? Or do you mean the one when I was with my mother? Or my actual first Christmas, when I was with my father?"

Katherine and Mitchell both looked even more perplexed. "I understand what you mean by the first two," Katherine said. "I know you remember things from your mother's pregnancy. But I have no idea what you mean by the last one. Isn't that the same as the first one?"

Angilia shook her head and took a deep breath. "No. It was the Christmas before I was with my mother, 1994. My mother got pregnant on Easter Sunday 1995. I—my soul—came to my father on Christmas Day 1994, on the balcony of this room. That is technically my first Christmas." Everyone was hearing this for the first time. Juanita and Alejandro looked at one another as they sat on the sofa across from Eric and Angilia. Susan, Daniel, and Roger had no inkling what Angilia meant, since neither she nor Eric had ever mentioned anything about this before. Eduardo felt more bewildered than anyone. Matthew was the only one who knew anything, because he had picked up some of the story early that morning as he sat with them in this room.

Angilia looked at her father, and he nodded. "We might as well tell them everything. I'll tell my side of it, and then you fill in the rest," Eric stated. "Marisol and I were in this room on Christmas morning 1994. She was standing in this area, her back toward the balcony, and I was over there near the tree and the balcony. I thought I had seen people out there, which kind of threw me since this is so high off of the ground. I stepped onto the balcony and looked around, but didn't see anyone. Suddenly I felt a gentle push against my chest and stumbled back a step or two. Something felt different. I just stood there for quite a while before I turned and walked to Marisol. She looked at me, smiling, but asked me what was wrong because I looked so serious. *'We are going to have a beautiful daughter. Next Christmas you will be pregnant with her,'* I told Marisol. She was. Angilia was born nine days after Christmas Day 1995."

Everyone looked as confused and concerned as they possibly could, except for Matthew. He knew just enough of the story and just enough about Angilia to accept this as truth. Angilia took a deep breath and told the events from her perspective. "The soul is eternal, always existing, sometimes centuries before someone's physical birth. God knows when each soul will be born. My first memories are of being in a part of Heaven called the Unborn Children Sphere, where manifested souls wait to be born. When souls manifest, they take on the physical appearance the person will have on earth. When souls are born, they simply disappear from the Unborn Children Sphere.

"Michael—the Archangel—took me from the Unborn Children Sphere to the Angels Choir in Heaven before I was born. I had a purpose for being there, for being an angel, but that is another story for another time," she explained and smiled at her father. Eric smiled and agreed. "Anyway, one day Michael told me that God had instructed him to take me to earth so I would be with my father before I was born. God wanted my soul to enter my father so that we would know one another and solidify our bond," she said, again smiling at her father.

"Michael brought me here, to the balcony of this room, where my parents were, on Christmas Day 1994. We were standing there, and I knew Daddy saw us, even though he wasn't supposed to. Michael flew us out of his sight, and helped me shed my manifested physical form and become my soul form. While Daddy stood on the balcony, my soul flew into his heart. That is what he felt push him. That was my soul entering him. God sent me to Daddy on Christmas Day."

"My real-life Angel came to me in this room 18 years ago today," Eric softly said, smiling and holding his daughter.

"Mi nieta, then you really are an angel. I always wondered about that," Juanita said, moving to sit next to her granddaughter. "Something in my heart knew that about you. Something in you told me it was true. The rest of you can call me silly if you want to, but I knew it. I have said it before, too."

Alejandro leaned forward and smiled at his granddaughter. "You really are ordained by God, mi nieta. You really are a miracle. You were different from the moment you were born. We all saw it and we all knew it. Sometimes I wondered if I were crazy. I thought I heard you say words before you should have, but I never said anything. I thought people would lock me away if I told them my newborn granddaughter could talk."

Eric laughed uproariously, never knowing others had heard her, too. "Are you telling me those really were words?" Susan asked Eric. "I thought I was crazy or delusional, too. One day when you were at a meeting and I picked her up, she said my name, I swear she did. And when you got home and walked upstairs, she heard your footsteps and I know she said '*Daddy*'. Please tell me I didn't imagine all of that."

Mitchell cleared his throat. "If you two are crazy, then so am I. I heard her say '*Daddy*' the day after she was born, on those videos we watched. At the end, when she woke up from her nap. Did anyone else hear that?"

Angilia sat quietly, neither confirming nor denying anything. Eric, though, smiled and put their minds at ease. "You heard her talk. I never questioned it or doubted it. It happened the first day, and just somehow seemed so normal and natural, although nothing about her is truly normal or natural. That first day, the day she was born, I held her after Mamá and Papa left the hospital, and she smiled at me and said '*Daddy*' for the first time. I now know that she was a mature soul when she was born, not an infant soul. Everything about her was formed in Heaven and remained with her soul when she came to earth. You are right, Mamá, our Angilia is a miracle."

Matthew watched and listened intently, his amber eyes lit from within. So very much now made perfect sense. Her talk of destiny, God, death, eternity, evil, divine punishment—it was all from her experience as an angel in Heaven. She knew the truth, the absolute truth, because she had lived it. She had known it. Angilia was God's gift to Eric, a Christmas gift. Matthew smiled at the pure beauty of that.

§§§§§

Lunch was casual, a buffet in the sitting room, with the twinkling lights of the Christmas tree and the fireplace bathing the room in a magical glow. Stories continued throughout lunch, inspired by the earlier conversation. Each person took turns telling his or her earliest memory. A familiar voice suddenly joined the others, and Angilia leapt from the sofa to greet Mr. Brennan and Ginny. She kissed his cheek, and held his hand while Ginny pushed his wheelchair close to Eric.

Eric stood and hugged him. "Merry Christmas, Mr. Brennan. We are so happy you are with us today. Please, help yourselves to lunch and jump right in. Everyone is telling their earliest memories."

Mr. Brennan smiled, and Ginny went to get him some food. "Oh, I'm not like the Princess here. I don't remember hardly anything before two or three years old. And that is not very exciting. I remember my mother carrying me outside to the yard in the spring. A butterfly landed on a vine near us, and I tried to grab it. A butterfly chase is my earliest memory."

Everyone smiled, and Angilia knew that was essential for his memoir. His book would indeed be interesting, historical, and heartfelt. How could anyone not enjoy Mr. Brennan's stories and experiences? "What kind of butterfly? What color was it? What made you try to grab it?"

Eric threw his head back. Mr. Brennan laughed. "Oh, Princess, I have no idea. I just remember flitting images of my mother carrying me, seeing the butterfly, and trying to grab it. I do not remember things the way you do, in great detail, at least not things from so long ago."

"No one remembers things the way she does," Eric commented, his head still resting on the top of the sofa cushion.

"Yes, they do. I'm not the only person with hyperthymesia, Daddy."

"Forgive me. She's right. There are twenty-one known cases, including Angilia, in the entire world. But you are still very different from the other twenty. I know that none of their earliest memories parallel yours, Angilia" Eric smiled.

"No one's memories do," Mr. Brennan agreed. "Our Princess is unique in this world. Something tells me that she is not of this world." Eric immediately sat bolt upright and looked at Mr. Brennan. "Oh, I didn't mean to offend you, Sir. I am sorry."

"You haven't. What do you mean, Mr. Brennan?"

"Well, she knows so very much about what lies beyond this world and this life. That is not mere faith and belief, as others might claim. She has first-hand knowledge about Heaven, I know she does. Call me daft and tell me to leave if you must, but I am certain the Princess is from Heaven," Mr. Brennan said.

Roger dropped his cookie onto the floor. How did Mr. Brennan know this, when he had just met Angilia recently? Roger was shocked, even frightened, and looked around him. "Relax, Roger. You won't be struck by lightning," Angilia wryly said to him. "I knew that Mr. Brennan had figured it out, though." She looked at him. "You are correct, Mr. Brennan. I am from Heaven." She and Eric repeated the story for him, and he smiled, relieved to know that he was not insane, either.

"Well, now we can stop watching what we say, at least," Eric sighed. "It's time for Christmas gifts now." Angilia followed him to the tree, thinking that she still had to be aware of what she said around Matthew. Until the time she revealed their shared past to him, she had to remain on her guard.

Everyone gathered around the tree, and handed their gifts to the recipients. Katherine's present to Angilia made her cry her happy tears and hug Katherine in gratitude. Katherine had finally found a set of the Eric and Marisol wedding dolls that Angilia had seen in the time capsule in August. They had been difficult to locate, but she had, and she was thrilled to see the girl so ecstatic. Angilia's love for her parents was beautiful and inspiring, and Katherine shed a few tears as she watched Angilia show them to her father.

The gift exchange culminated with Angilia's gift to her father. He beamed at her when he opened the box and saw a pastel portrait of Patrick, as she had seen him: sitting on the ledge near the clouds. Angel Patrick. She had to answer lots of questions about the portrait and whether she had known her uncle in Heaven. Roger was speechless, staring at the portrait, seeing Patrick as he had looked that last day, July 19, 1977. The same clothes, the same face, the same slanted smile that reminded most people of Elvis. Patrick was an angel? Angilia assured Roger that Patrick was indeed an angel and remembered him. She told him the story of Patrick rearranging Gabriel's sheet music, and Roger laughed. He could see Patrick doing that.

Eric stood the portrait on the mantle, making his brother part of the festivities. He returned to the tree and handed Angilia her gift from him, and she threw herself against him in tears when she saw it. "Thank you, Daddy. They will stay with me always." Eric held her for quite a while, her emotions heightened by the extraordinarily poignant day. Finally she loosened her arms and kissed her father's cheek. She stood the double picture frame on the table near them, and smiled.

"I finally located those pictures, and Muriel's staff at the museum framed them for me. That one is your great-grandfather Stefan at the age of sixteen. The other is him holding your Uncle Patrick at his christening. Your two special angels," Eric tenderly said, holding her as she fingered the pictures. Angilia smiled at him and kissed him again.

After Angilia and Eric's emotional exchange, Matthew cleared his throat. "I have one more gift to give, but it isn't here. It wouldn't fit through the doors, so it's in one of the back rooms in the stable." Everyone was abuzz, wondering who it was for and what it could be.

Eric shrugged his shoulders. "Let's go, then." Alejandro, Juanita, Angilia, Mr. Brennan, and Ginny took the elevator, while everyone else walked downstairs to meet on the patio and begin their jaunt to the stable. Matthew led everyone to the back of the stable to a large storage room.

Matthew stood in front of the huge sliding door and faced everyone. "Since it's for Angilia, I want her to be the first to see it," he announced. She looked surprised, and she took her father's hand and walked with him to the door. Matthew slid the door open, flipped a switch, and Eric's recording of "Sunshine on My Shoulders" loudly blasted forth.

Angilia could hardly believe what she saw, and her hands covered her face in her surprise. Eric looked in and could not believe it, either. He turned away and muttered, "Good grief." Roger stood next to Eric, his arm around him, and laughed joyously. The giant jukebox float from the Jubilee pageant filled most of the room, and its lights blinded them.

"This is awesome! I asked Mimi if I could buy this float, and she told me someone else already had. I was heartbroken. Thank you!" Angilia leapt at Matthew and grabbed him in a hug, much to his embarrassment, surprise, and pleasure. He wanted so much to put his arms around her and hold her close to him. He dared not, for he did not trust himself.

"You're welcome. I heard you say you wanted it, so after the pageant I asked the committee about buying it for you, and I did. It's been in here ever since, and Joseph managed to keep this room tightly locked until this morning. I'm glad you like it," Matthew said.

Angilia giggled. "Like it? I love it!" Matthew took a deep breath as she pulled away and took his hands in hers. I love you, Angilia, and soon I will tell you that, he thought.

§§§§

After the excitement over the giant jukebox, which Eric said could not be dismantled and reassembled in the ballroom, the family and friends returned to the sitting room. Antoine had hot cider waiting for them, and Angilia got cups for Mr. Brennan and Ginny. Everyone settled near the fireplace, chatting comfortably. Angilia, though, stood across the room staring at the photographs her father had given her, of her Great-grandfather and Uncle Patrick. She loved them so very much, and she knew they felt her love.

Matthew watched her, knowing more than ever how important her family was to Angilia and why they were so close. He had envied her relationship with her father, which made him feel sinful. That relationship was as pure, loving, trusting, and blessed as any human relationship could ever be. Matthew no longer felt envy, but rather happiness. He was happy for Eric and Angilia, and for himself. He was lucky—blessed—enough to share their lives and to witness their love. That itself was a special gift.

Matthew walked to her, and she smiled at him. "Thank you for the float. That was very sweet of you," she said to him.

"I wanted to do it for you. It was a tricky surprise to keep for four months, but with Joseph's help we did it. I wasn't going to say anything, but I told the committee that I wanted to buy it for you, so they negotiated something and what I paid was donated to your father's Open Heart foundation. I thought you'd like to know that, just because it matters so much to you," Matthew told her.

"Thank you, Matthew. That makes it even more special."

"I'm glad." Just ask her, he thought. "Can we go somewhere else for a little while, where we can sit and talk in a bit of quiet?"

Angilia motioned him to follow her, and they went to the elevator. She pushed the fifth floor button and led him to a staircase in the northwest corner. He had rarely been on the fifth floor, so the staircase was a surprise to him. He wondered where it went, and followed close behind her as she climbed the staircase, ready to catch her if she slipped or fell. A minute later, they were in a circular tower, which contained an iron table and chairs, as well as a telescope. The watch tower.

Angilia and Matthew sat at the table, the cool breeze slightly shocking after the warmth of the fire. "Thank you for letting me share part of this morning with you and your father," Matthew said. "That was very special and beautiful. I hope I didn't intrude."

Angilia shook her head and glanced at him. "You didn't. The poem my Mommy bookmarked drew you in for a reason. Nothing happens by chance, Matthew. You were supposed to be there. I'm glad you were."

Matthew's heart skipped a beat. "You are?"

"Sure. You're my friend. It was right that you were there," Angilia replied.

"You know, almost ten months ago when we met, my father was right about one thing," Matthew said. "It took him a few days to recognize it, but he later told me what he saw. He was right."

Angilia cocked her head, looked at him, and asked, "About what?"

"He said he had never seen any doctor fight so much for a patient, do so much for a patient, stay constantly with a patient, look at a patient the way I looked at you. When I told my parents that I was leaving Oxford and coming here, they knew. I have never said anything except to one person, but they knew." He paused and stared into her eyes, making her a bit nervous.

"They knew what, Matthew?"

"That I love you, Angilia. I do love you. I have loved you from that very first second when you looked at me as I lifted you onto the gurney." Matthew leaned forward and took her hand in his. "I love you."

Angilia had never expected this. What was she supposed to do? What should she say? This was the one thing with which she had absolutely no personal experience. She knew Matthew. He was her best friend. Or rather, he had been her best friend in the Unborn Children Sphere. Was he still her best friend? She felt confused and lost.

Matthew knew this was a bit much for her. "Angilia, I am not asking anything of you, nothing at all. I just had to tell you. I've kept it to myself for the most part for nearly ten months. I love you. I will always love you. I know you need to discover how you feel. I will wait for you to do that, however long it takes. Wherever your heart takes you is where you are meant to be, even if it's not with me."

She looked at him and placed her other hand over his. "I don't know exactly what I feel yet. I don't know when I will know. I need time to uncover it, find it, understand it. This is one thing I have never dealt with before, Matthew. I don't know what to do, to think, or to say right now. I don't."

"It's all right, Angilia. You don't have to right now. I just wanted to tell you so that I didn't have to fight it around you any longer. You have no idea how difficult that has been for me. I know you need time, and I will wait. That's not the issue. I will never rush you or pressure you. I know my love is real, so waiting is not a problem or concern for me."

Angilia took a deep breath. "Thank you for understanding that. You told my father. He's the one person you told."

"Yes. I had to talk to him before I dared approach you. I mean, you are not quite seventeen, and this is new to you. I couldn't just throw this at you without his knowing. Besides, it wouldn't be right to exclude him. He told me he saw it, too, but that ultimately it's up to you," Matthew confessed.

"Thank you for talking to him first. That means a lot to me," she told him with a small smile.

The air was a bit colder, and the sun was beginning to set. "We better go back in now," Matthew said, standing and helping her up. He continued to hold her arm as they walked down the stairs to the fifth floor. They took the elevator to the first floor, knowing dinner would begin soon.

Eric watched as Matthew held her chair for her, obviously curious what had been said. He took his seat and looked at her carefully. She smiled at him, as she always did, and placed her hand over his in a tender squeeze. "Today has been a wonderful Christmas, hasn't it, Angel?" he asked her softly as the table filled.

"Yes, Daddy, Christmas has been most wonderful from the stroke of midnight. My 18th Christmas with you has been amazing," she smiled at him.

Everyone settled at their seats, and Antoine served the dinner. The day's comfortable chatting continued through dinner, Mr. Brennan spending his time happily talking with Eric. Angilia did not eat much or talk much. Halfway through dinner, Eric looked over and noticed, which made him wonder more than ever what had been said between Matthew and Angilia. Eric looked at Matthew, his face asking how it had gone. Matthew shrugged, which did not encourage Eric.

After dinner, Antoine announced that a desert buffet was ready in the sitting room, so everyone reconvened there moments later. Angilia, Mr. Brennan, Ginny, Alejandro, and Juanita took the elevator, as usual, and walked in together. Alejandro hugged and kissed his granddaughter as they did, grateful to God that she was with them on this Christmas day. She kissed him, too, and as everyone went for desert and drinks, she picked up the photographs her father had given her and quietly left the room.

§§§§§

Matthew got a piece of pie and took a bite while he scanned the room looking for Angilia. She was nowhere to be seen, and he began to wonder why. She was the only person not there, which he thought unusual. Eric was surrounded by a group of people, playing host. She was not part of the group. Where was she? Matthew placed his plate on the cart and left to find her. He was concerned that he had upset or offended her, even though she had not appeared to be either. Still, his confession of love had taken her by complete surprise and shock.

He ran down the stairs and went to the chapel, her go-to place when she had a problem. The chapel was empty. Matthew ran up to the third floor and peeked in her sitting room. It, too, was empty. He gingerly walked across the carpet and looked into her bedroom. His stomach lurched. She was lying on her side, clutching a teddy bear and crying. Something was wrong.

"Angilia? What's wrong?" Matthew asked her. She turned her face to the bed. Matthew went to her and got on his knees beside the bed. "Where does it hurt? What's wrong?"

"Nothing," was her muffled reply.

"You have to tell me, Angilia. Are you in pain?" he persisted. She shook her head. "Are you sick? Tell me what's wrong."

"No, I'm not sick."

"Something's wrong. What is it?"

"I just need to talk to someone," she said.

"Can I help? I want to help you," Matthew said, his voice gentle. She shook her head. "You said you trust me. I'm here for you."

"I can't. Not to you," she said, crying even more. This was one thing she could not talk with Matthew about.

"Should I get your father?"

"No. Yes. I don't know. I don't know if anyone here can help me," Angilia answered, crying even more now. Matthew looked at her, wondering who she could want who wasn't there. Suddenly he knew. He went to the hall and texted Eric and told him to come to Angilia's room. She needed to talk to him.

Eric excused himself from his friends and family and ran to the third floor. Matthew stopped him and whispered, "She's upset about something and I think she misses her mother right now." Eric nodded and clapped Matthew on the shoulder.

Eric sat next to her on the edge of her bed and gently brushed the hair off her face with his hand. "I'm right here, Angel," he softly assured her.

"Oh, Daddy, I've never needed Mommy as much as I do right now," she cried.

"About Matthew?"

"Yes. This is all so new to me. I'm so confused and scared. All of a sudden I don't know what's real and what's not. Have I been projecting my memories of our past onto our present? I know I said he's the same Matthew, but is he really or is that my wishful thinking? Do I want him to be the same so much that I've convinced myself that he is? How do I know?"

"Angel, Mommy would tell you that you will know when you are in love. Your heart will tell you. When it happens, your heart will let you know. It will happen when you are ready. Mommy would tell you to follow and to trust your heart always," Eric told her, his voice tender and loving.

"I'm sorry, Daddy. I never meant to upset you on Christmas day."

Eric lifted her into his arms and cradled her against him, stroking her hair. "You haven't upset me, Angel. To tell you the truth, I am totally amazed that this is the first time this has happened. You have been so strong during your 17 years. Listen, Angel, it's okay to feel this way. You are still so young, and you need time, space, love, and patience. If a relationship between you and Matthew is meant to be, then it will happen. You know that, right, Angel?"

She nodded and sat up, looking at him. "I do know that. Somehow I let myself fall victim to my doubts and fears, and I know better. I'm sorry."

"You might have been an angel, but you are human now. You are allowed to have human emotions, baby. It's okay, believe me. Okay?"

Angilia smiled at her father and gently placed her hand over his cheek as she had done when she was a baby. "Okay. You're right. It will work itself out when God intends it to." She looked into his eyes. "Daddy, do you believe that there is only one real love for each of us? I do. That's one reason this is so scary if I am confusing the past with the present."

Eric held her hand. "I do. I believe marriage is once in a lifetime, for life, with that one special person. Once you know in your heart, the fear goes away forever. You are left with love and happiness."

"Like you and Mommy," she smiled at him.

"Yes." Eric fingered his wedding band.

"Daddy, what about the throne, though?"

Eric was confused by her question. "The throne?"

"Yes. You are not married. I am your only child. If something happens to me, you will need an heir."

"Angilia, baby, I know—we both know—what happened this year. You are far more important to me than the throne. You know that."

She sensed that the topic hurt and even angered him, so she asked her next question. "What about you, Daddy?"

"Me? What do you mean?"

"You are alone except for me, and the few family and friends we have around us. I know you said one marriage for life, but aren't you ever lonely?"

"Never. I've had love and romance, and Marisol made me very happy and fulfilled and loved. I don't need that again. It would never be the same anyway. Marisol is my one love. And I have never been lonely." Angilia looked at her left ring finger, at the purity ring she had worn for nearly six years. Eric understood her implication. He had remained celibate since Marisol's final illness and subsequent death. He still wore his wedding band. He had never even thought of dating anyone else. He knew people speculated and talked about his lifestyle choices, and he knew his daughter had read and heard all of that, too.

"Angel, that ring is very special for many reasons. I am so proud of you for staying true and strong to your morals. Believe me, I know first-hand it is not easy when people attack us for our beliefs and morals. They judge us for not conforming to what they perceive is right and moral. I think things like your work with COC are putting an end to some of that. Your mother is very proud of you, too, Angilia."

Angilia looked at him as tears fell down her cheeks again. "I just want God, you, and Mommy to approve of me, Daddy."

Eric smiled at her. "I do. Of course I do. And I am pretty sure God does, too, Angel. I know Mommy does. I never told you, but that was her purity ring. She wore it until our wedding day. She was 40 when we married, and she still wore the ring and upheld her moral standards. She wore it until her wedding day, just as you will do, I know."

Angilia hugged him. "Thank you, Daddy. You are my everything. You have eased my heart. You have made everything right."

"I love you. So does Matthew." Eric held his phone in one hand and texted him to come in. Matthew entered and sat on the floor next to her bed.

"You know this ring, which you removed from my finger in the ambulance?" Matthew nodded. "It was my Mommy's ring."

"So you carry that part of her with you, too," Matthew said with a smile. Angilia smiled back, pleased that Matthew understood and accepted her beliefs.

"Marisol chose to wear it with her engagement ring, but you don't have to, Angel. Most people don't," Eric told her.

"There's plenty of time to think about that," Matthew interceded. Eric smiled, happy that Matthew upheld his commitment to give her time and space.

"I'm sorry I couldn't talk to you earlier. I didn't want you to think I don't like you. I do. Besides, I trust you implicitly," Angilia explained to Matthew.

"I understand, and I'm glad. I know how hard trusting any doctor is after everything you've been through. No one will ever hurt you again," Matthew insisted.

"Never," Eric reiterated. "And this year will be over in a few days, and then it will be your birthday, Angel." She didn't notice the look exchanged between Eric and Matthew. "Why don't we join the others before Christmas 2012 is history?"

The three of them rode the elevator to the second floor, Angilia between her father and Matthew. Eric's arm was protectively around her, and Matthew held her hand. The two men would love and protect her for all time. Matthew was confident that he and Angilia would marry, though he could not know when. Eric had known for some time that Matthew and Angilia were destined to marry. Her heart and soul would tell her when it was her time to love. Angilia would learn that when God wanted her to, Eric knew that. She had taught him so much about destiny, God's will, and faith.

§§§§§

Eric, Angilia, and Matthew rejoined everyone in the sitting room. The friends and family sat together near the fireplace, talking, relaxing, and enjoying Christmas night. It was close to midnight, and Christmas was nearly over, when Ginny and Mr. Brennan left. Eric and Angilia walked them to their car, and then resumed their places in the sitting room with the people they loved most.

Shortly after 2:00 in the morning, Angilia fell asleep in her father's arms, her head against his right shoulder. Eric smiled at the sight of her, so young and peaceful. Everyone sat quietly for a few moments. "She really is my miracle. God gave her to me and kept her with me. I saw everything that day," Eric suddenly said.

Roger knew what Eric meant, yet he was taken aback by the unexpectedness of his friend's comments. "Eric?"

"I saw everything that happened to her. It happened so quickly, but it felt like slow motion. She pushed me backwards as I felt my shoulder on fire. I saw the first bullet hit her, then the second, then the next one in the center of her chest. Blood was gushing from her. The guards were shooting, running around, yelling for me to stay down, but she was still standing. She was looking at me, and I was trying to get up. She said, "*No, Daddy*," and threw herself down on top of me, covering my body and my head. She said, "*Don't move, Daddy.*" I felt warm wetness soaking me. Her blood. My daughter's blood. Then the guns were quiet and Mike and Tony were running to the shooter. Tony was on the phone calling for help. I slowly rolled her onto her back. All I could see was blood. So much blood. I grabbed the picnic blanket, and she tried to take it and put it over my shoulder. I pressed it to her chest with all of my force.

"She looked at me, and put her hand on my shoulder, "*Daddy, you're hurt.*" I was so scared. "*I love you, Daddy.*" Then she wasn't breathing. I couldn't feel her heart beating. She was dead. My baby was dead. I just kept screaming at her, begging her to come back to me. Then you got there, and Mike stood up," Eric looked at Matthew. "I was holding her, I was yelling at her, I was crying. Suddenly she opened her eyes, and I could barely hear her say, "*Mommy.*" It didn't make any sense then, but she was alive. She was alive. She told me very early this morning that her mother had forced her soul back into her body at that moment. Marisol brought our daughter back to me that day."

They all sat in stunned silence for several minutes, not knowing what to say. They believed Eric. Like Marisol had written in her letter to Angilia, Eric's intensity, seriousness, and belief convinced people. Connecting this to everything that they had learned earlier, they more fully understood the true miracles that had blessed Eric and Angilia.

Eric spoke again, connecting that tragic yet miraculous day to a long ago tragic yet miraculous day, both of them involving Angilia. "I was there when my brother Patrick was killed. I saw the whole thing." Eric looked at Roger. "We were standing on the riverbank, we and the crew, when the boat crashed. I swam out to him and helped bring him to shore. The doctors did CPR. There were no signs of life. None. I couldn't just let them stop. I couldn't. I couldn't just give up on my brother. Every time they wanted to stop, I told them no. They couldn't. I just stood there, not moving, just praying to God to let Patrick live. They finally told me there was nothing they could do. Patrick was dead. One of them said Patrick must have died instantly.

"I stood there looking up at Heaven, and I heard myself scream in agony. My little brother was dead. That couldn't be true. He was only nineteen. He was so full of life. He couldn't be dead. Not Patrick. I kept looking up, crying, my heart shattered. I saw a beautiful girl walk out of the clouds and down to Patrick. She stood there, beautiful and full of light, across from me. A tear slid down her cheek as she looked at me. Her eyes—they were my eyes. Exactly. Angilia. She was Angilia. God sent her to me that day to comfort me, to show her to me and give me hope, and so she could guide Patrick into Heaven. That's why her name is Angilia. She is my angel."

Juanita, Alejandro, Eduardo, Susan, and Katherine cried, feeling Eric's pain and joy as he spoke. Matthew looked at Eric, then at Angilia, and felt love and awe. Eric had mentioned once that his daughter had a way of turning tragedy into joy. Angilia had done that for her father long before her birth, turning his pain into hope. She had been an angel for that purpose, Matthew realized that. So did the others as they processed and connected the two events, the two most wretched days of Eric's life.

"Roger, will you please go to the office and get my bound diaries for 1977 and 2007? Bring them to me," Eric requested. Roger nodded, and a few minutes later he returned and handed the diaries to Eric. Eric held the 1977 diary out to Mitchell. "Will you please read aloud the entry for July 19 for me?" Mitchell hesitated for a moment, unsure whether he should intrude upon something so personal. "Please."

Mitchell took the diary and opened it, and then read Eric's words aloud to everyone:

19 July 1977

I never thought I would write this. Patrick is dead. My little brother is dead. It happened so fast. But why? Why Patrick? Letting him go was the hardest thing I have ever done. I will never see him again, talk with him again, be the victim of his practical jokes again. Nothing. Just the past, just memories. This felt like such a bad nightmare. Until I had to return home, without him, and tell Father and Mother. Father just seemed to go lifeless, just sat in a chair, his back straight, staring ahead. Motionless. Mother crumpled into a heap on the floor, screaming, crying, wailing. Both of them ripped out what was left of my heart. They are devastated. And I am devastated.

Now I have to be the strong one, ignore my own pain, and plan my brother's funeral. Dear God, this is too much. How am I supposed to remain stoic and strong, when I am drained of everything? I don't know if my brain understands all of this. What was real today? All of it? None of it? Was today merely a dream? I don't know.

I almost feel as if I am not me, that I am not in my body, that I am an actor in a tragedy and the real me is watching this play. None of this makes sense to me.

Especially the girl. Who was she? Where did she come from? She seemed to come out of nowhere. No. She came out of the clouds, she stepped out of the clouds. Then she was standing there across from me, next to Patrick. She was crying. For Patrick? For me? For us both? I don't know. I've never seen her before. Was she real? She seemed real. She looked real. So beautiful. Like an angel. An angel with long ash blonde hair and bangs, pink lips, and my eyes. My eyes. How is that possible? No one in recent generations of my family had these turquoise eyes. Is she an ancestor? Did I inherit my eyes from her? Is she an ancestor who came for Patrick's soul? To escort him to Heaven?

I don't know. But she won't leave my mind even in the pain. I've never seen her, but I feel like I know her. Like I love her. Insane.

There is just too much in my brain right now. I can't think. I feel empty. What am I supposed to do now? God, help me. Please.

Mitchell closed the book and handed it to Eric amidst more stunned, emotional silence.

"I never told anyone about this. It wasn't until 2007 that I truly admitted to myself who that mysterious girl was. On Angilia's 11th birthday, it just became true to me as I watched her and looked at her. She was the girl who came when Patrick died. The face, the hair. The eyes. My eyes. She is the girl, the angel, who came to me and Patrick that day," Eric told them as he opened the 2007 diary and read the entry aloud, his voice resonating with a lifetime of emotions and love:

3 January 2007

Today, my beautiful daughter Angilia celebrated her 11th birthday. I know now, beyond all doubt, that I knew her long before I thought I did. That angel who walked out of the clouds, out of Heaven, the day Patrick died, was not my ancestor. She was my daughter. She was Angilia. She was my Angel. My baby was sent to me on the worst day of my life. God sent her to me that day. I remember her tears. I remember the look in her eyes when she looked at me—it's how Angilia looks at me now. Eyes filled with love. I remember feeling that I knew and loved her. I did, I do, I always will. I was 22 when Patrick died. I was 41 when Angilia was born. 19 years. It was 19 years before I saw her again. Angilia—Angel. My Angel. She is my angel. My beautiful angel. I treasure her more than I ever imagined possible.

Eric closed the diary and kissed Angilia's head as she still slept against him. Juanita was sobbing, shaking as Alejandro and Eduardo held and comforted her. Katherine cried, too, feeling and sensing the love and warmth Eric had for his daughter. As tragic as Patrick's death, the truth was not painful. The truth was beautiful, hopeful, and loving. Eric's daughter loved him enough to bring him hope, comfort, and love at his lowest moment. Angilia's love for Eric really was immense and eternal.

Roger leaned forward and smiled. "So that is who you described a couple of years before Patrick's death, too, then." Eric looked at him, puzzled and confused. He did not remember what Roger referenced. "When we were driving along the coast, talking about what we wanted to do and who we wanted to meet. You said something about a girl you were going to meet again in the future. You described her completely. I thought you were crazy, and it never clicked until now—you described her, Angilia. You described your future daughter.

"And I always wondered what happened that day with Patrick. You just stood there, staring ahead, even though there was nothing there. I thought maybe you were in shock or something, but I didn't do anything. You were so distraught that I didn't know what to do. But you just stood there, staring, and you stopped yelling and crying suddenly. Instead, you looked awe-struck or something. I never saw her. But I saw you that day, and I know you did. It's like you imagined her or dreamed her and she became real."

Eric smiled, now remembering that conversation. "I did not dream her, Roger. I did not imagine her. I sensed her, I suppose. More likely, God allowed me to see an image of her. God had already created Angilia for me, to be my daughter. We were always destined to be father and daughter. We both know that. We are both eternally grateful to God for that ultimate blessing."

CHAPTER 12

ngilia woke up and looked at the clock on the bedside table. 6:00. She yawned and sat up, just as she heard a gentle knock on her bedroom door. "Come in, Daddy. Good morning," she smiled. Eric entered, smiling, carrying a breakfast tray. He placed it over her lap and bent to kiss her nose.

"Happy birthday, my beautiful daughter Angilia. Happy 17th birthday." He looked at her smiling up at him, and thought how very much had occurred during the year since her 16th birthday.

"Thank you, Daddy. Stay with me?" Eric smiled and pulled a chair next to her bed while she ate her fresh fruit breakfast.

She noticed the white rose and envelope on the tray and smiled. He had written her a birthday letter, his first in five years. She would read it after he left, when she was alone. "I'm so happy. Abuela and Abuelo are staying here with us, and so is Uncle Eduardo. Our small but love-filled family is together now," she sighed happily.

"I know, Angel. Our close friends have increased in number, too, over the last year. Mitchell, Katherine, Matthew, Bonnie, and Mr. Brennan are with us, too. We are very blessed, aren't we?" he asked with a smile.

"Yes, we are, Daddy. You are the greatest blessing I will ever know," Angilia said as she finished eating, moved the tray, and leaned forward to kiss her father's cheek. He pulled a gift from his pocket and handed it to her. "Oh, Daddy, your gifts always make me cry, they are so wonderful and beautiful." Angilia removed the paper and stared at the engraved plaque in awe as she read the words:

--Jeremiah 1:5

♥♥♥♥♥♥♥♥♥♥♥♥♥♥♥♥

Happy 17th birthday my beautiful daughter Angilia,

You are my blessed gift from God.

I love you for eternity.

Daddy

3 January 2013

Angilia began crying, and Eric moved next to her and held her close. "It is beautiful, Daddy. I love you." She did not know that the plaque was connected to another gift Eric would give her that day.

"There is a lot more to come today, Angel. This is an exceptionally important birthday, you know that. Today is yet another miracle, because you are here with me. People are already outside the gates waiting to see you and celebrate your birthday." Eric smiled and kissed her forehead. "You come downstairs when you're ready," he said, picking up the tray and winking at her as he left. Angilia watched him leave, her whole being so full of love, peace, and happiness. She was not afraid of death, but she was grateful to be with her father.

Angilia took a shower, brushed her teeth, dried and styled her hair, and dressed. Smiling, she picked up the rose and letter, and went to her sitting room window seat. She looked up at the sky and knew Uncle Patrick and Great-grandfather were watching them. She smelled the fragrant rose, and then picked up the envelope, which he had sealed with red wax and his signet. Angilia slit the top open and carefully removed her father's letter. Happy tears slid down her cheek as she looked at his elegant handwriting and read his words to only her:

3 January 2013

My Beautiful Daughter Angilia:

I love you more than I ever thought it was possible for one man to love. You are my heart and my soul. You are my life.

You are my blessing, my only reason for living. I know that. I've known that since Patrick died. I've known that since I first felt your soul on Christmas Day 1994—the holy day when we celebrate Jesus' birth, you came to me. You went from Heaven's light to my heart. You brought that light into my heart. You are my heart-glow, as you call it. You are my miracle, Angel.

You have taught me how to find the beauty and joy in even the most horrific and painful moments. You taught me what love—real, eternal love— feels like and does. That love is more than a feeling. That love is action. You showed me love.

Angilia, when the day comes that you ascend to the throne of Valdavia, you will inarguably be the best, most compassionate, intelligent, righteous monarch to bear the title and the duties. Oh, I know I have had my part in preparing you, as my father did me. But you were born and ordained to lead and to guide this country, and to shape this world, in every sense.

You are light when there is darkness, hope when there is despair, joy when there is sorrow, peace when there is unrest, love when there is hatred. You are everything this country and the world need as we march through this tumultuous 21st century.

More importantly, you are my little girl, my beautiful daughter. And today marks 17 years since your birth. I love you more than I loved you yesterday, but I love you less than I will love you tomorrow.

Happy Birthday, my much beloved, beautiful Angel.

You own my heart,

Daddy

Angilia smiled and reread his letter to her. Their bond and love were stronger than ever, and she treasured him above all other people.

Angilia placed the letter in its envelope and walked to her desk, where she placed it in a drawer with her mother's letter from 1995. She opened another drawer and removed a small velvet jewel box. She quietly walked across the hall and placed it atop her father's pillows. She smiled, wondering what he would think of her little gift for him, knowing he would probably find it that night as he prepared for bed.

§§§§§

Angilia walked into the sitting room and kissed and hugged her grandparents and uncle and greeted her friends. She beamed at her father, and sat beside him on the sofa. She put her arms around him, relishing just being with him. Everyone understood the importance of Angilia's 17th birthday. Ten months earlier, she had nearly died. That she was alive, celebrating her 17th birthday, was a miracle, they knew that.

Roger drew their attention to the morning news. "Look, it's the birthday pictures," he said as Laurie and Franklin shared the official birthday pictures with the country. Bonnie had taken several, including a formal portrait of Eric and Angilia, he in his white military uniform and she in a lovely white and gold gown. Another picture showed Angilia in the same ball gown and jewels sitting on the steps of the throne, an informal pose that reminded people of Diana's famous wedding portrait from 1981. Franklin commented on the similarities and even showed the two portraits side by side. Another picture showed Eric and Angilia with Starlight, both of them informally dressed in jeans and white shirts. The last picture was of all five family members in a smiling, happy embrace.

"Those are stunning, just stunning," Katherine said. "I love them all."

Angilia smiled at Bonnie, who blushed. "Thank you. These were the easiest portraits I have ever taken. There was no work involved for me, except to focus the camera and push the button."

Susan was sobbing, something she had done often during the past year. That was understandable, though, given the fear and emotions each of them had felt. "They are beautiful, really they are. Happy birthday, sweetheart."

"Thank you, Susan," Angilia said. She went to Susan and hugged her. When she married, she would ask Susan to be her maid of honor. She would ask Bonnie to take the pictures. She could not ask Katherine to be a bridesmaid. Katherine would most likely become her mother-in-law, Angilia thought with a smile. Over the past nine days, Angilia had prayed and received her message from God that everything was pre-destined and would happen when it was supposed to happen. He had brought Matthew and Angilia together for a purpose. They were destined to be together. Angilia's heart felt calm and confident as she smiled at her family and friends.

§§§§

Even with the windows closed, they could hear the crowd outside screaming for Angilia. Eric looked out and smiled. People loved his daughter so much. Hundreds stood outside waiting to see her and to wish her a happy birthday. "Angel, they want to see you. Let's go to the fifth floor and surprise them," he said, taking her hand and smiling at her. She smiled and went with him on the elevator to the balcony.

He pulled back the thick velvet drapes and opened the wide double doors, and when people noticed, the screams increased in intensity. Angilia held her father's hand, and they walked onto the balcony. The hundreds of people below screamed, cried, chanted, and played her music. She and Eric waved, much to everyone's delight. Angilia turned to Roger, who had followed them, and told him to have her grandparents and uncle join them.

Roger accompanied them in the elevator to the fifth floor balcony, where they were stunned and a bit timid to step out. Angilia left the balcony long enough to take her grandparents' hands and walk with them onto the balcony while Eduardo followed. Alejandro and Juanita smiled at Angilia, joyous to see again how many people loved and admired their granddaughter. They kissed her, which drew applause, and waved to everyone who had come to wish Angilia a happy birthday. Eduardo waved, too, amazed by the experience. One year ago he had not known he had a niece and now he stood on a palace balcony with her.

"We want Angilia! We want Angilia!" people chanted, and Eric suggested they go down and greet everyone as they had done one year ago. Juanita and Alejandro enjoyed that, and were happy to meet people. They left the balcony, and Roger helped Eric close the doors and drapes. They took the elevator to the main floor, while Roger called Susan and told her they were doing a walkabout at the gates. She met them at the main entrance, inviting the others to come along if they wished.

The Taylors knew no one wanted to greet them, but they wanted to watch the meet-and-greet from the courtyard. They went with Susan and Daniel to the main entrance. Eric opened the front door and took his daughter's hand as they walked into the courtyard to an eruption of screams. People jumped, reached through the gate bars, waved signs, and shouted for Angilia's attention. She and Eric walked to the gate. "Unlock the gates so they can come in and talk to everyone," Angilia suggested to the guard on duty. He looked at Eric for approval, and Eric smiled and nodded.

The guard unlocked the gate and opened it wide. Angilia motioned for people to come in and join them. Her birthday walkabout turned into an informal garden party on the courtyard. People handed Angilia cards, flowers, gifts, and wished her a very happy birthday. Susan, Roger, and Daniel carried piles of gifts into the foyer, as they had done the previous year. Fans produced copies of the <u>Heart-Glow</u> CD for Angilia's and Eric's autographs. Copies of the day's birthday pictures they had printed from the palace web site were also proffered for autographs. The whole-family picture received autograph requests from all five family members, which pleasantly surprised Alejandro, Juanita, and Eduardo.

Angilia stepped aside and made a quick call to Antoine. Within ten minutes, he appeared with a cart and two assistants. Eric looked at Angilia, surprised but pleased. She had asked Antoine to bring one of her birthday cakes outside, with paper plates, napkins, and plastic forks so that everyone could have a piece of birthday cake. Before they let Antoine cut the cake, the people sang the birthday song to Angilia and applauded her.

"Thank you all so much," Angilia smiled at them. "Your being here means so much to me. Enjoy the cake and feel free to mingle." As Antoine cut pieces of cake, she asked for plates that she handed to each of the guards on duty that day. They all smiled at her, knowing how thoughtful and compassionate the princess always was.

Billy made his way through the crowd to Angilia. "Happy birthday, Princess darling," he smiled up at her.

"Billy! Thank you. I'm so happy you are here. Please have some cake."

"I will. First I want to give you your birthday present." Billy handed her a card, a bouquet of flowers, and a wrapped gift. "Please, can you open it now?"

Angilia smiled at him, and said, "Of course I can, Billy." She tore the paper off to see a framed drawing Billy had done of Angilia and Eric standing side by side, surrounded by a sunray halo. Angilia showed her father and smiled at him. "It's the heart-glow, Daddy," she said, and Eric beamed and kissed her cheek. Angilia bent down to Billy and kissed his cheek. "Thank you, Billy. This is so beautiful. Thank you."

"You are most welcome, Princess darling," Billy said and put his arms around her neck while he kissed her cheek. Everyone clapped and many took pictures of the sweet moment. Angilia made sure that Billy got a piece of cake with an icing flower on it. She knew he liked icing.

After nearly two hours, Eric thanked everyone for coming to wish his daughter a happy birthday and for sharing her special day with them. "I wish we could stay out here all day, but we have the family birthday party to start soon. We love you all, really we do. Thank you."

"I do love you all. I am honored you shared today with me. Thank you so much," Angilia said as people wished her well and left the courtyard. Soon she, Eric, and the others were all inside the palace freshening up for lunch. Angilia and her grandparents took the elevator from the third floor to the first floor and entered the dining room together.

Angilia smiled when she saw her cake in the center of the table, a huge white sheet cake decorated with several dozen colorful flowers, sculpted from icing. "It looks like the most beautiful garden," she said. Eric came up behind her and hugged her.

Eric held her chair for her and everyone took seats around the table. Antoine served Angilia's favorite lunch, her grandmother's couscous green stuffed peppers, with steamed carrots and pearl onions. Eduardo sat next to his niece and looked at her constantly throughout lunch. When his parents, Eric, Matthew, and Mitchell had told him the details of what had happened to her last year, just one day after she mailed the letter that freed him, he had felt sick and disgusted. Angilia had never mentioned it to him. She had nearly lost her life to save her father's life. She had risked her safety to engineer his freedom. He could never doubt her angelic background.

Angilia smiled at him when she caught him staring at her. "I am so happy you are staying with us, Uncle Eduardo. I prayed for you every day."

Eduardo felt tears choking him. "I never want to be anywhere except with my family. The day I arrived, I called you my angel. You are my angel. You saved me. You saved your father. You risked your life for both of us, you know that. Writing that letter was quite dangerous." The look on her face startled him. She looked perplexed. "You never considered that, did you? Had that letter fallen into the wrong hands or the contents been revealed, you would have been the target of the terrorists. What you did for me, Bonnie, and the others was very dangerous, but you did it. You thought of others before you thought of yourself. You protected your father and not yourself. You are the most selfless person. You are a real angel, my niece Angilia."

Angilia smiled at him but shook her head. She started to speak, but Eduardo gently placed a finger over her mouth. "Do not say that you did not do anything. You did. I can never doubt that you are a real angel. You are. You prove that in everything you do.

You always think about what is best for others, you always do things for others, and you always have kindness, love, and patience. I am so honored that you are my niece and that I am blessed enough to know you," Eduardo smiled at her. He leaned over and hugged her. Eric and his parents smiled as they watched.

Angilia smiled at her father and grandparents. She loved her family more than her words could ever say. She prayed they knew how much she did love them. Eric placed his hand over hers and winked at her as Antoine and his assistant cleared the plates and set the table with desert plates and forks. It was time for the cake. Seventeen white candles protruded from the cake, which Antoine moved in front of Angilia. She would blow out the candles and cut the first piece.

Eric stood and lit the candles, and Angilia stood and took a deep breath. Ten months after the shooting, when her diaphragm and heart had been injured severely, she took a deep breath and blew out all seventeen candles with that one breath. Eric and Matthew smiled at one another, knowing what a major accomplishment that was for her. She was so much stronger than they had anticipated. Eric hugged and kissed her. Matthew walked to her and congratulated her, knowing more than anyone how impossible that simple act should have been. He even leaned over and lightly kissed her cheek.

Angilia smiled at them. She knew why they were so happy for her. She had died twice that day, she knew that, and both of them had remained beside her for three months as she struggled and suffered. She owed them both so much, and she was grateful to them both. No, Angilia did not fear death, but she had not wanted to leave her father behind yet, not when he was still in danger. She, too, was elated to celebrate another birthday with her father.

Angilia cut the first slice, with a red rose on top, and placed it on her father's plate. She smiled at him and hugged him. "I love you, Daddy. Thank you for being my life force." Eric held her as everyone dabbed at tears. Katherine dried her eyes and finished cutting the cake. Finally Eric and Angilia sat and nibbled their cake, too, before everyone would reconvene in the sitting room for the party and gifts.

Eric carried her on his back, piggy-back style, to the third floor, so she could wash up and change for the informal party. She giggled, which was such a joyous sound that filled his heart with love. She kissed his cheek and went to change from her suit to the cute outfit she had worn on her grandfather's birthday. Her friends from COC were coming; Eric had invited them all, including Darlene. Angilia told her father that Darlene had framed the invitation he had written and kept it next to her bed. He had rolled his eyes.

Angilia stood the plaque her father had given her that morning on the top of her bookcase with her family souvenirs. She reread it, feeling her whole being swell with love and warmth. Eric tapped at her door just as she felt real warmth surrounding her, and she turned and smiled at him. She motioned him to come to her, and as he did he, too, felt the warmth and looked at her. He smiled and held her arms, both of them knowing that Patrick was there. He had come on her birthday, a total surprise to both of them. Roger called to them that the guests were arriving, and they felt a swish around them as Patrick left.

"I told you he comes often, Daddy. I thought I sensed him and Great-grandfather earlier. They were watching us."

"That's my brother the angel," Eric giggled as he picked her up and carried her down to the second floor. They reached the sitting room just as her friends from COC came up to the room. Darlene gasped when she saw Eric standing there smiling. Scott and Amy poked her and whispered for her to get herself under control.

Angilia hugged each of her friends and thanked them for coming. Eric shook their hands, although he cringed when Darlene neared him. She tried not to look at him, but that only caused her to misstep and fall forward—into Eric's arms. He helped her to stand up, and she screeched and fainted. "Mitchell, we need you," Eric called.

Mitchell came to the door, saw Darlene on the floor, and sighed. He revived Darlene and covered her eyes as he helped her to her feet. He led her to a chair in the corner, hoping she would remain safe there. He even rearranged a potted tree to provide more cover for the besotted teen. He just hoped she did not choke on her cupcake later.

Scott apologized for Darlene, but Eric told him not to worry. "I'll just try to keep a distance. I don't want her to faint all afternoon," Eric grinned. He could not neglect to invite the poor girl when he had invited all of her COC friends, but she seemed so distressed around him. Eric just prayed Darlene did not suffer so much this time.

"I see you are still dealing with the love-struck teenager," Mr. Brennan said as Ginny pushed him down the hall.

"Mr. Brennan! I am so glad you came!" Angilia said and bent to kiss his cheek. "My birthday would feel incomplete without you."

"You are too kind, Princess. I am honored to be invited. I was most excited to receive the engraved invitation from your father. Is your birthday a nice one thus far?"

"Oh, yes, Mr. Brennan. Our family and friends are here, which is everything to me," Angilia smiled. "Please come in and join everyone." Angilia took Mr. Brennan's hand and stood beside him while everyone chatted and mingled. "Excuse me, everyone. I just want to share something with everyone, especially Mr. Brennan." The room fell quiet, everyone curious. Angilia looked down at Mr. Brennan with a huge smile. She removed an envelope from her back pocket. "I received this letter today from Shirley Watson, editor-in-chief at Cantor Press. Mr. Brennan, your memoir will be published by Cantor Press this fall."

Mr. Brennan took hold of Angilia's arms and pulled her down to him. He hugged her as tears filled his eyes. Everyone stood and applauded, so happy for Mr. Brennan. Eric knew what this meant to Mr. Brennan, particularly because Angilia had suggested the book and written the manuscript. She had completed it in November, in just three months. The final page count of the manuscript was 613 pages, which stunned Eric.

Everyone congratulated Mr. Brennan, saying they were excited to read his memoir. Finally Eric had a chance to bend and hug his friend. "Congratulations, Mr. Brennan. You and Angilia did an amazing job on the manuscript. I want a copy, too, you know, signed by both of you. In fact, I think we should have a book signing here, at the palace, when the book is released."

"Sir, I am flabbergasted. I never once dreamt of anything such as this, and now my life is a book thanks to the Princess and you. Thank you both. If ever there was any doubt, I know for certain that both of you are touched by the hand of God," Mr. Brennan said as tears slid from his eyes. Ginny, too, was crying.

Angilia hugged him again. "Thank you for indulging me and letting me do this, Mr. Brennan. It is I who owe you thanks."

After another round of applause and congratulations, everyone helped themselves to birthday cupcakes and beverages from the buffet. Ginny finally had a moment to add Mr. Brennan's gift for Angilia to the mountain of gifts on the table. Everyone talked and laughed for a couple of hours before it was announced time for Angilia to open her presents. Susan and Daniel brought the presents to the table in front of the sofa where she sat between her father and uncle.

The first gift Angilia opened was from her COC friends: Shannon, Amanda, Amy, Nicole, Darlene, and Scott. The lovely card they gave her had a scripture from Psalms by King David. Their gift to her was a huge book, a photographic history of Robert the Bruce, which they were sure she would enjoy. "Thank you so much. This is wonderful for me."

"We still think you should write that book about the story you told us on Halloween," Shannon said. "I went looking for a book about that for myself, and that's when I came across this book and we decided to make it your birthday gift."

Ironically, Mr. Brennan's present was the second which Angilia picked up and opened. His card had a butterfly on the front, a reference to his earliest memory that he had shared with them on Christmas. Atop the tissue paper cocooning the gift itself, Mr. Brennan had placed a short note which explained that the item was a family heirloom from the 18th century that he wanted the Princess to have. He knew she would treasure it and make it part of her growing family archives. It was a letter opener that was a replica of Robert the Bruce's sword. "Mr. Brennan, this is completely astounding. I can't. . . ."

Mr. Brennan held up a hand to shush her. "It is yours now. It belongs with you, rightly so. Besides, I want you to have it." Angilia stood and kissed him again.

Susan's gift was next, which brought a huge smile to Angilia's face. The large box contained new riding boots. "I know you will need those now, since you can ride Starlight again soon. Happy birthday, Angilia."

"Thank you, Susan. I can hardly wait to use them. They are lovely, really perfect," Angilia smiled at Susan.

Angilia picked up a gift no one in the room recognized except for Eric, who had received it by special currier at the end of December. He had kept it locked safely in his desk until moments before the party. Angilia read the card, stunned, and showed it to her father. Eric nodded, smiled, and said, "I know, Angel. Isn't that wonderful of him? Open it. I don't know what it is, either, just who sent it."

She removed the lid from the box and saw an envelope addressed to her on top. She removed the single sheet of parchment and read the letter. She looked at her uncle and smiled, and then motioned for Bonnie to come over. She handed the letter to them, and they were just as surprised. "The Prime Minister of Israel fell under your enchanted spell, too, my niece. You encouraged him to do what everyone thought impossible, and you touched his heart. I am not surprised that he remembered your birthday," Eduardo smiled.

"Neither am I, Angilia," Bonnie added. "We now know that many powerful people tried for twenty-two years to gain our release, but you did it with one heartfelt letter. You are very special, indeed." Angilia shook her head, but they, like Mr. Brennan, did not allow her to argue or to protest. She hugged them both.

She wiped tears from her eyes and removed the Prime Minister's gift to her, a Bible from the Holy Land, the gift page at the front containing their names and the date. She would cherish the Bible for the rest of her life. She replaced it in the box and handed it to her father. He kissed her cheek, knowing that others saw the hand of God on his daughter, too.

He smiled when Angilia opened Daniel's garnet and diamond earrings. Garnet was Angilia's birthstone. She thanked him, kissed him, and told him, "These are perfect for all of my business suits, Daniel. Thank you."

Roger's gift added to her personal library with a signed first edition of Willa Cather's novel My Ántonia. Angilia had liked the novel so much she had written one of her DPhil research projects over the novel's themes. "Thank you, Roger. You remember how much I adore this book. How did you ever find a signed first edition?"

"If I told you, the book would disintegrate in ten seconds," he smiled. "Seriously, I e-mailed book dealers until I found one. It only took five months."

Everyone giggled, and Angilia picked up an envelope. Inside was a card from Eduardo, Bonnie, and the other journalists, wishing her the happiest birthday. Included was a cashier's check made out to her Learning for Life Foundation in the amount of €5000. Her eyes filled with tears and she showed it to her father. Eric smiled and wiped her tears with his handkerchief. "This is truly amazing," she said. "You are amazing," she said and hugged Eduardo and Bonnie again. "I will have to send long-distance hugs to the others. You are each too kind. Thank you."

"We have a strong role model, Angilia," Eduardo softly said as he patted her back. Bonnie was crying, her emotions raging out of control.

Another large box had a card from Katherine and Mitchell, which had a poem by her poet Shelley on the front. She smiled at them. "You remembered my poet," she said as tears filled her eyes again. She removed the wrapping paper to see the famous orange Hermès box. Susan, Bonnie, and the COC girls gasped, instantly recognizing the iconic brand. Every woman, it seemed, dreamed of owning one of those handbags. The women and girls all but swooned when Angilia removed a pink Birkin handbag from the protective sleeve. The famous locked bag was the envy of any sane woman. Katherine and Mitchell knew, of course, that pink was Angilia's signature color. The bag had to be pink.

"I don't know what to say," Angilia managed to say. "This is beyond gorgeous. This is probably the loveliest handbag I have ever seen. And it's pink," she giggled. "Thank you both," she said and went to hug them. Katherine and Mitchell wanted Angilia's 17th birthday to be extra special, expecially since she had come so close to never celebrating another birthday.

Angilia wiped her eyes again and picked up a gift from her Abuelo. Inside the slender box was a gold fountain pen. Eduardo recognized it. How appropriate that it go to the writer in the family. He could imagine her signing copies of her books with that pen. "Mi nieta, that pen belonged to my grandfather, your great-great-grandfather. It has stood too long unused on the desk in Spain. You use it, mi nieta. You are a writer. You should have the pen," Alejandro said.

Angilia went to him, and he pulled her onto his lap and hugged and kissed her. "Abuelo, I will treasure it always, and it will be passed down to your great-grandchildren and great-great-grandchildren for many generations," Angilia promised him. "Thank you, Abuelo."

Matthew felt tears stinging his eyes suddenly, especially when Alejandro said, "God willing, I will live long enough to see my first great-grandchild, Angel."

"You will, Abuelo, I am sure you will," she smiled at him. "Which one is yours, Abuela? I want to open it next." Juanita reached for it and handed it to Angilia.

Angilia slid into her grandmother's arms in tears at the sight of Marisol's ivory lace shawl. It was so beautiful and delicate. Juanita smiled and slipped it over Angilia's shoulders. "It looks so beautiful on you, mi nieta. So beautiful. You wear it to your balls and parties, yes?"

Angilia nodded and kissed her grandmother's soft, wrinkled cheek. "Yes, Abuela. Perhaps pinned with her cameo Daddy gave me one year ago." Juanita kissed her again and scooted her back to Eric, who had tears in his eyes. He hugged and kissed her, knowing how happy Marisol was as she looked down on their daughter that day.

Eric took out his handkerchief and dabbed the tears from her face again. She took a deep breath and picked up another gift, which Eduardo had put together for her. How appropriate to open it now, he thought. His card had the Lord's Prayer on the front and a personal note from him inside. She kissed his cheek and opened the box. Inside was a photograph album.

Angilia opened it and gasped. Eric was looking at it, too, and he looked at his brother-in-law, a smile on this lips and tears in his eyes. Eric and Eduardo held hands behind Angilia as she looked at pictures of her mother that spanned Marisol's life. Alejandro and Juanita had helped Eduardo locate the pictures, so they had known of his gift. They smiled as Angilia wore Marisol's shawl and sat between her father and her uncle looking at pictures of her mother. The circle was complete, they thought. Marisol's spirit was with them, they knew that for certain thanks to Angilia.

Angilia bent her head and cried, overcome with emotions. Eduardo leaned over and held her, and Eric put his arms around the two of them. They sat that way for several moments, sharing a silent, reverent love for Marisol. Angilia clutched the album to her heart with one hand and hugged her uncle with the other arm. She put her chin on his shoulder and spoke softly into his ear. "Thank you, Uncle Eduardo. You know what this means to me. I love you so much."

Eduardo choked out an "I love you, my angel" as he hugged her and smiled at Eric. The afternoon could not possibly be any more emotional than it was at that moment.

Two gifts remained, and after Angilia regained her composure she picked up the smaller of the two, which the card said was from Matthew. The card had an angel on the front, and she smiled at him. It should have two angels, she thought. His gift was a white devotional book dated 1792, the year her poet Shelley was born. Matthew had bought it years earlier at an antique shop in Oxford, though he had no use or need for it. He had never understood until now why he had purchased and kept it. It was the perfect gift for Angilia.

Its pretty cover, with a pastel depiction of angels, was pretty and delicate. There was a page for each day of the year, and Angilia smiled as she read today's page. "Thank you, Matthew. This is one of the most beautiful books I have ever seen. The cover is stunning. I will read it every day and think of you," she said, which caused him to smile. Eric covered his smile with his fingers, for he knew what would happen in a short while. Angilia had no idea of her comment's impact.

"I knew you would like it. I bought it just for you," he said, which he knew now was the truth.

Angilia smiled and reached for the last present. Eduardo stood and lifted it in front of her. Angilia tore off the paper and suddenly her smile was huge and her eyes shone. Inside a custom white 16" by 24" frame was a portrait of her father. He was dressed in blue jeans and a white dress shirt, untucked as usual. He stood on the sitting room balcony against the rail, his arms and legs crossed informally. A lone cloud was in the sky behind him, a symbolic inference to Uncle Patrick. His smile was as charming as ever, and his bright turquoise blue eyes glowed. He looked straight at her. Bonnie's imprint was in the lower right corner of the picture.

Angilia leaned the frame against the coffee table and reached for Bonnie. Eduardo stood and switched seats with Bonnie, who hugged Angilia. "I could not imagine a more perfect gift for you, Angilia."

"It is perfect, Bonnie. Thank you for this. This will go next to the portrait of my Great-grandfather over my desk," Angilia said, turning her head to smile at her father. "I know you don't like doing this sort of thing, Daddy. Thank you for letting Bonnie do this for me." Eric smiled, knowing it made his daughter happy. That was all that mattered to him.

"Can we see it, too?" Katherine asked with a huge smile. Eduardo held up the portrait. Everyone admired it. Darlene stood from her seat behind everyone else to get a better view. She should not have. Darlene mumbled what sounded like "So handsome" and fainted.

Roger fought his giggle by stuffing a cupcake in his mouth. Eric covered his face with his hands and said his trademark, "Good grief." Mitchell revived Darlene yet again and suggested she should go home, take an aspirin, and get some sleep. "Doctor's orders," he told her. She reluctantly said her goodbyes and apologized to His Majesty, who waved goodbye without looking at her. Everyone sighed after that dramatic moment, relieved that Darlene would not have a fit of the vapors anymore that afternoon at least.

"You can never let her see or hear that giant jukebox in the stable," Roger giggled. "That would probably kill her."

"That's not funny, Roger," Angilia said and gave him a stern look. "Darlene is trying to control it." Angilia leaned down and whispered to her father that he could sit up now. "I'm sorry, Daddy. I know she tries not to do that."

"I know, Angel. This is just a bit too weird for me, though."

"Poor Eric. You're cursed with handsome looks, charm, and talent. You have girls throwing themselves at you and fainting at your feet. It sounds wretched," Daniel giggled. Eric picked up a couch pillow and threw it at Daniel, hitting him. "A reluctant superstar. I get it already." Roger laughed, too, and Eric threw another pillow at him.

"Now can we please get serious for a few minutes, please? There is one more gift for Angilia." Eric stood and said he would return in a moment. He ran to his office and unlocked the safe to remove his gift for Angilia. He returned a few minutes later and sat beside her on the sofa.

Eric took her hands and smiled at her. "There is no one else on earth with whom I would rather share my life than you, my beautiful daughter Angilia. Happy birthday." He placed a red velvet jewel case in her hands. She smiled at him, knowing his gift would send her emotions into the stratosphere yet again. Angilia unlatched the front of the case and lifted the front to reveal the most breathtaking pendant she had ever seen.

Tears once more filled her eyes as she looked at this unique symbol of their family's love. A citrine heart entwined with a garnet heart, the two connected hearts surrounded by round-cut emeralds. Dangling from between the bottom of the two hearts was a small gold cross. Angilia grabbed her father and held him tightly. Eric held her, too, and they were as tightly connected as the hearts that represented them. Angilia cried while Eric gently rocked her, neither of them speaking. No one knew yet what Eric's gift was, but all that mattered was the love they witnessed that afternoon.

After several minutes, Angilia lifted her head and kissed her father's cheek. "You, Mommy, and me together forever. Thank you, Daddy." Eric smiled and lifted the necklace from its case. He fastened it around her neck, where the pendant hung over her heart. Eric kissed her nose. Angilia lifted the pendant and looked at it, turning it over to see an inscription engraved on the back:

Jeremiah 1:5

E, M, A

"I love you, Daddy," Angilia said and hugged him again.

Juanita, Alejandro, and Eduardo smiled when they saw the heart shapes in Eric's citrine birthstone, Angilia's garnet birthstone, and Marisol's emerald birthstone. Everyone admired the necklace, especially Angilia's friends. The girls talked in whispers around Angilia, saying again how wonderful her father was and how beautiful their love was. No one had ever done anything so personal or loving for them, they sighed. "Your dad is so cool and awesome, Angilia. He really is. I don't think there is another father like yours anywhere," Amanda said.

Angilia thanked them and smiled. "There is no one like my father. He is one of a kind, and I love him more than life."

§§§§§

No one had noticed Roger sneak to the hall to make a quick phone call. He rejoined them a moment later, just a few minutes before the last major surprise of Angilia's birthday. A chorus of male voices boomed out with a boisterous "Happy birthday, Angilia!" Everyone turned to see who was there, and Angilia seemed to bubble with delight.

"Sam! My guys! Oh, I am so happy you are here!" Angilia met them in a group hug, and they all smiled joyfully, thrilled to see her again. "Come in and join us. I think you know everyone except Valdavia's newest author, Mr. Brennan, and Ginny," she proclaimed as she introduced her band and producer/manager to her friends.

"The Princess is too kind. I just told her a bunch of jumbled up stories and she wrote my memoir. This one is very special," he smiled and patted her arm.

"She most certainly is," Tim agreed, and the others echoed him.

"We need to get Daddy in the studio again so he can record his album," she told them as they chatted.

Eric overheard and looked like someone had slapped him. "My what? I'm not recording anything else, Angel. I told you that."

"I know, but you will. You have to. One song is not enough for all of your fans. They want more, and you can get in and out of the studio in one or two days. It's not a big deal, you know that. I think if you select ten or twelve of your favorite songs and record them, you'll have another smash hit," Angilia smiled at him. She hugged him and looked up at him. "You know how much I want you to."

"Yeah, Eric, you know Darlene needs more than one song on her smart phone," Roger giggled. Eric gave him a stern look.

"Actually, an album is a great idea, Eric. Think about it," Sam winked. "Before you protest, we want to give Angilia her birthday gift," he added and handed her a black velvet jewel case.

Angilia opened it and gasped. "Sam, John, Tim, Greg, Joe, this is gorgeous! And very extravagant! Thank you!" She kissed each of them.

"It's also very symbolic," Sam said.

"I know diamonds are for 60th anniversaries, but what else are they for?"

"You'll see," he smiled. We have something very special for you. But first, we have something for you," he nodded at Eric.

"Me?" Eric was confused.

"Yes. Sir, this is for you," Joe said and placed a large package before Eric.

Eric tore off the silver paper to reveal a framed award. "A gold record?" he asked in surprise.

"No. A diamond single award, Eric. Your recording of "Sunshine on My Shoulders" has sold at least 2,000,000 downloads. Congratulations!" Sam announced. He and the band applauded.

"Are you serious? Me?"

"Absolutely!" Greg said.

Angilia smiled at her father with tears in her eyes. "Oh, Daddy, no one deserves this more! Your song has always been my favorite, you know that." She kissed his cheek. "I love you."

"Wow, now this is serious business, buddy. Congratulations!" Roger beamed and hugged his best friend. "You really do deserve this."

"Congratulations, Eric. She's right. You deserve this," Daniel added and also hugged his friend.

"I told you that you sing better than all of those people out there, Sir. You should record an album now," Mr. Brennan smiled and shook Eric's hand.

"Mi hijo Eric, you are blessed. You have a gift. Congratulations, my son," Juanita said as she hugged and kissed him.

"You have always made us happy and proud, Eric. Yes, you deserve this, son," Alejandro told him. The two men hugged, and then Eduardo embraced Eric.

"Congratulations, my brother. Hearing you on the radio last summer was one of the biggest surprises for me. I am very happy for you," Eduardo smiled.

Bonnie congratulated him as she continued taking pictures of the day, at his request. Angilia talked him into posing with his award for a few pictures, much to his chagrin. He did anything to make her happy, though, which is why she knew he would eventually record an album. If this award did not convince him how talented and appreciated he was nothing would, Angilia thought. Susan, Katherine, Mitchell, Matthew, and Angilia's COC friends took turns congratulating Eric, who was amazed and stunned.

"Thank you all, really. This has got to be the most unexpected presentation I have ever received," Eric stated.

"There's more, though," Sam said. "Angilia, we cannot be any happier than we are to present these awards to both of you on this special day. Eric, it's rare to receive a diamond single, especially in less than one year. Congratulations." Sam shook Eric's hand. "As astounding at that is, what I have for our Princess is even more amazing."

Tim placed another large silver-wrapped present in front of Angilia. She looked completely surprised, but then said, "Oh, I get one, too, only because I played the guitar on it." Tim turned and smiled at his band mates and Sam, knowing how wrong Angilia was. Indeed, hers did not look like her father's award at all. Sam noticed her confusion and stepped forward.

"I want to read the plaque on this to all of you," Sam said, with a huge smile and love for the young lady he had first met when she was a mere six years old.

Presented To

Angilia DeBruce Martineau

This Diamond Record Award Commemorates

the sale of more than 10 million copies of the

Stone Canyon Records

Album

"Heart-Glow"

Congratulations, sweetheart! Just so you all know what a big deal this is, <u>Heart-Glow</u> is the fastest diamond-certified album in the awards' history. The album was released in May 2012 and certified diamond in December 2012," Sam informed them.

Everyone applauded and stood, except of course Mr. Brennan, although he did put his fingers in his mouth and whistle with the applause. Eric was not surprised. He was happy, and he was yet again amazed that his daughter had made history. He pulled her into a hug and kissed her cheek. "Angilia, you really are remarkable, baby. You blow my mind at least once each day. I love you, Angel."

"It's all because of you, Daddy, you know that. If I am your heart-glow, then you are my life force. I am here because of you. Thank you," she told him and reached up to kiss his cheek again.

Her friends and family applauded again, and soon were crowding around her to hug, kiss, and congratulate her. Several minutes later, they all settled comfortably for a late afternoon relaxing and talking. Mr. Brennan started another round of sharing memories by telling everyone about his favorite birthday present. Everyone else followed suit, to much laughter and a few tears. When the stories concluded and the conversation took off in another direction, Eric caught Matthew's eye and winked at him, a silent signal. This was the moment for which Matthew had waited what felt like an eternity. He felt his heart rate increase, and he prayed to God.

"Angilia, will you and Matthew go to the stable and check the horses? Joseph is away on errands, and I know you'll enjoy seeing your Starlight," Eric smiled at her.

Angilia giggled and kissed his cheek. "Of course, Daddy," she said, although she knew he was up to something. Still, he was right that she would enjoy seeing her beautiful boy. Angilia and Matthew took the elevator to the first floor and walked to the stable.

In the sitting room, Eric excused himself and said he had to attend to something important, but would return soon. He ran up to the watch tower, unbeknownst to Angilia and Matthew. He was certain what would happen, and his heart beat quickly and excitedly. He saw them enter the stable together.

Angilia greeted each horse with a sugar cube treat and a hug. Finally, she hugged her Starlight and gave him his sugar cube before she opened his stall and put on his bridle. "Do you mind if I walk him for a little while?" she asked Matthew, who smiled and shook his head.

They leisurely walked him in the paddock, neither of them speaking. After two passes around the paddock, Matthew did speak. "Angilia, I do love you. My love for you is real and strong. I know that. I know that you are still young, and yet you are so wise in so many ways, far beyond your earthly age. I will wait, just as I said I would, as long as you need and want me to. I need to ask you something." Matthew stopped walking and stood in front of Angilia, forcing her to stop. She looked up at him. Matthew removed a ring box from his pocket. "Angilia, would you do me the honor of wearing my promise ring?"

Angilia looked into his eyes, the tears in them screaming his love and begging her to say yes. "Since Christmas, I have examined my heart and I have prayed for God's direction and advice. I have never loved anyone in this way, and it is all new to me. Will you, can you, be patient and understanding with me while this matures within me?"

Matthew stared into those hypnotic turquoise eyes of hers. "I will be. Before I met you, I never would have been able to, but I can now, for you. For us."

"Yes, Matthew, I will wear your ring."

Tears fell from Matthew's eyes and he removed the ring from the box. He held her left hand and slid the ring next to her mother's purity ring. Angilia looked at it and smiled at the significance. The narrow gold band was engraved with the words True Love and had a small diamond heart. The inside of the band was inscribed *Matthew & Angilia 2013.* She looked up at him, her smile telling him how happy and pleased she was. As Eric watched from the telescope, Matthew leaned down and kissed Angilia's cheek.

Starlight whinnied and reared onto his hind legs, as if offering his congratulations. Matthew and Angilia laughed, and they petted him. A moment later, they returned Starlight to his stall and gave the horses extra sugar cubes to celebrate the happy occasion. They walked slowly back to the palace, not needing to talk. When they entered from the patio, Eric was standing there, and they smiled, knowing he had watched them.

"Well?" Eric asked.

"She said yes," Matthew smiled at his future father-in-law.

Eric smiled and pulled Angilia close to him. "I am happy if you are happy, Angel."

Angilia smiled up at him. "I am, Daddy." She reached up and kissed his cheek and whispered in his ear. "You will always be the love of my life, Daddy, always."

Eric's eyes filled with tears and he held her close and kissed the top of her head. "Ditto, baby." A few minutes later, he cleared his throat and smiled at both of them. "We better go break the news to everyone." The three of them took the elevator to the second floor and entered the sitting room with huge smiles.

Everyone looked at them, knowing something had happened. "Ladies and gentlemen, it is my honor to announce the pre-engagement of my beloved Angilia and her best friend Matthew." The room exploded with cheers and screams. Most of them had seen the romance budding, and to them this was not a major surprise. Angilia's friends and Mr. Brennan, however, were stunned.

Mitchell and Katherine joined their son, Eric, and Angilia for a family hug. They already felt like family. "I wondered when this would happen," Katherine admitted through her tears. "I am so happy for both of you."

"So am I," Mitchell said, hugging his son and kissing Angilia. "It's a relief, actually, I must say." Mitchell recalled his first sight of Eric, covered in his daughter's blood and terrified. None of them knew then that the tragedy of that day would unite the two families forevermore. Mitchell smiled and grabbed Eric into a rousing hug.

Juanita, Alejandro, and Eduardo joined them, equally unsurprised yet ecstatic. Alejandro hugged Matthew and told him it was about time. He smiled at his granddaughter and kissed her. "I love you, mi nieta. I want only your health and happiness. Are you happy?" She smiled, nodded, and kissed him. "Good. Then all is well," he smiled.

Eduardo grabbed his niece and cried. "I missed all of your other milestones, although I suppose your milestones were not the typical milestones," he giggled. "I am grateful to share this one with you, my Angel. I love you."

Angilia kissed him and held him close for a moment. "I love you, Uncle Eduardo. I am grateful you are with us."

"Let me see mi nieta," Juanita demanded through her tears. "You are very special, Angilia. You are destined for many more great things. You are happy?"

"I am, Abuela," Angilia answered and kissed her grandmother.

Juanita turned to Matthew and took hold of his arms. "You know you have to be patient, understanding, and gentle with her, yes? If your love is real, as you say it is, you will be."

Angilia smiled. "I have already told him that, Abuela."

"I will be. I promised her, and I promise you," Matthew assured her, and then kissed her cheek.

Susan, Daniel, and Roger took their turns hugging, kissing, and congratulating Angilia and Matthew. Susan cried, of course, commenting how happy she was for Angilia. Bonnie stopped taking pictures and also hugged Angilia, congratulating her. She and Eric had welcomed her and made her feel like family. What a wonderfully beautiful day, she thought.

Ginny pushed Mr. Brennan to the young couple, and he beamed as he reached for Angilia. She hugged him, he hugged her, and he cried. "I have seen many such events from a distance, Princess. I am blessed and honored to be among those who share this special moment with you. You are going to be a remarkably wonderful wife, mother, and queen," he told her. He took Matthew's hands. "Congratulations to the future king consort, my boy. You do right by this one. She does have God on her team, you know," Mr. Brennan smiled.

"Thank you, Mr. Brennan. I know she does, and I want only to make her happy and loved," Matthew said as he smiled at Angilia.

Finally, her COC friends gathered around her for a group hug. "We are so happy for you, Angilia, really we are," Shannon said. Scott shook Matthew's hand and kissed Angilia's hand. They admired her ring. "Now that is the most perfect promise ring ever," Amy smiled at Matthew.

"Yes, it is. Not every man is as understanding of things like this, you know. This means more than you know," Amanda commented. Angilia and Matthew smiled at one another, both of them happy, content, and confident that God was in complete control of their lives.

§§§§

That night, after the guests had left and everyone else had settled in, Angilia sat in her nightgown and robe, brushing her hair in front of her vanity mirror. Her 17th birthday had been a whirlwind of memorable moments, all of them duly written in her 2013 diary. She still wore the necklace her father had placed around her neck early that afternoon. She touched it, stood, and walked across the hall to her father's suite. Although the main door was open, she tapped lightly. Angilia heard his muffled "Come in," and could tell he was crying.

Angilia stood in his open bedroom door for a moment, looking at him. He was still dressed in his jeans and shirt. He sat on the edge of the bed, his head bent, looking down. "Daddy?" she asked softly as she stepped in.

Eric looked up at her, smiled, and extended his right arm to her. Angilia went to him and he pulled her into a hug next to him. "What's wrong, Daddy?"

"Nothing is wrong, Angel. Everything is right." Eric smiled at her. "You are amazing, baby. I cannot believe how special this ring is. How. . .when. . .?" Eric gently ran a finger over the necklace he gave her that afternoon. "I never told anyone, except the jeweler who made it for me, about this necklace. He worked on it for two months, and I picked it up last week and locked it in my safe. Only he and I saw it until you opened it. How? This ring is so similar."

Angilia smiled. "The idea came to me on your birthday, and I wanted to give it to you today. It had to be today. You, Mommy, and me. We are connected by our love forever. Our souls remain connected. God wanted us to be a family, and we are, for all time."

"So we both had the idea around the same time. Wow." Eric lifted the ring box and looked at the ring: one band of citrine stones and one band of emerald stones, with an oval-cut garnet centered over them. "Will you put it on my finger?" Angilia removed the ring, took her father's right hand, and slipped the ring onto his ring finger. "It is beautiful, Angilia. I will wear this ring forever," he said and kissed her cheek.

Angilia touched the necklace and lifted it to look at its symbolism. "It is perfect, Daddy. Your citrine is my sun, my warmth. Mommy's emerald is my life. My garnet is my blood. The hearts are our love, entwined for eternity. The cross is Jesus, our eternal lives. Together, we are one soul." She looked at her father with that look of love in her eyes that had taken ownership of his heart thirty-five years earlier. He had taken ownership of Angilia's heart that day, too, just as God had known.

Eric sighed. "That is so beautiful, Angilia. You and I entwined, surrounded by Mommy's soul. Always together, with Jesus protecting us."

A lone tear slid down her cheek. "Always." She kissed his soft, warm cheek. "I love you, Daddy."

"I love you, Angilia."

"I am so grateful and blessed that God made you my father. I am so very happy."

"I am, too, baby, on both counts. I cannot begin to imagine my life without you. Without you I have no life," Eric softly said.

"You will never be without me, Daddy. You are my heart and my soul."

"And you are mine, Angel."

"Today has been perfect and beautiful. All I feel today is love, and peace, and joy." Eric smiled, his own soul full. "We are fine, Daddy. We are healed. We are protected. The pain, fear, and guilt are forever banished. Now we have love, peace, and joy forever. Even when something painful happens, we will be fine. Our love and faith are far too strong now. They are our shield. We have each other, and we have God. I do love you both, Daddy, you and God, my two fathers," Angilia said.

"We are fine, baby. Remember Winnie the Pooh? *'You are braver, stronger, and smarter'* than you realize. More so than even I realized until this past year. You take my breath away."

"Oh, Daddy, you are going to make me cry again. All happy tears," Angilia smiled.

Eric took her hand and walked with her to his bedroom balcony. "Happy tears. You used to say raindrops are the angels' happy tears."

She smiled up at him. "Angels can never be sad, only happy. Like Mommy and Uncle Patrick."

"You are my Angel, my beautiful daughter, and you are my happiness. Happy birthday, Angilia."

Sheilah R. Craft is an English professor, writer, blogger, poet, artist, ardent genealogist, and book lover. Born and raised in the Midwestern United States, Sheilah was born surrounded by a close family—including several educators—books, and animals. She began reading and writing very early, and has published short stories, articles, and poems. <u>Heart-Glow</u> is her first full-length novel.

Web Site and Exclusive Content

Please visit the companion web site, which contains additional information, pictures, and exclusive features. Those who purchase this book have access to specific password protected content on the web site. To access the exclusive content, please visit Heart-Glow: A Novel at **http://www.heartglownovel.org**

On the protected pages, when prompted for the password, please enter **heartglowcraft16***